A NEW SONG

"A fast paced, exciting plot developing real Muslim and Jewish characters with great love and care. This is what our interfaith world needs."

— Dr. Laleh Bakhtiar
translator of *The Sublime Quran*

"Sarah Isaias' successful first novel...is a fast-moving, page-turning adventure tale, but it is also very much more: an exciting exploration of relationships between Judaism and Islam, a delicately portrayed love story, some erudite but accessible conspiracy theories, and even a couple of medical mysteries, all converging to a beautiful climax. I was deeply moved by this book."

— Rabbi Jonathan Omer-Man
founder of *Metivta:
a center for contemplative Judaism*

A NEW SONG

A Novel

A New Song

A Novel

Sarah Isaias

Derusha Publishing LLC

Derusha Publishing books may be purchased for educations business or sales promotional use. For information please write: Special Markets Department, Derusha Publishing LLC, 2637 East Atlantic Boulevard #16749, Pompano Beach, FL 33062.

First paperback edition published 2011.

ISBN 978-1-935104-05-6

לבעל שלי ומשפחה שלנו
לרבי ואשתו
עם אהבה

...all these religions, all this singing.
One song.

– Jelal al-Din Rumi

Blessings and thanks to Daniel Matt for providing the Aramaic translation on page 23.

Thanks and blessings to Rabbi Reuven Firestone for providing the Hebrew translation on page 173.

TABLE OF CONTENTS

OPENING

And God created a human being in His image, in the image of God He created it; male and female he created them.

Genesis 1:27

O humanity! Be Godfearing of your Lord, Who created you from a single soul and from it created its spouse, and from them both disseminated many men and women.

Quran 4:1

Cordoba Synagogue, Spain

11:00 pm. Thursday, July 20th 1391

After the screams and crying at last died down, a young woman, no more than sixteen or seventeen, crept quietly from her hiding place in the water cistern on the roof of the synagogue. She'd managed to escape there soon after the mob invaded, but not soon enough to avoid witnessing the brutal slayings of her parents and her young brother. She'd cowered there in the mostly-empty cistern during the forced baptisms and additional murders that followed, until, at length, the angry voices finally retreated into the night. In the silent dark of the aftermath, she stumbled, weeping, down the stairs and out the synagogue door.

Surprisingly, she returned an hour later, bearing a parcel and wearing a travel cloak. She was no longer crying. Though it was still deep night, light from the fires outside flickered in from the twelve windows above, and in the illumination provided by its glow, she made her way to a small niche in the western wall of the synagogue. There, she squatted down, placing her parcel next to her and removing a metal plate from the floor with a harsh scraping sound. She leaned into this space up to the shoulder and retrieved a small box. Sitting back and placing the box in her lap, she opened it carefully, examining its contents for a moment. She then pulled her parcel towards her, fumbling around in it for a moment before removing a piece of paper, which she exchanged for an item inside the box. Closing its lid and reaching back into the gap in the floor, she returned the box to its place and replaced the metal plate. She then put the item she'd removed from the box into her parcel, tied it up, and slung it over her shoulder. With no further ado, she slipped out the door and was gone.

Cairo, Egypt

5:00 pm. Wednesday, September 30th 1994
Week of the portion[1] of בראשית, "In The Beginning"
Prof. Yakub and Ibrahim al-Shadi

Yakub returned home to Cairo for the first time in a decade to attend the funeral of his father, Ibrahim. With bitter sadness and some considerable guilt at his long absence, he travelled the many thousands of miles from San Francisco to his home city with his wife, Rawiyya, and his teenage sons, Farid and Mahmud. They arrived just in time for his father's death.

Arriving at the side of his father's hospital bed, Yakub was shocked at the toll the cancer had taken on him. When he'd last seen him, Ibrahim had been a vigorous man, at the height of his poetic career. Now, Yakub encountered the sunken-cheeked and hollow-eyed visage of a skull.

Momentarily, his father revived, opening his eyes and fixing them upon Yakub. Seeing his son there, he had clutched his arm with a sudden, bruising grip, struggling to speak. His mouth opened, his lips pursed, and yet the air that passed his larynx gave rise only to a sigh. Mute, his eyes beseeched Yakub with some indecipherable warning. Soon afterwards, they closed once again, and his last breath, too, passed from him minutes later.

Following this appalling death, Yakub experienced not only profound grief but also intolerable curiosity. What had his father been trying to tell him? Only some dark family secret, long held in disquiet silence, could lead to this type of deathbed confession. If only Yakub had visited more often! Perhaps his father would have found the opportunity to divulge his secret before now?

Yakub's relatives tried to reassure him that death was always distressing and traumatic. But Yakub knew it was more than that. He could not forget the fear in his father's eyes. All through the memorial service and burial, he played the scene over and over in

---

[1] The Torah, the first five books of the Hebrew Bible, is divided into 52 weekly portions, each portion (*Parasha*) corresponding to a specific 7-day period. Thus, time may be measured by the progress through the annual cycle of Torah portions.

his mind. *What had his father been trying to tell him?*

Later, at the funeral reception, hosted at his Aunt Rima's house, he found out.

Standing in Rima's living room, he became aware that someone was watching him. His eyes were drawn to an odd little man, one he had not seen at the funeral. He was tiny, enveloped entirely in white robes and headscarf. This left only his face uncovered, a mass of wrinkles dominated by piercing blue eyes. With a start, Yakub recognized the face from his childhood.

Seeing Yakub return his gaze, the man made his way over.

"Are you…" began Yakub.

"I'm Muhtadi," said the man, "Your uncle." His voice was strong and melodious, despite his tiny frame, and Yakub recalled that he, like his father, had been a poet. "Do you remember me?"

"Yes," nodded Yakub. "But I haven't seen you since that day, so long ago…it must be forty-five years or more."

"The day you left Shaddad."

"Yes."

"You are correct. We have not seen each other since that day."

Yakub nodded.

"Your father forbade me to see you," said Muhtadi.

"What?"

"He forbade me to see or speak with you."

"He…?"

"Fortunately for me, our sister, Rima did not agree with him on this point. It was she who invited me."

Yakub stood in silence, so many questions rising up in his mind and replacing each other that he couldn't speak.

But his uncle shook himself, saying, "I forget my manners!" He bowed, *"Ahlan wasahlan,"* he greeted Yakub in formal Arabic, "I am Muhtadi ibn Mahmud al-Shadi, *achu abuka*—your father's brother."

"Izayyak," responded Yakub.

Muhtadi embraced him, and Yakub felt his uncle's bony shoulders and ribcage through his clothing. He had often wondered why his father never mentioned his relatives in Palestine. Now, apparently, he was to find out why.

Muhtadi was openly examining him. Yakub laughed self-consciously, saying, "As I recall, uncle, you are a poet."

"Yes," Muhtadi nodded.

"I have also been blessed, or perhaps cursed, with poetry," said Yakub.

Muhtadi looked at him sharply. "No curse," he said, his brow furrowing in disapproval.

Quickly, Yakub replied, "My apologies. Perhaps it's a habit I developed in America, to make a joke of everything."

"Perhaps," said Muhtadi, sternly. He scrutinized Yakub, his gaze sweeping his face and body, taking in Yakub's western clothing of suit, shirt, and tie. "So you are a poet. Will you recite one of your poems for me? A recent one?"

Surprised, Yakub felt sweat break out on his face and his heart begin to beat, as if this were a kind of test. Regardless of his literary success in America, bolstered by the recent popularity of the great thirteenth century Persian poet, Rumi, he was not sure his work would measure up. "I suppose," He said reluctantly, "I could do that. This poem is not really finished, though."

"What kind of poem is it?"

"A *qit'ah*, an elegy. For my father. Rhymed on the syllable *eem.*"

Muhtadi nodded. "Please go ahead."

Realizing there was no escape, Yakub closed his eyes and took several deep breaths. Reopening them, he began to recite:

Wa'aktub shi'r 'an Ibrahim, abiyy al-habeeb wa'al-kareem,
Mithla ab Isma'il wa Itzhaq, abd al-rahman al-raheem...[2]

He continued the poem, the stream of words swirling out, circling the one rhyming syllable, *eem,* in a tantalizing harmonic current.

As Yakub chanted, Muhtadi listened, eyes closed. When the poem was done, his uncle opened his eyes and placed his palm briefly on Yakub's cheek. His expression of disapproval had disappeared, and his face now bore a look of quiet pleasure.

---

[2] "I write a poem of Ibrahim, my father, beloved and generous, like the father of Isma'il and Ishak, a servant of the Merciful, the Compassionate..."

و أكتب شعر عن ابراهيم, أبي الحبيب والكريم
مثل أب إسماعيل وإسحْق, أبد الرحمن الرحيم

If there had been a test, apparently Yakub had passed it.

"Come, come!" said Muhtadi, his mood shifting as he gestured, impatiently, towards an empty space on one of Rima's couches. They both sat down, and Muhtadi turned to Yakub, grasping his forearm and staring into his eyes with intensity. "Tell me more of what you remember from those days."

Yakub paused, casting back through mental images from his distant childhood. "I remember the last time I saw you. I was about five, I think." Muhtadi nodded his agreement, and Yakub continued. "It was when my father first got the job in Cairo. A car came to pick us up, at the camp in Jericho. I had never been in a car before." He paused, looking away as he reconjured the scene in his mind's eye. "We passed you on the road as we drove away." He looked back at his uncle now. "I was sad," he said.

Muhtadi nodded again, releasing Yakub's arm. "Your father was the first in the family to leave the Bedouin life and go to the city. But he was a great poet, even then, and how much more so since he came here." Muhtadi looked at Yakub, and then said, an enigmatic smile on his face, "And you, Yakub. It appears you also have the gift. As I knew you would, all those years ago."

Yakub could not prevent a flush of self-conscious pleasure at his uncle's words. "Do you still live in the tents?" he asked, to change the subject. He remembered how he used to sleep, side by side, with his father as a child in a tent made of goat's hair. If you touched the walls, they were warm, not cold like the plaster of their city home in Cairo.

"No," said Muhtadi, shaking his head. "We have built houses now, in place of the tents." But Muhtadi seemed impatient for something else, and his gaze was boring into Yakub with a curious urgency. "Tell me more, please. What else do you remember from that time?"

Yakub thought a moment, and his mind conjured another memory, a vision of his uncle all those years ago. "I remember," he began slowly, "the story you told me, just before we left." He flashed to the image – a dark night, the stars thrown out onto the black expanse like a million sparkling jewels. He and Muhtadi were alone by the fire. It was a recollection from early childhood, formless and indistinct.

Muhtadi nodded, clasping his hands tightly against his chest. "You told me something. I had forgotten until now..."

Yakub tipped his head back under the force of the memory, his eyes distant, as if even now, he could see the desert sky above. He looked back at Muhtadi.

"Yes? Yes?" said Muhtadi.

"You said there was a family legend."

Muhtadi took a breath in but did not release it.

"Something about a poem."

"What about this poem?" said Muhtadi, in a tight whisper.

"You said that when we find this poem, the world will be redeemed and…"

"…*and the heavens will crack open, and all humanity will see paradise!*" Muhtadi concluded. "Yes!" He looked away from Yakub's face at last, moving his gaze up towards the ceiling. "*Al-hamdu lillah.* Thanks to God. I prayed you would remember. And, *insha Allah,* God willing, your father will forgive me from beyond the grave." Muhtadi surprised Yakub then by turning to him and grasping his shoulders tightly in both his small hands. "You must come with me to Jericho, immediately, tomorrow morning."

As if the subject were already settled, Muhtadi released his grip on Yakub and stood up. "I have found evidence, since I last spoke to you as a boy. This poem is *not* a myth. Your father wished to protect you from this truth. But there is no protection, in the end."

He would say no more on the subject, no matter how much Yakub pressed him. "But how can I go with you?" Yakub queried from where he still sat on the couch. "I have plans to return to San Francisco tomorrow with my wife Rawiyya and our family. The new semester at Berkeley begins next week. I have classes to teach and my students expect me to be there."

Muhtadi shrugged.

"And what about my sons? Mahmud and Farid start back at school on Monday…"

As Yakub went on in similar vein, the realities of his everyday life began to settle on him like a heavy blanket. In fact, the poem he'd written about his father was the first verse he'd set down in over two years. Was this how it was to be, now that he was fifty, middle age looming ahead? Was there no more joy or passion to be had, no momentary glimpses of glorious unity shimmering just below the surface of what seemed to him, now, to be a mundane and tedious reality?

"Alright," he said, standing up. "I will go!"

Muhtadi smiled, his teeth as white as his eyes. "I have waited many years to hear you say that."

The next day, Yakub sent Rawiyya, Farid, and Mahmud home to California, joining Muhtadi on his trip back to Jericho.

At 5:00 am, Yakub and Muhtadi climbed into the Volvo station wagon of his cousin, Kareem, Aunt Rima's son, beginning the first leg of the two-part journey to Palestine. They would travel by car from Cairo to the Suez Canal and from there across the Sinai Peninsula to the Israeli border. After passing through customs, Muhtadi's grandson, Khalid, would pick them up and drive them the remainder of the way to Shaddad, Muhtadi's tribal village near Jericho.

Yakub wondered if there might be trouble with his passport at the border.

"You have an American passport?" asked Muhtadi. Yakub nodded, pulling out the small blue booklet with the imprint of an eagle on the front. Muhtadi took it and, turning on the overhead light, leafed through its pages. He grunted when he saw the name. "With this Arab name, they will likely interrogate you at the Israeli border. It will help that you are with me, and I am an Israeli citizen in good standing. Do you have any other identification with you? Perhaps a university credential?"

Yakub nodded. "I have my UC Berkeley faculty card. Will that help?" He passed this over to Muhtadi as well. The photo, revealing a smiling man with short-cropped black hair and clean-shaven face, was reassuringly Western in appearance.

"Yes," said Muhtadi. "This should also help."

Muhtadi handed Yakub's identification papers back to him, and after this, the three men became quiet. They wove through the tortuous streets of Cairo and its outskirts, entering the straight highway leading towards the Suez Canal. The landscape, flat and sandy, was familiar to Yakub from his youth. He dozed throughout this portion of the journey, surrendering to the fatigue resulting from the extended travel and the grief of the last several days.

The group arrived at the Ahmed Hamdi Tunnel at the Suez Canal just as the sun was coming up. Ahead, Yakub could see the first morning rays strike the water, the canal a bright ribbon stretching in both directions through the yellow sand.

After just a few minutes in the tunnel, they emerged on the far side. Kareem then directed his car to the road leading towards the sandy expanse of the Sinai. Despite the time, it was already growing warm, and the three men rolled down their car windows. Kareem turned on the radio, and the air blowing about them was filled with the sound of popular Arabic music. In anticipation of the journey before them, Yakub felt his excitement rising, his curiosity about the poem possessing him, despite his grief for his father. The hours passed quickly, with little conversation.

By noon, they reached the Israeli border, and Kareem let them off at the Egyptian customs station. Muhtadi had anticipated no trouble here, estimating that it would take them an hour or so to get through. But Yakub became dismayed as the time stretched on: ninety minutes, two hours. By now, he had grown quite hungry.

He stepped outside the customs station. The air was warm but not too hot. He found several food stands, protected from the sun by canopies. Selecting one, he bought two sandwiches and a large plastic bottle of lukewarm water. He shared the sandwiches with Muhtadi. They were almost inedible: stale white bread with a single slab of dry, shiny meat in the center, no vegetables or condiments. His uncle ate a bite or two before setting it aside.

As Yakub finished his sandwich, a group sat down at the table next to them: a middle-aged man, his wife, and two daughters. The women were all garbed in *abayas*, the loose black robes worn by Arab women, their heads and throats covered by *hijabs*, head-scarves. By eavesdropping on their conversation, Yakub was able to deduce that they were Palestinians, returning from a visit to a family member in Cairo. Yakub noted that the daughters, despite their loose clothing, were young and shapely. One, in particular, had a fresh and lovely face, which the *hijab* only further ornamented.

He wondered, momentarily, what it would be like to start over again in life with a new wife, new family. He shook his head. The idea of re-living the early days of marriage with an immature woman did not appeal to him at all. Yes, it was true that, according to Islamic law, he was permitted up to four wives, assuming he could provide for all of them. But this was, of course, against the civil laws in most countries and, Yakub admitted to himself, in the absence of some kind of overwhelming population disruption, likely contrary to modern standards of human decency. In any case, complex as their relationship might be, he loved his wife and never wanted another woman.

Just as Yakub's impatience was reaching the boiling point, the customs officers returned with their passports and waved them on, gesturing to a battered bus that was filling up with travelers. Yakub and Muhtadi boarded and, soon afterwards, arrived at the Israeli customs station.

As Muhtadi had predicted, after submitting his passport, Yakub was taken into a back room by two young Israeli soldiers, searched thoroughly, and then interrogated for over an hour. The young men drilled him with questions, their body language betraying their skepticism of Yakub's responses: who was he visiting in Israel? What was his purpose there? Had he ever been friends with people known to be terrorists? They showed him pictures.

To the question of his purpose in Israel, Yakub could not be one hundred percent truthful. Could he really say he was here to view evidence confirming the family legend of a poem to redeem the world? No, of course not. Instead, he explained that he was visiting his Bedouin family in Jericho, in the wake of the family patriarch's death. Yakub showed them the obituary. This explanation seemed to satisfy the border guards, and, at last, they stamped his passport and approved his entry to Israel.

It was 3:00 pm when Yakub and Muhtadi left the building and entered the parking lot. There, they found Muhtadi's grandson, Khalid, the son of Muhtadi's deceased only son, Kamal. He was dressed in jeans, t-shirt, and sneakers and stood next to an ancient Toyota Camry. Khalid was taller than Yakub, about five foot ten, and Yakub estimated his age at around twenty-five. He smiled when Muhtadi introduced him to Yakub, giving him a shy embrace.

"*Ahlan wasahlan,*" he said, and then in English, "It is nice to meet you. I did not expect a visitor!" He reached in the car and rearranged the items on the back seat.

Muhtadi got in the front seat while Yakub climbed into the back. Soon, they were on the road. Through his car window, Yakub saw eerie evidence of recent warfare: twisted and rusted remnants of Egyptian tanks, signs warning of unexploded land mines, villages with battered houses, each and every one damaged by explosives. Finally, the devastation gave way to the empty, yellow landscape of the Negev.

As they drove, Yakub spoke with Khalid, whom he learned was a student at Tel Aviv University. After several minutes, Khalid made a phone call on his cell phone, letting his grandmother know that they would have a guest for dinner, explaining who it was.

"She was thrilled," said Khalid, after hanging up.

The conversation ebbed, and Yakub went back to staring out the window and thinking about the poem. Khalid switched on the radio. Chanted verses of the Quran floated back to Yakub, haunting and ethereal.

They drove past Beer-Sheva then travelled up to the southernmost tip of the Dead Sea. The landscape to their left turned rocky and mountainous, and eventually Yakub saw the unmistakable shape of the plateau of Masada. As a student at Cairo University, he had studied its remarkable history, the self-sacrifice of Jewish zealots in resistance to Roman conquest. He had not known, at the time, how critical the topic of self-martyrdom would become to those of his faith, Islam, in current years.

Soon after, there were signs to Ein Gedi, and Yakub saw the trees leading away from the highway towards the base of the mountains, the river hinting of the lush oasis above.

At last, the Dead Sea gave way to the river Jordan on their right and they turned off the main highway, navigating a series of small paved roads, ending up bouncing along a narrow dirt lane.

Yakub's knees were stiff and his backside sore from many hours of confinement and the vehicle's inflexible shock-absorbers. Despite his fatigue, his heart beat rapidly when he saw the small grouping of stucco-sided houses ahead.

It was already early evening when the car stopped and Yakub opened the door. Warm air rushed in, fragrant with jasmine and the smell of roasting lamb. He spied a young boy leading a group of goats up the road and smiled broadly, feeling as though he had come home.

A bell on the door jingled when they entered Muhtadi's house. The smells of cooking lamb and fresh bread overpowered them as a tiny woman exited the kitchen. Wrapped in *hijab* and *abaya*, she was even more diminutive than Muhtadi, her face etched with a multitude of tiny wrinkles and smile lines. These deepened as her husband spoke, introducing her as Samiha and telling her details about their honored visitor, a "great poet from America," as Muhtadi described him. She grasped Yakub's hand in both of hers, smiling and bowing her head, wishing him *"Ahlan wasahlan!"* and repeating *"al-hamdu lillah!"* over and over as tears streamed down her cheeks.

Soon, more relatives began to show up to greet Yakub, inhabitants of the village of Shaddad, the cousins and more distant relatives from the surrounding houses. They sat in Muhtadi's small living room, ate sweets, and drank strong coffee, served from a silver pot, speaking in Arabic smattered with Hebrew. Yakub accepted their condolences and found comfort in speaking the Bedouin Arabic he remembered from his childhood. He was happy to be with his family again, happy to feel the joy of homecoming among people who still loved him, despite his long absence. Some older relatives even remembered him as a boy. They asked him questions about California, and laughed in amazement as they heard his stories of the land of milk and honey, freedom and opportunity.

At last, as the night became fully dark, most of his relatives left, embracing him strongly before exiting. They invited him to visit them, admonishing him that he should come home more often. Several relatives stayed on for dinner, including Muhtadi's cousin, Adnan, and Adnan's daughter, Insaf. Muhtadi's daughter-in-law, Najma, also remained, as she and her son, Khalid, had lived with him since her husband, Muhtadi's son, Kamal, had died fighting in the Israeli army in the Yom Kippur war in 1973.

With the lead-time of Khalid's phone call, Muhtadi's wife and daughter-in-law had been able to prepare a lavish meal. The women emerged from the kitchen with silver trays loaded by plates piled high with food: hummus, falafel, Arabic bread, and dishes of steaming *mansaf*, the Bedouin main course of rice and nuts topped with spiced lamb meat. The women set the trays down in front of the men, who settled themselves on the floor in a semicircle. The men dished food into the bread, which they ate with relish. Yakub joined in happily, recalling similar meals from his remote childhood.

When they had finished, the women removed the trays, replacing them with dishes of baklava and *zarad*, round cookies filled with dates.

At last, after all the food was consumed and removed, Muhtadi's wife, Samiha, returned with a tray containing a silver coffee pot and a number of small cups. This was the *qahwa saada*, the "plain coffee" that Yakub remembered as a ritual the men participated in when he was a child. Samiha left, and Muhtadi poured portions of the bitter unsweetened brew into each of the small cups, handing them one by one to the men assembled.

Muhtadi continued to refill their cups until each man signaled, by moving the cup back and forth between his thumb and middle finger, that he was done. Yakub felt his heart racing. He wondered if it was the coffee, or the anticipation of revelations about *the poem,* still to come.

At last, coffee ritual complete, the time had arrived for the telling of stories. The women returned to clear the trays and then retreated again to the kitchen, with the exception of Insaf, who, Yakub noted with some interest, sat down on a cushion next to her father and remained with the men. He wondered about this.

"So!" began Adnan. "Tell us what has brought you here to us, so far from your civilized roads!"

Yakub looked across at his relative. The light of the kerosene lantern, the sole illumination in the darkened room, danced on his face. Yakub's eyes moved to Muhtadi with a question and Muhtadi nodded.

Yakub looked back at Adnan. "My uncle tells me that there is a poem."

All eyes were on Yakub.

"This poem will bring about the redemption of the world, paradise on earth."

Adnan was nodding his head.

Now, Insaf spoke, her voice high and pleasant. "Yes. But do you know the whole story?"

"No," replied Yakub, turning to her and adding, wryly, "That is why I'm here."

"Insaf will tell the story," said Muhtadi. "She tells it best." And now, Yakub understood why she had returned to sit with the men.

He looked at Insaf more carefully. As was customary, her head was covered by a scarf. This left her face free for scrutiny. She was, Yakub estimated, about forty. He had learned she was a widow, childless. Emotions moved across her face as she drew the story up.

She directed a question first to Yakub, speaking in precise and flawless Arabic. "You do, I imagine, still read the Quran, though you live in America?"

Yakub nodded his head. "Of course."

"Then you perhaps know the verses, '...In the Book, you shall tell of Isma'il: he, too, was a man of his word...and his Lord was pleased with him.'"

Yakub thought a moment, and then said, "*Surat Maryam*," referring to the *sura*, the chapter of the Quran, that contained these words.

"Yes!" Insaf gave him a smile, pleased. "Isma'il was a prophet, well loved by God, and the first son of Ibrahim. After he was exiled from his father's camp by Ibrahim's wife, Sarah, he and his mother, Hagar, fled to the wilderness, near Beer-Sheva. There was no food or water, and Isma'il became mortally ill. It is said that Hagar grew so distressed by the imminent death of her only son that she began to run, desperately, back and forth, searching for water. And this is when the first of the miracles occurred." She paused as everyone watched her.

"Hagar's feet pounded so hard, the world turned inside out. Afterwards, she found herself and her son in a vastly different location. Not the Negev in Palestine, but a strange new place, the Hijaz, in Arabia. She was still running, but now, she ran between two hills, Safa and Marwa, in desperate search of water for her boy. Afraid at what she might find, she went to where Isma'il lay and saw that his heel had dug a trench. Within it, water welled upwards. She gave this water to her son, and the boy lived. This became the well of ZamZam, which still gives water to this day, near the holy house of *Allah*, the *Ka'ba*."

Yakub was familiar with this story from his schooling, though he had not heard it quite this way before. "And you will tell me, I assume, how this relates to our poem?"

Insaf smiled with some amusement in her face. "I am getting to that part." She took a swallow of water and continued. "Isma'il grew up there, in the place we now call Makkah. When he became a young man, he rebuilt God's house with his father, Ibrahim, who used to visit his family in Arabia on the divine flying horse, al-Burak, the very same horse, as you know, that transported the prophet, Muhammad, peace and blessings upon him, from Makkah to Jerusalem on the night he ascended from the stone at the heart of the world to the seventh level of paradise.

"Isma'il was a handsome man, lean from all the running he had done with his mother, Hagar. He was an accomplished bowman. His family never went hungry, despite the many children his wife, Fatima, bore him. Truly, he was accomplished at everything he did, a rare leader, despite his scarce words. For he said little, aside from the prayers to *Allah* he spoke and taught to others, and aside from the poems, which he created in great number. And they were of a beauty never before heard by the ears of men. People came from all over Arabia to listen, and they remained on with him afterwards. The land around God's house grew crowded.

"But Isma'il was often absent from his home. He hunted, it was true, but more often he spent time in the caves in the mountain high above the camp. The few people who ascended those heights heard strange noises: the voice of Isma'il repeating words, experimenting, playing with the sounds of his mother's tongue, Arabic.

"Isma'il discovered amazing things. He could make the words sound like one another. He could arrange words with one, two, three accents, put them together in ways that evoked streams running or birds flying. He spent his happiest hours in the cave, evoking one after the other of God's creations with his poems. He controlled his voice, breath blowing through his mouth, his teeth, tongue, lips, and larynx to create the beautiful sounds.

"Isma'il also kept a secret gift, one he'd received from God at the time his mother had turned the world inside out with her pounding feet. He found this thing in his mind after he drank the saving water at ZamZam. It was a mark, long and straight, and when he saw it behind his eyes, he drew it in the dirt by using a stick. After this, he drew it many times, and it reminded him of God, even when God's face seemed far away. He believed the mark had something to do with his poetry, but he had not yet discovered the connection. This was the inheritance he would pass on to his eldest son, Nabit.

"Isma'il did not know that, ages hence, this mark, the Arabic letter *Alif,* would blossom into the most beautiful bouquet in the hands of his descendent, Muhammad. That was all for later. For now, he accomplished all that was necessary with the simple instruments of air, tongue, and throat.

"Each night, by the fireside, he would sit and spin his words together, speaking of God and God's most precious creation, the human being. At such time, people would listen in silence, stunned, as visions formed before him, rising in the air to join with God above."

Insaf stopped and rubbed her eyes, as if she too were attempting to bring these visions to life.

Yakub said, "And was one of those poems the one we're

looking for?"

Insaf shook herself, as if to loosen herself from the grip of her internal vision. "It is possible, but we do not know. It was all so long ago. Almost four thousand years. And written Arabic did not arise until some two thousand years later, so all of it would have been passed along in oral form by word of mouth."

"But what happened next?" asked Yakub. "In the legend?"

A shadow seemed to flit across the room, and everyone moved uneasily. Insaf's father, Adnan, sniffed once, then said, "Beauty does not always inspire beauty."

"What do you mean?" said Yakub.

Insaf's father, Adnan, spoke now, picking up the thread of the story: "One night, when Isma'il was reciting his poetry, it is said that another was watching. A stranger. A man of cunning and ambition. As he listened to Isma'il, he grew disheartened, and his face fell. He had tried to speak as Isma'il spoke, but he did not have the gift. His words were flat, dull, like heavy weights. One could not say he did not love God, because he did. Other men worshipped stone idols. This man loved the One. But he was possessed by a burning love that would not be shared with others. He cried that he could not speak to God as Isma'il did. Jealousy and hatred overtook him.

"He vowed that if Isma'il used words for beauty that he too would use words, not for beauty but for power. He thought, 'I have seen how words can influence people. I will put together words in ways that cause others to do what I desire. When I am great and powerful, then God will love me far more than Isma'il.'

"The legend says that this man's name was al-Qayana."

Yakub lowered his eyebrows, repeating the name, "al-Qayana. As in 'metal-smith' or 'forger'?"

Adnan nodded. "And it is interesting, isn't it, in the context of words, if you take the second meaning."

Khalid, who had said nothing for some time, spoke up, saying, "Well, whoever he is, I have some friends who'd like to punch him in the nose." This brought laughter from the assembled group.

Yakub said, "But who was this al-Qayana? Where did he come from?"

Muhtadi now spoke. "Unfortunately, we know very little about him. Legend says he was from the North, from the barbaric territories, and not from Arabia.

"And yet he believed in the One God," mused Yakub.

"With himself as God's self-appointed apostle," said Muhtadi.

Adnan spoke, saying, "Allow me to tell you just a bit more about al-Qayana. According to legend, this man did what he said. He used words to turn the men around him away from the truth of God, and he led the people of Arabia away from the light into a prolonged darkness, *Jahiliyya*. This continued until the time of the Prophet, Muhammad, when, at last, light returned to the Arabic people. But even during this time of darkness, some people continued, secretly, to practice the faith of Ibrahim and Isma'il, and these were called *Hanifiyya*, true believers. Our family, the al-Shadi's, were among these."

"But what about the legend of *the poem?*" probed Yakub. "When did that first appear? At the time of Isma'il?"

"We don't know," said Insaf, regret in her melodious voice. "But it makes sense that the legend would arise then, when the people in Arabia first appreciated the power of man's words through poetry. Whatever the case, al-Qayana and his descendents believed in the legend and sought, with great ferocity, to prevent the creation or discovery of *the poem*. And the most devilish thing is, the family was able to survive and even flourish, since they never got their own hands dirty with blood but only incited others to violence."

"And how, exactly, did the al-Shadi's, our family, figure into this?" asked Yakub.

Adnan said, "By legend, the al-Shadi's are descendents of the line of Isma'il, and so inherited his gift of words. As *Hanifiyya*, the people of our family have always maintained their focus on God. As I'm sure you know, from the poetry of your father."

Yakub nodded. "And al-Qayana? What has happened to this family?"

Muhtadi replied, looking grave. "Sad to say, they still exist, though the family has taken another name now. 'Smith.' They use this ubiquitous name to hide among the peoples of the world, but in truth, the family composes only a fraction of those who bear the name. They are a small tribe, made so by inbreeding and the maladies that creates. But it does not take many people to continue a contagion of words. And they have family members spread throughout the world, in many nations and religious sects. They do not follow those religions, but rather, their own twisted interpretations of the holy texts. And furthermore, they know, with meticulous precision, who is a member of their tribe and who is not. Maintenance of genetic purity is a major concern of this family."

"And what do they do? These Smiths?" queried Yakub.

Muhtadi said, with unexpected bitterness: "Destroy truth. Massacre hope. Incite war."

"For what purpose?"

"Ah, a very excellent question!" said Muhtadi, sipping from his cold coffee and grimacing. "We believe, after much discussion and argument, that they are attempting to create the conditions for the coming of the Day of Judgment, the *yawm al-din*."

"What...I don't understand," said Yakub.

"You see," continued Muhtadi, "They do not envision paradise for all. Certainly not. According to them, only their people are worthy of paradise. So it is imperative to them to turn people from the right path, the way of truth, towards the wrong path, the way of crookedness. They incite people to hatred and war rather than love and peace, so that they may bring about the war that precedes redemption."

"And they do this with words," said Yakub.

The assembled at the table nodded.

"And the poem we seek would do the opposite."

They nodded again.

"Alright," said Yakub. "I understand."

The discussion had brought them far into the night. Insaf and Adnan took their leave to return to their home, while Khalid, Samiha, and Najma went off to bed upstairs, leaving Yakub and Muhtadi alone at the table. The lamp still burned in the dark dining room, sending wavering light toward the shadowed ceiling. Across the table, Muhtadi's eyes appeared solid black in their sockets, the lines on his forehead deep.

"And this is the secret my father did not wish me to know?" asked Yakub.

He saw his uncle nod. "Your father wished to bury this dangerous secret as far in the past as possible," he said, "for your sake."

"But is it really so dangerous?"

"The Smith family is more dangerous than you can possibly

imagine. Many of your ancestors have died mysteriously over the years. Including my own son, Kamal."

Yakub emitted a sound of disbelief.

Muhtadi's head jerked up. "Do not scoff. This is the reason why, even before my son's death, your father fled to Cairo and abandoned our family, though it caused him great pain. He did this for you, because he saw that you were among the gifted. If you stayed here, you would try to write this poem, or to find it, whichever may be the case."

Yakub was arrested by this detail. "You mean, it's possible that the poem has not yet been written?"

"Yes. The words of the legend are ambiguous."

"But what does the legend say, then?"

Muhtadi stood up, his chair scraping against the floor with an eerie screech. "I will show you." He walked across the dining room, gesturing that Yakub should follow him.

He led him back to a small room behind the dining room, evidently once the third bedroom but now, judging by the books and papers arrayed on the desk and the single bed, serving as a make-shift office. There, he turned on one of the few electric lights in the house, a rickety table lamp. He removed the wall panel of what looked like a crawl-space vent, revealing a dark alcove. Out of this space, he pulled a shiny metal chest. He unlocked this with one of two brass keys he kept dangling from a chain around his neck, flipping open the top.

Inside, Yakub saw a roll of parchment, nearly black in color, with many cracks along its edges and a number of small holes and perforations in its outside roll. Muhtadi cleared a space on the desk among the papers which, Yakub noted with interest, were covered with the distinctive markings of Arabic poetry. *Was his uncle trying to write the poem? Even now?*

Meanwhile, Muhtadi carefully removed the scroll and laid it down. Leaning over the desk, he held the bulk of the roll with one hand while he carefully pulled back just the edge with the other, revealing the words *"Tehillim,"* Psalms. Standing behind him, Yakub drew in his breath sharply.

Letting go of the parchment with great gentleness, Muhtadi turned back to Yakub, gesturing to the single wooden chair by the desk. Yakub shook his head, indicating that Muhtadi should sit, while Yakub himself sat down on the floor. He looked up expectantly at his uncle, who began in a hushed voice:

"I found this scroll of Psalms when I was still a young man, soon after you were born. It was back in 1944, before the state of Israel was created, and before they discovered the Dead Sea Scrolls. When shepherding the goats, I used to amuse myself by climbing up into the caves to explore. It was quite difficult, the cliffs were very steep, and I had no ropes or equipment. But I was, of course, more agile back then…" a wry smile marked his wrinkled face, and Yakub smiled too.

"One day," Muhtadi continued, "I was out with the goats. I saw a new cave, very, very high up in the cliff. I recall it was hot that day, but I decided I would climb up anyway. By the time I reached the cave, I was completely exhausted. I remember tumbling through the opening and lying in the cool darkness for a long time. Little by little, I revived.

"As my eyes adjusted, I perceived an odd shape in one corner. It did not have the jagged form of a rock, but was round and smooth. When I went to investigate it, I found a single clay pot." He paused, lost in this youthful memory.

"What did you do then?" prompted Yakub.

Muhtadi looked back at Yakub, blinking, then said, "I took the jar out into the sunlight, cradling it carefully so I would not break it. There, on the ledge outside the cave, I removed the lid and looked into the mouth of the jar. Inside, I saw this rolled up parchment. And there was something else in the jar, too."

"What?" said Yakub, trying hard to control his impatience.

"The greater treasure," said his uncle, mysteriously. He arose once more and, returning to the alcove, retrieved a smaller box. He opened this with the other key around his neck. Inside, protected further in a plastic folio, Yakub saw a white sheet of parchment, about the size of a postcard and completely square. Unlike the scroll of Psalms, the edge of this parchment was pristine, neither cracked nor uneven, without evidence of damage by insects or mold. As a student of poetry and ancient languages, Yakub recognized the writing as Aramaic. The Hebrew characters stood out boldly, the script beautiful and clear. Yakub translated it as follows:

I tell of a poem of ancient wisdom, a creation understood in the house of Abraham and his sons, Ishmael and Isaac. When the truth of this poem fills the world, immediately it will be redeemed. The heavens will be sewn to the earth and God's name (YHVH) will be one.[3]

Muhtadi showed Yakub where the name for God, *YHVH*, was written in a more ancient form of script, a characteristic of authentic manuscripts from the era of the Dead Sea Scrolls. This testified that the manuscript was written sometime near the time of Jesus, almost two thousand years ago. Yakub gazed at the parchment for several minutes. At last he breathed, "So it is true! But what is the significance of the scroll of Psalms?"

"I don't know yet. I have examined this scroll carefully, and it appears to be merely an ordinary, though extremely valuable, version of Psalms, chapters one through ninety-six. There must be something in these Psalms that the recorder of the legend felt important to connect with the manuscript."

"Hmmm," said Yakub, thinking. "Psalm 96. What does it say?" He stood and carefully rolled back the bulk of the scroll from its edge, then peered down at the darkened parchment. *"Shiru l'Adonai shir chadash,"* he read aloud, *"Shiru l'Adonai, kol ha-aretz.* Sing to the Lord a new song, Sing to the Lord, all the earth…Could this 'New Song' be referring to our poem?"

"My assumption," said Muhtadi.

"And the *legend* captured in the manuscript uses the same word, *shir*, albeit in Aramaic."

Muhtadi nodded. He took a deep breath and sniffed. "When he was fifteen, I showed my son, Kamal, this manuscript." He directed his gaze towards a photo on his desk, a dark young man in an Israeli army uniform

"This is your son?" asked Yakub, picking up the photo.

Muhtadi nodded. "Yes. Kamal, named for beauty. Dead many years now."

"I'm sorry," said Yakub. "And he was in the Israeli army? But he was a Muslim, no?"

---

[3] חוינא על שירתא דחכמתא עתיקא, עובדא דידעין ביה בביתא דאברהם
ובנוי ישמעאל ויצחק. וכד קושטא דהאי שירתא מלייא כל ארעא ביה שעתא יתגלי
פורקנרא בעלמא ושמייא יתחטטן לארעא ושמא קדישא יי* יהא חד.

* YHVH, acronym for *Yud-Hey-Vav-Hey*

"Many Bedouin ended up inside the lines of the Israeli border, and so are Israelis. We serve our country, like good citizens."

"What happened?" Yakub said, looking up from the photo and over at his uncle. He saw tears collecting along Muhtadi's eyelids.

"My boy was just a little younger then you. Born in 1946. He was 27 at the time of the Yom Kippur war. Because he spoke Arabic, they assigned him to work in espionage, across enemy lines. He was killed in Syria. We learned later that my son was betrayed by a 'friend,' someone who informed on his movements to the enemy. We tried to launch an inquiry, but nothing came of it."

"And you believe the Smith family was involved? Why?" Yakub could not keep the skepticism from his voice.

Muhtadi sniffed and wiped at the tears with the back of his small hand. "My son was among the gifted, like you. After he saw this parchment, all his efforts were focused on writing this poem. While here in Shaddad, his work was comparatively private, but once he was in the army, his activities became more public. I am sure someone in that Smith family took note of this, with the inevitable outcome. Believe me, they are aware of the poetic genius of the al-Shadi's. Other such incidents have occurred over the years."

"But, I can't believe…" this story seemed to Yakub far-fetched.

"Why not? This is exactly the method they use! Whispering, informing, inciting others to do their killing work for them."

"Well…" said Yakub, still unconvinced, "There are lots of ways he could have died, in war…"

Muhtadi directed a burning gaze at Yakub. "My boy," he said, "do not underestimate the Smith family. Trust your own father, who was evidently convinced enough to move you far away from Shaddad and our family's legend."

"But why," queried Yakub, "doesn't the Smith family just come and wipe out the whole al-Shadi village? Make an end of it once and for all?"

"Ah," said Muhtadi, his face breaking into a mirthless smile. "First, the Smiths do not resort to the kind of violence you describe. Their method is to incite others to violence, through use of words."

"Even so," said Yakub, "they could have found a way,

through their own methods, to destroy us."

"That is true," admitted Muhtadi, "But they are torn. Like us, they do not know whether the poem already exists or is yet to be created. Yes, they would like to ensure, at all costs, that no one writes such a poem. On the other hand, if it already exists, they know that members of our family are most likely to find it. They wait for us to lead them to it, so they can destroy it, or use it in some manner for their own gain."

"So why do you think they instigated the murder of your son, Kamal?"

"I suppose his behavior convinced them that he had become a liability."

Yakub shook his head, still skeptical. "It all just seems so unlikely."

"Believe me or not, that is up to you. I warn you only that interactions with the Smith family are inevitably deadly." He looked at Yakub. "And you, Yakub, you have moved even farther away than your father. All the way to America. But you cannot, and should not, escape our family's destiny."

"Why not?"

"Because God has given us a sacred task . You are a poet. That means more than just publication, fame, and livelihood. Yes, pursuing the legend brings great danger. But also the possibility of inestimable reward, for the sake of humanity."

Yakub nodded, but he was still unconvinced about the Smiths and his uncle's conspiracy theory. The whole thing just seemed too outlandish. He admitted to himself that he wasn't even sure that this 'Smith" tribe truly existed.

Muhtadi sighed, stood, and began packing up his treasures, replacing the parchment and the larger scroll of Psalms back in their cases and relocking them. He put the two boxes back in the niche then shut and locked it as well. He then sat back down heavily in the rolling desk chair, rubbing his eyes.

Yakub looked at his elderly uncle, noting to himself that he appeared exhausted. "You have had a long trip and should rest."

"Yes," said Muhtadi. He rose again, now unsteadily, and Yakub stood up to support him. "I am sorry I haven't succeeded in finding or writing this poem," said, Muhtadi. "I don't know how to do it. God is very far from me." He gestured weakly at the papers on the desk, tears flooding his eyes once again.

Yakub looked away for a moment, considering. His gaze settled on the window, its opening now just a black rectangle containing his own reflection. Perhaps he had already been looking for this poem himself, he thought. Perhaps he had been looking for it all his life.

"I will help you," he said.

KINGDOM

London, England

12:01 pm. Thursday, November 2ⁿᵈ 2006
Mr. Smith, to Eugene Smith (journal entry)

My dear son – as a result of a worsening infirmity, of which I know you are aware, a sudden pressing need has come upon me to pass on certain knowledge to you, in case God should decide, in His wisdom, to take me to Him sooner than expected. I fear that my remaining days on this earth will not be many. Just yesterday, I passed quantities of bright red blood from my intestines. Something is amiss, but I no longer trust the doctors to diagnose or treat this most recent malady. And so I set this down, so you may learn about me and take to heart the wisdom I have gained in life.

Because you are not yet twenty five, I have not told you the full, secret history of our family. But it is nearly time, and if I pass before you reach the age, I would like you to learn these things from me. So I begin.

Know this my son. Words! I must tell you. I love them. They are ours, they belong to me and to you. I delight as they leave my pen and splash out onto the page behind my hand! And I have worked so hard, so hard, to master them. Years of study. I can see my diplomas from where I sit in my bed. Oxford, Harvard. And not just ordinary degrees. Advanced studies. Ancient languages. Hebrew, Aramaic, Arabic, Greek, Latin. Of this you are aware. It is necessary to know these things, for the holy purpose of our family, the Smith family, once al-Qayana. You must also learn them, and I know that you are doing so, in your studies at Cambridge.

The word *al-Qayana* means "the metal smiths," in Arabic. And once, we did work with metal. Now our material is *the word*. Eons ago, our fathers discovered the power it contains. Foolish men use spears, arrows, swords, guns, bombs to fight the wars. But everything begins and ends with words. Words start the wars. Words incite people to kill. Words spread rumors, gossip, libel. It was the Jew Maimonides who said that evil speech, *lashon hara*, is worse than murder or rape. Too bad that he himself used words in a futile attempt to further the doomed cause of his people!

Yes, my son, sad to say, they are doomed. As are all those not chosen, as we are, by God, to enter the gates of heaven in triumph while others remain behind to spend eternity in torment.

Our forefather learned, in ancient times, from God Himself, that it is only the true believers who are destined for salvation. The holy texts speak truth. But others misinterpret them, to their detriment. There will be a great war and a messiah and then salvation. But only for the worthy. And we must work to bring this war, the war to end all wars. We are almost there.

There is an equally ancient evil that bedevils us. A poem, said to contain the power to transform the souls of those who read it. When this occurs, the world and all its people will be redeemed. But my son! We cannot allow this. It is OUR family that loves God, and the others must not be saved. And so, if we are to successfully pave the way for our Armageddon, we must locate and destroy this cursed poem.

Since ancient times, there have been others who have known about *the poem*, have sought to discover or to write it. They are poets by trade. Poetry. It is not the medium of the Smith family. In fact, it is the work of the forsaken and the damned. They think that poems stand alone as things of beauty. They are foolish and misguided. Words are not an end in themselves but simply a means to power. I am happy to report that we have destroyed countless of these witless *poets* through the eons.

But now my stomach ails me, and I must stop. The doctors said it was a lack of cavities and passages in my gut at birth. A simple thing to fix, but it seems they made a hatchet job of it, citing "inborn errors" and "mutation." After the surgery, I was strong, but now, in my later years, my gut is tethered and I cannot leave my bedroom. Has it been ten years already since I last walked under the sun? But not to worry, my dearest boy. I can accomplish all I need from here, with my words alone, just as I did last time, when that Englishman picked up on the trail. How easily I dispensed with him!

Here, I console myself with the things I love. My library, my books, stretching from floor to ceiling on all sides, here in my own room. I see the titles now: Apion's *History of Egypt,* Ibn Hazm's *Fisal,* Machiavelli's *The Prince,* Hitler's *Mein Kampf,* Jacob Frank's *Sayings,* Abu Ishaq Al Ibiri's *Ode Against the Jews.* Some of these writings, these masterpieces, are from the pens of your very own family. Know this well!

And son, remember above all else, that though I may reprimand you and, at times, have resorted to the harsher disciplinary methods used by my own parents, I have done these things solely out of concern for your mortal soul. The days of confinement and forced meditation in dark places break the bridling spirit and allow for entry of God's divine grace, that luminous elixir uniquely formed and created for the select of our chosen clan. Through seclusion and self-mortification, we learn to overcome our desire for earthly love, leaving place only for the love of God. Do not despise me, but respect me, as I learned to respect my own parents, once the fear and loathing had passed.

San Fancisco, California
5:30 am. Thursday, November 2nd 2006
Dr. Rachel Roseman

The day I met Yakub began with a small but annoying mishap. Out for my morning jog, I was speeding along my usual four-mile route through the Presidio when something unexpected occurred. What I took to be a log beside the trail in the pre-dawn gloom suddenly sat up, emitting a distinctly non-pastoral string of obscenities and revealing itself as a human being.

"*Look Out!*" I yelled, startled from my runner's stupor. At that moment, the toe of my shoe caught on the top of a tree root, tripping me and sending me, arms outstretched, sailing through the murk into the eucalyptus leaves piled alongside the trail. There, my right hand connected with a broken bottle, resulting in a sharp pain at the outside of my palm.

I struggled to sit up among the leaves, dismayed to see that I had a deep cut that might need stitches. Meanwhile, the person whose sleep I'd inadvertently disturbed continued to rail.

"'Smatter with you? Can't you see when a person's sick? Gotta go smashing through the woods like some kinda damned rhinoceros?"

"Zeke?" I said. I could barely make out the outlines of the man in the darkness, but it sounded like him. "Is that you?"

"Depends."

"Depends? Depends on what?"

"Depends who's asking."

"It's Rachel. Doctor Roseman."

"Doc?"

I stood up, brushing the leaves and dirt from my sweat

pants, wincing at the pain in my right hand. I touched my wrist, which was wet with sticky blood. I took the sweatshirt I'd tied around my waist earlier and, holding my injured palm against my thigh, wrapped it around my hand in an attempt at a compression dressing.

"You okay?" said Zeke.

"Fine," I replied. "What are you doing here?" I knew Zeke's usual spot was over on Funston, in the trees along the strip by Park Presidio.

"Couldn't make it back home last night. Leg was hurtin'."

I groped my way through the gloomy light to where Zeke was lying. Though it was hard to make things out, I saw that his legs were inserted into a sleeping bag.

"What's wrong?"

"Got another one of them…whadda ya call 'em?"

"Abscesses," I said. "We call them abscesses."

"Yeah. One 'a them."

"Gosh darn it, Zeke! You've been skin popping again?"

Zeke didn't answer, but I saw his head nod.

Of course, I didn't usually have conversations with homeless people in dark and deserted public places, but Zeke had been one of my regular patients at the family medicine clinic over at County for over eight years now.

I reached my left hand down to check his forehead.

"Zeke," I said, "you're burning up!"

"I know. I feel like shit."

"We've got to get you into the hospital," I said.

"God damn it!" said Zeke. "I hate that place."

"That abscess will need to be drained," I said.

"Yeah. But I ain't takin' no ambulance. Feel like a friggin' idiot."

"Well, you can't take the bus in your condition. I'll go home, get changed, and come back to get you with my car. I'm about a mile and a half from here. I should be back within forty-five minutes."

"You'll give me a ride in your car?" he said. I could hear the incredulity in his voice, and saw his face, an indistinct and pale oval in the growing light, looking up at me.

"I'm heading to work anyway."

"I don' wanna go."

"I know," I said, sympathetically. "But with that fever, this abscess can't be good. Promise me you'll stay here until I get back."

Zeke mumbled.

"Sorry? I couldn't hear that. What?"

"Okay, I promise."

I pulled the sweatshirt tighter around my injured hand, and ran the twenty blocks back to my apartment at Sacramento and Pierce. Darn. When would I possibly have time for stitches?

When I arrived home, I showered, carefully dried my injured hand, and then taped the wound shut with butterfly bandages, promising myself I'd take care of this later. I dressed and grabbed my things for work, and then jumped in my car and headed back to pick up Zeke.

Zeke had been a heroin abuser for as long as I'd known him. From a distance, he could pass for the classic California surfer type: blond hair, blue eyes, dark tan. But when you got up close, you saw the prematurely aged look of the long-time drug abuser: yellow hair greasy and thin, skin leathery, tan splotchy and uneven, an unintended side effect of living on the street.

Despite his drug habit, though, Zeke was one of the sweetest men I had ever met. And he was a poet. He always brought me scraps of writing when he came in to see me in the clinic. I found this endearing and had kept all of these poetry fragments. In some crazy way, his words often made more sense than any of the other things I read.

Recently, Zeke had blown out all his usable veins and resorted to skin-popping, the practice of injecting directly into the skin. Unfortunately, this led to lots of skin abscesses. Sometimes, they cleared on their own, but often, they required surgical drainage. Zeke was a pretty hardy guy. If this one had slowed him down that much, I imagined it was bad.

I drove up Sacramento, turning right at Presidio. Soon after entering the gate, I turned left onto the small road that skirted Julius Kahn playground. I saw Zeke, sitting with his bags, leaning up against the Presidio wall. I pulled the car over and got out. Zeke was slumped over, dozing. He startled when he heard me, then looked at me blearily, his eyes filmy.

"Doc?" He said. His face was covered with sweat, despite the chilly San Francisco morning.

"Let's get you going, Zeke," I said. I opened the hatchback

on my Honda Accord and threw in his stuff. I'd worry about the mess later. I opened the passenger door and helped Zeke in, then got in myself on the driver's side, noting the characteristic smell that Zeke exuded: an odd mixture of dust and body oil.

Zeke continued to doze as we drove the twenty minutes over to County. At one point, near our destination, I heard him say, "You're a angel, doc."

I pulled up next to the outpatient building and, putting on the flashers, ran in, located a wheelchair, then went back out and collected Zeke. We took the elevators up to the third floor, where the family medicine clinic was located.

The receptionist raised her eyebrows when she saw me.

"Morning!" I called as I entered the double doors to the clinic and rolled past her down the hall.

It was still early, 8:30 am, and clinic didn't start until 9:00, so all the exam rooms were empty. I left Zeke in Room One then ran back downstairs to get his stuff.

When I returned, I saw Lenny Goldstein, my boss, at the far end of the hall. "Lenny!" I called.

He looked down the hall at me and called back, "Hey, Rachel, what's up? You been camping?" He'd noticed the sleeping bag.

"Not exactly," I said. "Can I talk to you?"

Lenny came down and I let him know about Zeke.

"I gotta go park my car," I said.

Lenny said, "No worries. I'll have one of the nurses check his vitals. You can call the surgeons when you get back."

I went and took care of my car, which, fortunately, had not been towed. When I returned, I found Lenny in Room One with Zeke, who had in the meantime changed into one of our paper hospital gowns. Lenny was examining Zeke's leg, appearing grim. When I entered, he looked over at me and grimaced.

I took a look myself. Zeke had a lump the size of an orange on the outside of his right thigh. The skin on top and surrounding the mass on all sides was bright red.

Zeke was looking away, averting his eyes from the abscess. I didn't blame him.

I called the operator and asked for the on-call surgeon. When he came on the phone, I informed a Doctor Gary Black, whom I had never spoken to before, that we had a patient with an abscess that needed draining, over in family medicine clinic. Dr. Black said he had no idea where that was, so I explained how to find us. He said he'd be over in about an hour. Meantime, we should draw some blood, collect some urine, and do a physical to make sure the patient was okay for surgery.

I wrote orders for the lab work, then went back and did a full exam on Zeke, listening to his heart and lungs and palpating his belly. Zeke submitted to this examination silently. At the end, he said, "Thanks, doc. I'd be dead a long time without you."

"That'd be a shame," I said. "Who'd write me poetry then?"

I left and went to go see my other patients, now late for my morning clinic. As I went to check my schedule, Lenny came to find me.

"Everything okay?" he asked.

"Yup, the surgeon, Dr. Black, will be over to check on Zeke in about a half hour."

"Excellent. Rachel, that was above and beyond the call of duty."

"You should talk," I said. "What time'd you go home last night?"

"Oh, I don't know. Maybe 10:00? 10:30?"

"Ah! An early night!" I said.

I was giving Lenny a hard time, picking up on a familiar theme of conversation between us. He spent virtually all his time at the hospital, caring for San Francisco's poor, sick, and underserved, much to the disgruntlement of his live-in girlfriend, Rebecca. Lenny had been a close friend of my husband, David, back in those days. Truthfully, Lenny was about the best doctor I'd ever met.

"Yeah, well, we're both up there at 10 out of 10 on the 'workaholic' scale, I'd say. Anyway, gotta go. Mr. Abelson will add another four complaints for each minute I delay..."

He headed down the hall, knocked on one of the exam room doors, called out, "Mr. Abelson? It's Dr. Goldstein." I heard a muffled reply from inside, and Lenny entered the room, leaving me alone in the hallway.

I went to the nurses' station to check the schedule for my morning clinic that day. *Ay-caramba!* A patient every fifteen minutes. Ah well, I sighed. What else was new? I draped my stethoscope around my neck, stuck my prescription pad in my pocket, and dove in, pulling the chart off the front of the first exam room door.

Inside the room, I found my patient, Cresencia, a sixty-year-old Filipino woman with diabetes whom I had the less than pleasant task of informing she'd need to go on insulin today.

When I entered, she gestured to the side counter. "Doctor!" she said, "I brought you something!"

I went over to have a look. A pecan pie! Seeing its glistening top, studded with sugary nuts, reminded me that I was famished.

"Cresencia! Just what I needed for breakfast!" The smell of the buttery crust and still-warm caramelized sugar was making my mouth water.

She beamed. Even though she could no longer enjoy these treats, she loved it when others did so.

My empty stomach grumbling, I sat down on the stool across from Cresencia, doing my best to put a positive spin on the news of the cataclysmic changes that would be affecting her life, referring her to a nurse specialist who would teach her how to do all the needle-intensive activities now necessary. Cresencia looked scared, but not surprised. This had been coming for some time. I tried to relieve her of the misconception that all of this was her fault. Really, the truth was she'd been dealt some pretty lousy metabolic cards.

After twenty minutes, I bid Cresencia goodbye and, taking the pie with me, went to my office. There, I enjoyed a big, juicy slice, accompanied by my second cup of coffee for the day. Aware of my caffeine weakness, the nurses always kept a fresh pot going in my office.

I rinsed my hands and face, thus destroying all evidence of my dietary crime. I then went to see my second patient, an infant boy in for his two-week "well child check." While the baby was generally in good health, he had not gained as much weight as expected. His mother, a young Irish woman with exquisite porcelain skin and lustrous black hair, was having trouble nursing, and was in a near nervous-breakdown as a result. I spent another twenty minutes counseling her, reassuring her that there was plenty of help around for just this problem. Before finishing the appointment, I called to arrange for a nurse come to her home to assist her with her efforts to breastfeed. I then left her, advising her to bring the baby back in next week for a quick follow-up.

Between my second and third patients, I went to check on Zeke, but found out that the surgical team had already taken him over to the hospital for incision and drainage of his abscess. It seemed a little strange to me that the surgeon, Dr. Black, hadn't come to find me to let me know he was taking Zeke, but oh well. Family docs like me were not as high up on the food chain of medical specialties as surgeons. But I knew that Zeke would be in good hands with the docs here at County.

I finished seeing the patients in my morning clinic, went and grabbed another cup of coffee and a sandwich, then dived into my afternoon patients. It was more of my cadre of familiars: a random mixture of pregnant women, sore throats, pap smears, chronic diseases, well child checks, depression, substance abuse. As always, I was captivated by the human beings that waited for me on the other side of each exam room door.

After I finished up with my last patient, a pregnant woman due in February, I went over to check on Zeke. The surgical ward was on the second floor of the main hospital, in a different building from the outpatient clinic where I worked. I'd checked with hospital admitting. Zeke was in room 248.

When I walked in, Zeke's face lit up and he smiled, revealing a number of missing teeth. "Doc Roseman!" he said, "How come you look prettier every time?" Apparently, Zeke was feeling better.

I couldn't suppress a grin at his goofy expression but then assumed my serious doctor face. "Zeke, compliments will get you nowhere. Why'd you go and get yourself another abscess, anyway? I thought you'd had enough of this place by now."

"Doc, if I didn't get sick, when would I ever get to see you?"

"News flash! You don't have to get sick just to see me! In fact, I'll see you anytime when you're *not* sick, right here in my very own clinic!"

Shifting uncomfortably at the reminder of his poor clinic attendance, Zeke changed the subject, saying, "Hey, I noticed before. Your hair's gotten real long since I last saw you."

I readjusted the elastic band in my ponytail, wincing at the pain in my neglected laceration. "Well, it's had a chance to grow a lot, considering you missed your last two discharge appointments."

Zeke looked at me, concern now erasing the guilty look on his face. "How's your hand? I'm sorry about that, doc."

"It's not your fault."

Zeke frowned. "You gonna be alright?"

"Sure."

We were quiet for a minute as I took a look at Zeke's vitals board. Still a little fever, but not bad. Good pulse and respiratory rate, good I's and O's (inputs and outputs). Aside from his drug habit, Zeke was doing great.

As I hung up the vitals board, Zeke blurted out, "Hey, guess what?"

"What?" I replied, coming up to take a look at his wound. It was covered with gauze and tape, which I carefully pulled back from one edge. The wound looked good. The abscess had been opened and packed with iodinated gauze. A small strip of white peaked out from the abscess opening. This would help prevent recollection of abscess fluids.

"I been working on another poem!"

"Really?" I said, pulling a roll of silk tape from my pocket and refastening the dressing.

"I brung it with me." He started getting up, succeeding in removing only one bony leg from the bed before I could hold him off.

"Hang on," I said quickly, putting a hand on his shoulder. "How about if I get it for you?"

"Sure, Doc. It's in the pocket of them jeans, over there on the chair." He pointed, lying back down in the bed.

I spied a pair of jeans on a pile of other clothes, all folded up tidily by the nursing staff. I picked them up carefully, concerned about dislodging any lice. When I moved the pants, they emitted his familiar oily smell. Favoring my right hand, and feeling a bit squeamish about what I might encounter, I plunged my left hand into the dark pocket. The paper was easy to locate, so I quickly pulled it out, thankfully with no insect passengers. On it were seven short lines in pencil:

I see the angels
every day
on the street corners
where I lay
filled with light
when they play.
Their rose is clay.

I thought about it for a minute, then said, "Zeke, why is their rose clay?"

Zeke looked a little puzzled, or worried, or maybe that's just how he looked when he was thinking hard. He stuck out his bottom lip and lowered his eyebrows.

"I don't really know, Doc. But it rhymed, right? Anyways, I'm still working on that poem."

"I like this a lot already. Can I keep it?" I said this knowing that he wanted me to have it. It was the ritual.

"It's for you, Doc. I copied it." Zeke kept his own copy of every poem.

I waited as a nurse came in and rechecked Zeke's vital signs. It was one of my favorites, Adele Swan, a stocky African American woman who'd been working the surgical ward for the past five years or so. We'd shared a few cases up here over that time, mostly Zeke Halvorson, who'd probably been in three or four times over the past year alone.

"Hi, Adele!" I said. "How are you?"

"Well, doctor, considering I'm doing double shifts from now to kingdom come, I'd say, I'm doing as well as can be expected." She leveled a gaze at the paper I held in my hand. "That one of his poems?" she asked, inclining her head towards it.

"Yup," I said, folding the paper and putting it in my pocket.

"Mmm-hmm," she said. She finished taking Zeke's temperature, blood pressure, and pulse, and recorded them on his bedside clipboard.

"Need anything?" Adele asked Zeke, checking the cup of ice chips by the bed, emptying it and refilling it with fresh ice.

"No, ma'am!" he said.

"Okee-dokee," she said. "Then I will see you in two hours, Mr. Ezekiel!"

"I'll be here!" he said, saluting.

I turned around and noticed for the first time a patient in the other bed. His skin was deep brown, his thick hair black and sprinkled with gray. I estimated his age at sixty to sixty-five. A fine sheen of sweat covered his entire face, and he was breathing through his mouth. His eyes were closed. He didn't look good.

I turned back to Zeke. "When did this fellow come in?"

"Gosh, I can't say, Doc. He was here when I got here. He's been looking pretty bad, though. Sleeps almost all the time, and when he wakes up, he don't say much."

"Do you know what's wrong with him?"

"They say he's got a abscess, just like me. That's why he's up here on surgical. The nurses said we were paired up, two pus-balls in one room." Zeke laughed.

I went over and glanced at the vitals sheet. Holy cow. "Man, his temp is up there," I said. No spikes, just a steady temp of between 101 and 102.5 Fahrenheit. I noticed his name: Yakub al-Shadi.

"I saw someone in here visiting him earlier today. Looked like it mighta been his son? He was trying to cheer him up, I think. The son was talking about the garden. He said the roses were all blooming. That seemed to make his dad happy, 'cuz he smiled. After that, he's been sleeping."

"Hmmm. Interesting." I put the man's vitals board back on its hook. "Zeke, I just hope that whatever he has, it isn't catching!"

"Amen," said Zeke.

"Hey," I said.

"What?"

"Thank you for the poem."

"Doc," said Zeke, "you're welcome."

I left the room, heading for the parking garage. I took Zeke's poem out of my pocket to read it again. A rose of clay. Hmmm . . . I really wished I knew more about poetry. My dad had loved writing it as a hobby, but, like most things related to my parents, I'd totally ignored this. And now it was too late to ask him.

I put the poem back in my pocket, distracted. Something else was nagging at me. Something I'd missed. I went through a mental analysis of my patients from that day but couldn't think of anything.

San Francisco, California
8:30 am. Friday, November 3rd 2006
Dr. Rachel Roseman

The next day before clinic started, I headed up to the surgical wards to check on Zeke again. My sense of having missed something had persisted. What was it?

When I walked into the room, the curtain was around Mr.

al-Shadi's bed. I saw the feet of what looked to be a group of people, and overheard a man talking. I recognized the voice. It was Dr. Ferguson, a visiting hand specialist from England or Europe or something. I wasn't really sure, since he'd been hired by the surgeons and my family medicine department had nothing to do with it. I focused on my own patient and tried not to eavesdrop.

Zeke was asleep. I picked up his vitals sheet and looked through. Uh-oh, fever today. I guessed he wouldn't be going home. Correction. Since he had no home, I guessed we wouldn't be sending him back out to Funston Street. Zeke had tried a few shelters and preferred the solitude and freedom of the outdoors.

I tried not to wake him up as I peeked under the sheets at his leg wound.

"Hey, Doc, are you trying to get into bed with me?" said Zeke in a sleepy voice. Despite his fever, he could still manage a small smile, made silly by the presence of some dried breakfast beside his mouth.

Laughing, I handed him a Kleenex and pointed to the spot of food by his mouth. "My husband's only been dead for six and a half years now. What do you take me for?"

Zeke wiped his mouth and said, "Well, you'll let me know when you're over all that, right? It's about time." Now he looked at me and his face became serious. "I mean it. And not about me. That's just a joke. But about someone to marry. I want you to be happy, doc."

I nodded. Zeke had gotten dangerously close to an uncomfortable truth. So I changed the subject. "How are you feeling today?"

Zeke thought for a minute, going through an internal checklist of pros and cons. "Well, let's see. As compared to usually, I'm in a nice soft bed with sheets, talking to a pretty doctor with great legs, three squares on the menu for today. That's all good. On the other hand, my thigh feels like someone dropped a grenade on it, and I'm a little sweaty. And also, the Jell-O last night sucked." He grinned.

The discussion around the next bed was getting loud, making it hard to ignore. Dr. Ferguson was speaking at a forceful volume, overriding another male voice, which was slightly accented, a nationality I could not identify.

"No, no, we really have done all the diagnostic testing that is appropriate," said Dr. Ferguson in his aristocratic tone. "Sometimes infectious processes can progress in this manner. Abscesses can require a second drainage if there have been areas of loculation that we weren't able to access in the initial debridement."

I wondered if the person he was speaking to knew what *loculation* or *debridement* meant. Like most medical terms, these things could have been said with simpler words, like *pocket* and *surgery*.

"But he looks very sick," the accented male voice said. "Are you sure an additional drainage will help?"

"I must confess, I'm a bit worried about the finger. I don't want to alarm you by saying this word, but I'm afraid that an amputation may be necessary."

I thought I heard a female gasp. Then silence.

Dr. Ferguson cleared his voice. "Well, please don't worry. I expect things will go well. But we shall have to operate as soon as possible. Can you please help your father to sign the release?"

The accented male voice said, slightly thickly, "Yes."

"Here you are." Another pause. "You can read English?"

"Of course." I heard murmuring voices. The sound stretched on for several minutes.

"Do you really need to read the whole thing? We have to get on to other patients," said Dr. Ferguson, impatiently.

"Yes, I just wonder what this means here—"

"Mr. al-Shadi, really, it's all just routine. Anesthesia has its risks."

I heard the sound of a pen scratching on paper, and then the *bling* of the metal rings as the curtain slid back. I saw Dr. Ferguson and several other doctors, male and female. Ferguson wore a long white coat; the others were dressed in the short white coats of interns and medical students. They raced along after him as he left the room, surgical consent firmly in hand, white coat trailing out behind him. He did not acknowledge me, or perhaps he didn't see me.

In his wake, beside the bed on the other side of the room, I saw a dark thirtyish man in one of the white caps I'd seen Muslims wear. I also saw a woman in a filmy blue head scarf. The man had his hand clamped across his mouth and appeared angry. The woman looked distraught.

He glanced over and saw me standing watching him. I made my "sorry" face. It was obvious that Zeke and I had heard the conversation.

"Is that how you doctors get a patient's consent here in the United States?" the man said.

"I'm really sorry," I said, coming closer. "The surgery staff here is so overworked --" It sounded weak. "Anyway, I could answer some questions for you, if you want."

"No, please, don't bother yourself."

"Well," I said, "I'm sorry about your dad."

In one of his classic non-sequiturs, Zeke chimed in: "I heard your dad's a gardener."

Taken aback, the man smiled slightly. "Among other things."

"Other things?" Zeke asked.

"Actually, he's a poet," the man went on, as if glad to talk about something else, something pleasing to him and his family. "He was a Professor of Middle Eastern Studies at Cal Berkeley until just a few months ago. He's published several books."

"No way! He's a poet?" Zeke was thrilled. "Well, now, that's too much! Two abscesses and two poets in one room! Unbelievable!" If there was a connection between poets and abscesses, Zeke did not elaborate.

Not knowing quite what to make of this, the man across the room looked down.

Something that had been hovering in the back of my mind struck me now. "Does your dad grow roses?"

The man looked back at me. "Yes, that's his specialty these days. Why?"

"Do you think he could have gotten a prick from a rose thorn somehow? Did he mention that to you, by any chance?" I felt my heart begin to pound.

Uncertain about the reason for my abrupt questioning, the man said, "It's quite possible. He often pricks himself with thorns. He doesn't like to wear gloves."

The woman looked over. Her face was delicate, dark and beautiful, but now her eyes were red, with puffy pouches below them. When she spoke, I noticed the same accent. "He did complain of a thorn injury several weeks ago."

The son said, "This is my wife, Hana. She spends a lot of time with my father. Is this significant? This rose-thorn injury?"

"It could be very significant," I said. *Argonauts!* I'd finally discovered what had been nagging at me all night! The roses! "Do you mind if I take a look at your father's hand?"

"Not at all," said the son. "By the way, my name is Farid."

I walked over to the bed and looked at the man lying there. Despite his dark skin, he had a pallor that I knew well. He was still covered with sweat and was breathing through his open mouth, eyes closed. Serious infection makes you look like this. It scares the hell out of doctors when they see this.

Hampered slightly by the continued pain in my own injured hand, which now had that day two "am I infected?" look, I took the bulky bandage off his left hand. It looked bad. Very bad. I put the bandage back on and went down to check the medication sheet. Mr. al-Shadi was on a medicine called vancomycin, which we use to cover a particularly bad-acting form of drug-resistant bacteria called *Staph Aureus*. This would have been fine if they were treating that bacterium. But I was increasingly convinced that we were not dealing with Mr. Aureus, but with someone else, an intruder from a whole different kingdom altogether.

I feared we were dealing not with any Kingdom Bacteria, but with Kingdom Fungi. Which requires a very different kind of treatment. And with the way Mr. al-Shadi looked, I also worried about dissemination, that is, infection spreading around the brain or in the lungs. The only thing that would cure this would be a drug called amphotericin. Amphoterrible. Not vancomycin, and not surgery.

There was a good reason why we called the drug amphoterrible. It had the most protean side effects of any antimicrobial currently in use. The benefits sometimes did outweigh the risks, but only because the illnesses it treated were so severe.

I walked over to the cupboard briskly, looking for a culturette. Then I thought better. *What do I think I'm doing? This is not my patient!*

And I realized I was facing a big problem. I was going to have to do something I did not enjoy. Something I usually tried to avoid at all costs. I was going to have a confrontation. With surgeons. Oy.

When I came back to the patient's bedside, I saw that his eyes were open. *His eyes are the color of the ocean!* I thought with a shock. The deepest, clearest green I had ever seen.

"Mr. al-Shadi . . . Farid . . . your father's awake!"

Farid went and leaned over his father. After the two made a few exchanges in what I now assumed must be a middle-Eastern language, probably Arabic, the elder Mr. al-Shadi looked over at me, and I felt the green of his eyes wash over me.

"Hello!" I said.

"Baba, this is . . . actually, I didn't get your name."

"I'm Dr. Roseman." I went a bit closer, so they could see my name tag: *Rachel Roseman, MD, Assistant Professor, Family Medicine.*

"*Tasharrafna*, Dr. Roseman," said Farid. "That means nice to meet you. Do you speak Arabic?"

"No, I'm afraid I don't. Just English, and a little Hebrew. Oh, and medicalese." I laughed.

"What is that? Medicalese?" asked Farid.

"Like 'loculation'—you know, what the other doctor said. Instead of 'pocket'."

"I see what you mean," said Farid, nodding.

I looked at the patient. "How are you feeling, Mr. al-Shadi?"

"Could be better," he said. I noticed how his tongue finely articulated the T's, a soft percussion of air forced around the delicate point of the tongue on the roof of the mouth, rather than the muddy D sound so often used in America. "Please, call me Yakub. I would shake your hand, but it appears you have an injury. . ." he gestured to my bandaged right hand. "My son says you have some thoughts about what is wrong with me?" His voice was weak but his diction clear.

Eagerly I said, "Actually, I'd really like to ask you just one question."

"Only one?" his remarkable green eyes sparkled, and I noted that the illness had not erased a fine irony from his speech.

Looking at his eyes, I felt a sudden, bizarre disequilibrium, as if I'd fallen and was plummeting through space. I closed my eyes and shook my head, but the feeling did not abate.

Sensing something amiss, Farid prompted me, "What was the question?"

"Oh. Yes. The question was this: do you remember getting a stick from a rose thorn at any time in the past few weeks?"

Interest sparked in Yakub's eyes. His voice grew stronger for a moment as he spoke. "Yes, I did. There was a single rose. White. It was perfect, just in the middle of a bush with big thorns. I had cut it off and was removing it. I suppose my hand was in kind of a fist. One of the thorns stuck me in the bottom of my little finger, and it broke off in my skin. I had to go inside to get some tweezers to remove it." After speaking, he had a fit of coughing that wracked his bony frame.

"How long have you had the cough?" I asked, alarmed.

His eyes were closed following the exhausting coughing spell. "Another question?" he said, weakly. "I thought you said one."

"Sorry," I said, "it doesn't really matter." What mattered was that he had the cough at all.

Farid looked at me with concern. "Is this bad?"

"I don't know yet," I said, "but we'll know a lot more after surgery. I'll quit talking now and let your father rest." I didn't want to tell them, since that was his surgeons' job, but now that I'd seen Yakub's hand, I knew that no matter what kind of medicine he took, it would be too late to avoid amputation of his finger.

At that moment, one of the young men who'd been with the group of surgeons came into the room, their rounds apparently over. His name tag said he was a first-year resident in surgery, Dr. Gary Black. Ah! The famous Doctor Black, he of the 'take your patient and abscond' variety! He looked at me, puzzled as to why I was standing by his patient's bed.

Unaware of decorum, Farid came immediately to the point, blowing my plans for diplomacy. "This doctor here, Dr. Roseman, is concerned about another kind of infection."

"Excuse me?" said Dr. Black. He was about my height, five-four, short and muscular, like he might have been a wrestler in college.

"And what, exactly, do you think it is, Dr. . . . ?"

"Roseman. I spoke with you yesterday about my patient here." I pointed to Zeke, who waved.

Dr. Black nodded, unimpressed. I continued. "Anyway, I just overheard a few things that made me wonder about sporotrichosis."

"And you heard these things while you were taking care of YOUR patient?"

"Yes, I guess so."

"Well, I think that's a pretty good idea. Taking care of YOUR patients, that is, and not worrying about the patients on my service."

I started to get a gnawing feeling in my stomach, and my heart pounded more fiercely than before. "Dr. Black, there is a lot of evidence in favor of the diagnosis of sporotrichosis. I really think that—"

"And this is from your vast experience in infectious diseases? That you've gotten in family practice?" He was talking in that kind-of-joking tone people use when they're blowing you off. "Dr. Roseman, we're really, really busy, and this patient needs to be prepped for surgery. If spor...spora...whatever...was an issue, our team would've picked it up." He zinged the curtain shut, leaving me staring at faded white canvas.

I spoke through the cloth, feeling rather ridiculous. "Dr. Black, you really should consider the evidence before you just dismiss it."

"I can't hear you," he called, "I have my stethoscope on."

"Then how did you know I said anything?"

"I didn't," he said.

Now I heard Farid chime in. "Excuse me, young man, but you really do need to hear what this doctor has to say."

"Mr. al-Shadi, I'll pass it on to my attending, don't worry."

After a few minutes, whether or not he actually used his stethoscope, Dr. Black completed his pre-op physical, opened the curtain, and, not looking at me, left the room.

"Let me know what your attending says!" I called after him, but he didn't reply. I looked over at Farid.

"That was not very satisfactory," he said.

"No, it was not very satisfactory." I headed out of the room after Dr. Black. Walking down the long hallway towards the nurses' station, I saw him sitting at the desk with his back to me. He was talking to another resident, Dr. Wells. They were laughing. As I got a little closer, I could catch what he was saying.

". . . so I'm like, 'Hey, Dr. Birkenstock, stick with your drug-addicts, okay? Let the real doctors take care of sick people, like Ali Baba in there.'"

The other resident said, "She's probably hot for the guy's son. I bet she hasn't gotten laid since her husband died."

"Excuse me!" I said when I got close enough. "Are there any *doctors* around here? Ones that actually give a SHIT about their patients?"

They looked over at me, startled. Adele, who was standing

nearby, looked up sharply. "Dr. Roseman!" she scolded, "That's not like you!" She was right. I couldn't remember the last time I'd used curse words around here. Or anywhere, come to think of it.

"Adele, I'm just wondering, if a doctor from another service had a friendly and well-meaning concern about one of your patients, would you at least take the time to hear about it?"

"Hey, girl, don't you involve ME in this. You fight your own battles!" she said with a laugh, but I knew she was on my side. She got tired of the puffed-up egos of doctors, too.

Unfortunately, the two puff-ups had recovered from the chagrin of being caught talking about me, and I wondered if they even felt any embarrassment about their off-color comments concerning their patient, Mr. al-Shadi. In any case, they were back to full hot-air mode now.

"Dr. Roseman," began Dr. Wells, "surely you can understand that we can't just take advice from someone peripherally involved in the case. If nothing else, there are liability concerns."

"I'd be more concerned you're going to get your asses sued off for missing a diagnosis here," I said, dismayed to hear my voice shaking.

"Be that as it may, Dr. Roseman, we don't feel you're qualified to be giving advice in this case," said Dr. Wells, acting very grown-up now despite his earlier juvenile comment about my sexual status (which, alas, was correct).

I shut my mouth and stared at the two of them. Then I looked over at Adele, who just shrugged and made a face like: what can you do?

"Okay," I said. "I'm going to call your attending."

He, at least, would not act like a juvenile idiot. Maybe a grown-up one, but I could handle that.

I went around the desk and picked up the phone. When the operator came on, I said, "Can you please page Dr. Ferguson for me?" I gave her my cell phone number and then, feeling uncomfortable toe-tapping there with the two jerks, walked back down the hall to Zeke and Yakub's room. Halfway down the hall, my phone rang.

"Hi, this is Dr. Roseman," I said.

"Yes, did someone page me?"

"Hi, Dr. Ferguson, yes, I did." My heart was pounding again. "I'm having a little problem, and wanted to bring it to your attention." Oh, jeez, that sounded lame.

"Problem? Who is this?"

"Dr. Roseman, a faculty member in the Family Practice department."

"Family Practice?" It sounded like he'd never heard of it.

Resisting the impulse to give him a definition, I said: "This involves your patient, Mr. Yakub al-Shadi. The fellow with the hand abscess."

"Oh, yes. And what is your connection with the patient?"

"Well, this is the strange part. None, really, but one of my clinic patients is in the same room with him. And something came up when we were talking that I thought I should bring to your attention."

"You should probably call the third year resident and talk about this. I'm quite busy, and about to go into surgery."

"Well, that's the problem. I already tried that, but he didn't much want to hear what I had to say."

Silence.

I struggled on. "Here's the thing. I just happened to find out that Mr. al-Shadi is a gardener, and he says he did, actually, get a puncture from a rose thorn in the past week or two. Also, I noticed he was coughing, and so I was concerned about sporotrichosis, possibly disseminated."

Dr. Ferguson cleared his throat. He sounded annoyed when he said: "And all of this has come to your attention through haphazard observation?"

"Well, yes, I suppose it was rather haphazard, but I don't really see what that matters in the overall picture."

"It does matter, Dr. Roseman, it matters very much. We have been approaching this case in a systematic manner, and we don't need untrained interns coming in and subjecting us to possible claims of liability."

"Dr. Ferguson, I'm not an intern but a full member of the medical staff here. I would not call myself 'untrained'."

"Nevertheless, this is really very irregular."

"All I'm asking is that you send a culture for sporotrichosis when you go into surgery today."

"I will think about it, but I doubt it. Thank you, Dr....uh..."

"Dr. Roseman. And Dr. Ferguson, I..."

But he had hung up.

I threw my phone back into my pocket, noticing my hands were shaking. This was a feeling I didn't like and tried to avoid at all costs. Anger.

Arriving back at Zeke's hospital room, I spat out the words: "Crapping sphincter-snapping assholes!" I looked around to see four faces staring at me.

Zeke had his mouth wide open. "DOCtor ROSEman!" he said.

Yakub was looking at me, too, and I had that sudden strange sensation again of falling.

What is going on with me? I wondered.

His look told me to come over next to him. I could tell he was too weak to speak loudly, so I went and squatted down by him, my ear close to his lips. Despite his debilitated condition, the scent that came from him was pleasant, like cinnamon and oil, the lanolin from the wool of a lamb.

"Dr. Roseman," he said, his voice soft, and I was surprised that he remembered my name. "You should not get so angry. It isn't good for you."

"Yes, you're right, but I'm more worried about you than about myself."

"That's because you are a good doctor." I didn't feel like a good doctor right then. Far from it. "Did the men ignore you?" he continued.

"They don't want to hear what I have to say."

"Don't worry. I'll tell them," said Yakub.

What? This was crazy. The patient was going to tell the surgeons what to do? This was all mixed up. I felt the urge to cry. I hadn't cried in this hospital before, *ever*. Crying was not for me. I stood up quickly, walking over to where Farid was sitting in the chair by the bed. "I'm sorry, they just won't listen to me."

"My father is right. We'll make sure they do what they need to in order to check for this fungus. Don't worry."

"Okay," I said, feeling silly that they were reassuring me, rather than the other way around. "I'm sorry I swore a few minutes ago. I never do that, but I was just so…upset."

Farid laughed. "It felt good that someone cared that much, actually!"

Just then, a couple of orderlies came in and told us that they were there to take Mr. al-Shadi to surgery. Farid and his wife Hana followed them out of the room.

I stood and watched them go. "Guess I'd better get going, too. See you later, Zeke. Sorry again for my language."

"Hey, doesn't bother *me*," he said. "Take care of yourself, Doc! Get yourself some tea."

"But I'm supposed to be taking care of you!" I said. "Not the other way around!"

"Don't worry about that doc. I'm feeling fine. Better every minute. Go ahead, I'll be good here. You go."

"Okay, I will," I said. And I did.

It was now about noon and I was due in clinic at 1:00. I had intended to do some reading in the doctor's lounge after my morning rounds, but instead I walked toward a small cafeteria I liked to visit on the top floor of one of the outpatient buildings. It was quiet, and the manager, José, made sure there was plenty of fresh, strong coffee at all times. Today this location had an added advantage—there was little chance I'd run into Drs. Black or Wells there.

As I walked, I felt shaky and sick. I still had the feeling of falling, as if I had somehow become untethered from time and space. My feet walked on the ground, but my body seemed to be plummeting downward through some unfamiliar dimension under the power of an unseen current. At the same time, my system reeled from frustration, anger, and worry about Yakub. *Oh, my God, what if he dies?*

At the cafeteria, I uncharacteristically ordered tea rather than coffee, as Zeke had suggested. It sounded just perfect right now, reminding me of times with my father as a child, when he used to make us all English Pekoe with granulated sugar and milk, served in a blue and white teapot with a woolen cozy, just the way his mother had served it to him as a child growing up in Surrey. There's nothing quite like a hot cup of tea on a rainy Saturday afternoon in Brooklyn.

I thought about my father and missed him again. I thought of all the other people I'd loved who were now dead: my mother, Miriam; my husband, David. The only one still alive in my entire family was my sister, Ruthie, who fortunately lived nearby in Palo Alto. The two of us had been orphans since I was in medical school when, ironically, the first case of cancer I'd diagnosed had been in my own mother.

I sat in the empty cafeteria, sipping the warm, sweet tea and feeling sorry for myself, wondering whether I'd now also be responsible for the death of Yakub al-Shadi, a man I hardly knew.

FOUNDATION

San Fancisco, California
1:30 pm. Friday, November 3rd 2006
Dr. Rachel Roseman

After finishing my solitary cup of tea, I went back to my other patients, but was distracted all afternoon, thinking constantly of Yakub and how he was faring in surgery. I prayed that he and Farid had somehow convinced the surgeons to check for the fungus, *Sporothrix schenckii*, may it rot in hell. After my clinic ended, I hurried back over to the surgery ward to check on him.

When I got to room 248, I saw that Yakub was back in his bed, Farid sitting beside him. Zeke's bed was empty, his things gone. I flinched when I saw Dr. Black there, too, standing holding Yakub's vitals sheet. When he saw me, he said:

"Hey, doctor. Guess what? Your patient walked. What'd you do to make him mad?"

"I wasn't the one who made him mad."

"Guess what else?" Dr. Black continued with irritating cheerfulness. "The fungal stain was negative."

"Great," I replied, my annoyance at his tone overridden by the relief I felt to learn that they'd tested for the fungus after all. "But you know, that's only positive about twenty percent of the time. It's usually diagnosed by culture."

"Hmmm. Interesting," he said, sounding anything but interested. "I bet his culture will also be negative."

"Want to put money on that?" I said.

"Hey, I don't bet. My wife would kill me."

"Okay." At least we weren't throwing scalpels at each other or something. "How did the surgery go?"

"Really well! But as I was just telling the patient's son, we did, unfortunately, have to amp . . . er, remove the fifth ray."

I tried not to look shocked. Rather than amputating just the finger, as I'd hoped, they had been compelled to remove not only the finger but also the hand bone at the outside of the palm, excising the tissue at the side of the hand all the way down to the wrist.

"Unfortunately, there was lots of necrosis in the tissues around the infection, along with severe damage to septic metacarpophalangeal and distal interphalangeal joints."

Our forgotten roommate, Farid, spoke up and said, "Excuse me, doctor. Translation, please. I don't understand medicalese." He looked at me and gave a small smile.

"Oh, yes, sorry. There was . . . pus in the two joints here and here." Dr. Black pointed to his own fifth finger. "And lots of dead tissues in the areas around these joints. Dr. Ferguson got everything out, and all the remaining tissue looked good."

Yakub was asleep, still under the influence of the anesthesia and the pain medicines he'd received post-op. I wondered if he knew yet about his finger, resting in some dark freezer in the pathology lab.

Dr. Black felt his pulse, took another look at his vitals sheet, checked the bandages, and, apparently satisfied, left the room. I walked out into the hall after him.

"Hold on a sec, Dr. Black," I called, catching up. "So! Never let the sun set on undrained pus, huh?"

"That's right." I was surprised to see him smile.

"Thanks for sending the fungal culture."

"The patient requested it. He's pretty persuasive. Anyway, it'll be negative." He looked at me and gave me another smile, more rueful than spiteful.

"We'll see," I said. "But thanks anyway. I'll see you later."

And that's how it is in war, religion, and medicine. You took sides, you broke into factions, you got in fights, but later, sometimes, you made up.

Recalling that I needed to write a note in Zeke's chart, I went back to room 248. Farid was holding his father's good hand, whispering to him in Arabic. I sat down on Zeke's now-vacant bed, all remade and ready for the next victim. I needed to write my note but was distracted by Farid and his whispered recitation of what sounded like highly rhythmic and melodic verse.

When he finished, I said, "That sounded beautiful. Was it the Quran?"

Farid looked over, surprised to see me there. "No, no, not at all. It was a poem. One of my favorites, written by my father."

"Really? What was it about?"

"My mother. My father wrote it for her when they were young. It became quite famous."

I wondered about Farid's mother. I hadn't seen her here in the hospital.

"And your mother, is she…"

Farid looked at his father and, all at once, seemed to come undone, his face disintegrating into a mask of despair. He covered it with one hand, and I saw his shoulders convulsing.

Stricken to have precipitated this emotional outburst, I remained frozen on the bed, unsure of what to do next. Giving Farid a hug seemed inappropriate. So I sat and watched helplessly as he sobbed silently for a minute or so. At last, he stopped, uncovering his face and wiping it with both hands. I jumped up, grabbed the box of Kleenex and went to offer it to him.

He looked at it and, as if in a daze, took a tissue and blew his nose. He then sat gazing blindly forward.

I sat down silently nearby him, on the ledge below the window.

After a several minute interval, Farid spoke, his voice catching. "My mother was killed by terrorists. She was on a trip overseas—"

I remained at a loss for words. All I could think of to say was, "That is terrible. Really terrible."

Farid stopped and swallowed, and his jaw set. He looked over at me, his expression scary now, a mixture of grief and anger. His eyes still held tears, but his jaw muscles clenched. "Yes. It *has* been terrible for our family."

I nodded, feeling awful. Even though I was used to counseling patients about medical tragedies, I had no idea how to respond to this horrific revelation.

Farid went on. "She was going to meet a friend, traveling from Madrid to Cordoba. To get to the central station, she took a commuter train. It was one of the ones blown up in Madrid on March 11, 2004. I don't know who those people were trying to kill, but they managed to kill my mother, a devout Muslim." Agitated, he jumped up and stood by the window, gazing out at the darkness. He stood silently for several moments, then went on.

"These people, these terrorists, say they are fighting on behalf of Islam, but they are, in fact, *muharibun,* people who wage war on society, a terrible crime. They are a tragedy for Islam and for the world." He drummed his fingers against the window pane.

Farid's agitation seemed to affect his father, who groaned and kicked his feet. His eyes were still shut, but his forehead was furrowed as if he were in pain.

I went and soaked a small towel in cool water and brought it to Yakub's bedside, folding it carefully across his brow, which seemed to bring him some relief. Farid came over next to me and sat back down, taking his father's hand and leaning forward to murmur in his ear. Concern and tenderness now erased the anger on his face.

I sat down again on the window ledge, watching Farid and his father for several minutes. Farid appeared calmer now.

I asked, "Is your father a faithful Muslim, like your mother?"

Appearing relieved to have something to speak of other than death, Farid answered readily. "Actually, he was a very faithful Muslim until two years ago. Now, he...well, he is very angry. And you? Are you religious?"

Surprised by his question, I found myself reluctant to tell him I was a Jew. It was scary to think I might alienate him. Would he hate me right away?

I hesitated so long that Farid offered his own answer. "Well, you said you know some Hebrew, and with a name like Roseman, I figured you were probably Jewish. Or your husband is Jewish, anyway."

"Was. And yes, I am Jewish, or getting there, at least. I sort of recently figured that out."

"Was?" said Farid, still hung up on the first word.

"Oh, yeah. My husband, David, died almost seven years ago." I felt the tears coming on again. *What is going on with me?* I thought. *I never cry!*

Farid looked up, compassion in his face. "I'm very, very sorry. That's a hard thing for a young woman. But have you not remarried?"

"No."

"But why? You are beautiful, compassionate. I would think men would be flocking."

I laughed. I hadn't noticed any flocking. "Guess I'm a one-man woman," I said.

"Not to pry too much, but do you have children?"

"No, no children." That was a whole other story, but not one I chose to talk about very much.

Farid nodded. "I have three—a baby, an eight- and a six-year-old. Sometimes I'm not sure that was such a good idea!" He laughed.

Relieved as I felt the threat of tears pass, I said, "Well, that must keep you pretty busy." Farid agreed with another nod, then sat gazing at his father.

I looked at Yakub too, and now, focusing on him, something about his appearance disturbed me. What was it? He wasn't coughing, and his color wasn't too bad. But something was wrong. I thought to myself, *all right, genius, just remember the basics. ABC—airway, breathing, circulation. Airway's okay. Breathing?* That was it! His chest was rising and falling too rapidly. Without letting on to Farid, I quietly glanced at my watch and began counting his breaths, the quickest and cheapest way to assess lung function and oxygenation: *one, two, three...* I counted for a full minute. Yakub was taking twenty-three breaths per minute. Not terrible, but still, too high.

I went over and took Farid's hand. I wasn't sure if this was allowed in Muslim etiquette, but it was vital in the language of my calling.

"Farid, I am really sorry about your mom. If there's anything I can do to help you, I want you to tell me. Will you do that?"

Farid nodded his head briefly and looked down. I let go of his hand.

"I'm going to head home now, since there's not much more I can do here tonight. We should have results on the fungal culture by tomorrow or the next day at the latest."

I didn't tell him I was going to go find the on-call team to let them know about Yakub's worrisome respiratory rate. "Make sure you get something to eat. It never helps patients when their family members make themselves sick."

Farid smiled, and I felt the temperature of the room go up a degree again. "Okay, Doctor. I will follow your orders."

I laughed and turned to go.

"Oh, Dr. Roseman?"

"Yes?"

"Your patient, Mr. Halvorson, left this for you." He handed me a folded piece of notebook paper with Zeke's familiar writing on the front: *"Poem for Dr. Roseman."*

"Thanks!" I slipped the paper in the pocket of my work slacks. "See you tomorrow!"

"Good night," he replied, turning back to his father, worry suffusing his face once again.

I left the room and headed down the hall, cringing at the thought of another encounter with team Wells/Black. Then I realized that by now, a covering on-call intern had likely taken over Yakub's care anyway.

When I got to the nurses' station, I saw that Adele was on duty again. I told her my worries about Yakub.

Adele joked with me. "Doctor Roseman, aren't you getting kind of attached to a guy who's not your patient?"

I laughed at myself. "Yeah, I know. Please, save your concerns for a time when I'm not so tired."

Adele peered at me, then said,

"You go home. Don't worry. I'll call the intern, make sure he checks out that patient. I'll be sure to call you at home if anything changes." I thanked her and left the hospital for the evening.

Outside, it was dark, the moon almost full, adorned by small wisps of cloud illuminated like gossamer veils. When I saw the moon now, it reminded me of the time last year when I had scribed a letter in our congregation's Torah. My letter, "*Hey*," had been in the sixteenth verse of Genesis One, in the words "*ha-M'or ha-Katan*," the "lesser light," otherwise known as the moon. The scroll was now complete and rested, with two others, inside the arc at our synagogue. It made me feel happy to think I was part of the moon in our congregation's holy scroll.

As I walked, I felt a sudden twinge of pain in my right side. I knew this feeling well: the beginning of ovulation. Right on cue, twelve days after the beginning of the last period. Over the next twenty-four hours, the twinges would increase and then settle as a boring pain occurring whenever I moved. I would also feel twitchy spasms on that side, the involuntary contractions of my defective fertility apparatus. And when I woke up in the morning two days later, the pain would be gone. One more egg, poof.

Ovulation. What a joke.

My brief good humor evaporating, I got into my car, and left the lot, turning right on Cesar Chavez and getting on 101 North. I exited at Ninth Street, crossing Market and heading up to Pacific Heights. My bitter mood left me craving something beautiful. I slipped one of my favorites CD's into the player: an old recording of

Arthur Rubenstein and the Chicago Philharmonic, playing the Rachmaninoff second piano concerto, Opus 18, second movement. The music began in a minor key, the piano making slow beats like the footfalls of a hesitant traveler, the volume and tempo building quickly, swept up by a wash of strings. I imagined the climax as the end of a heroic journey, a fateful meeting of two lovers.

As I listened, I couldn't stop myself from thinking about "the big unmentionable subject" again: my infertility, documented in full 2-D finality on x-ray when I was only twenty-nine, just a few months before David died. For the millionth time I asked myself, *why did this happen to me?* Was it a punishment for some unknown sin, brought down on me by the judgment of God?

You must have brought this on yourself somehow, my mind said, like one of Job's hapless companions. *It was your own fault. All that running you did. Or maybe you ignored some pain, too busy to take a break from your idiotic pursuit of success.*

The one thing I did know for sure, which I suspected no one else really believed, was that my tubal scarring was not due to a premarital sexually transmitted infection. As a doctor, I understood completely why people might doubt me on this. I had learned to maintain skepticism myself regarding a patient's explanation of their sexual history. The price of missing a pregnancy or sexually transmitted infection was simply too great. So I could tell that my doctors, and maybe even David himself, thought my claim of premarital virginity could be just the tiniest, the most wee bit, in doubt.

"These things don't just come from nowhere," they were thinking. But they were wrong. David was the only man in the world I had ever slept with.

I did wonder, secretly, about David and whether he might have been the one to pass on an infection to me, something he'd picked up before we were married. Or even afterwards. But when I questioned him, his look told me unequivocally: *Don't go there.* And I did know that his cultures had come up clean during our infertility workup, so I had all good reason to believe him.

The music continued, now in measured strokes, up up up, one after the other, like the rhythm of sex itself, the notes of the piano stopping for just an instant of aching beauty at the climax, and then rolling backward into the decrescendo, released, falling, full of grace, longing, regret.

A single musical note spoke the divine perfection of the moment of conception. And I thought, in one crazy instant, that if there was a God, then God must have created us just to hear that single note.

San Francisco, California
8:00 pm. Friday, November 3rd 2006
Dr. Rachel Roseman

When I entered my apartment no dogs bounded over to greet me, no people called out, "Hey, how was your day?" I didn't even have a lousy plant to water. I went and checked my message machine. Two messages. One a hang-up, the other a call from the dry cleaner's, explaining that they were unable to remove a coffee stain from one of my shirts. Great.

Since David's death, I hadn't let my mind dwell on being alone. At first I'd felt like he was only out for a few minutes and would be right back. Later, I realized he wouldn't be back but felt he was still with me. I spoke with him in my mind, asking him questions, and he seemed to answer. Today, when I spoke to him, he was silent. *Where are you, David?*

I roused myself from my spot in the hall and went to make myself a salad. I liked the ready-made kind I could just dump in a bowl. I'd throw on some croutons and Italian dressing. I could make dinner this way in less than sixty seconds.

I took my salad into the living room with me. Just as I was lifting my fork, I remembered it was Shabbat. In this renewed funk about my infertility, I had completely forgotten. This was bad. I made a mental apology to my rabbi and went to get my candlesticks, candle, bread, wine, and wineglass.

As I went about these preparations, I mused about the recent changes in my life. Practicing Shabbat was certainly something we'd never done while I was growing up, even though my mom was Jewish, which made me officially Jewish in the eyes of the orthodoxy. My Dad was a Christian, it was true, but not an observant one. Religion was basically a non-entity in our household.

I'd begun to explore religion only in the years after the attack on the World Trade Centers, when it struck me that it seemed to be the cause of so much trouble in the world. I decided to read the holy texts so I could figure out where in these books it said that we ought to be blowing up little children to accomplish God's will. So, during a three month sabbatical last year, I had sat down to read all the sacred texts of the Abrahamic traditions: the "Old" and "New" Testaments, and the Quran.

What happened to me was not what I'd expected. Not at all. Instead of finding flaws and errors, I'd been drawn into the stories, as though they were somehow connected to me. When I was done, there was a voice in my mind. It seemed to speak to me repeatedly:. "Hear, Israel. You! Yes you! I mean you, the one sitting there in the sweat pants and the San Francisco marathon t-shirt! Hear!

"The Lord is One!"

It was as though I'd been woken from a long slumber, like some kind of Jewish Rip Van Winkle. Though I'd come to the holy texts as a skeptic, in the end, I had simply fallen in love with the Torah.

Which wasn't to say I'd given up my worries about the religions and their dangers. Much to the contrary. In fact, in response to my own misgivings about the idea of "chosen-ness," I'd been prompted to create something   I called my "Religion Inventory," a list of ten things that people could ask themselves to see if they might be harboring some potentially toxic religious beliefs. I was still refining this list.

Though I'd never set foot in a synagogue for the first 35 years of my life, that had also changed, in concert with my growing love of Torah. I often went to Torah study on Saturday mornings, and when my work schedule made it possible, I'd been going to the Friday evening service at the synagogue, and I sometimes stayed on for the festive *oneg Shabbat*, the congregational dinner afterwards. But I also enjoyed the solitary ceremonies I performed on Shabbat evenings when I was by myself. It felt like I was having a private dinner, just me and God.

Musing on these unexpected changes in my life, I slowly set up the candles, opened the wine, and covered the bread. Then I said my first blessings for the day: "*Baruch atta Adonai*, blessed are you, O Lord," I began, acknowledging the first gifts of Shabbat: sanctification by the commandments, light, wine, bread. No children to bless.

I felt the presence of Shabbat descend upon me as I ate my salad in silence. When I was done, leaving the candles burning, I went to take a shower. The water usually took a minute or two to get hot in this old apartment building. After I'd turned on the water and taken off my clothes, I looked at myself in the mirror. Though it was becoming clouded by fog, I could still see myself reflected clearly enough: long dark hair, blue eyes, muscular body, not much fat. A runner's body, I thought, still youthful, unaffected by motherhood.

Actually, I thought I looked pretty good for a woman in her thirties, but then again, I'd resigned myself to the reality that it was impossible to compete with the ripening curves of the recently pubescent girl. This I knew was just nature's brilliant method of ensuring ongoing procreation. Going head to head with this was a losing proposition. And the idea that you could surgically achieve this effect was just another sad delusion of modern life.

I thought about something I'd seen last year in an introductory book I'd read about Islam. Muhammad had married an older woman, Khadija, fifteen years his senior. He had been devoted to her throughout his life, though she'd died when he was in his fifties. This, to me, spoke volumes about the goodness of the prophet.

After my shower, exhausted, I got into bed. This was my very favorite time of day. I picked up the novel on my bedside, Adhaf Soueif's *A Map of Love,* and stared at the cover for a few minutes. Feeling the first stages of sleep coming on, I put it down and turned off the light.

It may have been that my own animal brain was active that night, primed by the rising hormones of ovulation in my bloodstream. Whatever the cause, in the near-waking state of early sleep, I found myself floating in a pleasant nebula of sensual awareness, my body receptive to the imagined coming of an unknown lover. I fell into a deep sleep.

A dream came. I saw a woman. Her form was slim, her eyes dark, her hair black and shiny as midnight. She brushed it slowly, pulling the brush over and over through the luminous strands. As she did, her hair reflected lights that shimmered like stars. Someone must have spoken with her, though I could not hear the words. The woman began to take off her clothes, deliberately, one piece at a time. As she removed each article, I felt that I myself was becoming unclothed, my actions shadowing the woman's in mirror image, until finally, the woman, or I, sat completely naked. The unseen

observer was always present, and I could feel his desire, a palpable
force.

Sensing the watcher, I woke up. My bedside clock read
midnight. As I drifted back to sleep, I thought I detected the faint
smell of cinnamon.

San Francisco, California

7:00 am. Shabbat, November 4th 2006
Week of the portion of לך לך, "Go Forth"
Dr. Rachel Roseman

I woke up again on Saturday morning, remembrance of the
dream more a feeling than a thought, a kind of longing, bittersweet
and nebulous. It lingered as I drank my morning coffee and read the
weekly Torah portion in my mother's small Hebrew-English
Tanakh[4]. Usually, I would have gone to Torah study and then the
morning service at the synagogue, but today, I had to perform
another religious duty, visiting my sick friend: Yakub.

I showered and left for the hospital. On the way, I thought
about what I might confront when I got there. In the best-case
scenario, Yakub would be better, the surgeons right, his problem
due to a common skin infection. If this were so, removing the
infection by amputating his finger would prove curative. While this
might be a blow to my ego, it would be by far the best outcome. On
the opposite extreme, if he did have disseminated sporotrichosis, all
I would find when I arrived would be an even sicker Yakub and a
bunch of obstinate surgeons.

What I actually found when I got there was something else
entirely. Arriving on the ward, I found room 248 deserted, Yakub's
bed empty. There was no sign of Yakub or anyone in his family.
Feeling fear grip me, I ran down to the nurses' station, where Adele
was back on duty. "Adele!" I shouted, foregoing any greeting.

---

[4] The Hebrew Bible, known by its acronym for the three sections
that compose it, "Torah, Nevi'im, Ketuvim," that is, Torah (the five books of
Moses), Prophets (Joshua, Judges, Samuel 1 & 2, Kings 1 & 2, Isaiah, Ezekial,
Jeremiah, and the 12 'minor' prophets), and the Writings (Psalms, Proverbs,
Job, Song of Songs, Ruth, Lamentations, Ecclesiastes, Esther, Daniel, Ezra,
Nehemia, Chronicles 1 & 2).

"Where's Mr. al-Shadi?"

"Hey, Dr. Roseman! Don't get your panties all tied up in knots! They took him down for an x-ray about forty-five minutes ago."

"Oh, thank God!" I said, leaning over the counter and taking deep breaths.

"When Dr. Ferguson went on his rounds this morning, he was in a lather to see that the patient had been tachypnaic all night. The doctor took a listen to the patient and said he heard something, sent him down for a STAT chest x-ray."

"What did the intern say last night when he came by to look at the patient?"

"Well, he thought the man's lungs sounded just fine. 'Clear as a bell' were his exact words, I believe. I guess Dr. Ferguson is going to have a little talk with that young doctor."

"Did Farid, the patient's son, go down to x-ray with him?"

"Fellow in the hat? Yes, I think so. Do you think that guy's a terrorist?"

"Adele," I scolded. "They're not all terrorists, you know!"

"Hey, girl, I got a right to a little prejudice, too!"

I laughed. "No, I don't think he's a terrorist. Actually, he's a victim himself. His mom got killed a couple of years ago on those trains in Madrid."

Adele opened her eyes wide. "No!" she said.

"Yup."

"Good Lord Almighty!" she said, "What in the world is *wrong* with people?"

"I don't know," I said, shaking my head.

Adele peered at me, narrowing her eyes. "You don't look too good. Why don't you go get yourself some coffee? I'll call you when he gets back."

"Well, you're aware he's not my patient—"

"Kinda hard to forget that," Adele said with a laugh.

"Oh, great, have the surgeons been gossiping?"

"Who listens?" said Adele.

I sighed with resignation. "Yes, that would be great if you could call me when he gets back to the ward. And hey, Adele?"

"Yes, Doctor?"

"You're working awfully long hours, aren't you?"

"Saving up for a vacation. I'm gonna take a *long* one this

time!"

"Good! You deserve it!"

Adele nodded, never one to argue with the truth.

I went to my favorite coffee shop again and sat reading the *New England Journal of Medicine*. Just as I finished wading through all the ads, I got a call from Adele.

"He's baaaaack," she sang.

"Thanks, Adele. You're awesome."

I headed to the ward, wondering whether the fungal culture had grown anything.

When I got to room 248, I found quite a bustle of activity. Dr. Black was there, along with Drs. Wells and Ferguson. Yakub was awake but looking ill and extremely tired. Nevertheless, when he saw me, he smiled. The others completely ignored me and continued what appeared to be a tense conversation.

Dr. Wells was speaking. "I did some research. It looks like we start with amphotericin B and can then switch over to itraconazole when the patient improves."

Dr. Ferguson responded with "That's all very well, but I also want an infectious disease consultation. Get them on the phone before beginning anything. The consultant should take a look at his chest radiograph, as well. We'll need some advice about our therapeutic alternatives."

"My sources said that sometimes surgical treatment of lung infections is required," offered Dr. Black.

"Well, that is precisely why we require specialty advice," snapped Dr. Ferguson. "And now I am going to go see if I can find that intern who was covering last night. There is no excuse for waiting on a chest radiogram until this morning."

He left the room as always, long white coat flying out behind him, clipboard in hand. Dr. Wells went out with him.

With both of them gone, Dr. Black apparently felt he could acknowledge me.

"Oh, hey," he said. "Good thing I didn't bet. I was right, my wife would've killed me."

"I assume you got the culture results back?" I said.

"Yup. *Sporothrix schenkii*, as you suspected." He gave me an apologetic smile, and I was glad to think that there might be another future surgeon who would think well of us family docs.

"Where's Farid?" I asked.

"He went to make a phone call. Wanted to tell his wife that the diagnosis had changed. I imagine he'll be back soon."

Farid walked in at that moment. "Doctor Roseman!" he said, his voice transmitting several messages at once: friendship, gratitude, worry. I could tell he knew that his dad wasn't out of the woods yet.

Meanwhile, Dr. Black was talking to Farid's father. "Mr. al-Shadi, I'm going to go give the infectious-disease fellow a call to consult about your case, if that's okay with you."

Yakub nodded his head.

Dr. Black left the room.

I went over and sat down next to Yakub in the chair at the head of his bed. He was lying on his side, facing me. His chest still rose and fell rapidly, and he said with some effort, "Dr. Roseman, you should not be here. It is Saturday. Shabbat, I think?"

"How did you know...?" I said.

"That you're Jewish? You said your name was Roseman..."

I nodded, amazed that he had remembered, given all else that was happening to him at the moment.

I said, "Anyway, this kind of visit is what we call a *mitzvah*, visiting a sick friend in the hospital. Since you're not my patient, it doesn't count as work."

Yakub smiled. "In our tradition, the prophet has a saying: 'Show compassion to those on earth, the One in the heavens will show mercy upon you.'" (1)

"Beautiful!" I said, and then I remembered something myself. "In Judaism, there's actually a specific name assigned for visiting the sick. It's called *Bikkur Holim*."

"You know a lot about this, it seems!" said Yakub.

"Not so much. Like most things, I put on a pretty good show."

Yakub looked at me, and suddenly all I could see were his eyes, infinitely green, and I became dislodged once again, like my body was suddenly in the force of a strong magnetic field. As though in a trance, I saw my injured right hand reaching forward to grasp his uninjured hand, which lay above the bed sheets beside him. I don't know what compelled this breach of cultural etiquette. When our hands touched, it felt like a million small electric crackles sparked. Warmth suffused my hand and lanced up my arm to my heart, striking it with a shock of joy. The world contracted in that moment to the space between us, and all that existed was the feeling in my hand and the expression of surprise on Yakub's face. And then Adele entered the room and the moment was over. I removed my hand, which was still pulsing.

Adele carried a clear plastic IV bag with a label on it. Yakub's antifungal medication.

Cradling my right hand with my left, I mouthed, "Amphoterrible?"

She nodded her head and grimaced. The side effects of amphotericin were legendary. This drug might cure him, but it also might knock off his liver, kidneys, and bone marrow. Not to mention making him feel nauseated and miserable.

Great. Now I would have another reason to worry to death about Yakub. Would this never end?

Palo Alto, California
7:30 pm. Shabbat, November 4th 2006
Dr. Rachel and Ruthie Roseman

My experience of connection with Yakub had been so brief and surreal that my memory soon had me doubting its veracity. It hadn't really happened, had it? And yet, I was soon faced with yet another bizarre occurrence.

After leaving the hospital and returning to my apartment, I took a shower. In preparation, I removed the bandage on my hand. To my surprise, I found that the laceration was completely gone, as though it had never existed. No wound, no scar, just pink, healthy skin, with only the tiniest hint of a remaining electric "buzz." Of course, my scientist's mind was soon jumping in with lots of plausible explanations.

"I guess I must have exaggerated the severity of the cut," I thought to myself. "Or maybe these modern bandages really *do* heal you up more quickly, like the ads say."

The possibility of a miracle was just not viable. I soon packed the whole episode away into a deeply submerged pocket of my unconscious mind, where it was welcome to hang out with all the unexplainable childhood memories, libidinous impulses, and souls from past lives, for all I cared.

In the evening, I drove down to visit my little sister, Ruthie, at Stanford. Though in her early thirties, she was already an associate professor in the Department of Physics and was doing undoubtedly brilliant research in her area of expertise, though its meaning completely eluded me, like all things physics-related. It was something about movement of electrons at very low temperatures.

We never spoke about work anyway, since Ruthie was perennially interested only in my love life, or lack thereof. She herself was between boyfriends. She'd just recently broken up after a six month fling with a man five years her junior, an investment banker and mountain climber. He was a little too intense, and when the conversation turned to marriage, Ruthie balked. I guess she had a few more wild oats to sow. In the area of love, we were just about as different as two people could be.

When I arrived at Il Fornaio, the waiter seated me at a table for two. I ordered a Diet Coke, settling in for my usual ten- to fifteen-minute wait for Ruthie. She arrived, on cue, exactly twelve minutes late and sat down across from me. With barely a greeting, she immediately launched into, "So, Rachel! What's up in the romance department?".

"The usual," I said. I grabbed a piece of bread and disconsolately stuffed it into my mouth.

"Omigod," she said. "We have nothing to talk about!"

"How about you?" I said, chewing on the bread. "That is always *something* to talk about."

"Still in between men, I'm afraid," said Ruthie. "It's just not that easy to meet people in low-temperature physics."

"Try meeting some of the people I get to hang out with at the hospital!" I said. That made me think a minute, though. What about Yakub? I looked down suddenly and paused, no longer able to keep up the glib patter.

"What!" said Ruthie. "Hey, don't look like that without expecting to tell me something!"

I picked up my menu, unsure what to say about Yakub. With her characteristic good-natured-yet-cynical laugh, Ruthie said, "Come on, Rachel, you know that menu by heart."

I put the menu down and looked at my sister. "I'm just not really sure what this is," I said.

"How come?"

"You're going to think I'm weird again."

"So what else is new?"

I sat and looked at Ruthie a moment, musing on our differences. Two years younger than me at age 34, she was my height but a little curvier, more densely muscular. She'd always enjoyed the team sports, while I'd been into the loner things like distance running. She had inherited a head of dark, curly hair that sprang off the sides of her head and rested on her shoulders like a living creature. She looked like the kind of woman who would have great conversations and do adventurous things, like climb mountains and jump out of planes, both of which she had done. She'd been involved in a five-year long relationship that hadn't ended in marriage, leaving her single in her late twenties. But she never had problems finding men. Unlike me. Miss Quiet-go-home-read-and-run-thirty-miles Roseman.

"C'mon, quit stalling," she said. "You're not getting off the hook here about that guy."

"Did I say there was a guy?" I laughed.

"Hey, if you think I can't read that Rachel-has-a-secret look you've had since you were a little kid, you're sadly mistaken." Ruthie had always been more perceptive in reading my emotions than I was myself.

"Okay," I said, realizing there was no escape. "There's a guy in the hospital. He's really, really sick. He's also . . . a bit older than me. I saw his chart; he's sixty-two."

"Is he your patient? Because in that case, I'd have to agree with you, it's weird."

"No, no, he's on another service. Surgery. There's something about him that is really attractive. Exotic, in a way. He's Egyptian. He speaks Arabic and writes poetry."

"So come on, what else about him?" pressed Ruthie.

"Well, it's just really odd, but I feel kind of . . . disoriented around him. Kind of silly or something, like almost having a crush, but even weirder. When I first saw him, it felt like my life came . . . unstuck, or something." I picked up my right hand and looked at it, considered telling Ruthie about the cut and the mysterious healing, but then decided against it, saying, "And now do you think I'm even weirder than before?"

"Yes, but I still love you anyway."

The waiter came and brought our food: capellini with garlic and sun-dried tomatoes for me, filet of sole Meuniere for Ruthie.

Life was good in the San Francisco Bay Area.

As we ate, Ruthie continued to pester me about Yakub, but I really didn't know any more about him. Finally, she hit me with a hypothetical. "What do you think Mom and Dad would have thought about him?"

The big question. We seemed unable to escape it, even now that they'd both been dead for over a decade.

"I don't know. I'm not sure how Mom would have felt about me hanging out with a Muslim guy. It's true, she never was an observant Jew herself, but she was a very *Jewish person*, if you know what I mean."

"Yeah, I do." Ruthie mused, "Also, she was crazy about David. She always prayed I'd land a doctor, like you."

"Yup," I agreed.

"How about Dad?" She said.

I snorted. "Dad would be more concerned about his ranking in the Fortune 500."

"Come on, Rachel! Don't always be so weird about Dad."

"Well it's true!" I protested. "Nothing I ever did was good enough."

"As I recall, miss perfecto, you were plenty good at everything you did," argued Ruthie. "Dad knew that better than anyone."

"Not really," I said. "And he liked you better anyway."

"You always say that!" said Ruthie, "But it isn't true."

"Well, you could always talk to him."

"Yeah, well you were too busy bringing home trophies to stuff in his face." Ruthie grabbed her last bite of sole with an irritated jab.

We sat in tense silence as the waiter removed our plates, placing dessert menus in front of us without a word.

As usual, Ruthie broke the silence with a laugh and a shake of her head. "Forget it. We'll never figure Dad out. I just wish I'd paid more attention to them both, back then when I had the chance. I still wonder what Dad was up to, the year before Mom died."

"I know," I said.

"All those poems he wrote," mused Ruthie. "What was he doing?" We'd hashed this over a million times before.

"Something about mom," I said.

"Then he went and just burned them all. Jeez."

I nodded.

"Strange…"Ruthie shook her head.

"That drove David crazy," I said. "He couldn't stand that Dad would write all that poetry and then destroy it, without even ever letting us see it."

"Well, Dad and David never really got along that well, anyway," Ruthie said.

"Still, David hated to see him acting so crazy, that last year before Mom died. He saw the toll it took on me."

Ruthie nodded. The waiter came and we ordered dessert, moving on to other topics: Ruthie's new house, people she knew at work, her dog. Afterward, Ruthie wanted me to go with her to a jazz club to dance and meet some single guys. "Maybe you should look for someone younger, rather than older than you," she said.

"I'm not really looking for anyone," I said.

I went home while Ruthie headed over to the jazz club on her own.

San Francisco, California
9:00 am. Sunday, November 5th 2006
Dr. Rachel Roseman

Though Sunday was another day off for me, I went into the hospital again to visit Yakub. I did not stop to examine my motives in depth. Why was I spending my days off visiting a patient who was not my patient? Why did I care so much for this man, to the point where I was losing my professional boundaries? Why was I so strangely disoriented around him? And what had happened to my hand? The more I tried to solve these riddles, the more the answers evaporated, diffusing like San Francisco fog. Simpler to focus on the specific issues and problems. Like how was Yakub doing?

The answer was immediately evident when I walked into room 248. He was not doing well. I detected the acid smell of vomit and could hear Yakub's breathing, deep and hollow.

Farid and Hana sat in chairs by the bed, looking worried. A third person also occupied a chair in the room, a man with a head covering similar to Farid's. He looked to be twenty-five or thirty, with dark hair and green eyes like Yakub's. Farid's younger brother?

"Hi, I'm Rachel," I said, offering my hand, which he shook

firmly, and I marveled that it hurt not even the tiniest bit.

The young man looked at me, curiosity and warmth in his eyes. Though he was a handsome man, he looked quite shy. "I'm Mahmud. I've heard about you. I think we have you to thank for saving my father?" He cast a worried glance at him in the bed.

Ignoring this compliment, I said, "How is your dad this morning?"

"My father has had a hard night. He complains of pain in all his joints. He has a fever. Also, he has been sick to his stomach a number of times."

Yakub himself spoke up then. "It's true, Dr. Roseman, I'm no party guy right now."

"Guess I'll have to cancel our reservations at the Top of the Mark," I joked. But I was thinking, *I know what the problem is. Amphotericin B.*

"Has Dr. Lee, the infectious-disease doctor, been in yet today?" I asked.

"No, not yet," answered Farid.

I checked the vitals board, then took out my cell phone, dialed the operator, and asked her to page Dr. Lee for me. I didn't give a darn about hospital protocol at this point. Whatever intern was covering the post-op floor today would certainly know less about this patient than I did.

Dr. Lee called back and I spoke with him briefly. When I got off the phone, Yakub and his family looked at me inquisitively.

"The infectious-disease doctor thinks it's okay to switch medications. I believe the amphotericin B is what's causing Yakub's problem now. The vital signs indicate the lung infection is improving. He said he'd call in the order for a different medicine."

I looked over at Yakub's family. They all had the same expression: furrowed brow, corners of their mouths turned down, chins propped in their hands.

"Will he be all right?" asked Mahmud.

"Actually, I think so! As soon as they get rid of this." I pointed to the clear plastic bag, still dripping medicine into his vein.

In a few minutes, Adele came in, a plastic pouch in her hand. I saw the label "Itraconazole." She also had an IV kit with her. "Okay," she said, "you guys go get some coffee. I'm going to change his IV and his medication. I bet you he'll feel better already when you come back."

Relieved, I said to Yakub's family, "I'll take you to the best coffee shop in the hospital, if you want. Do you drink coffee?"

Mahmud smiled, revealing a set of very white teeth. "You are asking Arabs if they drink coffee?"

After saying goodbye to Yakub and Adele, I took them to the café in the outpatient building. José had, as usual, outdone himself on the coffee. It was strong enough to singe your eyebrows. My new friends were impressed. We sat down at one of the wooden café tables.

I took the opportunity to do a little detective work about Yakub and his activities. "What will your Dad do when he goes home? I think you mentioned he retired from his work at Berkeley?"

"Yes," answered Farid, "last year. Now, he mostly tends the garden."

"Does he still write poetry?"

Farid shook his head. "Not recently. I don't know why. But he says he can't right now. I guess that's how it is, with poetry." His brow furrowed and he looked worried, but he didn't say more about this.

Mahmud said, "We all hope he'll start traveling again. He used to go frequently, back to the Middle East, where many members of our family live. You know that our family is Bedouin?"

"No!" I said, "I didn't know that!" This struck me as hopelessly mysterious. "Did you all grow up in tents? In the Sahara Desert?"

Farid laughed and shook his head. "No, no, our family tribe is from the Middle East."

"Is that where you grew up?" I asked.

"No, we lived in Cairo until I was about seven. My grandfather moved away from Palestine when he was young, to teach poetry at Cairo University. That's where our father grew up, though he did spend his first five years in tents."

"Does the family in Palestine still live in tents?"

"No, even they have now succumbed to modernity. They live in a small village of houses, near Jericho. We've visited several times, since my grandfather died when I was a teenager. Of course, my father used to go back quite frequently, that is, until my mother died. It was all part of his research."

"Research?" I asked.

"Ah!" Farid said, "My father had been researching a poem, one that has been missing from our family for thousands of years, they say. But he is quite secretive about its nature. Only my mother knew anything, and she wouldn't speak about it either."

"We believe," said Mahmud, "That her trip to Spain had something to do with this research." He looked down, his eyes blinking rapidly, as though he had been gripped by a sudden and crippling pain.

"I'm sorry about your mother," I said.

He looked up, his green eyes swimming in tears. He wiped them quickly with the back of his hand.

Thinking of their remaining parent, Farid said, "What do you think about our father? Will he be alright?"

I felt my heart go out to these men, who had just lost their mother and now were at risk of losing their father as well. I did feel optimistic about Yakub, however. I had the sense that he had turned the corner and was on his way to recovery.

"Yes, I do think he'll be alright now," I said.

Looking relieved, Hana said, "Why? He was so ill this morning."

"That was a result of the medication. He needed it in the beginning, but now he can move to a safer antibiotic."

We sat in silence for a few moments, sipping the dark coffee.

Changing the subject, I asked Mahmud "What do you do?"

Farid spoke on his behalf. "Mahmud's working on his PhD in physics at Berkeley. He's four years into it now, and no end in sight yet."

Mahmud laughed, saying, "I don't know about that."

"My sister's a physicist too," I said. "She's at Stanford. Ruth Davidson. Have you heard of her?"

"Low temperature physics?" said Mahmud. I nodded. "Yes, I know her work. Brilliant." He continued, "It is very nice of you to come in and watch over my father on the weekend. You don't have to be in church today?"

I laughed and shook my head. "No, not today. If anything, it would have been yesterday."

"Yesterday? You mean Saturday? Oh yes, Farid told me you are Jewish."

I nodded, once again concerned that I might alienate this

nice young man, who was obviously a Muslim like his brother and father. But again, I saw no hostility in his eyes, only interest.

"You know, we share the same patriarch!" he said, his smile making his face even more appealing.

I laughed at his enthusiasm. "Abraham. Yes, I guess we do!"

"But then it all splits off," he said.

"Splits off?"

"Yes. You've heard of Ishmael and Isaac?"

"Of course." Who could forget Isaac? The one-time near-sacrifice of his own dear old dad?

"Did you know that in Islam, Ishmael is the intended victim of the sacrifice, and not Isaac?"

"Really? I don't remember seeing that in the Quran."

"Hold on," said Farid. "You've read the Quran?"

"Only once. In English, of course."

"That's one more time than I've read the Bible," remarked Farid. "How about you, Mahmud?"

"I've read it," he said. "I loved the Songs of David. The Psalms."

Farid shook his head with a rueful smile, looking at me.

"What?" I asked.

"My brother!" he replied. "If it weren't modern times, I believe he would be wearing wool!"

"Wool?" Now I was really confused.

Mahmud smiled at me, saying, "What my brother is referring to is the practice of the Sufis, the Islamic mystics, who, by legend, wore plain woolen garments in their pledge of poverty. He believes I am a Sufi."

"And are you?" I asked.

Mahmud considered, then said, "I'm neither wise enough nor pure enough to call myself by that name."

Farid continued to chuckle, saying, "My brother. The only hard core scientist and religious fanatic I know."

"Hardly a fanatic," said Mahmud, "I merely seek truth in the world God created, using whatever means are available. And now, let us go see how our father is doing!"

Hana agreed. "Yes," she said. "We should go. I imagine he'll be missing us by now."

We all got up, put our dishes in the bussing bin, and started out of the cafeteria.

"Thanks for the great coffee, as always, José!" I called from the doorway.

"*De nada, doctora! Mañana,* I will make it strong, *fuerté.*"

"Then I'll be back!" I said.

Back at room 248, we found Yakub looking a bit less uncomfortable.

"Hello, Dr. Roseman!" he said. He seemed happy to see me. "Have you been keeping my family entertained?"

"More to the contrary! And please, call me Rachel."

"All right, Rachel," he said. And this was the first time I heard him say my name.

After I had convinced myself that Yakub really was on the mend, I left him to spend some time alone with his family. As I often did on weekend days after rounding on my inpatients at the hospital, rather than heading straight back to my lonely apartment, I decided to stop at Peets for some more coffee and a snack.

Driving my car uptown to Pacific Heights, I thought back on what Mahmud had told me about Ishmael and Isaac, running through their family story again in my mind.

It all began when Abraham and his wife, Sarah, left Babylonia at God's command: "*Lech Lecha,* go forth!" They traveled around the fertile crescent, ending up in Canaan. While there, they experienced a famine and had to go down to Egypt to find food. They returned with many possessions, including, among them, Sarah's new hand-maiden, Hagar.

Like so many of the biblical matriarchs, Sarah could not conceive, and so she gave her hand-maiden to Abraham, in the hope that she would bear progeny on her behalf. God did, indeed, bless Hagar with fertility, and she soon became pregnant with a son. This only seemed to turn the blessing into a curse for Sarah, who soon perceived her former servant to grow haughty and elevated above her own position. So Sarah oppressed Hagar with harsh labor, and her maidservant ran away in desperation, only to return at the urging of God's angel, who appeared to her at a well on the road back to Egypt, promising her a son named Ishmael.

Later, Sarah miraculously conceived her own child, Isaac, the one, according to Torah, selected by God to receive Abraham's inheritance. With a mother's ferocious protectiveness, Sarah knew that there wasn't room in this hierarchy for two. Furthermore,

Hagar had not lived up to her end of the bargain by relinquishing her son, Ishmael, to Sarah as her own. And so Sarah commanded her husband to send Ishmael off with Hagar into the desert to die. With God's blessing, Abraham followed his wife's instructions.

Aside from all of the obvious problems in this story, one little detail that had seemed to me particularly strange was God's response to Hagar. Far from rejecting her as an outcast and usurper, when Hagar receives the news of her coming son at the well in the wilderness during her flight from her oppressive mistress, the angel also confers on her a blessing similar to that of Abraham himself: "I will greatly multiply your descendents; they shall be too numerous to count."[5] But the following story, the story of Ishmael and his auspicious lineage, was not expanded much in our Torah. I always sensed this great story must have picked up somewhere else.

And now, Mahmud had given me a clue as to where: the Quran! But while this was provocative and fascinating, nevertheless, it caused me worry. I could see how this dynamic, the "selection" of one son over the other, could be perceived as a kind of giant sibling rivalry. And sibling rivalry on the level of nations was a terrifying prospect. This scenario of "selection" seemed to imply that one story usurped the other as the only "true" story. But wasn't there some other way, some different metaphor that would allow for the coexistence of two mutually-exclusive stories?

Beyond this, I admitted to myself, I felt a kind of visceral, protective impulse towards my own patriarch, Isaac. I realized that I'd always had a very special connection with him that started when I saw a movie about the Bible with my father at the age of seven. In the movie, I'd seen Abraham and his son, Isaac, walk to the top of a mountain. When they got there, Abraham took a rope and tied up his son, laying him on top of a woodpile and raising a knife. In horror, I realized the dad was planning to kill him. I'd looked up at my own father, wondering, *would he ever do that to me? He wouldn't. Would he?* For some reason, I'd identified with Isaac ever since that day, despite the gender difference. Weird.

When I got to the counter at Peets, I ordered a double-espresso and a blueberry scone. I stuck my hand into my pants

---

[5] Genesis 16:10

pocket and pulled out some dollar bills. Along with the money, I saw a folded sheet of paper, the words *A Poem for Dr. Roseman* scrawled in Zeke's familiar writing.

Zeke's poem! In my concern for Yakub, I'd forgotten all about it. I picked up my coffee and scone and headed to a table by the window, where I sat down, unfolding the scrap of paper. It contained the following:

"Dear Dr. Roseman. This is a better version of the poem I gave you yesterday. I will try to stay out of this place for awhile! From Zeke."

And the poem:
I see the angels
every day
on the street corners
where I stay
the gorgeous light they
 hide away
inside the rose. And
now I say.
that you must fix vav
yud, two hey
and watch for scaries
on your way.

What the heck? With the small amount of Hebrew I knew, at least I recognized that these were Hebrew letters: *Yud-Vav-two-Hey.* If rearranged, these would compose the four-letter name, *YHVH,* the holiest, most intimate name of God.

Since learning about it recently, the idea of this name had perplexed and intrigued me considerably. For reasons I hadn't yet fully grasped, you couldn't actually say it out loud, in fact, we didn't even really know how to pronounce it. When it came up in Torah, we'd use another word instead, like "Adonai" or "Lord." My rabbi had tried to explain it to me this way: the name, *YHVH,* was distinct from any other name of God because it contained God's *essence.* In other words, it was not *about* God but actually *WAS* God. Unlike the other names of God, which could exist only after creation, this name existed before time, before creation, before separation of any kind from God. At the other end of time, the time of redemption, all names would fold into this single name, and thus creation would be unified. Or something like that.

But really, beyond all these mind-bending ideas, , I also figured that the unpronounceability of "the name" made ultimate, cosmic sense. If God is completely beyond understanding and definition, then saying God's true name would be an actual physical impossibility, given the constraints of our finite vocal apparatus.

On the heels of these thoughts, several other questions followed: how in the world did Zeke know these letters? Was he a closet Jew? And when he said "you" did he mean me? And if so, how in the world was I supposed to fix these letters? And what did he mean by "scaries"? And finally, why was I spending so much time worrying about the thoughts of strange people like Zeke?

I sat, sipping my coffee and pondering all these mysteries.

San Francisco, California
8:00 am. Monday, November 6th 2006
Dr. Rachel Roseman

Monday morning, I arose at my usual early hour and did my jogging loop through the Presidio, watching out for Zeke as I ran the trail along the Presidio wall. There was no sign of him.

After I showered, I drove over to the hospital, heading up to check on Yakub first thing. He'd continued to improve since yesterday, and was sitting up in bed eating breakfast when I entered.

"Doctor Roseman!" he said when he saw me, putting down his fork and pushing the bed-top table away. I was struck by how handsome his face looked, now that he had recovered some vigor.

"Ah! I see you're feeling better!" I said. "Your appetite is back! That's a good sign!"

"Yes," he admitted. "I must be better. Even the hospital food tastes delicious. And how are you? I trust you had a chance for some rest yesterday?"

"Yes, I did. Thanks. And I had a really good time talking with your family. You've raised some wonderful sons."

"Thank you. But it certainly wasn't my doing."

"Mahmud seems very smart."

"Ah! Mahmud! The Sufi scientist!" said Yakub.

I laughed, recognizing the similarity of this description with what Mahmud's brother, Farid, had said about him yesterday. "Actually, Mahmud did say something very interesting about religion."

"What was it? I can only begin to guess!"

"He said something about how Ishmael is the intended sacrifice in Islam, rather than Isaac."

"Really. Hmm! I won't ask how that came up!" Yakub smiled, his expression betraying amused affection for his unusual and gifted son. "Well, that point is not 100% settled, but most Muslims do agree with that conclusion, yes."

I thought a minute. "I really want to know more about Abraham. I have this feeling that if all of us Christians, Muslims, and Jews could understand those stories about him and his family, we'd figure out some big secret about how to get along."

Yakub looked at me and nodded, but did not say more. I had the sense he knew a lot more about this than he was saying, but I did not push him. It just didn't seem like the place or time. Also, I was in a bit of a rush, since I had a clinic full of patients waiting for me.

"Well, I better get going," I said. "I have to go cure some people."

"And I'm sure you will," said Yakub.

"I'll come by and see you again tomorrow. Have they told you when they're discharging you?"

"It will likely be tomorrow afternoon."

"So I'll be sure to come by in the late morning to say goodbye." The last word caused an unpleasant clenching in the pit of my stomach.

I left, heading over to my clinic, trying not to think too much about Yakub's impending discharge.

Tuesday, my morning clinic was even busier than usual. In addition to my familiar retinue of physicals and blood pressure checks, I had a couple of left-fielders that morning. First, my 45 year-old hypercholesterolemic patient, Andy Chu, happened to mention as I was leaving the room that he'd been having a little pain in his left leg. On further questioning, I found out the pain had started after a long plane ride back from Hong Kong. This prompted a battle with the ultrasound lab to secure an immediate venous Doppler study checking for deep vein thrombosis. After several phone calls, we were able to convince the chief radiologist that we needed the test, and off Andy went, returning a half hour later with a positive reading. Fortunately, this was something that could be treated as an outpatient these days, but nevertheless required extensive education and follow-up.

Meanwhile, my last patient, Rita Blandenstein, slated as a "foot problem," came in with a raging paronychia, an infected ingrown toenail requiring an immediate surgical procedure in our office. All the time I was scrubbing up, doing the digital block anesthesia, and performing the toenail removal, I was thinking about Yakub and the fact that he was being discharged today. *What if he was already gone by the time I got there?*

When I was finally done, I raced over to the surgical ward, pausing outside the door to room 248, my heart pounding, terrified my knock would bring no answer. Finally, I lifted my hand and rapped twice. To my immense relief, I heard a voice from the other side of the door. "Come in?"

Entering, I found Yakub standing over by the window, still attached to his IV pole.

Noting my flustered condition, Yakub said, "What's that matter! Are you alright?"

I put a hand to my head, smoothing my disheveled hair. "Yes! I just had a really busy morning. I was afraid I might miss you."

"Well, not to worry! As you see, I am still here! The wheels of progress do not move so fast in a hospital!"

I nodded, taking a deep breath and smiling. I looked at Yakub more carefully.

Seeing him standing up now, I could take him in as a person rather than a patient. Though he was quite thin as a result of his bout with illness, it appeared to me that he was well-built for a sixty-two-year-old, about five foot nine and trim. Despite his infirmity, he carried an air of dignity. He had somehow draped two hospital gowns around himself so that he was modestly covered. In the air, I detected once again the distinctive scent of spice and lanolin, no longer any smell of illness.

"How does it feel to be up out of bed?" I asked.

"It feels wonderful. To be alive, I mean. And it's thanks to you."

"Oh, I didn't do that much—"

"Don't be modest."

I looked down, not knowing what else to say. "And you're

going home today?"

"Yes," said Yakub, "as we thought."

Though this was the news I had expected, I still couldn't stop my feelings from rising to my face.

"What's wrong?" he asked, the smile leaving his mouth.

"Nothing. Why do you think something's wrong?"

"It's the look on your face, as though a *jinn,* a spirit, flew over your grave."

"Well, I was just getting to know you and your family, and all."

"Yes, I know. That's why Farid insisted I invite you over for dinner this Friday. I argued strenuously with him, but he would hear of nothing else." Yakub was shaking his head and smiling mischievously. He went to the drawer by his bed and brought out a large sealed envelope. "Don't open it now!" he cautioned. "It's for you to read later."

"Okay," I said, trying not to smile too hard. Hesitant to believe in my good fortune, I said, "What time should I arrive on Friday?"

"How about 5:30 or so?"

"That's good. Just before sunset. It's Shabbat, you know."

"Yes, of course. Our neighbor is Jewish. He's a cantor. Sometimes we hear him singing. It's very beautiful."

"Don't you attend a Mosque on Fridays?" I asked. When I'd read about Islam, I'd learned that Muslims practice their most important communal prayers on Fridays. Each monotheism seemed to have claimed its own day of rest: Islam, Friday; Judaism, Saturday; Christianity, Sunday. Though the day for both Islam and Judaism begins at sunset, the Christian day begins at midnight. This meant there was no overlap at all between the weekly rest days of any of the three faiths. Though we couldn't find a way to avoid each other in space, at least our religions seemed to have figured out a way to avoid each other in time.

While I mused on this thought, I noticed Yakub's face darken. "Lately, I have not attended the mosque. Religion does more damage to humanity than repair." He did not elaborate further.

Fearing I might veer into tricky subject of Yakub's wife, I did not ask what had caused this change of faith, but instead said, "I thought about that a lot after 9/11, actually."

Yakub looked at me with interest. "You did?"

"Yes. I even wrote a list of ten things people could ask themselves to figure out if their religious beliefs were harmful to other people. I call it my 'Religion Inventory.'"

"Ah! You are a list writer!" said Yakub, as if this were significant. "Perhaps you could bring the list with you when you come to our home on Friday? I would like to see it."

"Sure," I said. "But you'll likely find I'm better at medicine than religion."

"We will see," he said. "And what do you think would be the end result, if people followed your advice?"

"Peace," I said. "Then redemption."

"Ahhh!" said Yakub, his eyes lively. "Redemption. I have a secret to tell you about that."

"What?" I asked, intrigued.

"You will have to wait until Friday to find out."

"Come on!" I said.

"Patience, Rachel," said Yakub.

Adele knocked and came in at that moment. "Mr. al-Shadi! Good afternoon! How are you?"

"I'm very well! Thank you!"

"Excellent! I have your discharge instructions. And I'm going to take out your IV."

"Very good!" said Yakub.

Sighing and giving up my questions about redemption, I said: "See you Friday, then Yakub? Oh—I don't know how to get to your house!"

"There are instructions in the envelope," he answered. "And Rachel?"

"Yes?"

"Bring your Shabbat candles."

"Sure!" I laughed.

Ignoring Adele's raised eyebrows, I left the room, clutching the thick envelope. I had a half hour before my afternoon clinic and decided to go read the contents in private, heading over to "my" coffee shop in the outpatient building.

The aroma of coffee struck me even before the elevator door opened. I followed the smell down the corridor.

"José!" I said as I entered, "*Muy fuerté!*"

"*Doctora!* I had an idea you might be back today." José went and stood behind the cash register while I poured myself a cup of the fragrant black brew. I ran my card through the machine then found a table.

I took out Yakub's letter. The envelope was wide and thick. I broke the seal with my finger. Inside were two pieces of paper. One was the card that went with the envelope. The other was a simple piece of white copy paper, and on it I could see an address and a map.

I turned to the card. My eyes were struck by a block of text in a strange calligraphy. The letters swooped and swerved about, with long bold lines like saber slashes interspersed with tiny squiggles and seedlike dots. My gosh! Could anyone understand this thing? How was it possible? I stared at it, uncomprehendingly. Before now, I'd only seen this script in photos and film clips of the Middle East, on banners and headbands borne by angry men.

On the reverse side of this card was a note, in English, from Yakub:

> My dear Doctor Rachel,
> How can I thank you for the gift you have given me and my family? My life. There is no earthly thing I could give you that would redeem me. Instead, I loan you something beautiful: the Arabic language. To me, these letters embody God.
>
> In your faith, you study the Psalms. I enclose here an Arabic rendition of my personal favorite, Psalm 23, 'The LORD is my shepherd.' So now you know both the meaning and the beauty of the Arabic words I enclose.
>
> With respect and admiration, Yakub

I turned back to the page of Arabic script, realizing that I did, after all, know the meaning: *The LORD is my shepherd, I shall not want . . .*

I finished my coffee and said good-bye to José, leaving the coffee shop with my precious letter.

As I went back to my clinic, I thought about Psalm twenty-three. Was I walking in the valley of the shadow of death? Would the Lord provide me comfort? It was so hard to know. Leave it to the fundamentalists to be sure about these things. As for myself, I would continue to grope around as best I could, not understanding or knowing much, if anything at all, about how this all came to be and what God really wanted from me.

SPLENDOR

San Francisco, California
7:30 am. Friday, November 10th 2006
Dr. Rachel Roseman

Friday morning, I was running late for the clinic and just rushing out the door of my apartment when I remembered that Yakub had asked me to bring my Shabbat candles for dinner at his home that evening. I hurried around locating them, then threw them in my bag along with my change of clothes.

Though I was impatient to see Yakub, once I got to work, I was drawn in, as always, by the special rhythms and rituals of my medical practice.

As a young doctor, I'd been consumed by the need to fix everything. Of course, fixing things was great. But as time went on, I discovered that sometimes things couldn't be fixed, and that what was really important was just to *be there* for my patients. Sometimes, my patients just needed someone to hug them. Or to say they were sorry about what had happened. To find out how everyone was at home. To joke and to laugh.

Now, a little more than a decade into my career as a physician, I had become as interested in the stories of my patients' lives as in the details of their diseases. I looked forward to discovering more about their personalities, the unique composition of their souls, which, in times of stress and illness, somehow peeked out from beneath the layers of protective covering more often than in everyday life. It became increasingly clear to me that no matter how a person might look when they walked in, whether dressed in head turban, baseball cap, *kippa*, or scarf, whether their skin was brown, black, yellow, or pink, the soul that appeared in the space between me and them in that sacred time was the same. Beautiful.

That Friday, my last patient of the day was Harry Blum. Harry was an obese sixty-seven year old man who visited me every three months to check his blood pressure. Usually, we just ended up chatting, since we'd already spent the first five years talking unsuccessfully about weight loss and there wasn't really much left to say about it. Today, we talked about the old days when Harry toured as a groupie with the Grateful Dead. Oddly, Harry remained healthy all this time, despite his obesity. Just the high blood pressure and that was about it.

Near the end of the visit, Harry said, "Well, what's up with you, Doctor? Worried about a patient?"

"No, no more than usual. Why?"

"You seem a little distracted. You missed my last joke, which I must admit, was hilarious. Usually, I can score at least a chuckle out of you."

"Sorry about that! I guess I have what you might call a 'date' tonight."

"A date! Enough with the jokes then! Hey doctor, get out of here and get going! We're done, as far as I'm concerned."

"Are you sure? No hand-on-the-doorknob revelations for me before I go? No lurking chest pains you haven't mentioned?"

"Nope, just feeling disgustingly well."

"Then I prescribe more of the same!" I said, shaking his hand.

"See you in three months?"

"Perfect."

At 5:05 p.m., I went to the doctor's lounge, where I showered, washed my hair, and put on my "Shabbat evening" clothes. Feeling clean and maybe even pretty, I left the hospital. I got in my car and headed south toward Bernal Heights.

As I drove down Potrero Avenue to Bayshore Boulevard, I noticed an unfamiliar feeling. Happiness! As soon as I recognized the feeling, however, my mind began offering its usual counter-remedies, nagging me with unwelcome doses of reality: *What do you really know about this man, anyway? His wife just died violently; he himself almost died last week, and, oh yes, he seems to belong to a religion that is, at current time, highly displeased with your own...*

Attempting to ignore this bothersome voice, I turned right at Cortland Avenue and followed Yakub's excellent directions, finding myself in a narrow lane of houses at the top of a hill in Bernal Heights. His instructions said I could park in his driveway, and when I found it, I turned in, leaving space in front for women to pass with their baby strollers, if needed. Noticing it was chilly when I opened the door of the car, I reached in back to get my sweater.

The house was a beautiful little Victorian gem, painted dark azure, with white and gold trim. On the roof, I saw a white railing and realized it probably surrounded a protected platform, a kind of urban widow's walk created to enjoy what must be an outstanding view. As I parked, I saw a curtain upstairs fall back into place, and in a moment, Farid was down at the door welcoming me.

"Dr. Rachel!" he said warmly, giving me a hug. Apparently this name was going to stick. "I'm glad you're here! Come in, come in!" Hana was there in the doorway, as well, in stockinged feet and head scarf. As I entered, a breath of warm air greeted me, aromatic with the smell of spiced cooking meat, and I realized that I was famished.

Removing my shoes, I said, "How is Yakub?"

"Come see for yourself!" Farid said, gesturing to the stairway.

The interior of the house was classic San Francisco Victorian, with delicate plaster moldings and plates around the light fixtures sculpted into graceful floral and fruit designs. Photographs of a foreign city decorated the walls along the stairwell, domes and minarets reflecting a very different culture. Farid saw me looking. "That's Cairo," he said, "my home town."

Near the top, I was arrested by a stunning painting of a hawk. Close-up, I saw the drawing was actually composed of letters which I now recognized as Arabic. I marveled for a moment at the way the artist had succeeded in creating perfect beak, eye, and wing, with swooping strokes of the calligraphy brush.

I looked up to see Yakub watching me from the banister above the stairway.

"It is a beautiful work, is it not?" he said. "The artist has managed to capture the *Fatiha*, the opening verse of the Quran, in a majestic bird of prey."

Seeing him, I felt the happiness return in force, a surge that reached its peak in a smile I could not prevent from splitting my face. I felt a tiny tingling in the side of my right hand.

Farid, Hana, and I followed Yakub through the door into what appeared to be a den. Mahmud was seated on a large brown corduroy couch. He jumped up when I entered, coming to greet me. Around us, lining every wall, were shelves filled with books, many of them embossed with Arabic on their spine.

There were dishes of food on several of the small tables in the den: juicy dates, figs stuffed with cream cheese, dried apricots. On the desk by the window was a small mound covered in a gold-rimmed maroon cloth. Bread? Beside it were several thin-stemmed glasses and, in a nearby wine bucket, a bottle of purple grape juice, its glass beaded with water.

Yakub stood beside me next to the desk.

"How are you feeling?" I asked him. To me, he looked marvelous.

"I feel very well, now that you have cured me," he said.

"That remains to be seen," I said with mock sternness.

"Did you bring the Shabbat candles?"

"I did." I reached into my backpack to bring out the candlesticks and candles. "Shall I set these up next to the bread?"

"Yes, please," said Yakub.

I set the candlesticks on the table, inserting the small white candles. Outside, the sun was down below the line of mountains, the sky pale along their tops, deepening to indigo above. Yakub put his hand into his pocket and pulled out a white crocheted head cover, similar to the one worn by Farid.

"I'm afraid I will need to ask for your help with this," he said. "It's a two-handed procedure."

I took the head covering from him and stood in front of him, reaching up slightly to place the cap over his thick hair. He was about four inches taller than me, so I had no problem pulling the woolen cap down over his head. I smoothed the wrinkles out by running my hands across the crown, forehead, and sides of his head several times. His hair felt soft, and I noticed it was clean and smelled like shampoo.

"This reminds me of a *kippa*, or what my mom would call a *yarmulke*. What do you call it?" I asked him, gesturing to the cap.

"We call it a *kufi*."

All of us assembled at the table. I asked, "Should I begin?"

Yakub nodded.

I had been doing this for about nine months now and so was fairly comfortable with the blessings. We lit the candles, and I showed everyone that we should pull the light in towards our eyes. I began the prayer: "*Baruch atta Adonai, Eloheinu Melech Ha-Olam*…Blessed are you oh Lord our God, Master of the universe, who has sanctified us with your commandments and commanded us to light the candles of Shabbat."

I poured the grape juice and offered the *kiddush,* the prayer that's recited over the wine in order to recognize the gift of the Sabbath day. Finally, I uncovered the bread, surprised to see a fresh Challah. I sliced it with a serrated knife, then said the third prayer, the *motsi,* and held a piece of bread out to Hana, gesturing that she should pull off a hunk. I repeated this with the three men. I put a piece of bread in my mouth, savoring its sweet, soft center and wondering where Yakub had gotten it.

As if reading my mind, Yakub said, "I asked my neighbor, Andy Levinstein, the cantor, to pick up an extra loaf when he went to the bakery earlier today. He became curious about why I was making this request. I told him I had a dear Jewish friend coming to celebrate Shabbat with me today." He smiled. I chewed the bread slowly as it released its earthy flavor. Closing my eyes, I thought of the seeds that had entered the moist soil, split and divided from one into many diverse parts. I pictured sun, fields, and waves of wheat blown by gusts of wind.

When we were done, Farid, Mahmud, and Hana went downstairs to finish preparing dinner, leaving Yakub and me alone. Standing looking out the window, Yakub took a sip of grape juice, then quoted something, speaking in the tongue I had come to recognize as Arabic. He translated:

The goblets were heavy
when they were brought to us
but filled with fine wine
they became so light
They were on the point of flying away
with all their contents
just as our bodies are lightened
by the spirits. (2)

I let the words sink in. "Who wrote that?" I finally asked.

Yakub turned from the window. "Idris ibn al-Yamani, an eleventh-century poet from the Andalus. In medieval Spain, there was a collision of monotheistic cultures, a brief flowering from the temporary reunion of the brothers, Ishmael and Isaac." He switched topics: "You know, as a Muslim, we are prohibited from drinking wine."

"Yes, I know," I said. "That's okay, I'm not much of a wine drinker. I've seen too many people in liver failure to want to go out that way."

Yakub nodded, then said, "We Muslims drink a different kind of wine." He began to speak in Arabic again, his voice musical, and then translated:

In memory of the beloved

we drank a wine;
we were drunk with it
before creation of the vine. (3)

"That one is by Umar ibn al Farid, a great Sufi mystical poet from Egypt."

We stood in silence for a couple of moments, and then Yakub said, "Please, help yourself to some food! Sit down!"

We both took some of the appetizers on small white dishes. The dates were sticky with sugar, perfectly sweet and soft. I avoided the cheese-stuffed figs, thinking the al-Shadis would likely be serving the savory meat I smelled, and wanting to avoid breaking the Jewish proscription against eating meat and milk at the same meal. My own version of *kashrut*, keeping kosher. I sat down on the corduroy couch, then looked at Yakub and said, "Didn't you say you were going to tell me something about redemption today? Some sort of secret or another?" I said it casually, but this question had been on my mind all week.

Yakub, who had sat down next to me, now looked at me sharply. "You remember that?"

"Yakub," I said. "Jewish people are obsessed with redemption."

"Really?" he said, with interest.

"Yes! Don't you know the story of the Exodus and God's redemption of the Jewish people from slavery? And we're always working on ways to get the world back to where we started, the Garden of Eden. You know. The *real* redemption."

"Of course," he said, looking hard at me, his green eyes probing my face, and I felt that drawing feeling again, like a current. Then he nodded. "Yes, I have a secret about redemption."

The words sent a thrill down my spine.

"I will tell you. But Rachel, do you know? I have only told one person about this before. Rawiyya, my wife. And now she is dead. As for the boys, they know very little about the family legend. But I will tell you. Since I told you I would." He paused.

I was about to reply when we received the dinner summons from below.

"Time to eat!" called Hana.

"We'll be down in a sec," I responded, agitated that I had not yet heard the secret.

Yakub paused a moment longer, laughing at my curiosity,

and I noticed how white and even his teeth were, how attractive his smile. He began, speaking very softly, "There is a legend." He paused.

I nodded enthusiastically, encouraging him to keep going.

"It's a legend about a poem," he continued.

"A poem?"

"Yes. My family has spoken of this legend for millennia. But twelve years ago, my uncle showed me true evidence of its existence."

"A poem?" I repeated, dumbly. "What kind of a poem?"

Yakub spoke, and I watched his mouth as he said, "A poem that will redeem the world."

Unburdened of his secret, Yakub stopped. He looked at me, gauging the effect of his words, the air still buzzing with electricity.

"And what was the evidence?" I said.

"A parchment my uncle found, in one of the caves near Jericho, in Israel. Near where the Dead Sea Scrolls were discovered later. He also discovered a scroll of Psalms, ending in Psalm 96."

"What did the parchment say?" I asked.

Yakub closed his eyes. Then he opened them and began to recite: "*I tell of a poem of ancient wisdom, a creation understood in the house of Abraham and his sons, Ishmael and Isaac. When the truth of this poem fills the world, immediately it will be redeemed. The heavens will be sewn to the earth and God's name (YHVH) will be one.*"

"Gosh," I said, trying to take it in. There was so much there. "Can you say it again?" I took a pen and a notebook out of my purse. Yakub repeated the words and I wrote them down, my mind already beginning to work on this legend and what it could mean.

When I was done writing, Yakub rose, saying, "And now, my dear Rachel, let us go down to dinner."

Distracted, I put the notebook back in my purse and followed Yakub down the stairs. My mind was racing. I was thinking about something my father had once said to me... trying to remember exactly what it was....

As we approached the dining room, the delicious aromas of meat and sautéed olive oil grew overpowering. My hunger returned to me in full force, pushing my feverish thoughts about the poem back for the time being.

"Welcome!" said Hana as we entered. "Please help

yourself!".

Dinner was arrayed on the top of a wooden sideboard. I saw steaming plates of food: a dish of stuffed grape leaves, a bowl of rice mixed with noodles, a plate piled high with crunchy falafel, and several assorted bowls of vegetables. In the center of the dining table, a large pitcher of lemonade sparkled with crushed ice.

I piled my plate high, promising myself that I would go on an especially long run this weekend.

Everyone else filled up their plates as well, talking happily as we sat down at the table. I began with one of the grapeleaf-wrapped bundles. My fork went through it like butter, and out spilled a redolent mixture of browned meat, rice, tomatoes, and spice. Cinnamon?

"That's called *warak enab*," said Yakub. "Do you like it?"

I nodded, my mouth full. "Mmmm."

"Have you ever been to Egypt?" asked Farid.

I swallowed. "No. I did go to Europe, Asia, and South America, though, when I was running competitively."

Mahmud was interested. "You are a runner?"

"Yes. Or I should say, I was. Now I just jog."

"Were you very good?" asked Mahmud.

"I was pretty good," I admitted. "One of the better runners in the country. When I was a teenager, I got to race in the Olympic trials. Unfortunately, I ruptured my Achilles tendon there, which ended my career." Reminiscing, I remarked, "In the paper the next day, it said that when my Achilles went, it sounded like a bowstring snapping."

They were quiet. Sometimes I forgot that not everyone was accustomed to these gruesome medical images.

Yakub broke the silence. "Goodness! You are fast as well as beautiful!"

I felt warmth rise to my face, unable to think of a witty comeback. Flustered, I asked, "Have you all lived here long?"

Yakub answered. "We moved to America from Cairo twenty-five years ago, when Farid was five, Mahmud three. First, we lived in Berkeley. But Rawiyya loved San Francisco so much, we decided to move here about fifteen years ago. The boys lived here when they were in high school. Now, of course, I live here by myself, since...since my wife passed away."

"Sometimes I sleep over," said Mahmud, quickly. "Like

tonight."

"I love the San Francisco Victorians," I said. "I've always
wanted one. But my husband, David, and I were both doctors, and
were both so busy we didn't have time or energy for anything but
medicine. We were always renters. " This comment, unfortunately,
raised the specter of my dead husband.

It seemed the ghosts of two dead spouses had joined us at
the table.

Changing the subject once again, Yakub said, "Rachel, you
said you were going to bring something for me to read! A list of
some kind?"

"Oh, yes!" I said, now feeling a little self-conscious about it.
"My Religion Inventory. It's in the notebook I left upstairs. I could
bring it down before dessert."

"Perfect!"

At length, everyone finished their food. It had been
absolutely delicious and I hated to quit, but I couldn't fit another
morsel into my stomach. We cleared the dishes away, carrying our
plates into the kitchen. I offered to help clean up, but Hana and
Farid sent me back out to the dining room. "Go keep that old
invalid company!" Farid said, in a loud voice so his father could
hear, and I heard Yakub laughing from the dining room.

I went and sat back down with him at the table.

"Yakub," I began.

"Yes?" He looked into my eyes, and I felt the disequilibrium
again, almost like our souls were overlapping. I wondered if he felt
anything like this. I couldn't tell.

"What you said upstairs, about the poem . . . " I said.

"Yes, I would like to talk about that. But first, I want to see
what you've brought. I know already that you have a large and
wonderful brain inside that head that you carry around so casually."

"I'll go get it." I got up and walked toward the door. "But
don't go thinking I'm a genius or something. I get by in the world
by reading everything over and over a hundred times."

"Rachel," said Yakub, "it would take a lot for you to
disappoint me now." I ran up the stairs, skipping a few here and
there. I grabbed my notebook and ran back downstairs. When I got
there, I handed the notebook to Yakub. He took it with his good
hand, sitting quietly as he read.

"Religion Inventory" Does my religion lead me to believe that....

Slavery – I am justified in taking away the rights* of any other person, man or woman?

Certainty – I know exactly what God is and everything in my holy book is literally true?

Hatred – I should hate or kill people who believe something different from me?

Imperialism – My religion is the only religious system for the whole world?

Separation – Our own group (family, tribe, nation) is superior to another?

Magic – I can learn and use magical forces for my own personal gain?

Fundamentalism – I should follow daily customs as they were at a perfect time in the past?

Rank – I am better than another person?

Evangelism – I should worry about others' salvation status and feel the need to convert them?

Exclusivity – Those who belong to my religious system are the only ones destined for salvation?

* Fundamental rights: life, liberty, the pursuit of happiness. Be wary of any "Yes" answers!

After about five minutes of silence, I began to feel uncomfortable. I thought about my list. Was it complete baloney?

At last, Yakub cleared his throat. "Well," he said, "this isn't poetry—"

"No."

"—so I'm not an authority," he continued. "And there are many, many people who would strongly disagree with you on some of these points, particularly *Evangelism* and *Imperialism*. Though I'm not one of them."

"That's a relief!" I said.

Yakub looked up, tilting his head back to scrutinize me. "This is very good, Rachel." He gazed at me a little longer. Then he said, "Your systematic thinking provides a good balance to the poetic mind."

"I don't know about that," I said. "But I do know my mind is already working on the question of how a poem might redeem the world."

"Really?" I nodded, and Yakub smiled broadly. "Excellent!" he said.

Hana entered the room with a plate stacked full of Baklava. Farid and Mahmud walked behind her, with cups and coffee. The smell of honey-drenched flour mixed with the pungent scent of coffee was overwhelming.

"What are you two up to?" asked Hana.

"Oh," I said, "we're just trying to solve the world's problem with religion."

"Haven't you fixed that yet?" said Farid. "Come on, get cracking, Dr. Rachel!"

"Okay, but just know my motto, Farid," I said.

"Yes?"

"Coffee first. Then save the world."

"Ahh! Then you've come to the right place!" Farid set down the five glasses of thick brown coffee, one at each place. "If you've never been to Egypt, you have never had coffee like this. So get ready for some serious world saving!"

Hana picked up the notebook Yakub had set down on the table, interest sparked on her pretty round face. "What is this?"

"It's something I put together last year when I began studying Judaism," I said.

Mahmud was circling the table with the baklava, putting a small plate in front of each of us, two diamonds of the sticky pastry on each one. I picked up my knife and fork and cut off a small piece. It was full of nuts and spices, drenched in sticky honey, still warm.

"Mmmm," I said for the umpteenth time that night.

I looked over at Hana, just as she put down the notebook. "Great!" she said. "But it's hard to imagine the fundamentalists ever giving up their own method of saving the world—that is, by converting everyone to their own faith, through persuasion or force."

I took a sip of the bittersweet coffee, a perfect accompaniment to the overpoweringly sweet baklava. "That's one conclusion I came to. I decided that some things can't be tolerated anymore in the world. Fundamentalism is one of them. Exclusive 'chosen-ness' is another."

"But you are Jewish," protested Hana, "and so a member of the group that invented chosen-ness!"

I shook my head. "You misunderstand the concept of chosen-ness. It doesn't mean the Jews are the only ones chosen for salvation. What they were actually 'chosen' for is something completely different from what people think."

"And what is that?" asked Hana.

"To bring honor to God's name."

"Really? How do you do that?"

"Hmm." I thought for a minute, trying to remember the most important things. "By following God's commandments. By loving God and showing justice. By testifying that God is One."

"What for?"

"So that *all* humankind can be redeemed."

"Really!" said Farid, finishing his baklava and wiping his mouth with the napkin. "So what am I chosen for?"

"Well, since you're a Muslim, I imagine it's much the same thing," I replied. "Loving God and acting justly. Testifying to the Oneness of God."

Farid nodded. *"Tawhid.* Yes. But we also have other important testimonials, such as belief in the Day of Judgment and the prophecy of Muhammad."

"Well, I'm not sure if you see your holy book, the Quran, in the same light or not, but we look at our Torah not only as a revelation but also a kind of covenant with God, a two-way promise, if you see what I mean. And there's something else kind of interesting about that."

"There is?" Farid picked up his coffee cup and looked at me expectantly over the brim.

I nodded. "There's more than one covenant described in the Torah. There's the covenant from Mt. Sinai, which includes all the commandments the Jews agree to follow, and then, there's the covenant of Abraham, called the covenant of circumcision. And there's also the covenant of Noah, which applies to all people. Have you heard of Noah?"

Mahmud raised a hand, swallowing his last bite of baklava. "He's the prophet of his generation, who survived by building an ark while all the rest of the people were drowned in a flood. His story is in the Quran."

"Yes, I thought so. Anyway, after the flood, God promises He'll never wipe everyone out again, as long as people follow certain rules."

"What rules?" asked Farid.

I paused for a minute, trying to remember. There were seven of them. "You're not supposed to murder, worship idols, blaspheme, commit adultery, eat meat from an animal while it's still alive...hmm. I can't remember all of them..."

"That last one is rather strange," remarked Mahmud. "I wonder what that means?"

"I take it to mean that we shouldn't be savages," I said.

"So if people follow this covenant, the covenant of Noah, they will be living righteously? Redemption isn't only for 'the chosen'?" said Hana. "Really?"

"Yes, really!"

"Very interesting," she said. "Tell me. Is there anything you'd like to know, some burning question about Islam? I've noticed you examining my head scarf, for example."

I looked down, embarrassed. Had it been that obvious?

Hana laughed. "Don't worry, I'm used to it! Western women are always curious about this. But please don't be concerned! I don't need any rescuing!"

I looked back up at her, openly examining her now. She wore an opaque blue scarf that was tight on her head and expertly tied so that only her smooth face showed through its opening. The color exactly matched that of her clear eyes.

"Understand this well," she said, pausing to make sure that I was listening. "It is my own choice to wear this scarf. And that's what makes the whole world of difference. I choose to wear it, so I can remember God. I do it for God and not for man." She looked over at Farid, and something warm, even intimate, passed between them.

I was still curious, though intrigued with her response. "But what does your hair look like?" I asked.

In answer, Hana untied the back of the scarf and pulled it away from her head. Her hair swung away in a black carpet to her mid-back, thick and lustrous. She was stunning.

Farid stood up and came to kiss her on top of her head. "My wife," he said, "is quite remarkable."

"One thing that young western women may miss," said Hana, "is the power of concealment. Revealing all is not so beguiling as they may believe."

Watching Hana gather up her hair into a thick knot and retie the scarf around her, I had to agree.

"But what about women's rights?" I said to Hana. "Here in America, you're free to do what you like. But what about other places in the Islamic world?"

Hana nodded. "Yes, many have misused the words of the Quran. There is subjugation and enslavement of women in a manner never intended by its laws. I worry, too, when I see television footage of mobs of angry men thronging the streets in Muslim countries, no women's faces in the crowd. A balance is needed, I believe. "

"But what can be done?" I asked.

"We women who have a voice must speak our part, from within the tradition."

"Hana is writing a book regarding Islamic law on women," said Farid. "She made a study of this when we were at Cairo University."

"You're writing a book?" I said, impressed once again.

"In between changing diapers!" laughed Hana.

"She has a publisher already," said Farid, gazing at his wife, his face alight. "American University in Cairo Press. As I said, my wife is quite remarkable!"

We all got up and began clearing the dishes. While Mahmud kept his father company, Hana, Farid, and I carried them into the kitchen, where we put everything in the dishwasher and turned it on. When the kitchen was all clean, the dishwasher whirring quietly, I followed Hana and Farid back out to the dining room, laughing at Farid, who had tied a flowered dishrag on top of his head with a large rubber band.

I joked, "Only in San Francisco could you find a Bedouin with a floral head scarf!"

Yakub and Mahmud laughed at the ridiculous sight, and at length, Farid removed the towel and bent to kiss his father on the cheek in preparation for departure.

"*Ma'es salaama,*" he said, *goodbye.* "We will see you tomorrow, when we visit with the children."

"*Allah yisal'mak.* Thanks to you and Hana for coming."

San Francisco, California

9:00 pm. Friday, November 11ᵗʰ 2006
Dr. Rachel Roseman and Prof. Yakub al-Shadi

After Hana and Farid left, Yakub asked me if I wanted to see his roof garden.

"Yes, please!" I said, resisting the temptation to clap my hands like a child.

"Don't be too long up there," Mahmud worried. "You are still recovering, Baba."

"I'll keep an eye on him," I promised. "I'm trained for that kind of thing!"

Climbing slowly up the three flights of stairs, Yakub did puff a little. I promised myself I wouldn't keep him out there too long.

At the third floor, we passed through the master suite, a large room with a small attached office. I caught a glimpse of the master bed but did not look long. This must have been Yakub and Rawiyya's bed. It always bothered me to see the private spaces of married couples. We continued up the stairs, reaching a door at the top. Yakub unlocked and opened it, speaking as he went.

"After Rawiyya died, I discovered that she had created this beautiful garden up here on the roof. I was rather shocked, actually, at this evidence that our lives had become so separate. Apparently, I had been so busy and preoccupied with my own work, I hadn't noticed. And then, of course, there was *the poem*. It wasn't until the end that I discovered Rawiyya had an interest in helping me with the search."

I stepped out onto the roof behind Yakub, immediately sensing the loamy warmth of growing things, the fragrance of roses and vegetation. My eyes took in the glorious view all around, the lights of San Francisco sparkling on the curving hills. Yakub walked to the chest-high parapet at the edge, leaving the roof in fecund darkness.

I followed and stood next to him, taking in the panorama. I said, "I really love this city. But I've had a lot of pain here too."

"Your husband?"

"Mostly."

"Farid mentioned you were a widow. How did your husband die?"

"David died in a house fire. On Christmas day, almost seven years ago. You can see the hill where our house burned down from here. Potrero Hill." I pointed over to a nearby hillside, the last one before the bay.

"What happened?"

"One of the Christmas lights short-circuited and set the tree on fire. David was the one to go check when we smelled smoke in the middle of the night. The firemen think his clothes caught fire…"

My voice caught, and the familiar bad feelings tried to flood upward, but I blocked them. I was tired of grieving, tired of being angry at David and missing him, all at one time. I didn't want to feel sad, up here on this rooftop, the smell of life all around me.

"I'm very sorry," Yakub said, and we stood in silence several minutes, taking in the lights and the fog. Abruptly, Yakub turned and said, "Rachel, what do you think of the legend I described to you?"

Grateful to talk about a different subject, I said, "It's amazing! And odd."

"Odd? Why do you say odd?"

"You won't believe this, but my father was studying something like that."

"Your father? What does he do?"

"Did. What *did* he do. Unfortunately, he died in a car accident about ten years ago."

"I'm sorry," said Yakub.

"It was all awhile ago now," I said. "Anyway, Dad was in commercial real estate. He was British, and he studied English literature at Cambridge before coming to the states. He always loved poetry, but, well, of course, he had to make a living."

Yakub laughed. "Yes, I understand all too well."

"Here's the really strange thing. Mom got breast cancer. When things started looking bad for her, the last year or so, Dad got a little strange. He started scribbling down poetry all day long. He was almost frantic, but at times incredibly animated. He was going crazy, I think. He'd say things like, 'If I could only write it, death wouldn't be a problem anymore,' and he'd grab onto my arm so hard it hurt." I paused, remembering my father's strange behavior.

"Was there anything else?" asked Yakub.

"Yes, there was. Just before Mom died, a package came. It was wrapped in brown paper, and had a fancy label that said *Cambridge University Library*. I thought Dad would literally burst when it arrived! He said to my sister and me, 'Girls! This is it!' Ruthie asked him what 'it' was. I remember exactly what he said: 'This package contains information about a poem that puts an end to death, bringing eternal paradise.' Of course, Ruthie and I thought he was completely nuts. He locked himself in his office." I paused, remembering the awful scene.

"And what happened then?"

"When he came out, it looked like someone had drained all the blood out of him. He didn't say a single word, just went and burned the papers in the fireplace. I remember they smelled awful...like disgustingly sweet almonds or something. Then he went and got his journals of poetry and burned them too. Two days later, Mom died of cancer."

"And those were the words he used?" said Yakub, "*a poem that puts an end to death, brings eternal paradise?*"

"Yes, those words exactly. I think he might have been trying to write the poem himself, because he was always scribbling things in his notebooks, but would never show them to anyone."

"Did you ever see any of the papers your father was looking at?"

"No. He was very secretive."

"But you say the label on the final materials he received said *Cambridge University Library*?"

"Yes."

"So we can likely obtain a record of the materials checked out by your father. As his heir and legal representative, you would probably be able to get this information. How do you think your father stumbled across this idea?"

"He mentioned it was something he'd first heard about when he was working on his thesis. At the time, he hadn't put much stock in it. It was only when he learned that Mom was dying that his interest was sparked again."

"And what did he study when he was a student at Cambridge?" asked Yakub.

Embarrassed, I said, "I don't know. I guess I never really talked to Dad much about himself. I could probably find that out too, though, by writing to the university."

"Yes, I imagine so."

I noticed that Yakub was rubbing his shoulders. It had become quite chilly, with a fine mist rising up and surrounding the houses nearby, condensing into a fog that drifted across the roof and penetrated through your clothes. My teeth began to chatter.

Yakub said, "Perhaps we should tour the garden now! The walking will warm us up!"

I nodded, stamping my feet to stimulate circulation in my numbing toes.

Yakub went back to the staircase, opened the door and flipped a switch. The lights came on, bathing the roof in illumination, and I was struck by an explosion of color. All along the roof were banks of wooden planters. At every three-foot interval was a long tub perpendicular to the others, giving the effect of a multi-layered garden of rosebushes. This was the life I had sensed behind me before, and it tumbled out in glorious and fragrant abundance all around.

Yakub returned to me at the parapet, gesturing that we should tour the rosebushes. As we passed each one, Yakub commented on its roses. I could see how much he had devoted himself to gardening since his wife died. Some of the roses were remarkable for their beautiful fragrance, others for the delicate blending of colors, and still others for the tightness of their buds.

Yakub showed me the rosebush that had pierced him, causing his malady. I had to admit, it did have scary-looking thorns, big and hooked, each one attached to the stalk by a thick base. I could imagine it would take some force to break one of these off. This rosebush no longer bore any roses.

Yakub asked, "Can you see the fungus on there?"

"No, I believe it would be microscopic," I said, "invisible to the naked eye." Regardless, I looked closely at the thorns. It struck me that, if not for these, I would not have met Yakub.

We continued walking the path through the planters, arriving at a species of fruit tree.

"What do you think this is?" asked Yakub. I looked at the familiar shape of the leaf, with its long central lamina and four associated lobes, picturing statues and paintings I'd seen in art history: Adam and Eve crying, the pitiful covering over their private parts symbolic of the shame related to their disastrous choice.

"Fig tree?" I ventured.

"Bravo!" said Yakub, reaching up to pull off a fig. He handed it to me. It was soft and felt slightly warm against my palm. "Try it!" he encouraged.

I placed it against my lips and opened my mouth. The skin was slightly fuzzy. The fruit burst as I closed my teeth into its soft flesh, and several drops of juice fell onto the roof below. "Mmmmm!" I said. It was sweet, the tiny seeds crunchy. I looked down at the remaining half of the fig in my hand. Its heart was pink and full of seeds, rimmed with a band of pale white. A tiny collection of juice pooled in my palm.

I handed the fruit back to Yakub. In exchange he offered me the fabric handkerchief from his pocket. I watched as he put the rest of the fig in his mouth, leaning his head forward so the juice droplets would not hit his clothing.

Yakub wiped his mouth. "Let me show you one more thing," he said. "My prize!"

We walked a few more feet to the center of the roof garden. There, I saw a planter box with another tree. This one had single-laminate leaves, tapered like fingers, and was graced with several red flowers. On a low branch, I spied one small red orb.

"I'm attempting to grow pomegranates," Yakub said. "But it is difficult in these cold, foggy conditions." He pointed to two heat coils, one located on each side of the tree's planter box. "I'm experimenting with some special measures. I haven't yet been able to produce an edible fruit, but I have hope for this one!"

It was warm, here at the center of Yakub's garden, and I felt heat penetrate my limbs. I noticed a small tea table made of white filigreed metal, two matching chairs beside. The table sat in a small alcove created by an overarching latticework trellis, small roses interlacing its wooden meshwork.

Noticing where I was looking, Yakub gestured towards the welcoming enclosure. I went and sat, noticing an even more concentrated fragrance within the protected space.

"I chose this species of rose," said Yakub, sitting down and gesturing to the flowers around us, "precisely because of its perfect aroma."

I inclined my nose towards one of the open blossoms and breathed in its fragrance, thick and luxurious with scent. I drew in several more intoxicating breaths.

Abruptly, Yakub said, "Rachel, I have an idea!"

Removing my nose from the rose blossom, I said, "Yes?"

"We should go to Cambridge together! Look at whatever it was your father was researching!"

"What, you and me?" I said. The idea struck me as bizarre. I didn't think we had established any kind of relationship that would qualify us for a trip overseas together.

"Yes! You see, until now, I've been researching this poem

among the Bedouin, and also in the archives of the Dead Sea Scrolls. But I can see that I may have been searching in the wrong locations!"

"So let me get this straight. You want to travel with me to Cambridge, England, to join you on your search for this...this poem?" I said. I felt a small quiver, down near my heart.

"Yes, that's right!"

"When would we go?" I couldn't believe I was actually considering this preposterous idea.

"Do you have anything scheduled right now?"

"Only my work," I said. "But I could probably submit a vacation request..."

"Yes! Well...when could you do that?"

"It would take some time to find coverage for my practice. I'd say, maybe a month?" I took a deep breath. "My God, I can't believe I'm actually thinking about doing this!" But really, I had to admit to myself, I was thrilled at the prospect of spending more time with Yakub, as ill-defined as our relationship might be at this moment.

Looking at Yakub, I now noticed how pale he appeared in the fluorescent roof lights, and recalled his recent illness. I was doing a terrible job of caring for him in his convalescence "We need to get you back inside!" I said.

"Doctor, you are bossy!" said Yakub, standing up nevertheless.

"Comes with the job."

Yakub turned off the roof lights and we descended the stairs, through the bedroom and on down to the den. There we found Mahmud sitting reading a magazine: *Journal of Applied Physics*. He stood up when we entered.

"I was beginning to get worried," he said.

"No need!" I remarked. "Your dad seems to be recovering beautifully!"

Mahmud looked relieved. "Do you think so?"

"Yes, he must have a strong constitution."

Yakub laughed, saying, "Well, I hope I still have a few good poems left in me, anyway."

It was 10:00 p.m., plenty late for a first visit. I said, "I'd better get going. I have early Torah study at the synagogue tomorrow."

"All right," said Yakub. "But Rachel, think about my invitation and let me know, will you?"

Politely, Mahmud stood and did not inquire what his father was referring to.

I said, "Yes, I will. And I'm going to put together one of my lists. And do a little of my own research."

Yakub nodded, then suddenly thought of something. "Rachel, be sure you don't tell anyone about this poem. It isn't...safe."

"Really?" I said. The idea of danger seemed preposterous, here in this comfortable house in San Francisco. Nevertheless, I shivered.

"Can I tell my rabbi about it?" I asked.

"Hmm. Yes, I think so. But only if you really trust him. Do you?" asked Yakub.

"With my life and soul," I said. In my mind, I pictured my rabbi. He was saying, *Roseman, you're taking yourself too seriously again.*

"Go ahead and talk to him," he repeated. "He may know something helpful. But don't tell anyone else, please."

"Okay," I said. "Don't we need to take an oath in blood or something?" I laughed. Yakub did not.

Mahmud spoke up then. "I assume you'll fill me in on all this cloak-and-dagger mystery, Baba?"

"Only what you need to know," said Yakub.

"I should be going," I said, a little spooked by Yakub's sudden caution. I turned to Mahmud. "Don't forget to change that dressing at least once a day," I was back on familiar ground, bossing people around with my doctor talk.

"Will you come back to look in on my father again?" asked Mahmud.

"Of course," I complied, all too readily. "When?"

"How about dinner next Friday?" suggested Yakub. "We can talk more about the . . . other subject then, too. See what you've decided."

"It's a date. Same time?"

"Yes, that's perfect," said Yakub.

I squeezed Yakub's good hand in farewell, gathering up my candlesticks and putting them in the backpack. Mahmud walked me down to the door. "My father really likes you," he said. "He has not been sociable *at all* since our mother died. I cannot remember when

I last saw him laugh."

"Well, I'm pretty easy to laugh at," I joked.

"All humor aside," said Mahmud, "thank you. For saving his life."

"I'm very glad he's doing better."

Mahmud, shy young physicist, awkwardly reached his arm around my shoulder and hugged me. We said good-bye, and I walked out the front door into the foggy night.

San Francisco, California
6:30 am. Shabbat, November 11ᵗʰ 2006
Week of the portion of וירא, "And He Saw"
Dr. Rachel Roseman

Though the next day was Saturday and a day off for me, I still woke up early, as I always did on Shabbat morning, to read the Torah portion before heading over to the synagogue. Today's portion was *Vayeira,* which included many stories about Abraham, including the most troubling one of all, the story of the binding of Isaac.

When I was done reading, I took a shower, got dressed, and then walked the twenty blocks down Sacramento Street to my synagogue. Despite the disturbing Torah reading that day, my mind was still preoccupied with the Yakub's legend. I was burning to discover something more about his intriguing "poem to redeem the world." My rabbi was the wisest man I knew. If anyone could shed light on this issue, it would definitely be him!

I arrived at the synagogue, entering through the security gate. The guards greeted me in a friendly manner, happily waving me through the metal detector. I hardly noticed these precautions any more, since they were now standard in all synagogues and Jewish buildings.

I arrived at the study room a few minutes before class began. When I walked in, the rabbi was engrossed in conversation with one of my Torah classmates, a tall man with a droopy mustache and many pins and ribbons attached as adornments to dress up his Shabbat clothing. The rabbi raised a hand in greeting when I entered, then returned to his conversation.

As I waited for class to start, I looked my rabbi over,

thinking about what I'd said to Yakub the night before, about how much I trusted him. He was such an endearing little person, maybe sixty years old, short and slight. Not at all how you might expect a rabbi to appear. No long beard, fringes, or black hat. Though he wore a dark suit today, on weekdays he usually preferred a fleece jacket and Levi's topped off by a *kippa*, the small disk somehow clinging to his hairless scalp by friction or some kind of mysterious glue.

In contrast to his shiny head, his face was decorated by a thick gray mustache, his cheeks appearing for all the world as though he'd shaved that morning with a pair of children's scissors. He had a fine, fuzzy down on his cheekbones, like peach skin. A multitude of tiny wrinkles radiated around his deep blue eyes, the color of the midnight sky on the night of a Passover moon. My rabbi referred to himself as a neo-Kabbalist. I was still trying to figure out what that meant.

After a few minutes, the rabbi ended his conversation and began a *niggun*, the wordless tune we sang before class each week. When the song was complete, he looked around. About twenty people were present. It took just a moment, but in that time, he managed to absorb something from each person and to impart a unique message to every one of us. I don't know what the others saw in his brief gaze, but I saw this: "What's up? You have a secret." Then his eyes moved on to the next student.

Surprisingly, the rabbi did not talk about the *Akeda*, the binding of Isaac, that morning, but about circumcision. He drew our attention to the order of the story, as presented in the Torah: first, Abraham *submits* to God's will by circumcising himself and his family, and only after that does he merit a visit from God and an argument with Him about justice on behalf of the people of Sodom and Gomorrah. In this, according to the rabbi, we see the very first implications of *covenant*: perfection of the world is a joint project between God and man.

"But what about Ishmael?" I asked.

"What about him?" said the rabbi.

"He was also circumcised by Abraham. Doesn't that mean he's part of the same covenant?"

"Different covenant," said Rabbi Lehrer.

"How do you know that?" I argued.

"Genesis 17. Abraham does argue with God on behalf of

Ishmael. God promises that he'll make a great nation of him, but says that 'it's with Isaac that I will establish my covenant.'"

"So Ishmael gets a different covenant."

"I guess you could say that," said the rabbi.

"Which one? Islam?"

"Could be, but I really shouldn't comment, since I know nothing about it." The rabbi looked over at me and fixed me in his stare. "Rachel," he said. "Let me just give you one caution. Don't get your religious wires crossed, okay? Be careful about mixing metaphors."

I nodded, taking this under advisement. I said nothing more about it, but wondered to myself why no one ever seemed to talk about Ishmael. According to the passage in the Torah, he didn't protest his circumcision at all, just submitted to his father's knife, even though he was thirteen years old, when most kids seem to argue with their parents a lot. Didn't Islam mean something like *submit?* So Ishmael already showed this quality of submission to God's will in our own Torah! I, personally, thought that was very interesting.

The class went on, but I daydreamed, thinking about the scene at the tent, when God and the angels arrived and announced to Abraham and Sarah about the upcoming and miraculous conception of their heir, Isaac. Had Ishmael been standing there in the tent as well, nursing his own raw circumcision? If so, he said nothing. In fact, I reflected, I didn't think that Ishmael ever said anything in the entire Torah. Odd, since the meaning of his name was "God will hear." Did God hear someone who never spoke? I was going to ask the rabbi about this, but kept silent, thinking he was probably getting tired of all these questions about Ishmael.

When class was over, we all headed down to services in the main sanctuary, a cavernous space with a soaring, domed ceiling and rainbow-colored glass windows that splashed the high walls with color. At the end of services, the strains of the *motsi* prayer still hanging in the air, people filed out to greet the two rabbis and the cantor at the entrance.

I also took my turn shaking their hands and exchanging pleasantries, then waited patiently as others went up, one after the other, to chat briefly with Rabbi Lehrer. Finally, everyone had passed by and entered into the foyer to collect their Challah and wine or grape juice, and the rabbi stood alone. I went back to speak with him. I wanted to ask him about Yakub's legend, and whether he'd ever heard about a poem like this.

"So, Rachel. Are you holding out on me?" The rabbi peered at me through his glasses and I noticed for the first time that one eye was just a little off. Only the right eye was actually looking at me; the left was gazing somewhere past my shoulder. I wondered what that eye was looking at. "What's your secret?" he continued. "Cough it up!"

"How do you know there's a secret?" I asked.

"Come on, Rachel. As they say in literary circles, your face is like an open book, there for all to read. And from the looks of it, this book is some kind of tawdry thriller."

"Well, it's a little bit involved," I laughed.

"*Involved* is my middle name! C'mon, let's go somewhere where we can sit down and talk in private."

Without waiting for a reply, the rabbi took off up the stairs at a rapid pace.

"Where are we going?" I said from behind, struggling to keep up.

"The library, up on the third floor," the rabbi called back down to me.

Winded, I arrived, at the third floor and joined Rabbi Lehrer where he stood in front of the glass doors to the library. There, I saw a small room lined with books, several tables occupying the center. The rabbi pushed open the library door, holding it open for me. The breeze produced by its movement carried from within the room the pleasant, slightly dusty smell of books.

"I've never been in here before!" I said, as the door shut behind us.

"Really!" said Rabbi Lehrer. "Ever been in any Jewish library at all?"

I shook my head.

The rabbi rolled his eyes to the ceiling, turning up his palms and raising his face to heaven in mock despair. When he looked back at me, he said, "I know you're bursting with some news or other, but first, allow me to make some brief introductions. It's important."

"Okay," I said.

He sat down at one of the tables, inviting me to sit next to him.

"So you know, I think, what Torah is."

"Yes."

"Describe it to me, please," he said. "Be specific."

"It's the first five books of the Bible," I replied. I loved easy questions. I even embellished a little. "Given to Moses by God at Mt. Sinai."

"Hmmm. We'll talk about that more some other time. Anyway, in the Torah, do you remember how God created the world?"

"In the beginning, God spoke and created light."

"Good!" said the rabbi. He jumped up and retrieved a Tanakh from the pile of books on another table. Opening it to the beginning, he read, "Genesis 1, verse 3: 'And God said let there be light, and there was light.' God spoke the word and the word *was* the light. So here's what I'm trying to say. It is impossible, absolutely impossible, to overemphasize the importance of language to the Jews. Got me?"

I nodded.

"Okay, lemme take that a step further." He put the Tanakh down on the table and walked to a seven-foot expanse of brown books. "This is called the Babylonian Talmud. It's a kind of elaboration on the Torah." He ran his finger gently along the spines until he reached the volume called "*N'zeikin*," which he pulled down and placed on the table in front of me, turning carefully to an entry whose page he apparently knew by heart. "Look at that," he said, pointing.

The page was a mess. In the center was a block of text in symmetric bold Hebrew script. Around it swirled additional text in various type styles and sizes. I could make absolutely no sense of this tornado of language.

Rabbi Lehrer laughed at my stricken expression. "Don't worry!" He pointed to the page adjacent to the one with all the Hebrew lettering. This page was an English translation. "What does it say?"

I read, "'Moses received the Torah from Sinai and gave it over to Joshua. Joshua gave it over to the Elders, the Elders to the Prophets, and the Prophets gave it over to the Men of the Great Assembly—'"

"Do you see what's happening here?" asked my rabbi.

I was thinking hard, but I couldn't come up with anything. I bit my lip and stared at the ground, but this didn't help me dig up a reply.

The rabbi thought of something and started flipping through the Tanakh. "Lemme help you out," he said. He quickly arrived at the passage he was searching for. "Here." He had opened to the book of Ruth.

"And these are the descendents of Peretz: Peretz begat Hezron, Hezron begat Ram," I read, continuing several lines further through a series of "begats," ending with the name David.

"What happens when people descend, one from the other, over time?" asked the rabbi.

"Well…they evolve, I suppose…" I said.

"Bingo!"

"So you're saying that Torah also evolves? Is that what the Talmud passage means?"

"What do you think?"

"But the words of the Torah don't change!" I argued.

"Is it possible they evolve but also stay the same?" posed the rabbi.

"But…" these paradoxes were twisting my mind into a pretzel.

Rabbi Lehrer laughed. "Okay, now that you understand that, let's hear your secret."

"Wait," I said, still caught up in the rabbi's argument.

"Come on, Rachel. You can think about that other stuff later. Let's go, before I die of curiosity. I've waited a long time already."

"But…"

"Come on, Rachel, spill! Or I'll be forced to resort to torture, tie you to the chair, go find Mrs. Finkelstein and make you listen to her current list of medical ailments."

I laughed. Sometimes my rabbi seemed more like a stand-up comic than a sage. Did this have some connection with the name of our patriarch, Isaac, which in Hebrew means "He will laugh?" This too was a mystery. Because just like his half-brother, Ishmael, who never spoke, Isaac never laughed in the entire Torah. Though his parents, Sarah and Abraham, did seem to laugh at inappropriate times.

"Rachel?" the rabbi prodded, "Mrs. Finkelstein's waiting,

just outside..."

"Okay! Okay! It's just that the person who told me this thing asked that I not tell anyone but you."

"Wow! Now I'm really interested!" said Rabbi Lehrer. "Tell me more!"

"Well," I dropped my voice, "I have a friend, actually, a patient I met in the hospital last week. He's a Muslim."

"Okay. Go on!"

"His name's Yakub. He's a Bedouin and a scholar. An expert in Arabic poetry. But the important thing is that his family has a really interesting legend."

"Beware of Bedouin men bearing legends..." said the Rabbi, as if to himself. Then to me, "Sounds intriguing! What is it?"

I reached in my purse and retrieved my little notebook, opening to the page where I'd written it down. I handed it to Rabbi Lehrer. He read for a few minutes in silence, and then whistled.

"Wow. So as I read this, there's a poem which is somehow connected with Abraham, Ishmael, and Isaac. When this poem is found, or possibly when it's understood, the world will be redeemed."

I nodded. "Have you ever heard of a legend like that?"

"Let me think for a minute." He ran his hands a few times over the top of his smooth scalp, as if to stimulate the activity of the gray matter beneath. He was looking down at the table in concentration, his moustache wiggling. Abruptly, he reached for the Jewish Bible and began flipping through the pages.

"I think . . . I think it's this one . . ." he said, ending at Psalm 96. "Yes, this is it."

He pushed the Bible over to me. I sat looking at it a moment.

"What is it?" said the rabbi, examining my expression. "Did you think of something?"

"Yakub said there was also a scroll of Psalms in the cave where they found the legend I showed you. It ended in Psalm 96."

"Hm," said the Rabbi. "Interesting! Go ahead and read the Psalm."

I started reading silently.

"Read it out loud, please," said the rabbi.

"*Shiru l'Adonai shir chadash,*" I read, "*Shiru l'Adonai, kol ha-aretz...*" I read the translation. "Sing to the LORD a new song, sing to the LORD, all the earth…"

"You know that, in Hebrew, *shir* means either song or poem. I thought of this particular Psalm because the 'new song' mentioned here is one that 'all the earth' will sing to the Lord. Not just the Jews, not just the Muslims, nor even just the Christians."

I said, "So the Psalms may also be prophesying a poem or song that will redeem us, allowing the nations to live in peace together?"

"It's possible."

"But Yakub's legend says it may already have been written."

"Well," said Rabbi, "if it has been written, it's most definitely been lost, destroyed, or mis-interpreted. Because as far as I've noticed, the world ain't been redeemed yet…"

"Nope," I said.

"…because if it had been, Bill Blatchley, my neighbor, would have returned my weed whacker by now."

I laughed. "Anything else you can think of I should look into?"

"Well, Abraham, Isaac, and Ishmael seem to figure prominently in this legend. I'd advise you to try to learn more about them. To unlock the puzzle, you're going to have to figure out what's important about these people and their relationships."

"Yes," I said. Judging from all the questions raised by my reading so far, including today's Torah portion, I knew this wouldn't be easy. "Do you have any suggestions about where to look?"

"I'd advise you to start with the Torah. That's always the best place to begin. After that," he gestured, waving his arm vaguely towards the books surrounding us, "there's all of these. The oral Torah. Evolution." He looked at me, giving me a sly wink.

"Ah!" I said, glad for another clue on that subject. "I see! Anything in particular you suggest I read, in relation to Abraham and his sons?"

He pointed to a two-foot expanse of blue books. "There's this," he said. "Genesis Rabbah. But first, I suggest you look at the Encyclopedia Judaica. Check under 'Abraham.' That's as good a place to start as any."

I nodded. "Okay, thanks."

Rabbi Lehrer sat a moment more, gazing at me. "Good secret, Rachel!" he said at last, putting his palms on the table and standing up.

"Yeah, I know." Then, I blurted out: "Yakub wants me to go with him to England, to check a source there."

The rabbi sat back down. "What do you think of that?" he said.

"I don't know."

"Do you trust him?"

"Funny. He asked me the same thing about you."

"And what did you say? No, no. Never mind, don't tell me. You probably said something dramatic or maybe embarrassing."

"Not too bad," I laughed.

"Anyway, how about the guy? Do you trust him?" Rabbi Lehrer repeated.

I thought for a minute, remembering his garden and the way he spoke about his dead wife, Rawiyya. The way he smelled. And his eyes. "Yes," I said, "I do."

"Are you two . . . an item?" asked my rabbi.

"Now you're getting nosy!" I laughed. "No, we're not 'an item.' I don't know what we are. We'll be sleeping in separate bedrooms, though, in case you wondered."

Rabbi Lehrer thought for a minute. "Rachel Roseman, you're one of the weirdest people I know. But most people seeking goodness are strange in one way or another, so I wouldn't let that bother you. You're going on a search for the hidden light. How could I, as a theoretically religious person and, more importantly, as your rabbi, say anything other than 'go for it'?"

I felt a strange excitement building. *I really might do this!* I thought.

The rabbi's voice broke into my reverie. "Roseman," he said sternly. I looked at him. Fixing me with his right eye, he said, "Be careful. Seeking righteousness is rarely comfortable and is, at times, extremely dangerous." He stood. "And now, I'd better get going. I'm supposed to have a meeting with a couple of Bar Mitzvah parents, and if I'm late, they'll send a posse out looking for me."

"Thanks, Rabbi!" I said as he walked towards the door.

Turning back to me, he said, "No, I should thank you! As the great Rabbi Akiva said when it came to teaching students, 'More than the calf wants to nurse from its mother, the mother wants to nurse her calf.'"

The door closed behind him, leaving me alone with the books. I sat for a moment, looking around, enjoying the sight of all of them, their many-colored bindings and varied heights and widths. All those books, containing all those words. Millions and millions of letters, little squiggles of black on white. Each volume exuded a personality, like a spirit hovering around the organic materials that composed it. The feeling of presence here was so great you could almost speak to it.

At last, I opened the Torah, flipping to Geneses 22. I had, of course, read this section of the Torah just that morning. But I scanned it more closely now.

Sometime afterward, God put Abraham to the test…Take your son, your only one, the one you love, Isaac, and go forth to the land of Moriah. Offer him there as a burnt-offering…" I looked up, thinking hard. There was something about this sentence that bothered me. A lot. Well, of course the part about offering Isaac as a sacrifice…

But that wasn't it….it was something else.

"Take your son. Your only one…" *ONLY???*

WHAT? What about Ishmael? Abraham had two sons, after all! Judging by what the rabbi had just said about the importance of words, I knew they didn't just happen by chance in the Torah. So what did this *"only"* mean?

All at once, like cooling molecules of water arraying themselves suddenly into an elegant icy lattice, the idea solidified: Hagar's message from God promising she would give birth to kings and nations; Ishmael's submission to the knife of Abraham and his own silent covenant; and now this word, *only,* implying that the two stories, the two sons, had, by this point in the Torah, already separated into two different religious realities.

The separation of Islam and Judaism didn't happen when Muhammad arrived, but millennia earlier, at the very moment Hagar first spoke to God's angel!

This division of things must be in God's design!

This made sense. Because if, as my rabbi had once said in his Torah class, God began as infinite nothingness, *Ayn Sof,* and somehow created "somethingness" from that "nothingness," that must involve things dividing. The Torah confirmed this. Light divided from darkness. Upper waters from lower waters. Woman from man. Many languages from one. Isaac from Ishmael. And yet, despite the division, somehow, God remained one. That was the fundamental religious paradox.

I stood up and closed the Torah. I had no idea how this

insight related to Yakub's legend, nevertheless, I left the library feeling as though I'd made a profound discovery.

London, England
8:00 pm. Sunday, November 12ᵗʰ 2006
Mr. Smith, to Eugene Smith (journal entry)

I cannot write much today, I am not well. My infirmities remind me that there is much I must impart to you. First, I must apologize for all of my complaints of a bodily nature. The torments of the flesh that we may endure in this life are as nothing next to the pleasures of the world to come. When I am gone, you must remember that. I will be in paradise and no longer suffering. But we must ensure that the unworthy do not contaminate that place. Yes, people may revile us, and even those closest to us despise us, but it is all for that single glorious goal. We will live with God, and we will be like gods to Him in the time to come.

I admit to some regret that women have not loved me. The traditions of our betrothals do not encourage earthly love. We engage in the pleasures of the flesh simply for the purpose of procreation and continuity of our sacred line. For this reason, marriage outside the family is not permitted. As you know. You yourself will soon be married. Alas, a cousin only, because your mother and I were not able to conceive a female. As your mother is past the age of fertility, this is no longer a possibility. So, you will not know the strange and curious pleasure of betrothal to a sister, as I did. Though, as I said, I have not known your mother's love.

Of course, the marriage to a sister, wrongfully interpreted as sinful by misguided readers of the Bible, is our holy obligation and sacred right. When we do this, we are like the children of the first parents, Adam and Eve. We return to a state of diminished sin and, when the time of redemption comes, we will rise yet another rung, beyond original sin to a condition of sublime perfection. Our holy unions in marriage allow us to ascend just below this level, even now. Only those in our family are capable of reading these signs within the Hebrew holy text.

But I must end this talk of love and speak now of our work. I cannot emphasize enough the importance of your job as sentry. I can see that you are growing restless. Your spirit yet protests the boundaries I have worked so hard to construct. I lament you are too old for further physical discipline, and must content myself with verbal means to reign in your restless spirit. I trust that you will see, in the words I write about our obligations, that these are not a prison but in truth, a means to set you free.

You wish to finish your education at Cambridge and go abroad, to study in exotic places. You feel your current task is dull and useless. No one ever seeks the document you guard, TS-AR.44.224. I agree, it has been quite some time, nearly a decade, since the English poet with the dying Jewish wife requested copies of that manuscript in his mission to conquer death.

I look back on that accomplishment with uncommon satisfaction, and delight in my own mastery! How easy it was to kill that man's enthusiasm! One look at *The Damaging and Futile Nature of Poesy,* my master work, and the spirit was sucked right out of him!

My son, you have the ability to write words of this or greater caliber. I believe you could surpass even the greatest commissioned work of our family, *The Protocols of the Learned Elders of Zion.* I know you have the gift. But you must be patient. You are young. You must continue your daily monitoring of TS-AR.44.224, go on with what you call your dull and stupid job as a librarian's assistant. As the rhythm of these things go, I can feel it is time for someone new to pick up on the trail. It will happen soon.

My son, with agony in my gut, I hope you will forgive me if, in the privacy of this journal, I make a small confession to you. Sometimes, I look outside, at the world beyond my window, and wonder why this heavy burden falls on us. Wouldn't it be wonderful, to run about as others do, unconcerned with the world's salvation for just a moment? To enjoy the food, the fruit and wine that God has made, to feel the sunlight and the spring breezes? To have a woman hold you in passion rather than claw at you in terror? To feel her love... Ah, love! I should not speak of it. We have a great and holy task, and this we must pursue.

San Francisco, California

November 12th - 16th 2006

Dr. Rachel Roseman

Sunday, I went for a long run out in the Marin Headlands,

which gave me the chance to clear my mind and really think about Yakub's offer to join him on his quest. By the end of the ten miles, bolstered by the rabbi's approval, I had made a decision: I would go with Yakub overseas.

As a first step, when I got home from my run, I sent off two e-mails to Cambridge University: one to the library, asking them to send me whatever circulation records they might have on my father, the other to the registrar's office requesting my father's transcript.

My next step was to work seriously on freeing myself up for the winter break. I would need to speak with my boss, Lenny Goldstein first thing Monday morning. I also realized that, given the uncertain nature of my relationship with Yakub, it would be best if I could find a kind of "chaperone" to accompany us, the obvious candidate being my sister, Ruthie. But how could I convince her to join me on this cockamamie journey?

Monday morning, I was happy when my patient Zeke Halvorson actually showed up in my clinic for his appointment. This was not the norm for him. I estimated he usually made it to about a quarter of his scheduled follow-up appointments.

When I walked into his exam room, I saw that Zeke had already garbed himself in one of our paper gowns. It crinkled when he stood up to greet me.

"Don't get up!" I said.

"It's okay, doc, chivalry ain't dead, after all."

"Well, you look very noble in that paper haberdashery! How are you doing?"

"Pretty good," said Zeke. "My leg's pretty much healed up, and I been staying off the drugs like you said. Dja get my poem?"

"Yes, I did! Thank you!"

"I don't really know where all that stuff came from; just kinda popped into my head."

"Where'd you learn the names of the Hebrew letters?" I asked.

"I can't really say," he admitted. "My mom was Jewish, before she married a Methodist. Maybe she told me, when I was a little kid."

"Where is she now?"

"Lives in Indiana, last I knew. I don't see her no more."

"How come?"

"Sorta wore out my welcome, I guess."

While he was talking, I took a look at Zeke's leg. It did look good, the skin just a little shiny and red where the abscess had been twelve days before. "So did you pull the packing out yourself, after you left the hospital?"

"Nope," said Zeke, "I guess it must've fallen out on its own. Day after I left, it was gone. Skin healed up about five days later."

I didn't see any fresh puncture wounds, and so asked, "Did you go back on methadone?"

"Yep," he said. "Hit the methadone clinic right after I left here last week."

I paused and looked at him warmly. "Zeke, that is great. I am really proud of you!"

Zeke smiled self-consciously.

"I wanted to let you know I may be going away for a little while. I'll be leaving in a couple of weeks."

"Where ya goin', Doc?"

"All the way to England."

"Wow! Cool! So you're taking my advice I gave you in my poem? Looking for the letters?"

I thought about that, remembering the words *You must fix these: Yud, Vav, two Hey.*

"I guess I am," I said. "But I have a question: when you said to fix those letters, were you talking about the name of God?"

"I don't know, Doc. I think so."

"So have you been working on this poem anymore?"

"Yup. Been out there looking."

"Looking? Looking for what? The letters?"

"Yup. Figured if I was going to ask you to fix 'em, I should get my butt out there too."

I noticed I was having a hard time catching my breath… *Get a grip!* "Did you find anything?"

"Not yet. Still looking."

I nodded. "So I'll see you again in a few weeks? I'd like to see you once more before I go." *To find out about the letters? Or to check on his health?* Brother, I was really losing it.

"Sure, doc. I'll be here."

"Great. See you then."

"Okay, Doc, bye!"

I left the room, musing about this strange turn of events. Whether he understood it or not, Zeke seemed to be looking for the letters of God's holy Name. What did that mean, and how would he know when he'd found them? Was he aware of the song we sang during Shabbat services, the Aleinu? I ran through the final verse in my mind:

As it is written in Your Torah: "Adonai will reign forever and ever." And it is said: "Adonai will be Ruler over the whole Earth, and on that day, God will be One, and God's name will be One"

At the time of redemption, perhaps the time alluded to in Yakub's legend, God will be One and God's name will be One. I wondered about how it was possible to repair these letters. I hoped Zeke could find an answer. Maybe someone who understood poetry could figure it out.

"Hey, Rachel!" said a voice. "What's the matter?"

I looked up and saw Lenny Goldstein standing in the hall looking at me. "What'd you say?" I said.

"You looked strange. Everything okay?"

He has no idea what strange can be, I thought to myself, considering the request I was about to make. *Yeah, sure, everything's great. And oh, by the way, can I have some time off to go redeem the world?*

Unsure how to approach this, I stalled a minute. "Yeah. Everything's great!"

"That's good."

I took in Lenny's concerned face, feeling a pulse of warmth towards him. Ever since David died, Lenny had made a special effort to look out for me. During the few years they'd worked together, he and David had become close friends, and we used to spend a lot of time with Lenny and his long-time live-in girlfriend, Rebecca. Since David died, my friendship with Lenny had taken on a more professional character, but was, nevertheless, very strong. If he hadn't had a girlfriend, I suppose I might have been interested in him myself, though that would have made work a little tricky.

Lenny certainly was good looking, in his early forties, five foot nine and fit, with dark hair and friendly eyes. Today, he wore his customary long white coat, weighed down in each pocket with a multitude of medical instruments, manuals, and pens. Lenny was always prepared for any medical situation that might come up. He was a great doctor and a greater boss. But noticing the dark pouches under his eyes, I got an inkling something might be wrong.

"And how are *you* doing?" I asked. "How's Rebecca?"

He took in a deep breath and puffed it out through pursed lips.

"That good?" I said.

"She's just kind of…fed up, I guess, with the life of living with a busy doctor."

"Are you two going to be okay?"

Lenny looked at me, his face serious. "Actually, I don't know."

I nodded and squeezed his arm once. "Let me know if there's anything I can do." *Like fix you up with my sister, Ruthie,* suddenly popped into my head.

"Thanks," he said, then, "But enough about me. How about you?"

I braced myself, then plunged in. "Actually, I was meaning to talk to you."

"Yes?"

"As my boss, I mean. I know this is kind of late notice, but I'm wondering if you might be able to cover me for the holidays this year?"

Lenny grimaced. Scheduling around the holidays was a notorious nightmare in the hospital. "You mean, over Christmas and New Year's and all?" he said.

"Yes," I said, then rushed on, "An opportunity has been offered to me that I just can't pass up. Also, I've worked every Christmas for the past five years, as you know, and haven't even taken any vacation since my sabbatical last year…"

Lenny put up a hand and I quit talking. "Okay, okay…I know you deserve it. It's just, can I swing it, is the question. What kind of dates are we talking about?"

I pulled out my cellphone and checked the calendar. "I don't know, maybe December 16th through January 2nd or so?"

Lenny retrieved an index card and wrote the dates down. "I'll see what I can do." He looked up. "So tell, me, what's this great opportunity?"

"Ummm…" I stammered. This was the hard part. "Well, it's kind of along the lines of the stuff I was looking into during my sabbatical."

"You mean trying to figure out about the world's religions so you could help everyone get along?" Lenny laughed. "Repair the world?"

I nodded, then broke into a self-deprecating smile. "Busted," I admitted.

Lenny shook his head, his smile betraying his affection. "Ah, Rachel," he said. "If anyone could do it, you could."

The rest of the week passed at its usual snail's pace as I waited again for Friday to arrive. I wanted so badly to talk with Yakub about our trip, since I'd decided to go forward with it.

Meanwhile, I did receive return e-mails both from a librarian in Cambridge and from the registrar's office at the university. We exchanged some further correspondence validating my claim to the information, and they both agreed to send me the desired documentation, including my father's college transcript and a list of the items my father had requested from the library.

San Francisco, California
6:00 pm, Friday, November 17th 2006
Prof. Yakub al-Shadi and Dr. Rachel Roseman

Friday afternoon, I drove over to Yakub's house once again. Farid and Hana met me at the door when I arrived. This time, two children poked their heads shyly around their legs and Hana held a baby in her arms. Farid introduced them. "This is Isma'il"—he pointed to the larger boy—"and this is Hisham. The baby is Zahra. Boys, this is Dr. Roseman. She is the one who saved your grandfather's life."

The two boys looked at me in awe. Feeling a little silly but not wanting to contradict their father, I shook their small hands. They had their mother's dark hair and brown eyes.

"Yakub is upstairs," said Farid. "We're going to head into the kitchen and keep on cooking. Come on, boys!"

"Are they helping, too?" I asked.

"Of course!"

I headed to the stairs and found myself bounding up, skipping steps again.

Yakub and Mahmud were sitting in the den, engrossed in discussion. They stopped talking when I entered, and both stood up.

"Dr. Rachel!" said Yakub.

"Did I interrupt something?"

"I was talking with Mahmud about something very . . . interesting that has come up."

"What is it?"

Mahmud spoke. "Have you heard of the five pillars of Islam?"

"Yes." I'd seen them mentioned in the book I'd read about Islam last year. I recited the list: "Witness, prayers, charity, fasting, and pilgrimage."

"Yes!" Mahmud smiled with pleasure at my unexpected knowledge. "Well, my father has been invited to fulfill one of these. He just received notice that his visa to visit Makkah for the pilgrimage, the *Hajj*, has been approved!"

I noticed that Mahmud was trembling with excitement. Yakub, on the other hand, looked troubled.

"When did you find this out?" I asked.

"My father just told me. Apparently, the document arrived today."

Yakub spoke, a deep furrow between his eyebrows. "Why now? I don't understand why the timing has worked out this way. I applied for those visas years ago."

"Is the timing a problem?" I asked.

He looked at me probingly, and the deep green of his eyes engulfed me. "I had hoped we might be going on a trip together."

"Why can't we still go on a trip?" I asked.

"My dear Rachel," said Yakub, "I'm afraid this is not a trip upon which you may accompany me. Only Muslims may enter Makkah."

"I know," I said, "but you could still go, after we visit Cambridge. When does the *Hajj* occur?"

"The official first day to move into Mina is December 29th," said Mahmud. "So we would want to arrive in Makkah by December 27th. That's just a little over a month from now."

Yakub motioned to me to sit, and I sank into the soft corduroy sofa. He joined me there and Mahmud sat down in the easy chair opposite.

"We were just discussing whether or not we would go," said Yakub. "There are several problems. The visas were issued to me and Rawiyya. I'm not sure if it is possible to get hers transferred to Mahmud at this point. Then there is the larger problem." Yakub took a deep breath. "I don't know whether I'm in the proper mental state to prepare myself for a religious pilgrimage right now, given all that has happened to us."

"You mean Rawiyya?"

Yakub nodded, looking down. "I still feel very angry. And those who undertake the *Hajj* must be in a tranquil mindset." Then he looked up, directly at me. "And what about our trip, Rachel? It sounds like you may have made a decision about that."

"Yes, I think I have," I said. "I don't really know why, but I feel like I have to go."

A grin transformed Yakub's face. He said "Then I have even further doubts about performing the *Hajj* at this time!"

"But why?" I asked again. "Like I said before, we could schedule our travel plans around the *Hajj*. You could fly to Makkah from England. I could stay on and wait for you there."

"By yourself?" asked Mahmud.

"Actually, I thought I'd ask my sister, Ruthie, if she'd come with us. Would that be okay?"

"Of course! Wonderful!" said Yakub.

"While you're in Makkah, Ruthie and I could stay in Cambridge, continue looking into whatever leads we'd found by then."

"Or," suggested Yakub, "you and your sister could visit Israel. Have you ever been there?"

"No, I've never been there before." I considered this a moment. "What a great suggestion!" The idea made me feel inexplicably happy.

Yakub was looking at me and smiling, his teeth even and white against his chestnut skin. He said, "So! We will make travel plans!"

We continued to talk about the upcoming trip, and I let them know that I'd requested time off from my boss, and that I'd heard back from Cambridge University and should soon be receiving the info I'd requested. The future seemed to open up in front of me with tremendous promise, and I felt happy and excited, such unfamiliar feelings in recent years.

Soon, we were interrupted by the sound of a sweet voice from below, one of Yakub's grandsons: "Jaddi . . . dinner is ready!"

Yakub stood and led us all down the stairs and we made our way to the dining room, where the side table was brimming with food that, if possible, smelled even better than last time.

The table had been arranged so that the two grandsons could sit near their grandfather. I was seated across from them. As we ate, Yakub began a small discourse on poetry, intended as much for his grandsons as for me.

"Do you have any idea of how long it was between the time Ishmael was sent off into the wilderness in your Torah and the time that Muhammad received his revelation on Jabal al-Nur, near Makkah?"

"Hmmmm . . . not sure," I admitted.

"Well, it is estimated that Abraham went out of Ur sometime around 1800 BCE or so and that Muhammad received his first revelation in around 610 CE. So that would be 2400 years, approximately. And over all that time, virtually nothing was written in Arabic script until a very few things beginning in around 300 or 400 CE.

"However, there was an extremely rich oral tradition throughout all these millennia. And the height of this oral tradition was poetry. What do you know about the Arabic language?"

"Nothing, really," I said.

Yakub shook his head, saying, "You know, that is a shame. Many great medical texts were composed in Arabic." He sighed, gazing at me for a moment, and then he shrugged. "Ah, well," he said, "let me enlighten you a little.

"Arabic words are composed of root letters. As a rule, each word has three. The root letters technically compose the verbs, nouns and prepositions. Each of these may be used at times as an adverb or adjective. So, when you look at any word, you can begin to guess its core meaning, even though you may not know its precise definition. In essence, each word flowers from its root, drawing meaning and nourishment from it. This is also true of Arabic's sister language, Hebrew."

"That much I knew," I said.

"Good! That will help you understand Arabic. Perhaps by this explanation, you can appreciate, as well, that both the Quran and the Torah, composed of words with infinitely deep roots, are actually alive."

The younger of Yakub's grandsons said, "The Quran is alive, Jaddi?"

"Yes, it is," said Yakub.

"Oh!" he said, eyes huge.

Yakub continued, "Did you know that the poetic rhyme was invented in the Arabic language?"

"No, I didn't!"

By now, Farid's younger son, Hisham, was squirming and looking like he wanted to jettison himself out of his chair.

"Time for dessert!" announced Farid, standing up and picking up his plate. The boys, apparently well-trained, collected their dishes and carried them into the kitchen.

Hana stood up too, and turned to me, saying, "Would you mind watching Zahra for a bit, while I clean up?"

"Not at all," I said, sliding over into the place that Mahmud had vacated so I could be closer to the baby's high chair. I looked at Zahra, a precious little bundle with soft wispy black hair and dark brown eyes. I took my napkin and put it over my head, then pulled it off in the timeless ritual of "peekaboo!" I was rewarded with several thrilling peals of laughter.

"You like children?" asked Yakub.

"Yes, I do," I said, unable to keep a trace of regret from my voice. "Luckily, I get to see them in my practice."

Yakub nodded but did not probe this statement. "I never had a daughter," he said, "and I do regret that. It is a great satisfaction now to have this young one here, a gift from God."

That aroused my interest, and I said, "You seem hesitant about the pilgrimage to Makkah, and yet you speak so much about God."

"God is not the problem," said Yakub. "It is the people and their religions that I find problematic." His look became dark.

I nodded, gazing at Yakub for a moment, and he looked back. His gaze made me self-conscious. I looked down. When I raised my eyes again, he was still looking at me.

"You are a funny girl, Rachel," he said. "Not like anyone I know."

"Is that good or bad?" I asked.

"Good. Why would I want to meet someone like everyone else?" He rested his chin on his hand. "Are you really serious about this trip?"

"Yes, I am," I replied.

"Do you really think I should go on the *Hajj*, too?"

"Well, I don't know too much about Islam, but I have a

funny suspicion that the *Hajj* may be the *only* way for you to resolve
the issues you're grappling with."

Yakub didn't reply but continued to look at me with a smile
at the corner of his mouth. I began to feel an irresistible urge to lean
over and kiss him on the lips, though I knew this was a bad idea at
this moment.

Just as I'd anticipated, Yakub's family reentered the dining
room at that precise instant, the boys proudly bearing plates stacked
with sticky pastries, Farid carrying the metal coffee pot, Hana
balancing delicate china on a tray. Farid poured strong coffee from
the metal pot.

After we finished eating dessert, I looked at the boys across
from me, and noticed they were almost sleeping. They were very
polite boys to sit quietly through this long, adult dinner.

Yakub looked over at them as well. "Ah! I can see it's time
for the young ones to be in bed. Upstairs, boys!"

"They get to stay at Grandpa's house tonight?" I asked.

"Yes, it's a special treat for me."

Hana and Farid went to put the boys and Zahra to bed
while Yakub, Mahmud, and I went into the kitchen together and got
busy putting the dishes in the dishwasher.

As we worked, I said, "About this *poem to redeem the world*."

Both men looked at me with interest. "Yes?" said Yakub.

"I thought of this while you were discussing the oral poetry
tradition of the Arabs, the descendents of Ishmael. If 'the poem'
were composed by a member of Ishmael's line in the two millennia
before they began to capture things in writing, then isn't it possible
that no-one ever wrote it down?"

"Of course," said Yakub.

"But then, how could we ever hope to find it?"

"With great difficulty. You're right. I spent my first ten
years searching for it among the Bedouin. I listened to countless
unwritten poems by dozens of firesides. Though this was quite
enlightening in its own way, I didn't find 'the poem,' nor any real
clue as to how to write it myself."

"So you're trying to write it?" I asked, intrigued. I'd been
wondering about this.

"I was, but now…" I saw his lips tighten.

"What is it?" I said.

He shook his head. "I'm too angry." I saw his chest begin to rise and fall and his face flush.

Mahmud dropped his washcloth and came to hug his father. I longed to do the same, but instead stood dumbly.

Releasing him, Mahmud said, "My father has not been able to write any poems since my mother was killed."

"I understand," I said.

At length, Yakub returned to his chore loading the dishes into the dishwasher. "In any case," he said, "I'm intrigued with the new lead we have from your father's research. I wonder what it was that he discovered?" He turned his head to look at me. I shrugged and made a "beats me!" face. He said, "Well, if we don't find anything, in Cambridge, we could always return to the Bedouin."

I had a sudden vision of riding across white hot desert sands, my throat parched with thirst, approaching an oasis guarded by a young man with an old rifle, pointed at my heart. Shades of *Lawrence of Arabia.*

Yakub laughed at my expression. "You forget that my own family is of Bedouin descent. We still have branches in the Sinai and in Israel. They are friends and family, no threat to us."

I looked at Yakub, his upright frame, strong shoulders, and dark skin. My mind's eye could see him in Bedouin garb: loose robes, long head scarf. His bearing spoke of quiet leadership, confidence, equanimity. I still had an intense urge to go over, take the dishrag out of his hand, and kiss him. The feeling of disequilibrium rushed back to me, and I clamped a hand onto the edge of the sink.

"What is it?" said Yakub in alarm. He came up next to me and looked at me with those deep green eyes, like the ocean…

I was being drawn into that powerful current, feeling, with a sense of terror, that I might drown. What was happening to me? This could never work! A Jew and a Muslim? One of us would have to convert, wouldn't we?

"I think I should go home now."

Yakub nodded. He bent down and gave me a kiss, right on the top of my head. It was in the category of "best kisses," despite its platonic nature.

I left then, my heart in a state of confusion.

ETERNITY

San Francisco, California
1:30 pm. Shabbat, November 18ᵗʰ 2006
Dr. Rachel Roseman

Shabbat morning, after Torah study, I had a chance to chat very briefly with Rabbi Lehrer and to let him know I'd decided to go on the trip with Yakub. He greeted this information with a nod, as though he'd already known I'd make this decision. Later, I arrived home to find my phone ringing. Who would be calling me today, I wondered? It was probably my sister, Ruthie, checking in about our plans for dinner that night. That was good. It was time to talk to her about the crazy idea I was hatching with Yakub, to see if she'd join up. I was pretty sure she would. This was just the kind of off-the-wall last-minute adventure she loved. When I answered the phone, however, it was not Ruthie but Yakub. I had never heard him on the phone before and he sounded strange.

"Hallo," he said stiffly, "May I speak with Doctor Rachel Roseman please?"

"Hi, Yakub," I said, "It's me."

"Oh, hallo! It's Yakub."

"Yes, I know." I said, then asked, suddenly worried. "Is everything okay?"

"Yes, yes. Fine," he said, distractedly, then continued, "Rachel, I've been thinking since our conversation yesterday. I'm sorry to call on the Sabbath, but I did not want to put this off."

"What is it?" I asked, terrified all at once that he had called to change his mind about the trip.

"It's about the poetry."

"What about it?" I said, relieved.

"You must know some Arabic, at least some letters, if you are going to help me with this search."

This floored me. "You called to tell me this today?" I said.

"It's important! Crucial!"

"But how am I going to learn enough Arabic in the month we have left before our trip? Even if I dropped everything, which I can't do, I wouldn't get very far."

"That's alright. As long as you learn the letters and a few simple words, that will be a tremendous help," he said.

"Tell me again why you think it's so important?"

"I can't really explain it, it's just a sense I have. I think my feeling is connected to what happened in the Andalus during the Golden Age, when so many Jewish people learned Arabic. This had a catalytic effect on the creativity of their Hebrew verse. You are so smart! I'd like to use your mind to help, solve this riddle. Arabic is somehow involved. As is Hebrew."

"So what do you suggest I do?" I asked. "Can you teach me Arabic?"

"No. I think it's best if you have a real language teacher. There may be grammatical rules and other things that I've forgotten. I know an excellent school, downtown, near the Ferry building. One of my former students is on the staff there. They are quite concerned with teaching proper grammar, and their purpose is non-religious."

"Well that all sounds good," I said.

"Actually, I already called and found out that they're starting a new session of introductory Arabic."

"Great!" I said. "When does it begin?"

"Well," he said, sheepishly, "It begins in about 45 minutes."

"What?" I sputtered. I'd been looking forward to a quiet time, perhaps reading some poetry, relaxing before heading down to Palo Alto for dinner with Ruthie.

"I'm sorry," said Yakub.

I took a deep breath and tried to think. Did I actually care so much about my plans for that afternoon? Not really.

"Okay, where do I go? And are you sure they have room for me?"

Yakub informed me that he'd already given my name to the instructor, in the good chance that I would agree to yet another of his crazy ideas. He gave me the directions to the school. It was down on the Embarcadero, about fifteen minutes by car from my apartment in Pacific Heights. I had just enough time now to make a cup of coffee and go.

"Rachel, this is wonderful!" I could tell from his voice that Yakub was happy. "You will not regret this!"

"We'll see about that. Will I see you again next Friday?" I asked.

"Yes, Friday," said Yakub. "We'll need to meet regularly before we go! You can show me some of the Arabic letters you've learned."

"Well," I said. "I'll try."

"You had better go now," said Yakub.

"Okay," I said, not wanting to hang up.

"Rachel," said Yakub.

"Yes?"

"You are very special."

"Thank you," I said. "So are you. But maybe a little weird."

He laughed. "Goodbye," he said, and hung up.

The Arabic language school was on the third floor of a waterfront building near the Embarcadero. I grew increasingly apprehensive as I approached, my mind preoccupied with images I'd seen recently on the television of suicide bombers and Hezbollah soldiers with checkered headscarves wrapped around their faces. What kind of people would be learning Arabic here, I wondered?

I parked my car and ascended the stairs, entering the classroom just a few minutes before 3:00 pm. The room was already almost full. The people looked quite ordinary. Some appeared to be of college age, while others were older, like me. There were about twice as many women as men. Nobody knew anyone else, so we all sat quietly, staring surreptitiously at the intimidating script on the posters around us.

At exactly 3:00 pm, a man entered the room and walked briskly to the stool at the front. He had short, dark hair, and was a muscular 5 foot 7. He did not smile. He introduced himself as Ahmad, and immediately launched into a discussion of the Arabic language and where it fit within the world's linguistic geography.

A student entered a minute or so into the talk, and Ahmad, without breaking or looking away from the blackboard, said "Of course, from now on, none of you will be late, because you wouldn't want to be disruptive to the class, I know."

Blushing, the student sat down, and Ahmad went on. He asked questions as he spoke, such as "Who knows what language family Arabic falls into?" and "Where does the English language fit in?" No one knew any answers to his questions. When he was done with the introductory lecture, he said, "Is all this clear?"

No one answered.

He turned and fixed his gaze on me. "You. What's your name?"

Terrified, I stammered out "Rachel."

"Is all this clear, Rachel?"

"Yes, I think so."

"You *think* so? Super." His words dripped with sarcasm. He turned to someone else. "Is all this clear?"

"Absolutely," said the other student, a short man with grey hair.

"Good!" said Ahmad. "Enough. Let's learn some Arabic! Please turn to page five of the workbook."

I flipped pages in my book until I got to page five. On one side, there were words in Latin alphabet; on the reverse page, words in Arabic script.

"There are ten lessons in this course," said Ahmad. "By the tenth lesson, you will no longer use the Latin script, but will read everything in Arabic."

This was clearly impossible.

"The one thing you should know right away is that in Arabic, every letter is sounded. This is unlike English, which includes words such as 'though,' using combinations of letters to form a sound. In Arabic, if you see an H you pronounce the H.

"Also, there are several new sounds in Arabic. You'll have to practice trying to make these sounds. Make sure you do this in a private place. Otherwise, your friends might think you are dying and rush in to give you CPR." Ahmad laughed at his own joke, though the meaning escaped all of us. "Anyone here speak any languages other than English?"

Several people raised their hands. Ahmad had them tell him the names of the languages.

"Any others?"

This time I raised my hand.

"Yes, Rachel is it?"

I nodded. "I'm learning Hebrew."

Maybe I imagined it, but I thought Ahmad's look changed. "Hebrew?"

"Yes."

"And why are you learning that?" he asked.

I hesitated a moment, trying to formulate an answer that wouldn't cause me to say the words "Bible," "Israel," or "Judaism."

It seemed I hesitated too long. "OK! Our student doesn't know why she's studying Hebrew! Don't worry, they make medications for things like this!"

Everyone laughed while I blushed. From this stellar beginning, we continued on to a kind of "round robin," where we went around the room in a chain of dialog, saying, "Hello, my name is…" and "Nice to meet you!" first playing one role with the person on our left, then continuing the chain by playing the other role with the person on our right. At one point, one of the students slipped up and mispronounced one of the words.

Ahmad shot over to him, "You don't want to make mistakes in Arabic. Certain people might even cut your tongue out."

At this, I pictured showing up at Yakub's apartment, blood stains on the front of my blouse, mutely mouthing an answer about what I'd learned in Arabic class that day. After another nerve-wracking fifteen minutes, we finally finished. Ahmad gave us our assignment for the next Saturday, and all of us, each nursing the particulars of our own bruised ego, got up and slinked away.

I retrieved my car, then drove South on 101 to meet Ruthie for dinner at our usual location in Palo Alto. What a train wreck that class was! Perhaps I was mistaken, but I really wondered what they thought about Jewish people there. I couldn't believe it, but I was actually afraid to "come out of the closet" about my Jewish-ness in that setting.

But maybe I was just reading it wrong. David had always said I was overly sensitive. He was probably right.

Ruthie was ten minutes late as expected, but I was perfectly happy to sit and sip Diet Coke, unwinding from the harrowing Arabic class and planning my own attack, figuring out how I might convince Ruthie to join me on this expedition with Yakub and Mahmud. I decided that I'd have to tempt her with romance.

Ruthie entered the restaurant, calling greetings to a couple of the waitresses as she came.

I hugged her, my mind working hard. I decided I would wait until the dessert before bringing up the idea of the trip. I hated to ruin what would otherwise be a pleasant dinner in case she gave me a disappointing answer.

We chatted about a number of subjects as we consumed the delicious food: chicken with shell beans and stuffed tomato for Ruthie, orechiette with pine nuts and organic peas for me.

Finally, entrees cleared, cappuccinos half way gone, I broached the subject, wiping my face with my napkin so Ruthie wouldn't notice I was sweating.

"Ruthie, do you promise you won't think I'm a complete weirdo?"

"Why should I change now?" she asked.

"No, this is even more weirdo than my usual stuff."

"More weirdo than the patient you told me about last week?" she said. I nodded. "Go on," she said. "I'm listening."

"Well, you told me you're still between boyfriends," I began.

"Yes?"

"How'd you like to check out some foreign men?"

"Still listening," she said.

"Yakub, the man I told you about last week, has asked me to go with him on a trip overseas. We'll probably leave December 17th and return the first week of January." I went on now in a rush. "I want you to come with us, Ruthie. I already checked the academic schedule here at Stanford, and that timing would work out perfectly for you."

"And where would we go, assuming I agree to this cockamamie plan?" said Ruthie, batting her eyelashes facetiously.

"Our plan would be to stop in England for a couple of days. See, Yakub and I are involved in a...research study." I wasn't sure I should tell Ruthie anything about *the poem*. Not without checking first with Yakub. After all, it was *his* family secret. "Yakub and his son, Mahmud, are going from there to Makkah for the pilgrimage. I thought we could go to Israel while they're doing that. We'd meet them back in England before coming home."

"Wait a minute, wait a minute," said Ruthie, holding out her hand like a traffic cop. "Pilgrimage? Makkah? Israel? What's going on, Rachel?"

"I know it sounds a little nuts, but don't worry, I'm not becoming a religious freak or something. This trip will be a kind of...quest, I guess you'd say."

Ruthie looked dubious. "A quest. To Israel. And Makkah."

"Yes." I was getting flustered again, but made an effort to look cool and collected.

"And you say there'll be handsome men."

Encouraged, I said, "Well, I can't guarantee it, but it's a strong possibility." Was there just a tiny ray of hope?

"And how about this guy, Mahmud. Is he single?"

I laughed. "He's pretty shy," I said.

"Never stopped me before," said Ruthie. She stared at me a minute. She took a sip of coffee. She smoothed a section of her unruly hair.

"I'm in," she said.

San Francisco, California
Morning of Sunday, November 19th 2006
Dr. Rachel Roseman

Sunday morning, in celebration of Ruthie's decision, I decided to go for a fifteen-miler out in Marin. Afterwards, I showered and dressed in my favorite frayed-up sweatpants, San Francisco Marathon t-shirt, and plastic sandals. Feeling clean and happy, I pulled out the Arabic workbook I'd received the day before in the class Yakub had set up for me. Ahmad had asked us to learn six of the twenty-eight letters of the alphabet that week.

I looked at the first letter. *Alif* (ا). Just like the Hebrew letter, Aleph, by itself, the letter *Alif* had no sound of its own. Paired with the proper dots, squiggles or preceding letters, it became a vowel or glottal stop.

I stared at the letter. If any single thing could convey the concept of "one-ness," this was it. A single line, from the top of the writing space to the bottom. As the first letter of a holy alphabet, I could think of no more elegant symbol of unity.

Feeling a little strange, I followed the instructions in the workbook, writing *Alif* after *Alif* on the five lines below the description. One vertical line after another, marching along from right to left. No human interpretation could alter in any way its stark message: *I Am One.*

I went on to learn that Arabic letters have different forms, depending upon where they fall in a word. Some connect on both sides and some only on one side. Alif connects only to the letter before but not the one afterwards (example: لـ). This symbolism too was striking: If Alif represented God, then God stands in relation to us but has no associates, no "others," beyond Him.

The very notion of connecting the letters was strange to me, after having studied Biblical Hebrew. In the Torah, letters do not touch. In fact, a scroll is considered defective, needing repair, if any letter touches another anywhere in the text. If this occurs, the letters need to be scraped off of the parchment with a blade, or if that isn't possible, the entire section of Torah has to be replaced. What did the difference tell me about these cultures? I had no idea.

I continued on to the next letters: *Baa, Taa, Thaa.* These were all of the same shape and followed the Alif in the alphabetical order. The stand-alone form of the *Taa* looked like a shallow bowl with two dots above, ﺕ. Slowly, I filled the lines of the page up with this letter, moving from right to left. When I was done, I looked back at my work.

It looked like a page full of smiling faces.

Despite the risks to life and limb (and tongue!), I was already starting to like this mysterious language!

Throughout the ensuing week, I continued to practice the letters, and to accustom my speech apparatus to make the very different sounds of Arabic, sounds that came from very low in the throat. I also spent time working out the details of my upcoming trip: renewing my passport and discussing details with the travel agent and my sister, Ruthie. Yakub had also suggested we travel to Cordoba, Spain, to follow up on the lead his wife had been pursuing before she was killed. After that, we would see where the clues led us.

On Wednesday, a letter appeared from Cambridge, England. It was an official-appearing document bearing the University crest and imprinted with the words "for recipient only" on the front. Inside, I found my father's college transcript, including course titles and grades. Feeling a bit like a voyeur, but also oddly and posthumously proud of my father's excellent marks, I searched the document for the title of his thesis. I found it listed under "additional details" at the end of the transcript: *William IX of Aquitaine, The Arabic Girdle Poem, and its Influence on European and English Literature: The Marriage of Romance and the Orient.* Intriguing, I had to admit, but I had no idea what it meant. I put the transcript in my purse so I could show it to Yakub.

Friday, I continued my new tradition of sharing Erev Shabbat dinner with Yakub and his family at his home in Bernal Heights. That evening, it was only me, Yakub and Mahmud, since Farid and Hana had another social engagement. I was elated to discover that Mahmud had been granted a *Hajj* visa. He was definitely coming with us. I let them know that Ruthie had also agreed to come, and that my boss, Lenny Goldstein, had been able to find me coverage. Yakub and Mahmud were thrilled. It looked like this trip was a go!

At dinner, we toasted our upcoming adventure with glasses of bubbly apple cider. Afterwards, Yakub and I went upstairs while Mahmud stayed in the kitchen to clean up. He said he had some work to do, and that I should stop by to say goodbye later on my way out. Yakub and I sat down on the couch together in the den.

"Rachel, there are a few things I wanted to talk to you about tonight. But first, show me some of your Arabic writing!"

I made a groaning sound.

Yakub pulled out a piece of paper and a marker. "Come on, Rachel," he coaxed.

"Is it always so scary?" I said.

"What?"

"Learning Arabic."

"What do you mean?"

"I don't know. Our teacher, Ahmad, said something about how they cut out your tongue if you say a word wrong."

"Ignore that," said Yakub. "Please. Show me some letters."

I started by writing the *Alif*. "That's an amazing letter," I said.

Yakub looked at me sharply. "Why do you say that?"

"Well, I was just thinking: if you're going to express unity, that's pretty much the best way I can think of."

He smiled at me, saying "Very good!" He patted my knee. I became distracted by the feel of his hand.

"Haven't you learned any more letters?" he prompted after a moment.

"Oh, yes," I went on to draw the other five letters I had learned, and then wrote a couple of words. *Baab* for door, *Ab* for father.

Yakub took the pen from me and wrote an *Alif*, then a letter I didn't recognize, and then a *Baa*. أحب

"What's that?" I said.

"That's how you write 'I love'."

"Oh," I said, wondering how you would add the *you* afterwards.

"To a poet, it is the purpose for which the Arabic language was created."

I laughed.

"Don't laugh," said Yakub, seriously. "It is through loving that we learn to know God."

I nodded.

"You've heard of the Sufis?"

"Yes, Mahmud and Farid were talking about them in the hospital."

"Well, I'm not sure if they told you this, but the Sufis write beautiful, mystical poetry. In my opinion, their greatest poems concern the love they feel for God, the endless pain of separation, and the ecstatic bliss of union, called, in Arabic, *Fana*. Love, human love, is a beginning for that self-dissolution. Have you read any Rumi?"

"No," I said.

"He is a Persian poet who wrote some astonishing poems in the Farsi language. Farsi, is an indo-European language, of the same family as English, though written in Arabic characters. It is very different from the Semitic languages of Aramaic, Hebrew, and Arabic. If we believe that *the poem* must have been written in one of these, the languages of Abraham, Isaac and Ishmael, Rumi could not be its author. But there could be clues from his poetry as to where to look or how to think."

"Clues! I hadn't thought of that," I said.

"Yes. I've deduced that we might find clues in any number of places, even in the holy texts, though these, as well, could not be the location of our poem."

"Why not?" I asked.

"This is a very important question," said Yakub. "It has to do with the difference between poetry and prophecy. Muhammad, peace and blessings upon him, made a clear distinction between the two. He said that poetry springs from man's desire while prophecy, including holy text, comes directly from God. Look here." Yakub got up and retrieved a book from the shelf. It had a blue cover and was ornately decorated with gold letters, some of which I now recognized.

"Is this the Quran?" I asked. Yakub nodded. I looked at it with interest. I had not seen an "official" copy before, just the paperback English edition I'd read last year.

Yakub flipped through the thin pages of parchment. In no time, he found the passage he was looking for. "Here!" he said, pointing to a block of text, "Sura 69." Yakub translated:

"I swear by all that you can see, and all that is hidden from your view, that this (the Quran) is the utterance of a noble messenger. It is no poet's speech...It is a revelation from the LORD of the Universe."

"So," I said, "Muhammad was not a poet. His inspiration came from God."

"Yes, and of that he had no doubt," said Yakub. "That's the difference. The prophets are compelled to utter the words of God. Some may even do so unwillingly, such as Jonah or Jeremiah."

I said, "So to clarify, the poem we're looking for can't be in one of the holy texts."

"No," said Yakub. "I believe it must be written by a poet, not a prophet. Its origin would be inspiration rather than prophecy. To use Muhammad as an example, he received the message of the Quran, but Muhammad never claimed to have written it himself. In fact, the style of the Quran is considered by Muslims to be unique, singular, impossible to imitate, as the Quran itself says in this famous verse: '*If men and jinn combined to produce a book akin to this Quran, they would surely fail to produce its like, though they helped one another as best they could.*'[6]

"As a poet, I would strongly agree with this. It is impossible to create anything close to the beauty, complexity, connectedness, spirit, voice, and internal consistency, of the Quran. It is God's creation, a language beyond language, if you will. It is connected with God, at its root."

I sat quietly, trying to assimilate all of this. "You realize that in Judaism, this excludes not only the entire Jewish Bible, including the beautiful poetry of the Psalms, but also the Talmud and even the Midrasheim. As my rabbi recently explained to me, all of these are considered holy text, derived from the revelation at Mt. Sinai."

"Yes, I know," said Yakub. "Perhaps *the poem* will come from a quite humble source."

I nodded, thinking for a moment. Remembering my father's thesis, I said, "What's an Arabic Girdle Poem?"

"Why do you ask?" said Yakub.

I reached down to retrieve my purse, pulling my father's transcript out and handing it to Yakub. "It was a phrase my father

---

[6] Qur'an 17:88

used in the title of his thesis. I got this from Cambridge in the mail a couple of days ago." I pointed to where the title of my father's thesis was printed.

"Hmm!" said Yakub. "Very interesting. So your father's research brought him from study of English literature to the mysteries of the orient! That explains a lot!"

"It does?"

"Well it certainly gives us some clue as to how he might have stumbled upon traces of our *legend*."

"What's a 'girdle poem' though? Was my father writing about women's lingerie?"

"No, no," Yakub laughed. "The term 'girdle" actually is more accurately translated as 'sash' or 'belt.' In Arabic, the word is *muwashshaha*. This is a poetic form that arose in the Andalus, probably in the tenth century or so. So your father's research drew him to study Medieval Spain, the time and place where Christian, Muslim, and Jewish culture collided. We have discussed this before. You know, Rawiyya was on her way to Cordoba when she died."

"Yes, I remember that. I wonder why she was interested in Cordoba, in particular?"

"Achh," said Yakub. "It's my fault. I don't know. I never paid any attention to what I considered her ramblings about female poets. She was intrigued with one particular poetess from Cordoba. I don't know which one," he sighed. "But Rawiyya's friend, Tatianne, will likely know more details. We'll be meeting her in Cordoba."

Looking at Yakub's troubled face. I wanted to take him in my arms, to smooth the worried lines on his forehead, to kiss him, but I felt the enormous space between us once again, the gulf separating our faiths appearing, at that moment, wider and deeper than the Red Sea itself. He must have sensed this himself.

"I should probably go now," I said.

"Alright," said Yakub.

I got up, collected my purse, and went downstairs to say goodbye to Mahmud.

San Francisco, California
11:00 am. Shabbat, December 2ⁿᵈ 2006
Dr. Rachel Roseman

The following Saturday, I received an e-mail from a Margaret Tibbs at the Cambridge University Library. Attached was a computer-generated record of the library withdrawals of William Davidson from the years 1965 through 1998. The list was extensive, beginning with the standard classics of the curriculum in English Literature: Homer, Plato, Shakespeare, Dante, Milton, and, of course, *The Bible*. Beginning in the year 1968, however, there began to appear books with titles like: *Hispano-Arabic Poetry,* and *The Poetic History of the Troubadours,* and *The Beginning of Hebrew Poetry in Northern Europe and France.* Evidently, resource material and background for his thesis on the "Arabic Girdle Poem."

The final entries on the list were as follows:

Taylor-Schechter Genizah Collection - Copy sent – December 2ⁿᵈ, 1998 - TS-Ar.44.224 – Letter. Addressed to Dunash ben Labrat by his son. Judeo-Arabic, parchment, composed of 2 leaves, slightly stained; verso blank.

Original sent – December 2ⁿᵈ, 1998 - Un-numbered document – Booklet. Title: On the Damaging and Futile Nature of Poesy. Author: Smith. Publication date: Unknown.

When I saw the title of the second document, I recalled, for some reason, the acrid smell of burning papers. Was this the document my father had burned that day, before he incinerated his own poetry?

I immediately called Yakub to let him know I'd received the list, and read him the last two entries which, given the ensuing events in my father's life, seemed the most relevant.

"Can you repeat to me the last entry?" asked Yakub. "What was the author's name again?"

"All it says is Smith," I replied.

There was a long silence at the other end of the line.

"Yakub?" I said, "Are you there?"

"Smith?" said Yakub. "You're sure?"

"Yes, it says it right here. Why?"

"I will tell you when you come this Friday," said Yakub, and then even more mysteriously, "Now I know we're on the right track.

Will you bring the list with you?"

"Sure. Of course."

"And also, could you please respond to the librarian in Cambridge and have her pull these last two documents in preparation for our arrival a week from Monday?"

"Yes, I will," I said, still wondering why Yakub sounded so spooked.

That Friday, a little over a week away from our travel date, I showed up once again at Yakub's doorstep on Erev Shabbat.

Before dinner, Yakub, Mahmud, and I sat in the den and planned the specifics of our journey. The two men had already met for several hours to prepare for their pilgrimage. They had set out the materials they would need: unscented soap and deodorant, a small pair of scissors, a paperback copy of the Quran, a prayer book in Arabic, small notebooks with tiny pencils, first aid kit, four bath-towel-sized white cloths.

"What are those for?" I asked.

"Those are called *ihram*," said Mahmud. "They are to wear during portions of the *Hajj*, when we remind ourselves that, rich or poor, we are all equal before God." He ran a hand over the cloths.

I noticed a thick guidebook, also in Arabic. From the letters I knew, I could make out the word *Hajj*. There was also a *Lonely Planet* guide to Israel. I picked it up.

Yakub said, "I got that for you."

I examined it closely. On the cover were clustered honey-colored buildings and above, puffy, milky-white clouds. *Israel*. I felt a thrill and I looked over at Yakub. He was smiling at me.

After that, we leafed through travel books on London and Cambridge, reading aloud the description of the hotel where we'd be staying, the Sherlock Holmes Hotel on Baker Street. The excitement was palpable. It felt like the early scenes in the adventure movies I'd loved as a child: Journey to the Center of the Earth, The White Tower, the Eiger Sanction. Did I forget, in my eagerness, that in these movies, usually something went terribly wrong? That on average, at least one person usually died?

At dinner, we continued talking about the trip. The entire family was there, even Hana's mother, Fatima, who had, as a younger woman, participated in the *Hajj* herself. She gave tips to Yakub and Mahmud: "Do not bring too much money! But be sure to get some *riyal* to give to the poor.", "Leave your valuable watches and jewelry at home!", "Decide on a place where you will meet if you get separated!", "Practice patience! There are many people, speaking many languages, and they will get tired. Help them when you can!"

Meanwhile the grandsons asked questions. "Is it very hot in Makkah?", "Will you sacrifice the lamb yourself?," "Which room will Doctor Rachel sleep in?"

To the last, Yakub explained that Doctor Rachel's sister, Ruth, was coming with us and that she would sleep in the room with me. This satisfied the boys, and they went on to further questions.

When she learned I was going to Jerusalem, Fatima said, "Oh! You are also going on a pilgrimage!"

I hadn't thought of it that way before. "Yes," I agreed, "I think you're right!"

She continued, "You must visit the Temple Mount, even if you feel uncomfortable or unwelcome there, since it is now a Muslim sanctuary. You cannot go into the al-Aqsa mosque or the Dome of the Rock, but you will get a sense of their power just from standing nearby. Do not worry what people say. Go there. But cover your head when you do so, out of respect." I looked into Fatima's brown eyes and saw kindness.

"I will," I said.

We all talked and laughed happily as we cleaned up, and I had the feeling that I belonged here. I had not felt this since I was a child in my own home. These people were becoming like a family to me. But what was my place in this family? That was still unclear.

After dinner, Mahmud, Yakub, and I went upstairs to talk a bit more about our trip. I reminded Yakub that we needed to look through the list of my father's library withdrawals at the Cambridge University Library. I went to my purse and retrieved the paper, handing it to him. He and Mahmoud perused it together.

"Look here!" exclaimed Yakub. "Look at this work by the son of Dunash. Your father checked it out twice! First in 1969, and again in 1996."

"So maybe 1969 is when he first learned about this 'poem to redeem the world,'" I said. "But who was that? Dunash ben Labrat?"

"You haven't heard of him?"

"No, sorry!"

"Dunash ben Labrat was a tenth century Hebrew linguist and poet, one of the first to thoroughly study the Arabic language and apply its poetic rules to verse in Hebrew. By doing this, he almost single-handedly revived Hebrew from near-death, resurrecting it from its position as a fossilized language of religion to the living language of poetry. Though his major contribution was as a grammarian, he is perhaps better known to the modern Jews as the composer of the well-loved Shabbat song, *Dror Yikra*, 'proclaim freedom.' He was also court poet at the palace of Abd al-Rahman III, the great Andalusian Caliph during the Golden Age of Spain."

"So is this what you were referring to, the day you told me I should study Arabic?" I asked.

"Yes! I don't know, but I believe some great creative force results from the intersection between the two languages of Hebrew and Arabic."

"Interesting!" Hesitantly, I changed the subject, saying, "How about this fellow, Smith? The one who wrote the other document? *The Dangerous and Futile Nature of Poesie.*" Mentioning the title triggered an uncomfortable feeling in my stomach.

Yakub remained silent for several moments. Then, looking from Mahmud to me, he said, "This name, Smith, causes me some considerable concern."

"Why, Baba?" asked Mahmud. "It is such a common name."

"Smith, or 'metal smiths' in Arabic, is *al-Qayana*. Do you recall that name, Mahmud?"

Mahmud considered. "I thought it was associated with the legend of the poem. An adversary of some kind."

"Yes, that's correct," said Yakub. "Our relatives in Shaddad mentioned this name to me. This family of 'Smiths' has, according to legend, set itself against the poem since the very early days. My uncle, Muhtadi, believes the family to be responsible for the death of his son, Kamal. They are the reason my father moved away from the rest of the family, in order to protect us. Until now, I was not convinced this 'Smith' family really existed. Now, the presence of this name among your father's records, so soon before his death, causes me to reconsider..."

"Hmm," I said. "This doesn't sound good." I felt fear whisper into the air around us.

"We will learn more when we see this document," said Yakub. "Until then, we will keep our eyes open."

Realizing it did no good to sit there and tremble, I changed the subject again. "I was thinking," I said.

"Yes?" said Yakub.

"Maybe we should have a going-away celebration, with your family and mine, before we leave next week! Invite Farid's mother-in-law and all your children and grandchildren. I'd love for them to meet Ruthie."

"Wonderful! Where?"

"There's a really nice restaurant close to my house. It's called the Magic Tuba."

"Shall we arrange to have lunch together on the Saturday before we leave?" asked Yakub. "That will give us time to complete any last-minute preparations for our trip the next day afterwards."

"Great! I'll call and make a reservation, if you want to go ahead and invite your family."

That settled, I bid goodbye to Mahmud and Yakub, who accompanied me to the door. They watched as I climbed into my Honda Accord.

Just before I shut the door, Mahmud called out, "Dr. Rachel!"

"Yes?"

"Be careful."

I shut the car door, the whispering fear returning as I drove the deserted streets.

London, England

2:01 pm. Monday, December 11th 2006

Mr. Smith, to Eugene Smith (journal entry)

My dear boy, I interrupt this chronicle of my life's wisdom to say to you: congratulations! The time you have waited for has come at last! You tell me that a woman has requested the document you guard, TS-Ar.44.224. And not just any woman but the daughter of that meddlesome man, the last one to seek the trail of this abomination. Her name: Rachel Roseman. A Jew, of course, like her mother.

She has the audacity to request the original of this document, and also, my own work, *The Dangerous and Futile Nature of*

Poesy. But you must not release this latter to her, for fear we lead her off the trail. For surely she will quake with fear and lose all hope, like her pathetic father, if she sees it. I would like to take a different strategy with the daughter, give this group an opportunity to lead us to this so-called "poem to redeem the world," since that seems to be their intention. If they are lucky enough to find it, we will be there to destroy it.

She arrives a scant week from now. When she comes, you must not lose sight of her. You must attach yourself to her like a lamprey. We will see where it leads. Perhaps to the very distant lands you so yearn to see. My son, the time is here.

San Francisco, California

Friday, December 15th 2006

Dr. Rachel Roseman

Friday was my last day of work before our trip. I had specifically arranged to see my most potentially-unstable patients that day, including the two women due to deliver in February, if you could call pregnancy "unstable." I wanted to make sure that they were not showing any signs of impending premature delivery or other pregnancy complications. Fortunately, outside of the discomforts of the third trimester, that is, heartburn, low back pain, and general ungainliness, both of them were feeling absolutely fine.

I also saw several of my patients with multiple-system disease, my infant patient with feeding difficulties, who was now two months old and still gaining weight more slowly than expected, and a woman with a suspicious finding on mammogram. I wanted to let her know that the radiologist had compared prior studies and ruled the finding benign. I didn't want her worrying the whole time while I was away. I called several other patients to see how they were feeling. No one seemed on the verge of hospitalization.

The very last patient scheduled that day was Zeke Halvorson. He was the one I was most concerned about. I hoped he wouldn't show up with some major illness today, as he often did. Unfortunately, it turned out he did not arrive at all. I suspected this meant he had gone back to his drug habit, despite his promise. I was sorry not to receive an update on his progress towards resolving his "poem." I wondered whether he was on the track of the letters, *Yud-*

Hey-Vav-Hey. Could that be why he was a no-show?

After I had completed writing my notes, I went to find Lenny so I could sign out my patients to him. His office was down the corridor from the clinic. The door was open when I arrived, and I knocked on the door jamb. He looked up. The dark circles under his eyes had only deepened since our last encounter. When he saw me, his sad expression transformed into a welcoming smile, and he gestured to me to enter, saying, "Rachel! Sit down, sit down! Here to sign out your patients, I assume?"

Plumping down into the wooden chair in front of his desk, I said, "Yup. Hope the load won't be too heavy…"

Lenny broke into song, "*He ain't heavy, he's my brother…*"

I laughed, but eyed Lenny with concern. "You look like heck," I said. "I hate to add to your troubles!"

"Not to worry, not to worry. I always love your patients."

Despite the light-hearted banter, I saw Lenny's forehead wrinkle into a frown, and the sadness return to his eyes.

"Lenny, something's wrong," I said. "What is it. Rebecca?"

He nodded, and I actually thought he might start to cry. Tears sprang into his eyes, and he said, "I moved out last Tuesday."

"What happened?"

"I just couldn't take it anymore. The constant resentment and disapproval. A person can't come home to that day after day after day."

"How was Rebecca about it?"

"Not great. She's pissed."

"So it wasn't really mutual?"

"I think it was, but Rebecca just hasn't figured it out yet. She thought we'd get married. But as I see it now, that would be the biggest mistake in the world."

"So are you living on your own now?"

He nodded. "Found an apartment on Potrero Hill. It's nice living closer to the hospital." He gave a sardonic laugh. "The odd thing is, I feel really sad, but at the same time, ecstatically happy." Looking up, he said, "Figure that one out!" He broke into a smile, and his face looked more appealing than ever. This re-sparked the idea in my mind. My devious mind. My matchmaker mind. But this was okay, wasn't it? After all, it was a mitzvah to help people find their mates. And here he was, a nice Jewish boy…

"Hey, Lenny!" I began, "Are you free tomorrow?

Lunchtime?"

"I think so…why?"

"We're having a 'going-away' celebration, at a restaurant near my apartment in Pacific Heights. Why don't you join us?"

"Who'll be there?"

"Oh, a bunch of people…the man I'm doing the project with, Yakub al-Shadi, his sons, Mahmud and Farid, plus their whole family, and then my sister, Ruthie…"

"Ruthie, huh?" said Lenny, too savvy to miss my intentions. "Is she single?"

"At the moment, she does happen to be single, yes."

"Sure," said Lenny, his smile growing further. "Why not! If she looks anything like you, I'm in luck…"

"She looks better than me. And she has the benefit of a couple more years of youth!"

"She can't look better than you," said Lenny.

"Compliments will serve you well," I said, "but they won't absolve you from hearing about my patients."

"Go ahead," said Lenny, "shoot!"

I proceeded to fill Lenny in about all my more worrisome patients: Zeke, the baby with failure-to-thrive, my two third-term pregnancies. The family medicine residents-in-training would be covering my clinic hours, with the supervision of the rotating attending staff, but Lenny would provide coverage for any of my patients who might be admitted to the hospital in my absence.

When we were all done, I rose to leave, saying, "So, we're meeting tomorrow at 1:00 pm at the Magic Tuba, Sacramento and Scott."

"I'll be there!" promised Lenny.

San Francisco, California

Morning of Shabbat, December 16th 2006

Dr. Rachel Roseman

Saturday, I walked the twenty blocks to my synagogue for morning services, my heart full of joy on this beautiful, sunny Shabbat morning. I had already packed the afternoon before, so I could leave the day free for rest, Torah study, and celebration with friends and family.

The Torah portion for the day was the beginning of the "Joseph novella," the story of the young patriarch's descent into Egypt after he was sold into slavery by his scheming brothers.

"I'd have to say," said the rabbi to his class of fifteen people, after we'd read the opening verses of the portion, "seems like Joseph's dad, Jacob, fails 'parenting 101,' doesn't it? 'Let's see...' he says, 'why don't I just give *one* of my kids a Hannukah gift this year? A really nice coat...'"

We continued on, through the story of Joseph's service in the household of Pharaoh's steward, Potiphar, and the adulterous advances of his wife towards the handsome young Hebrew servant. Joseph was able to escape her amorous clutches only by ripping out of the shirt she grabs to hold onto him.

"My own conclusion," said the rabbi, "is this. This story is all about garments, and what you really are underneath them. No matter what Joseph wears, whether multi-colored dream coat or the shirt torn off by Mrs. Potiphar, nevertheless, he remains what he is. A Jew."

He looked at me directly when he said this.

At the end of class, I stood up to go, but the rabbi called to me.

"Rachel," he said, fixing me with his good eye.

"Yes?"

"Don't run off after services today. I want to talk with you."

"Okay, Rabbi," I said, noticing his serious attitude. "Is there something wrong?"

"No, no. Just something we need to talk about."

"Will there be coffee?" I joked.

"You'll need something stronger than coffee," said the rabbi, ominously.

"Uh oh..."

"See you later. My office."

All through services, I sat fretting about what the rabbi was planning to say to me afterwards. It seemed we'd never get to the end, but at last, we finally reached the *Aleinu*, the *Kaddish,* and the *Motsi*, and I went out to collect my grape juice and Challah with the other congregants. After that, I made my way, with trepidation, up towards the rabbi's office.

"Are you Rachel?" said his receptionist. I nodded. "Ah, yes.

He wanted to talk with you." She looked at me sympathetically, then went to get me a cup of strong coffee and asked me to take a seat. I sat and waited, tapping my foot. After handing me my coffee, the receptionist gave me a sympathetic smile. "Don't worry," she said, "it only stings for a little while."

Several minutes later, the rabbi entered, and without a word, stalked across his reception room, gesturing for me to follow him.

He entered his office and sat down at the table, saying, "Have a seat, please, Rachel." His attitude was, if anything, even more serious than it had been before. "I'm not joking around anymore," he said.

"You weren't joking around in the first place! You seem so serious today!"

He looked at me, his good eye fixing me balefully. "This *is* serious, Rachel. Very serious. You're leaving tomorrow?"

I nodded.

"Okay, so here's what I wanted to say. *Be careful. You're playing with the big stuff here.* Where you're going, people really might hate you, just because you're Jewish." He paused for a moment and then continued. "And I happen to know that you are a person who *particularly* wants to be liked. Most people do like you. But some of the people in the places you're going, in Israel I mean, will not. They will dislike you, and some of them, yes more than a few, might even wish to see you splattered into miniscule pieces too small to find for burial."

Yuck. "Okay, Rabbi," I said, but he wasn't done.

"In my Kabbalah teaching, I tend to stay away from discussions about the evil side, but those forces are very real. They will oppose you in the work you've undertaken. Don't underestimate them. I know they're part of God too, but nevertheless, lethal. You get me?"

I nodded. The way he spoke and the words he said definitely put a chill on my heart.

"And there's one other thing," he said. "This man you're traveling with, what's his name?"

"It's Yakub al-Shadi."

"Yes. Well. I just wanted to check with you. With all of this interfaith...relationship thing going on, you're not thinking there's going to be one kind of big combined religion, are you?"

"No, Rabbi. Don't worry."

"Because I believe the message at Babel was that God intended to split us into many faiths."

"I know," I agreed.

"Good. But in regard to relations between faiths, you're going to run up against a few challenges, if this thing with your friend...Mr. al-Shadi...gets serious."

"Don't worry, Rabbi. As I learned in a poem I once read when I was a kid, that famous one by Robert Frost, you can't walk two roads at once."

"... *sorry I could not travel both, and be one traveler...*'" quoted the rabbi. "Good. Doesn't mean you can't learn something from Yakub. Remember what the sages say in the Talmud: 'Whoever says a word of wisdom - even if that person is from the nations of the world - is called a wise person.'" [7]

"Well, he's said plenty of wise things to me already, so I'm on board with that."

"I'm glad to hear it. And now, I have something for you." The rabbi opened up his jacket and reached into the inside pocket, pulling out a small package wrapped in gold paper. He handed it to me. It felt heavy.

I carefully removed the wrapping paper. Inside, I saw a tiny book, about the size of a business card and a half-inch thick. The cover was composed of a thin piece of silver, and there was a picture of Jerusalem embossed upon it, the letter Aleph outlined in jewels.

I opened it and, inside, found the word *"Tehillim,"* Psalms, in Hebrew. There was a little silk cord attached to the binding, the kind you can use to mark your page. I opened to the page he had marked.

"Careful!" said the rabbi. "Don't lose the page!" It was Psalm 126.

"When you get to Jerusalem, just before you pass the city sign, I want you to get out of your taxi or limo and read that Psalm. Then walk into the city. Okay?"

"Okay, I will."

"When a Jew first makes *Aliyah,* that is, 'goes up' to Israel, it's customary to say 'I hope you don't come back,' meaning, I hope

---

[7] Talmud B. Megilla 16a

you fulfill the dream of living in *ha-aretz*, the land. I won't say that to you, though, because my first concern is for your safety. So instead, I'll say, 'I hope you *do* come back. And here's a little insurance." He stood up and reached into his pocket, handing me a twenty-dollar bill. "This is the smallest I have. Take it with you to Israel, and give it to a worthy cause. Okay?"

I stood up, took the twenty, and folded it inside the book of Psalms, so I wouldn't confuse it among my other bills. "Okay. Thanks, Rabbi!"

My rabbi gave me a hug. He felt bony, and his mustache tickled my cheek.

Preoccupied with the rabbi's words, I walked the fifteen blocks to the Magic Tuba. There I found Yakub and his family already seated at a long table in the sunny atrium. Seeing Yakub, I forgot all about my rabbi's sobering words, and my heart flooded with elation. Yakub was wearing a dark suit and a vivid green tie, a spotless white *kufi* on his head, looking better than anything I'd seen in recent years.

At that moment, my friend, Lenny Goldstein, walked in, and I noticed that he, too, was wearing a head covering, a crocheted *kippa* which he had attached to his thick, dark hair with a silver clip. "Shabbat Shalom!" he greeted me, giving me a squeeze.

I introduced him to the al-Shadi's, and the men all shook hands. I seated Lenny on one side of me, leaving the spot across from him free.

After we were seated, I looked around the table at our group once more. Everyone was dressed up in their best clothes, the women wearing dazzling headscarves covered with sparkling pearly beads. None of the waiters could quite figure out what to make of us: a couple of Jews, obviously fresh from Shabbat services, and a small group of Muslims in their best clothes. Regardless of the eclectic composition of the group, however, it was clear there was a festival atmosphere.

Ruthie showed up then, hardly even late, and I went through our introductions one more time, ending with Lenny.

"So!" said Ruthie, taking him in with an appreciative tilt of her chin, "You're the famous boss of Rachel!"

"Guilty," he said, appreciation registering on his face, as he took in my sister, who looked particularly good today in pleated knee-length skirt and a purple silk shirt that accentuated her flat stomach and revealed just a hint of soft cleavage.

She sat down across from Lenny, and they were soon engrossed in an animated conversation, oblivious to the rest of us. It turned out they had attended the same college, though they hadn't known each other back then. Soon, they were exchanging ribald stories about their halcyon days of youth.

Meanwhile, I chatted with Yakub about our trip.

"I conducted a little research on the internet last night," I told him.

"Really? What were you studying?"

"I did a search for the name 'Dunash ben Labrat,' the poet mentioned in my father's list of library withdrawals."

"And?"

"I came across something really interesting," I said. "It turns out that Dunash had a wife."

"Well, that's not so surprising!" laughed Yakub.

"I know," I said, "but the surprising thing was, it appears she was also a poet!"

"Really? Are you sure?" said Yakub. "As far as I know, there were no Jewish poetesses whatsoever during that era. A few Muslim ones, but no Jews."

"Well, it really does seem like they found a short poem by this wife of Dunash."

"Fascinating!"

"I printed up the article. I'll bring it with me to the airport and show you tomorrow."

"Wonderful!"

"I'm so excited about this trip!"

"Me as well! I am curious about what it is your father found!"

Looking at him, with his vivid green eyes and fine-fingered hands, I hoped secretly that he was looking forward to more than the research.

At length, dessert and coffee finished, people started leaving. I made plans with Ruthie to meet her at the airport tomorrow, warning her that she should arrive early enough to allow for increased security. She promised she would, but I had my doubts.

I noticed that she and Lenny left the restaurant together.

Yakub and his family also departed as a group. All of them except Mahmud were heading back to Yakub's house in Bernal Heights, joining him there tonight as a send-off to his trip. Meanwhile, Mahmud was going home to Berkeley to pack. As I watched Yakub leave the restaurant, I felt a pang. Aside from a brief goodbye, there had been nothing more from him. I really had very little sense of his feelings towards me. Would anything change on our trip overseas together?

BEAUTY

San Francisco, California
2:00 pm. Sunday, December 17ᵗʰ 2006
Dr. Rachel Roseman

After my morning run on Sunday, I dressed in my favorite travel clothes, including a pair of blue silk pants that seemed impervious to wrinkles, a comfortable white rayon t-shirt, and a long, navy blue cotton sweater, all of which I knew, from experience, would hold up to the rigors of a twelve-hour plane flight. I loaded my bags into a taxi and headed to the airport. The plane to Heathrow left at 2:00 pm, and I was afraid there would be traffic. However, we sailed through town and onto 101 South, no problem, arriving at the international terminal at SFO two hours and ten minutes before my flight.

When I walked into the cavernous departures area, I found Yakub and Mahmud already there, welcoming me with big smiles. They each wore khaki pants and button-down shirts, and I noticed that they were not wearing their *kufi's*, likely in an attempt to avoid racial "profiling" at the security line. We waited a few minutes for Ruthie, but knowing her well, I figured she'd push it to the last minute as usual. "Let's go check in," I said. "Ruthie can fend for herself."

After we were done checking in, we still had an hour and a half to spare. We decided to go through security and go find some coffee before getting on the plane.

Despite their precautions, Mahmoud and Yakub were still subjected to extra security; they were both taken off to a private room for questioning by an impassive male guard. Fifteen minutes later, they emerged, the guard waving them on without a smile.

Despite this delay, we still had a good forty-five minutes before boarding would begin. We picked up some British pounds at the Thomas Cook ATM, and then headed down to the Rulli's café at the end of the terminal. There, we ordered espressos, and I ordered a doughnut. Krispy Kreme.

Now that we had the opportunity, I pulled out the article on the poem by Mrs. Dunash. I handed it to Yakub, and he read for a few minutes, silently sipping his coffee. It was a short article, less than a page, announcing, with excitement, the discovery of two poems, both contained in a single document. Apparently, it was a poetic interchange between the famous Dunash ben Labrat and his unnamed wife. She was protesting the impending desertion of her husband, who was apparently leaving her in Spain, for some unstated reason, with a babe-in-arms.

Yakub read out loud the plaintive reply from the errant husband:

Could I betray a bright young wife, one joined to me on High?
Perish the thought a thousand times! Would I not rather die?

"Very interesting!" he said, handing the article back to me. "But they don't include her poem here."

"I know," I said. "I searched for it on the internet, but couldn't find it."

"Well, we should be able to see the original at the Cambridge library tomorrow!" said Yakub. "We'll request it when we arrive."

We sat for several more minutes, finishing up our coffee, then headed down to the gate. Ruthie had not yet arrived.

As we approached, I heard them announcing initial boarding for first class and business passengers. I was now officially worried about Ruthie. But at that moment, I caught sight of her at the far end of the concourse, walking quickly towards us. Out beyond security, I saw a familiar person standing watching. He waved when he saw me from a distance. It was Lenny Goldstein.

That was fast! I thought.

Ruthie approached us, out of breath. "Hi!" she said. "Sorry I'm late! Traffic from the South Bay."

I hugged her. "Well, you're here, and in perfect timing. By the way, is that Lenny Goldstein I see?"

She turned around. Lenny waved at her.

When she turned back, I raised my eyebrows.

"He gave me a ride to the airport," she said.

"Wow! That's handy!" I said.

"Well we just…he just thought it was kind of a big deal that the two of us were going to Israel for the first time. He wanted to wish us off."

Even though I was giving Ruthie a hard time, in truth, I was secretly thrilled about this turn of events. Was it possible that my little matchmaking scheme had worked?

"Let's get on the plane!" I said, "Before someone steals our seats or, worse, uses our overhead baggage space!"

Ruthie and I were sitting in *Economy Plus,* the row immediately behind Yakub and Mahmud. I grabbed my computer and my Arabic book so I could read and study on the airplane. Ruthie pulled out some papers. When I glanced at them briefly, I saw they were spattered with odd symbols and notations. Physics equations.

I sat and gazed forward, glimpsing Yakub's hand on the arm rest of the seat in front of us. I thought about what it might be like to pick it up and kiss it.

"What're you thinking about?" Ruthie asked.

"None of your business!" I replied.

"You had this dumb smile on your face." Ruthie mimicked my vacant look.

"Leave me alone!" I joked. "Anyway, what's all this with Lenny Goldstein? Did he spend the night last night?"

"Of course not! What do you take me for?"

"But you like him."

Ruthie did a retake of my dumb smile, but this time, for real. She did like him.

"Too bad we didn't ask him to come with us!" I said.

"Yeah," said Ruthie, "but I'm sure it would've been too late. And also, he's covering your patients, isn't he?"

"That's true," I said.

Ruthie inclined her chin towards the row of airplane seats in front of us. "I like him," she said. "Yakub."

"Me too." I couldn't prevent a return of the goofy grin from before.

We were taxi-ing down the runway, and now the plane was ready to take off. In a gesture that demonstrated eloquently the power of humanity's scientific mastery, its giant bulk left the ground, and soon we were high up above San Francisco Bay. I saw the mountains on the east side getting closer, the Bay Bridge a silver ribbon below with cars sparkling like jewels, the Golden Gate Bridge and my beloved Headlands dark shapes around to the left. *Goodbye, I will see you again soon.*

I pulled out my Arabic book, opening to lesson five.

"What in God's name is that?" said Ruthie, looking aghast at the squiggles and dots that swooped around the page.

"Arabic," I said.

"You're learning Arabic?"

"Didn't I tell you?"

"No, you managed to omit that little tidbit."

She pulled the book over to her lap, peering at it more closely. "Can you read all these little lines?" she asked, in wonder.

"Can you read *that?*" I asked, pointing to the physics.

"Hmmm. Interesting," she said.

I retrieved my book, and we both sat quietly studying until the stewardess arrived with dinner. Then, we set our books aside, freeing up our seat-back tables for the proffered trays of warm airplane food, giving in to the vacation atmosphere, talking about any and all subjects that occurred to us as we ate.

Later, sometime after dinner, an idea popped into my head.

Could the poem be something like a physics equation?

No, that was dumb. But wait, I reasoned. It did fit some of the qualifications of a poem. It was composed of carefully-selected letters and symbols, had meaning, could be written or spoken. No, no, the purpose of the equation was not language but physical description. But I was beginning to sense that the difference between physical things and words was not so distinct after all. If objects were, as Einstein had first discovered, really made of energy rather than miniscule pellets, could that type of energy also be present at the heart of a poem? Interesting. I would have to run this by Yakub.

I looked up then and was startled to see his face, gazing over at me from the back of his seat.

"How long have you been looking at me?" I asked, worried I might have perhaps fallen asleep a little and snored, or even drooled.

Yakub came around and kneeled down next to me, in the aisle. "Not long. You look beautiful."

"Thanks! You can come with me on a trip anytime you want!"

"We'll see."

"Did you watch a movie?"

"No...did you?"

"No," I said, then remarked, *sotto voce,* "I was thinking about *the poem.*"

"Again?"

"Of course. Anyway, could *the poem* be something other than what you'd traditionally think of as a poem?"

"For example?"

"Well, like maybe, a physics equation. One that had a particular elegance or beauty, or solved some huge problem having to do with God."

"Hmmm. A very interesting idea I hadn't considered. You know, at the time of the Golden Age of Islam in Spain, there were some very great Muslim astronomers and scientists."

A passenger came down the aisle, and Yakub got up, moving into the space in front of his seat to let the person pass. Then he returned to crouch down next to me again.

"What are our plans after we get to England?" I said.

"Well, we arrive tomorrow morning at 9:00 am. I propose we take the train out to Cambridge while Ruth and Mahmud go to London with our luggage. We'll spend the day at the library. The following day, we can return if we need to, and then we'll travel down to Madrid that evening and on to Cordoba the following day, to meet with Rawiyya's friend, Tatianne, and follow up on that lead. After that, we're tentatively scheduled to return to London and to travel from there to Makkah and Jerusalem, respectively. But we shall see. It may be that our clues will lead us elsewhere!"

The stewardess was now coming down the aisle, and Yakub retreated once again to the space in front of his seat. After she passed, he leaned over the back of the seat, saying, "It's time for sleep. Goodnight, Rachel! Pleasant dreams!"

"Good night!" I said, yawning. I lowered my seat down all the way, covered myself up with the blanket, and rolled onto my side.

Cambridge, England
Monday, December 18th 2006
Dr. Rachel Roseman and Prof. Yakub al-Shadi

After we arrived at Heathrow, Yakub and I went and found the tube while Ruthie and Mahmud located a taxi to take them to our hotel in London. Yakub had decided to book the hotel there rather than in Cambridge, so Ruthie and Mahmud would have something to do during the day while we were busy with our library research. Cambridge was an easy hour-long train ride from London. We left our bags in Ruthie and Mahmud's care, carrying only our hand luggage. At the tube, we figured out how to get to King's Cross station and then out to Cambridge.

On the train, I watched the small brick townhomes and factories of London go by, the sight reminding me of my visits here as a child to see my grandparents before they died. After fifteen minutes or so, the buildings began to sort themselves into towns and open spaces, and eventually, we were riding through English countryside. It was a beautiful sunny day, a bit crisp, with puffy white clouds above. I should have been tired from jet lag, but everything seemed so fresh and full of hope and promise that I felt wide awake. *Would we find the poem today?*

I pulled the paper with the printed e-mail from the Cambridge librarian out of my pocket and looked at its two relevant entries again: the first, the letter attributed to the "son of Dunash ben Labrat," the second, that strange publication by the man with the name of "Smith," a name that, despite its blandness, had caused even Yakub to show fear. I felt the butterflies begin fluttering around my stomach. I put off thinking about this now, and was struck by a question. I turned to Yakub.

"What is the *Taylor Schechter Genizah Collection?*" I asked. "That's where the manuscript came from."

"The Genizah Collection? You haven't heard of it before?"

"No, I don't think so," I admitted.

"Ah! It is one of the great wonders of the literate world!" he said, then asked, "Do you know, generally, what a genizah is?"

I vaguely remembered something from the introduction to Judaism class I'd taken last year. "Something about God's name?" I said.

"Yes!" said Yakub. "It's a storage area in a synagogue, a place where all damaged Torah scrolls, books, and discarded papers are kept, since according to the Jewish tradition, anything containing God's name cannot be destroyed. Just to be safe, virtually all written materials are disposed of in these genizahs. They are emptied out at various intervals, their contents ceremonially buried in graveyards, almost like people."

"Gosh! That is weird!"

"Yes, it does sound a bit strange, I admit. In any case, there was one very special genizah, located at a synagogue in my hometown of Cairo, Egypt, the contents of which, for various accidental reasons, remained undisturbed for many centuries. The

Genizah was found to contain hundreds of thousands of documents, some of them very ancient. It is a window into the rich tapestry of medieval life.

"Because Cairo was a kind of nexus point for trade during the years of the Middle Ages, the Genizah holds documents from a wide variety of sources, including a lot of material from Andalusian Spain. So I'm not surprised it would contain letters of the sort your father was researching."

"So all these old documents were just jammed into some room at the synagogue?" I asked, picturing in my mind a huge mountain of moldering paper, containing hundreds of thousands or even millions of instances of God's name. Based on the Jewish belief in the connection of God's name with redemption, as articulated in the *Aleinu* prayer, this seemed like a very promising place to look for a poem to redeem the world.

"Yes, they were, *al-hamdu lillah*. Without them, we would know very little about life in the middle ages. Also, there's something else important about the Cairo Genizah."

"Yes?" I said.

"Over 40% of the material is in the form of poetry."

"Oh!" I said.

My excitement mounting, I looked out the window again, waiting impatiently as the last few stations passed before we arrived in Cambridge.

We took a taxi to the library, weaving through streets full of grey academic buildings with spires and turrets, most of which looked like monasteries or churches. The religion of academia.

The Taylor-Schechter Genizah Research Unit was located in the main library, a huge building with a central tower which we entered through the front door. Yakub and I greeted the librarian standing at the desk, a rotund, pleasant-looking middle-aged woman with a pale complexion and comfortable midriff. I consulted the e-mail I'd printed to double-check the name, and then asked for Margaret Tibbs.

"Well, you've come to the right place," she said, smiling, "Because you've found her! What can I do for you?"

"Oh, hello! I'm Rachel Roseman. I requested several documents in preparation for our visit?" I showed her the e-mail.

"Ah, yes!" she said. "Can you wait here just a moment?"

She disappeared behind the first bookcase, returning with a large grey box which she placed on the counter in front of us, removing the lid. Inside, I saw a three-ring binder, a hand-written note on top. The librarian consulted this paper. "I apologize," she said, "My assistant was not able to find the second document you requested, *The Dangerous and Futile Nature of Poesy.*" She was frowning, the sides of her mouth pulled down with distaste. "Hmm. That *is* an odd name. Author: Smith. That doesn't provide much help."

I nodded, in truth relieved to have escaped encountering this book, connected as it was in my mind with the death of my parents.

Margaret Tibbs said, "I shall see what I can do to locate this document myself. On a positive note, I was able to locate the letter you requested, TS-Ar 44.224, which, interestingly enough, includes a poem on its second page." She put the top back on the box, then pushed a clipboard over to me. "Would you mind very much showing me your identification?"

"Sure," I said. As I rummaged through my backpack, I asked, "Do you know anything about that poem you mentioned? Is it written by the author of the letter?"

"As it turns out, a very interesting question!" said the librarian. "We know nothing about the letter's author, other than that he is the son of the famous Sephardic poet, Dunash ben Labrat. But the text of the letter points to a fascinating conclusion."

"Really?" Both Yakub and I were looking at Margaret Tibbs now.

"The poem appears to have been written by his mother. Most unusual for the era in which it was composed. Do either of you read Judeo-Arabic?"

"What's that?" I asked.

Yakub turned to me and explained, "Judeo-Arabic is the language most commonly used by rabbis and authors living in the Medieval Islamic world. They would write the Arabic language using Hebrew letters. It is a little-known fact that some of the greatest works of the Jewish tradition, such as Maimonides' 'Guide to the Perplexed' and ibn Paquda's 'Duties of the Heart' were composed in Judeo-Arabic."

He turned back to the librarian, saying, "As a scholar of the Semitic languages, I do know how to read it, yes."

"Wonderful. That will help tremendously."

I finally located my passport and wallet, pulling out my County Hospital ID card, which showed my University of California faculty status.

The librarian looked at these, then pushed them back to me, saying, "Ta, very much. Go ahead and sign the documents out, right here." She pointed to the next vacant line on the checkout sheet.

Yakub now spoke with the librarian. "So if the poem in our letter was written by the mother of the letter's author, then it would be the second known work of this poetess? The wife of Dunash?"

"That is correct!" said Margaret Tibbs. "You already know about the other poem?"

"Yes. In fact, we were hoping you might be able to locate it for us."

"Certainly!" she said. "But I will need some time to retrieve it from the archives."

"How long will you need?"

"I could have it here by tomorrow morning. Would that be sufficient?"

"Yes, that's fine."

The librarian then described to us where we could find a private reading room: through the main entrance hallway, down the stairs and to the right. We followed her instructions, heading through the spacious entrance, past display cases with Genizah documents enclosed, continuing on down the stairs and into a hallway, painted grey, with doors on either side. We chose one of the rooms on the right, entering a small private reading space with fluorescent lights and a large square table in the center.

I put the box down and looked at it. Such a plain box.

"Do you think *the poem* in the letter is the one we're looking for?" I said, "The poem to redeem the world?"

Yakub smiled at me, with fondness, I thought. "It is highly unlikely, because if so, your father would have accomplished his goal and saved your mother, not to mention all of us. But I am hopeful that it does contain a clue."

"So let me just clarify for a minute," I said. "Are we looking for a poem that's already written? Or a clue to help someone write the poem? Or a clue to help us decipher or decode a poem already written?" I pulled out my notebook and retrieved the legend. "It's not really clear from this, is it?" I quoted, "*I tell of a poem of ancient wisdom, a creation understood in the house of Abraham and his sons, Ishmael and Isaac. When the truth of this poem fills the world, immediately it will be redeemed…"'*

"I agree. There is a great deal of ambiguity. But to answer your question, I would say, 'yes.'"

"Yes?"

"Yes, it could be any of the above: a clue to help us write a poem which does not yet exist, or an existing poem that has either not yet been found or not yet understood."

"And I'm also a bit unclear about something else in the legend. What exactly does it mean, to 'redeem the world'?"

"You mean, what is paradise?"

"I suppose so…we don't really call it paradise, in my religion…"

"What do you call it?"

"We call it the *olam haba*, the world to come. Or, as my rabbi would say, 'the world that is coming'."

"And what is that like?"

"I'm not really sure. All I know is that it's a place where you're with God all the time."

"There's extensive discussion of paradise in the Quran."

"Yes, I know. All that punishment and reward stuff…"

"You're right. There's frequent mention of reward and punishment. However, as the great Sufi poetess, Rabia, says, 'those who know best seek the face of God for its own reward.'"

"What do you think redemption means then?"

"Relief from suffering. Peace."

"So if we find, write, or understand this poem, then we'll be at peace with one another?"

"That would seem to me the required starting place for redemption."

"Not some massive war, like Armageddon?"

"Not according to how I see it," said Yakub. "I would think our reward would come instead when we are at last capable of loving one another, as the scriptures say."

"Do you think you could write it? This poem?"

A wistful look entered Yakub's face. "To write such a poem…ah, that, to me, would be heaven, the most sublime act of creation. I would give almost anything for that…But as I've said before, I have been…well really, I've been too angry to write any poems at all. Until recently." a secretive smile danced across his lips.

"Really? You've written a poem lately?"

He nodded.

"Can I see it?"

"No," he shook his head. "Maybe sometime later," he continued mysteriously, "but not yet."

He turned from me and opened the box. Inside, I saw a simple three-ring binder. It contained three pages, the first a set of cautions about proper handling of the papers, the second two plastic folios with brown, frayed documents enclosed.

"We cannot touch these," Yakub commented, as he flipped past the first page, "or the oils from our hands would damage the fragile documents. That's why they are contained in these plastic folios, and can't be removed, except under protected conditions."

Yakub perused the letter, looking carefully at the first page, which contained three paragraphs of text in Hebrew letters. He then flipped to the second page, which held only six lines of Hebrew writing.

"The poem," I said. "The second one by Mrs. Dunash."

Yakub nodded, then popped open the rings of the binder and handed me the plastic folio. "You read some Hebrew, correct?"

"Ye-es," I said, uncertainly, "but not much…"

"Why don't you get a start on this, while I read the letter itself, which is in Judeo-Arabic."

I looked at the page Yakub still held. It was full of mysterious writing. "You can read that?" I said, with wonder.

Yakub nodded.

I went and retrieved notebook and pencil, and Yakub also pulled his out. We both bent our heads to the task, and the room fell into silence, with only the sound of our scratching pencils.

I looked at my own document, the six lines of poetry, written in a sturdy block Hebrew. The page was cracked and frayed around all the edges, with dark splotches, and a horizontal tear extending almost all the way across the page. Fortunately, almost all of the words were intact. I copied them one-by-one into my notebook. After that, I went and retrieved my small Hebrew-English dictionary from my backpack and began translating, line by line, as best I could..

We worked independently on our translations for some time. Every so often, I would sneak a look at Yakub, attracted by his face, so intent on discovering, here in this stuffy room in Cambridge, the answer to world redemption. Looking at his face, the thought came into my head: *heaven is somewhere nearby.*

After forty-five minutes, Yakub blew air through his lips and looked over at me. "Very interesting!" he said. "Very, very, *very* interesting! But first, what have you found?"

I pushed my notebook between us and showed him the six lines of the poem, fully transcribed. They looked like this:

לו יכולתי לשטוח עצמי עליך
כמו כתנת פסים כל כך קרוב לך
ידי קשת על צוורך
רגלי אבנט סביב לך

אי אפשר להבדיל סופי מראשיתך
אהיה כמזמור דוד דברי לובשים אורך

Yakub read aloud my translation in English.

If only I could drape myself upon you
like a many-colored tunic, so close to you,
my arms a bow upon your neck,
my legs a girdle around your waist.

Then you could not tell my end from your beginning.
I would be like a Psalm, my words clothing your light.

He paused after reading it, tilting his head to the side, his chin propped in his hand. He made a "hmm" sound.

"What are you thinking of?" I said.

"It reminds me of something…" he mused. "A Quranic verse…" He stood up and retrieved a worn copy of the Quran from his briefcase. Returning to the table, he flipped through it, arriving at the passage in question immediately.

"*They (your wives) are your garments and ye are their garments.*'" [8]

I sat letting the beauty of this vision sink in. "So your

---

[8] Quran 2:187

spouse is your garment…with you, wherever you are, separate but part of you…concealing yet revealing…permitting modesty…"

Yakub nodded in agreement as I spoke. "I see that the love between this woman, Mrs. Dunash, and her husband was very great."

"What does the letter say? The letter by her son?"

"It attests further to the love his mother felt for her absent husband."

"Really?"

Yakub nodded, pulling his translation over between us on the table. "Read it out loud," he prompted.

I began to read Yakub's English translation.

"To Dunash ben Labrat, ha-M'shorer ha-Gadol, your humble son, who venerates you, greets you.

I write you now with urgent news, uncertain if these words will ever find you. The rabbi here, who knew you when Cordoba was your home, recalled your destination, those many years ago, as the city of Fustat. So I write you there, care of the local rabbinate, in hope that, even if you are no longer in that place, they will, at least, know where you might have gone.

My mother is gravely ill and will soon die. If you wish to see her, I beg you, return at once, else she be cold before you come to her. My dear father, I must tell you, she has never ceased to love you, though she has become a great poetess with many followers. I hope you will bear with me if I include a bit more detail on my mother's life, because I admit to you, I am in dire need of your assistance.

As I mentioned to you above, my mother has attracted several pupils. Of one, I will write further here, as he is of remarkable spirit and origin, though mysterious fate, and this is what impacts upon my mother's soul at the time of her approaching death.

This man, called by the name of Said al-Shadi, was an Ishmaelite of the most gentle nature. He came to us from Palestine, drawn here by a poem. This was that self-same poem to which you yourself responded with like words of love. With its delicate rhymes and revelation of my mother's tender spirit, this small verse has found its way into the libraries of great rabbis, scholars, and poets. One such itinerant scholar, travelling through the holy land towards Aleppo, encountered al-Shadi, a humble shepherd yet member of a family of great Arab poets. There, this man revealed my mother's verse to al-Shadi, who was, at once, smitten to the heart, vowing that he would trace the poem to its source.

And so al-Shadi made his way to Cordoba, leaving his flocks and his tents behind, to find my mother here at the court of al-Zahra, and thus began a most remarkable relation. Though you, as many here, may wonder at the propriety of a pairing between a young and handsome Arab man and a woman long abandoned by her husband, yet I promise you, and vow on my soul, the relation that developed between them was the passion of a pupil for a teacher, a love of the highest order, and nothing in the way of elicit romance. Under its influence al-Shadi wrote many poems, inspired, he attested, by the power of love in the Hebrew verses of my mother, whose letters broke open the light within his own Arabic words. For I should tell you, father, that every poem written by my mother concerned her love for you and her never-ending hope for your return.

The relation between al-Shadi and my mother came to an end, and you might say with some irony, when al-Shadi, like you, abandoned us some ten years hence, during the wars of al-Mansur, the Hajib of Cordoba. Al-Shadi had made a discovery of some kind, a breakthrough in his poetry, and now must travel to the 'holy land' to complete the work. He promised to return, leaving his diwan in keeping with my mother until such day should arrive.

Alas, he never returned.

Now, my mother, in the delirium of her illness, rants about her fears for al-Shadi, her suspicions of foul play. She frets interminably about the fate of what she calls the 'poem to redeem the world.' 'What will come of it?' she asks, and grips my arm so hard her fingers bruise my skin. Over and over, she draws a strange talisman, a six-pointed star with many wavy rays, telling me that this was al-Shadi's destination. She extracts from me a promise that I will guard this diwan of al-Shadi, no easy vow to keep, given what I see as the inevitable conflicts ahead with the Berbers and the ever-encroaching Christian forces. I keep this diwan in safekeeping, though I know not what it contains, as al-Shadi used only the flowing characters of the Arabs, which I admit, as a humble tradesman, I cannot read. It is with this work that I so desperately need your assistance, to help me understand upon what ill-fated quest its author has embarked, so that I may ease my mother's wretched fears before her death.

My father, I do not know what mighty winds of fate have born you from us to cast you on those distant shores, or whether, God forbid, you yourself have passed beyond the veil. But if you, through God's grace, still remain among the living, know that my mother has kept the love between you alive in her heart these many years. I attach here a poem from her hand, one of the many flowing from that abundant wellspring within her soul.

Peace upon you, and may redemption come quickly and within our time. Sivan, 4763

I finished reading. "What is that?" I said, "A '*diwan*'?"

"It's a collection of poems, generally in Arabic or Persian, by a single author. Ach!" he said, putting a hand on his forehead, "Why did I not think of this before?"

"Think of what?" I said.

"Searching the Genizah database for my ancestral name? If I had only done that, I might have stumbled on this letter years ago."

Just then, a loud buzzer went off, and we heard the loudspeaker overhead announce that the library would be closing in ten minutes.

"Come on!" said Yakub, jumping up and replacing all the materials in the grey box. "Let's go do a little more research before they close!"

He walked quickly out the door, and I raced to keep up with him, as he ascended the stairs and reentered the main hall of the library. He looked over and apparently spied what he was looking for. He sat down in front of a computer, and navigated to the Genizah database, typing in the name "Said al-Shadi." The computer processed for a long moment, and then a single entry flashed onto the screen, the title in Hebrew letters, an English translation below: *Listing of contents, private genizah of Rabbi David II Maimonides.*

"Hmm!" said Yakub. He clicked a few buttons, and a nearby printer spewed out a page.

"Come on!" he said, grabbing the paper and our grey library box and heading back to the circulation desk.

I raced after him, calling out, "Who is that? Rabbi David Maimonides?"

"I'll explain everything later," he said as we arrived at the desk. Impatiently, he rang the little bell, pushing the small plunger down five or six times. Not long afterwards, Margaret Tibbs emerged from the office.

Spying us, she smiled, saying, "Success?"

"Yes!" said Yakub. "Would it be possible for us to request one more document?"

"Of course!" said Margaret Tibbs. "What document would you like?"

Yakub showed her the paper. Margaret pushed her spectacles onto her nose and took a look. She nodded as she read. "This shouldn't be a problem," she said. "Would you like me to put it in your box, along with the additional poem of Mrs. Dunash, tonight?"

"Yes please."

"Done," she said with a smile. As we were leaving, she called after us, "I hope you find what you're looking for!"

"So do I," Yakub called back, "for the sake of all of us!"

"Oh!!!!" she said, "You two are so mysterious!"

Yakub had asked the driver to return for us at the library at closing time, and true to promise, the cab stood by the curb at the bottom of the steps. Once inside, I pressed Yakub with questions.

"So, who was David Maimonides?"

"David II Maimonides," Yakub corrected. "He was the Nagid, the head of Jewry in Egypt and most of the Arabic lands during the latter half of the fourteenth century."

"Was he related to Moses Maimonides, the great rabbi and physician?"

"Yes, David II was his...great, great, great grandson, I believe. He was the last in the line of Maimonidean rabbis in Fustat. Scholars believe he left the city for a decade or so, in the last quarter of the fourteenth century, and perhaps returned after that to finish out his years."

"What do you know about him?"

"Well, of course, all of the descendents of Moses Maimonides were distinguished in one way or another. But I have always found David II Maimonides to be of particular interest because of his connection with Islam and the influence of Sufi thought upon his philosophical and mystical works. In fact, all of the Maimonidean *Nagidim*, beginning with Maimonides' own son, Abraham, were influenced by Sufi beliefs, and have even been referred to as 'Jewish Sufis' by scholars in our era."

"But why did this particular document come up when you entered 'Said al-Shadi' in the search engine? The document dates would be almost four hundred years after he left Cordoba."

"I don't know," admitted Yakub. "But with luck, we will find out tomorrow!"

"Yes!" I nodded. "I wonder what ever happened to that diwan of Said al-Shadi's?"

"That," said Yakub, "Is the question."

We arrived at the Cambridge station and sat down on a bench together to wait the few minutes for the train to King's Cross to arrive. The room was deserted. As we waited, I said, to Yakub, "What about this relationship between Said al-Shadi and Mrs. Dunash. Do you really think it was innocent? It seems to have affected Said so greatly."

"The love between a teacher and a student can be as intense as romantic love."

I nodded, thinking about this. "I can understand that. My rabbi once asked me, 'Who does tradition say is more important? Your parents, or your teacher?'"

"What was the answer?"

"The answer was: your teacher. Your parents are responsible for bringing you into this world, your teacher for bringing you into the next.'"

The train arrived. When we got on it, there was only one other passenger, embarking on the next car down the platform.

London, England
7:30 pm. Monday, December 18th 2006
Prof. Yakub al-Shadi and Dr. Rachel Roseman

From King's Cross Station, we took the tube to Baker Street and walked the few blocks to the Sherlock Holmes Hotel, where we met Ruthie and Mahmud and prepared for dinner.

Other than its proximity to the location of Conan Doyle's fictional character's townhome, and the many portraits of Holmes and his sidekick, Doctor Watson, on the walls, the Sherlock Holmes Hotel had little connection with that erstwhile detective. It was, however, a well-kept and tidy inn, with a cozy restaurant visible from the lobby, and spacious rooms with comfortable beds and large bathrooms.

Ruthie was fast asleep when I entered, having evidently surrendered to the jetlag that had now beset me in force. Resisting the temptation to join her in a nap, I woke her up so we could get ready for dinner. Initially groggy and bleary-eyed, she rallied with the promise of a good meal and the recollection of the phone call she'd arranged later this evening with Lenny Goldstein before leaving the states.

We dressed ourselves for dinner as best we could in the slightly wrinkled clothes from our suitcases. I wore my all-purpose dark-purple velvet dress with long sleeves and knee-length skirt, while Ruthie put on pin-striped hip-cut pants and a white elastic t-shirt that highlighted her slim middle. I thought we both looked pretty good by the time we were done.

We met Yakub and Mahmud downstairs at the restaurant. Yakub's face lit up, and his gaze followed me as I made my way across the dining room.

"Well!" he said, looking me up and down, an experience that made my face flush, "We are certainly the envy of the other men in this restaurant!"

He finally removed his eyes from my dress and looked at Ruthie. "You two look most exquisite!"

"Well, thank you!" said Ruthie. "I guess my little beauty rest was effective!"

We sat down, and the waiter soon arrived to fill our crystal glasses with ice water. I took a big swig, which did not do much to cool me down.

The four of us shared a delicious dinner together, staying on past dessert for a long time talking about our upcoming trip to Cordoba, until we finally couldn't resist the pull of fatigue, and parted reluctantly to head for bed. Yakub agreed to meet me the following morning at 7:30 am, so we could go back over to Cambridge to review the additional documents we'd requested. The plan was for me and Yakub to pack tonight. Mahmud and Ruthie would then meet us tomorrow afternoon at Gatwick with our bags. From there, we'd fly on to Madrid.

Back at our room, I packed my duffle, and then Ruthie and I changed into our pajamas and brushed our teeth. Ruthie's phone call with Lenny was scheduled at 9:30 pm our time, which I calculated would be just before the time his afternoon clinic began back home. I lay down in bed just as she began dialing, and drifted off to sleep to the sound of her murmuring and quiet laughter.

London, England
11:17 pm Monday, December 18th 2006
Mr. Smith, to Eugene Smith (journal entry)

My son, though it is perhaps difficult to tell from my behavior, I am so proud of you! Who would have guessed that, in addition to your immense academic and verbal capabilities, you would also have the makings of an outstanding spy?

You have told me, and I believe you, that you were able to tail al-Shadi and his girlfriend from the library to their hotel in London, and, undetected, to determine that they are analyzing several documents, including TS-Ar.44.224. They are, apparently, planning a trip to Cordoba tomorrow. Well done!

Your diminutive and unassuming appearance likely aids you considerably in your espionage activities. Thank goodness, since you are still only twenty-four, you have not yet developed the distinctive silver forelock of our family.

I have been most fortified to receive your descriptions of this ill-fated couple and their entourage, who apparently dined sumptuously as they made their plans. You tell me the group included the two members of the al-Shadi clan, the Davidson woman and her sister. How this group managed to coalesce, I cannot imagine, though I sense the hand of God in this, assisting us as ever. We use these people at His will to bring about our successful Armageddon. I can only marvel at His irony in bringing together Jews and Muslims for this task!

My son, the only thing that worries me is your request for permission to slit their throats. There is in you a tendency towards physical violence, since you have not yet learned, it seems, the very first lesson, which is: never, never get your hands dirtied with blood! As God Himself says in Genesis four, "Your brother's blood cries out to me from the ground." Allow others to take this sin upon them, but remain pure of it yourself.

Wielding the knife or sword is not our method! Instead, we use our words to incite others to kill, to separate, as it were, the wheat from the chaff so that the righteous may ascend.

I do admit to great admiration regarding your tactic, so brilliantly conceived today, of slipping a copy of our family's master work, *The Protocols of the Learned Elders of Zion*, into the library case of al-Shadi before you left, in order to intimidate the woman. I envision, with near physical ecstasy, the expressions on their faces as they discover this surprise on their return to the library tomorrow! I fear they are not strong enough to withstand my own work, *The Dangerous and Futile Nature of Poesy*, and use of *The Protocols* should serve a similar, though less debilitating, purpose. This is the kind of intellectual method I encourage.

Tomorrow, you will follow them to Cordoba, and we will see, I can only pray, an end to this four thousand year long fiasco. As I've told you on the phone, you must keep them in your sight at all times, as distasteful as that may be.

London, England
7:30 am. Tuesday, December 19th 2006
Prof. Yakub al-Shadi and Dr. Rachel Roseman

After a quick run and shower the next morning, I found Yakub downstairs in the lobby. He was sitting in a comfortable armchair reading a book of poetry. His face lit up when he saw me, and he jumped up. "How is it possible," he said, "for you to look so fresh in the morning when it is now a quarter to twelve at night back home?"

"You should have seen me an hour ago!"

On the train to Cambridge, Yakub reviewed our plans once again. We'd spend the morning at the library, then take the train out to Gatwick and fly to Madrid, where we'd spend the night tonight. Tomorrow morning, we would ride the high speed train from there to Cordoba, where Rawiyya's friend, Tatianne, would meet us. We'd spend tomorrow afternoon exploring Cordoba.

In Cambridge, we re-entered the Genizah Collection, greeting Margaret Tibbs, who retrieved our box for us. "Here you are!" she said, smiling pleasantly. "Oh yes, I have a follow-up. I'm so sorry, but my assistant, Eugene, and I have not been able to locate the manuscript by 'Smith.' Apparently, the library sent the only existing copy to your father, back in 1994."

"Hmm," I said, thinking again of the papers my father had burned. "Thanks for checking."

"My pleasure."

We headed through the entryway then down the stairs, re-entering the same reading room we had used the day before. Yakub put the box on the table. Removing the top, he looked inside and let out an unexpected yelp. He was staring into the box, a horrified expression on his face, as if it contained a snake or swarming insects.

"What is it?" I asked, alarmed at his stricken expression. I looked into the box. There, in addition to the folio, I saw a small booklet, its paper yellowed, edges tattered. On its cover were the words *The Jewish Peril,* and below, *Protocols of the Learned Elders of Zion.*

"Oh!" I said.

"Who in *Allah's* name put this here?" Yakub's voice was shaking. Not looking at me, he grabbed the booklet, pushed a nearby chair away with a loud scrape and stormed back out through the door, opening it with such force that it hit the wall before slamming shut again.

"Where are you going?" I called out uselessly to the closed door. I got up and hurried out after him, but Yakub had already disappeared into the stairwell. Racing through the hall and up the stairs, I caught up with him at the librarian's counter. He was involved in a furious whispered conversation with Margaret Tibbs.

"What is the meaning of this?" he said, gesturing at her with the tattered book.

"Oh my goodness," said the librarian, her soft cheeks flushed. "Where in the world did that come from?" She was staring at the book in Yakub's hand, an expression of revulsion on her face.

"Is this some kind of prank?" Yakub continued in his infuriated whisper.

"I've no idea!" she said. "How dreadful!"

"You didn't put this in here?" Yakub continued, his voice beginning to mollify a bit.

"Of course not!" she replied indignantly. "I would never do such a thing!"

"Then who else would have access to our materials?" demanded Yakub.

"I'm afraid any number of people."

Yakub let out an exasperated breath.

Margaret Tibbs said, "I'll check with my assistant, Eugene, and see if he witnessed anyone tampering with the box."

"Please do so," insisted Yakub. "Immediately, if possible."

"I'm afraid Eugene doesn't come in until the afternoon. I'll check with him then. I am really terribly sorry."

I stood at the counter, uncertain what to say.

Yakub turned to me, compassion in his eyes. "I'm sorry, Rachel." He squeezed my shoulder. I looked down, unable to avoid a momentary flash of shame.

Shaking his head, Yakub left the librarian's desk, abandoning the pamphlet on the table. On impulse, I picked it up and brought it with me, following Yakub as he returned to the stairway. When we got to the door to our reading room, Yakub saw what I had in my hand.

"Why did you bring that with you?" he snapped.

"I've never actually read it," I said.

"Believe me, you don't want to read it."

"But I think I should. I'd like to know what kind of things people say about us...us Jews."

Yakub looked at the booklet with disgust. "Why, in this place, would someone care that you're Jewish? And how did they find out?"

I pointed to the Star of David hanging from a silver chain around my neck, a gift from my sister. "Maybe it's just this. I probably disturbed some latent anti-Semite, who crawled out from under his rock long enough to cause us a problem."

Yakub nodded, a dark expression on his face. He then shook his head from side to side as though to rid himself of negative thoughts and retrieved the folio from the case. "We should not permit some bigoted prankster to divert us."

He turned his attention to the first document in the folio, whose label said it was 'T-S NS 143.46.', and described it as a "letter from Dunash's wife." The page was covered on both sides with faded Hebrew letters. There were several holes and cracks in the paper, which wasn't surprising, given that the letter had been written over a thousand years ago.

Yakub began a slow oral translation, *"Will her love remember his graceful doe, her only son in her arms as he parted...?"* He took out his notebook and began to work on the translation.

Meanwhile, I took a look at the second document, the listing of the contents of David II Maimonides private genizah. This page, too, was written in a foreign language, but I could not decipher the letters at all. It appeared to be a table, listing titles and authors.

Yakub glanced at me over the tops of his reading glasses. He said, "That is Oriental Semi-Cursive, a kind of Judeo-Arabic script used by Jewish scholars in this era. It will be difficult for you to decipher."

I nodded.

"This shouldn't take me too much longer," he said. "After I'm done, we can go through that list together."

"Sure," I said.

Yakub returned to his concentrated study of the poem of Mrs. Dunash. Meanwhile, I surreptitiously picked up the booklet, *The Protocols of the Learned Elders of Zion.* Opening it carefully, I noticed that the pages emitted an acrid, sickly-sweet odor, like almonds. This was not the usual pleasant, dusty smell of old books.

"Are you reading that piece of trash?" said Yakub, looking up from his work again.

I nodded.

Yakub sighed and shook his head. "It's your choice! But let me warn you. You will be disgusted with humanity when you're done."

"I expect you're right, I said, but opened the booklet anyway. Turning past the title page, I began to read the text. Immediately, I found the language jarringly officious. The words outlined, in twenty-four sections, a series of sequential steps by which the Zionists would quietly conquer the world, subjugating all the non-Jews, the "GOYIM," as the book repeatedly referred to them in screaming capital letters, to slavery under the fascistic leadership of a descendent of King David.

Despite the clumsiness of the writing, the work had an uncanny, almost diabolical ability to draw upon recognizable detail and human paranoia, causing even me to wonder at times: "Could this be true?"

For example, one protocol claimed that the Jews had planted minions in all the universities. The purportedly Jewish author of the protocols proclaimed the following: "In order to effect the destruction of all collective forces except ours we shall emasculate the first stage of collectivism - the UNIVERSITIES, by re-educating them in a new direction. THEIR OFFICIALS AND PROFESSORS WILL BE PREPARED FOR THEIR BUSINESS BY DETAILED SECRET PROGRAMS OF ACTION..."

Another protocol claimed that the Jews owned and manipulated the entire world press: "In the hands of the States of to-day there is a great force that creates the movement of thought in the people, and that is the Press...It is in the Press that the triumph of freedom of speech finds its incarnation. But the GOYIM States have not known how to make use of this force; and it has fallen into our hands. Through the Press we have gained the power to influence while remaining ourselves in the shade; thanks to the Press we have got the GOLD in our hands..." And this GOLD would, of course, be used to actualize their sinister plot for world domination.

And on and on and on, in suffocating detail.

Most unnerving was the revelation by *The Protocols* that those things most valued and sought after, that is, freedom, universal education, suffrage, even peace, were actually just devious methods used by the Jews to destabilize and destroy governments for the ultimate purpose of world conquest by a Jewish elite: "In all corners of the earth the words 'Liberty, Equality, Fraternity,' brought to our ranks, thanks to our blind agents, whole legions who bore our banners with enthusiasm. And all the time these words were canker-worms at work boring into the well-being of the GOYIM, putting an end everywhere to peace, quiet, solidarity and destroying all the foundations of the GOYA States..."

At length, the tone of the writing, its pomposity and spurious authenticity, grew so wearing that I could not stand to read any more. I was beginning to feel ill, the coffee I had finished hours ago a bitter bile in the back of my mouth. Disgusted, I skipped to the last paragraph, the final promise of complete ascension of the "King of the Jews" to the peak of diabolical power. When I turned the page, I saw the words, scrawled in blue ink: *WE KNOW WHAT YOU ARE DOING!*

Horrified, I examined this entry more closely. It looked like it had been written recently.

"Yakub!" I squeaked.

He looked over at me, alarm in his face. "I told you!" he said.

"No, it's not that! Look at this!" I showed him the entry in ball point pen.

Yakub took the booklet, his nose wrinkling with disgust at the acrid odor. After examining the scrawled writing closely, he said, "Someone appears to be giving us a message. And not a very nice 'someone,' judging by their reading material."

I nodded.

"Well, anyway," said Yakub, "that message could mean any number of things. Let's forget it for now, and get on with our work. Our time is limited." He pushed *The Protocols* away with a dismissive hand, moving his notebook into its place. "Look at this!" he said, his voice changing, infused now with interest and curiosity.

I read the poem out loud.

Will her love remember his graceful doe
her only son in her arms as he parted?
On her left hand he placed a ring from his right,
on his wrist she placed her bracelet.
As a keepsake she took his mantle from him,
and he in turn took hers from her.
Would he settle, now, in the land of Spain,
if its prince gave him half his kingdom?

I felt my spirit lightened by these words of beauty, rising up from the dull, dark place of dread induced by those in the rancid booklet.

"'*She shall be a garment to him, and he shall be a garment to her,*'" I said, quoting the Quranic verse Yakub had read yesterday.

"Yes," said Yakub, smiling in pleasure at my recollection. "And it is quite amazing that Mrs. Dunash wrote this poem, just at the time when her husband was beginning to use the Hebrew tongue in the manner of Arabic poetry. She has mastered it already in this very early poem." He leaned over the folio. "See here, how it is rhymed: two stanzas, all four lines in the first rhymed with the female possessive 'ah,' and two alternating lines in the next stanza also matching this rhyme. And see, how this poem is all about relation between people. In their exchange of things most precious, it is as if they become unified."

I looked below, where Yakub had transcribed the response of her husband, the one quoted in the article we'd read at the airport in San Francisco:

Could I betray a bright young wife, one joined to me on High?
Perish the thought a thousand times! Would I not rather die?

"Apparently, Mrs. Dunash's husband didn't leave her as a result of a paucity of feeling," I said. "It appears to me their separation wasn't voluntary."

"I agree. And there's something else quite intriguing about all this. You know, Rawiyya was always convinced that the 'poem to redeem the world' was written by a woman. Her friend, Tatianne, whom we are meeting in Cordoba tomorrow, was the one who suggested Rawiyya visit her there. Apparently, she knew something she wanted to pass on to Rawiyya. Perhaps it was this 'Mrs. Dunash' she was thinking of. After all, this poetess did live in Cordoba."

"But did Mrs. Dunash write the poem we're looking for, or did Said al-Shadi?"

"That still remains unclear."

"So, we either need to find this *diwan* of al-Shadi's, or some more poems by Mrs. Dunash. Do you think Rawiyya was on the trail of this 'wife of Dunash'?"

"When she died? It seems very likely."

I nodded, recalling, with a shudder, the scrawled message in *The Protocols*. "Do you think someone's trying to scare us off?"

"I don't know," said Yakub, anxiety stirring the depths of his green eyes. "We will have to be careful."

He turned his attention now to the listing of contents in David II Maimonides' private genizah, which he perused for several minutes before letting out a satisfied grunt. "Here it is!" He ran his finger across the plastic folio cover as he read: "*Said al-Shadi. Diwan: Ma'ana al-Tazaawuj. Arabic, in Arabic script.*"

"What does that mean..." I looked down at the paper, reading, "'Ma'ana al-Tazaawuj?'"

"The meaning of ...I guess you would translate it 'marriage,' but it has a more subtle meaning in this form, as well...more like, 'to form a pair,' or to 'come together to form a pair' or 'intermarry.' There's something in it of the coming together of two unlike properties, almost like metaphor itself. A very fascinating word, to say the least.'"

"But why was David II Maimonides hiding all these books, including al-Shadi's *diwan*? And, more importantly, where *is* this genizah?"

Yakub didn't answer, and I looked over at him. His expression had grown distant. He was staring off into space, absently flipping the page back and forth between his hands, allowing it to flop from side to side on the metal rings of the notebook.

"Yakub?" I said.

He started. "Rachel! Feel this!" He guided my hands onto the two sides of the folio. "Tap it back and forth!" I did so. "Now, try it with another page." I did as he said. "What do you feel?"

"Is the genizah list...heavy?"

"Yes!" he said, "Brilliant! What do you think would make it heavy?"

"Hmmm..."I said, uncertainly.

"Could it be because it is actually *more* than one sheet of paper?" Yakub suggested.

"You mean, there are two sheets here? Stuck together?"

"It happens all the time! Come on!" he said, taking the folio from me and putting it back in the box, along with the booklet, *The Protocols of the Learned Elders of Zion.* "Let's go talk with our helpful librarian! Oh, and bring all your things with you. We'll leave for the airport from there."

We headed back upstairs. Yakub tapped impatiently on the bell once again, and out came Margaret Tibbs.

"Ah!" she said when she saw us, "It's my two mysterious sleuths! Watson and Holmes is it? Or Tommy and Tuppence?"

"Oh," said Yakub, "MY doctor is of a much higher caliber than Watson!" he smiled at me. "More like Miss Marple, but far prettier!"

Margaret Tibbs looked at me, raising one conspiratorial eyebrow. "I see. Well. What can I do for you both?"

"First," said Yakub, opening the box, "take a look at this. Or a feel, I should say." He demonstrated his discovery to her, as he had done for me several minutes ago. "Don't you agree? There seems to be a second page here."

She nodded. "Yes, I do agree. Shall I submit it to the lab for you? It should be a relatively simple matter to separate the pages."

"Yes, please!" he said.

We made arrangements to have the librarian fax the resulting documents to me at a number that would arrive at my e-mail address.

"Anything else?" she asked, after she'd taken down the information.

"A question. Do you know of the location of the private genizah mentioned in this listing?" He opened the folio and showed her the document outlining the contents of David II's genizah.

She shook her head regretfully. "I'm sorry, no. No one has been able to locate it, as yet."

Yakub sighed. "I was afraid of that."

"You could try some other libraries housing Genizah fragments. The Firkovitch collection in St. Petersberg, for example, has only recently made its Judeo-Arabic fragments available. Perhaps they've discovered something new that I'm not aware of."

"Very excellent suggestion!" said Yakub. "Oh, and one other thing. Would you mind making copies of the documents in the folio?"

"Of course. It will take about fifteen minutes, though."

" 'That's fine," said Yakub, "We'll wait here,"

"Actually," I said, "Can you tell me where I can find the Encyclopedia Judaica? I'd like to look something up while we wait."

She directed me to the location of the Encyclopedia, then left with our folio to make the copies.

"Do you mind if I go for a few minutes?" I asked Yakub.

"Not at all." He went and sat down on a bench by the wall, pulling out his poetry anthology.

Following Margaret Tibb's excellent directions, I found the Encyclopedia Judaica in no time. I had not read much about *The Protocols of the Learned Elders of Zion* before, and wanted to find out a little more detail. I pulled out the "P" volume and found the entry.

It seems *the Protocols* were written by an unknown author in Paris in the late 1800's. This mysterious author was apparently working for the Russian secret police, and his pamphlet was intended to turn the Czar, Nicholas II's, attitude against the Jews in order to discourage him from making reforms unfavorable to the establishment. The author hoped to convince him that these reforms would play into the hands of the "Jewish secret plot." The unknown author adapted a play by a fellow named Maurice Joly, whose dramatic work, *Dialogue aux Enfers entre Machiavel et Montesquieu, ou la politique aux xix siècle,* painted a picture of the world-dominating aspirations of Napoleon III. The author of the *Protocols* simply forged the entire work, replacing mention of the French emperor with reference to a conference of leaders of world Jewry.

These *Protocols* didn't have the desired effect on the Czar, who recognized them as a fraud. However, in the fertile setting of post-World-War-I Europe, and particularly in Germany, the ideas presented in *The Protocols* received new life, resonating powerfully and spreading like wildfire in the minds and imaginations of the populace, primed already by millennia of anti-Judaism.

The one ray of hope I found in the entire sorry history was the description of the actions of a certain Philip Graves, a non-Jewish reporter for the *Times* of London who, in 1921, wrote an article exposing *the Protocols* as a fraud and a forgery. His words disassembled the authenticity of the work piece by piece, and after reading his article, no one of conscience in England continued to take *the Protocols* seriously.

Out loud, I cheered for the assistance of my English forefathers. Here was at least one major triumph on the side of truth and goodness.

Sadly, despite this inspiring victory, some people still remained all-too-willing to overlook the obvious flaws of the work and accept it as truth. From the notorious publication of *The Protocols* by Henry Ford in the Dearborn Independent to their translation into virtually all of the world's major languages, to this day, *the Protocols of the Learned Elders of Zion* maintains its powerful hold on the imagination of the world's people.

This made me wonder. *Is it harder to stamp out a lie than it is to spread the truth?*

Checking my watch, I saw the fifteen minutes had passed already, and hurried down to meet Yakub. He was still sitting reading his poetry book, and a smile lit his face when he looked up to find me approaching.

"Did you find what you were looking for?"

I nodded, but didn't elaborate on the depressing subject of my research. We headed back to the circulation desk, collected our photocopies, bid goodbye to Margaret Tibbs, and left the library. I looked over my shoulder a few times, feeling, suddenly and inexplicably, as though someone were following us.

"What is it, my dear?" said Yakub, surprise on his face.

"I thought someone was there," I said, then laughed ruefully. "I guess all this reading about *the Protocols* has made me a little paranoid."

"I told you…" said Yakub.

"I know, I know…"

We went out to find the taxi waiting for us at the bottom of the library steps once again. I wondered, briefly, as we left, if Margaret Tibbs had informed her assistant about the incident with the pamphlet, and whether he had known anything about it.

On the train to Gatwick airport, Yakub and I went to the dining car to get some lunch. Despite my romantic visions of an elegant moving restaurant with white tablecloths and china, prompted, I suspected, by a few too many British mystery novels, the reality was less impressive: a Formica concession counter, with racks of potato chips and candy bars, the menu consisting of various combinations of processed meats and deep-fried potatoes.

Nevertheless, I was starving, and ordered fish and chips with a large coffee. Yakub ordered a cheese sandwich on whole wheat bread.

We sat down on the red plastic benches in a booth by the window. Yakub pulled the photocopy of "the letter from Dunash's wife" out of his backpack and reread the poem aloud, between bites of cheese sandwich. He then read her other poem, the one contained in the letter from Dunash's son.

"There is so much here about true love, the sacred relation between *azwaaj*, spouses. And then that word in the title of Said al-Shadi's *diwan*, al-Tazaawuj. There is some clue to this entire mystery in that," said Yakub.

I nodded. "But where do you suppose Said al-Shadi was going on the quest to complete the poem? It sounds like he was almost done with it!"

"I know."

"We have to find his *diwan!*"

"Yes, we do," said Yakub.

When we arrived at Gatwick Airport, we found Ruthie and Mahmud already at the *Iberian Airlines* counter. We all checked in and headed to the long security line. While we waited, we talked about our day. Ruthie had joined Mahmud for breakfast, and then the two of them had gone for an early visit to the British Museum.

Mahmud talked excitedly about all the things he'd seen there, but mostly about the famous Rosetta stone. "It was such an earth-shaking discovery!" he marveled. "Until they found it, archaeologists and linguists had not been able to decipher the hieroglyphics. This stone cracked the code, because it juxtaposed that unknown language, hieroglyphics, against a known one, Greek, allowing us to read all the inscriptions in the tombs and to uncover a vast and as-yet-unknown chapter of human history."

"You mean about the Pharaohs and the ancient civilizations of Egypt?" I said.

"Yes, that's right. It made me wonder. How would it be if we could add another unknown language, the genetic code, and so find the connection between words and biology? Could we begin to perceive the genetic code of God?"

Yakub was laughing and shaking his head. "Mahmud, you never fail to amaze me! You find the most fantastic connections between science and faith!"

As for me, I considered Mahmud's vision seriously. There was definitely something compelling about it.

"And how was your day?" asked Ruthie, breaking into my thoughts.

"Good and bad," I said. "We made a lot of progress on our research. But something really awful happened too." I described the pamphlet and the sinister scrawled message it contained. Ruthie looked worried.

"Do you think it's just general, common-or-garden anti-Semitism? Or do you think the person who did this has a particular problem with you and your research?"

"I don't know," I admitted.

"What, exactly, is this research anyway?" said Ruthie. "I should probably know a little more about it, if it's going to be running us aground of anti-Semitic creeps like that. Maybe somebody's gonna need a karate chop or a quick punch to the solar plexus?" Ruthie assumed a "crouched and ready" position. I laughed at her antics.

"Probably not a good idea, here in the security line," I warned. "Seriously, we're just doing some research on a poem. I don't see why it should have stirred up any anti-Semites."

"Hmmm. Well, keep me posted if you need any help," she said. "We're all in this together, you know."

"Yes," I agreed, "we are."

Madrid, Spain
7:00 pm, Tuesday, December 19th 2006
Prof. Yakub al-Shadi, Dr. Rachel Roseman, et al

We left London to a beautiful, rosy sunset, arriving in Madrid to rainy skies.

The four of us took a taxi to our hotel, entering the broad, rain-slick boulevards of Madrid in darkness. Our hotel, The Palace, was an elegant, grey building that took up a full city block, its entrance creatively placed at the corner. When the chatty desk clerk learned that we would be travelling to Cordoba the next day, he told us that the Atocha train station was within walking distance.

At the mention of this name, Mahmud and Yakub froze. Too late, I only now remembered that we had blundered into the epicenter of the recent al-Shadi family tragedy. Atocha was the central station where the commuter trains were heading when they exploded during the terrorist incidents of 2004. We walked in silence to the elevators, the expressions on the men's faces grim. Ruthie looked at me, perplexed, and I mouthed *I'll tell you later.*

We separated to go find our individual rooms. When we were alone, I told Ruthie the story of Rawiyya al-Shadi's untimely death.

"Gosh, Rachel. I wish you'd told me this before! Are you sure this is really a good idea, being here?"

"I don't know," I admitted.

We had a late dinner that night in the hotel restaurant. Yakub and Mahmud were silent through most of it. Mahmud excused himself early, indicating that he had a headache and wanted to go lie down.

After he left, Yakub said, "He didn't realize he would feel so badly being close to where his mother was killed."

When we went upstairs, I told Yakub I would get some medicine for Mahmud's headache. I briefly quizzed him to make sure there were no contraindications and, finding none, gave Yakub two tablets of naproxen from the small medical kit I always brought with me on trips. I instructed him to give these to Mahmud with a large glass of water. Later that night, I went to check on Mahmud.

When Yakub opened their hotel room door, I noticed he was wearing his *kufi* and, peeking past him, I saw a vacant prayer mat. Next to it, I saw Mahmud, forehead to the floor.

"Oh, I'm sorry!" I said.

"We were just finishing. Please, come in."

"Are you sure? I don't want to intrude…"

"Yes, yes. Please! Come in!"

I entered as Mahmud stood up and began rolling up his mat.

"Do you do this every night?" I asked.

"Of course!" said Yakub. "And when we're able, four more times a day as well."

"Oh!" I'd forgotten about this aspect of Yakub's life.

"You, however, only have to do something like this three times a day!" said Mahmud. "One each for Abraham, Isaac, and Jacob."

"Yes, you're right!" I said. "That's a midrash, I think. But how'd you know it?"

"There is a hint of this in the Quran, in the chapter about the prophets. It says that Abraham, Isaac, and Jacob established regular prayers."[9]

"Hmm. And how are you feeling, Mahmud? Is your headache better?"

"Yes. Thank you very much for the medication. It helped."

"Good, that's good," I said. "I'm glad. Well, I'll say goodnight then."

"Goodnight," said Yakub and Mahmud together. I left the room, feeling confused. Where did I fit in the life of a Muslim man who had lost his wife in a terrorist bombing?

The next morning, I arose again very early to get in my morning run, still befuddled about the direction of my relationship with Yakub.

When I returned, Ruthie and I packed up for our trip that day to Cordoba. We dragged our rollable-duffles down to the lobby, where we met Yakub and Mahmud. As we went out through the revolving door, the sun was just rising in brilliance over the buildings, sparkling on the sidewalks, and I saw Yakub stop and take a deep breath. He looked at me and smiled. I didn't know what this meant, but it raised my flagging spirits considerably, and I felt hope wash over me.

We walked the few blocks to the Atocha station. In front, there was a memorial to the terrorist victims killed in 2004. I watched as Mahmud and Yakub's eyes locked onto the plaque and then closed. I also prayed. *Baruch Dyan ha-Emmet.* God is the True Judge.

Our train was sleek and modern, one of the new high speed varieties that now streaks in smooth unbroken high velocity at over a hundred miles an hour through the country-sides of Europe. Yakub had booked us in the first-class compartment, so that we would, as he explained, have space and privacy.

Each car contained several seating areas for six around spotlessly clean dining tables. The train was remarkably trim and well-tended, unlike those I'd ridden in America. We were soon

---

[9] Qur'an 21:72-3

travelling rapidly through the Spanish countryside, plains of rolling yellow vegetation, with a low range of mountains visible to our left. The small castles on the hilltops reminded me that this was not California, though the landscape was otherwise quite similar.

After breakfast, I took out my little Psalter, the book of Psalms received as a gift from my rabbi, and read for several minutes. I was startled when Yakub broke into my thoughts, saying "What are you doing, Rachel?"

I showed him my treasure. He took it and carefully looked it over. "You know," he said, "I read these Psalms for the first time after my uncle, Muhtadi, showed me the manuscripts he'd found in the caves above Jericho. They are quite beautiful."

I nodded in agreement. Then, I said, "Yakub, I have a question..."

"Yes, my dear?"

"Dunash's son said he was going to guard his mother's documents in a safe place. So how do you think Said al-Shadi's *diwan* ended up in David II Maimonides' genizah, wherever that was, four hundred years later?"

"I don't know. Somebody may have fled to his home during one of the many Jewish persecutions in Spain."

"If he were going to hide documents like this, where do you think he'd put them?"

"I would venture to say, somewhere within the synagogue, under the watchful eye of the rabbis. Though not safe, it was at least more secure than other locations. Many Jewish people would bury forbidden books in the synagogues in those days."

"Aren't we going to visit the synagogue today?"

"Sadly, not the one that would have existed during the days of Dunash's son, that is, the early eleventh century. The only synagogue that still exists in Cordoba today was built in the fourteenth century, well after his death. However, it is quite probable that any of the valuable items from the original synagogue were removed before the building was destroyed and moved to the new building. So I would say our best bet is to look closely at the existing synagogue."

"And what are we looking for? If al-Shadi's *diwan* has already been removed, that is..."

"I don't know, precisely. The *diwan* mentioned in David II's list may be a different work by al-Shadi, and not the one left with

Mrs. Dunash. Or it could be a copy. Though remember, it would have to have been hand-scribed, as the printing press did not come along for another few centuries. Also, we are looking for more poems by Mrs. Dunash herself. Both she and àl-Shadi seem to have been on the track of the *poem to redeem the world,* so her poetry should contain clues as well. We should do our best to see if we can find anything in that synagogue in Cordoba."

"The one we're visiting today." I nodded. "So, were there...pogroms and things in Cordoba? Even after this current synagogue was built?"

Yakub nodded his head. "Sadly, yes. Violence against the Jews increased, as the Christian conquistadors controlled more and more of the country. There were terrible riots and massacres of Jews in Cordoba and other Spanish villages in the year 1391 in particular, during attempts at mass conversion to Christianity. And then, of course, the monarchs attempted to solve all their problems by expelling the Jews completely in 1492."

"I wonder how that would have affected members of Dunash's family. If they survived the massacres, isn't it possible they would have fled with the documents once again in 1391?"

"Yes. But it's equally likely that they did not survive the massacres, and that is why the poetry of Mrs. Dunash and Said al-Shadi, has been lost to us until now."

"Okay, so we'll search the synagogue thoroughly."

Yakub nodded. "Also, Tatianne, Rawiyya's friend and our guide, will tell us what it was that inspired her to invite my wife here in connection with the poem, back in 2004."

"How did Rawiyya meet Tatianne?"

"They were both students at Cairo University. Not surprisingly, as a resident of Cordoba, Tatianne was interested in Andalusian history. She went to Cairo to learn more about Islam and the history of Arabic culture. She is a very fine local historical guide."

I nodded, settling back in my seat. Glancing up, I looked at Ruthie and Mahmud, each reading articles from the selection of physics journals they had brought with them. The two, thrown together for long periods of time, had formed a good-natured friendship. Nothing romantic, of course. At this point, I was certain that Ruthie had something serious going with my boss, Lenny Goldstein.

The train pulled into the station at Cordoba precisely on time, and the conductor informed us that someone was waiting for us outside. I disembarked to see the beaming face of our guide, Tatianne.

She was about five foot six, with short, curly brown hair sprinkled with just a few streaks of grey and smile lines that radiated around her eyes and mouth. By these, I estimated her to be in her late fifties, though her bearing and energy were those of a younger woman.

"Welcome to the beeootiful city of Cordoba!" she said in heavily accented English when she spied us.

Despite our protests, she ladened herself with Yakub's suit bag and my roller-duffle. Tatianne had a ready laugh, and chatted on with questions about our journey as we navigated the spacious train station lobby towards the taxi stand, her English endearingly executed with a thick Spanish accent, many soft 'c's' pronounced with a lisping 'th.'

In the taxi, she said: "So we will leave your luggage at the hotel, eh? Then we will see Cordoba! Ohh, the Mezquita, so beootiful! And the Sinagoga! Ahh! You will see!"

After this, Tatianne settled back in her seat, directing her gaze towards Yakub, who occupied the front seat next to the driver. I saw her face grow serious as she said, "And Yakub, how does it go for you. You are alright?"

Yakub looked back over the seat towards Tatianne and inclined his head, raising his eyebrows in a gesture that said, "How could I be alright?"

Tatianne nodded, leaning forward and squeezing Yakub's shoulder. Then she turned to Mahmud, saying, "And you. The baby. How are you doing, eh?"

Mahmud shook his head and tried to smile, but tears jumped to his eyes, as they always did when the subject of his mother came up.

Tatianne let out an expletive below her breath, shaking her head and looking out the window.

We drove through a large gate and entered the Juderia. The streets were narrow, paved with cobblestone. As we bounced along, Tatianne remarked, "So, I have chosen your hotel carefully. You will be at the Hotel Amistad, in the Jewish Quarter, just a few steps from the Sinagoga and the statue of Maimonides."

We navigated the narrow lane to an iron-fenced entrance, the gate opening to a charming courtyard. I saw the facade of a small hotel, sided in yellow plaster and limestone, its windows and doors supported by graceful pillars, a semi-circular stairway approaching its entrance. I had to agree. Tatianne had chosen well.

After we checked in and brought our bags to our rooms, we returned to the lobby of the hotel to meet Tatianne. She looked at her watch, saying, "One-thirty! Time to see my city of Cordoba! I take you to the Mezquita, so beoootiful. It isn't far. Then, maybe you would like some lunch?"

Yakub said, "Yes, that would be nice. But as I mentioned to you when we spoke, we're really here to see the synagogue."

"*Yo sé, yo sé*. But I will not permit you to visit my city without seeing the Mezquita first. Then, we will do anything you want."

Yakub laughed. "Alright."

We left the courtyard of the hotel and walked through the narrow streets, white-washed buildings on either side. Tatianne told us she had just returned from vacation. Ruthie asked her where she'd gone.

"Ah," she said, "to the seaside and also…" her words were garbled.

"Excuse me?" I said.

"I visit Auschwitz," she said, "Omigot, poor people." She started to cry. We were silent as we reached the courtyard of the mosque, passing the bell tower, which encased portions of the ancient minaret. A tear rolled down each of Tatianne's cheeks. "Poor people," she repeated.

We entered the cavernous space of the Mezquita, which, though crowded, seemed to absorb its visitors in its enveloping silence. As we walked, the sound of our footsteps disappeared into the lofty spaces above. In every direction the geometric patterns of columns with soaring red-and-white striped lobed arches; stone and brick, old and new. It was stunning, knocking any words from our mouths.

The thirteenth century Spanish Catholic conquistadors who had wrested control of the city of Cordoba from the Muslim Berbers had asserted their victory by ripping a hole in the center of the mosque and building a cathedral. This was accessed through a door in a wooden wall. Inside, we were impressed by the ornate designs of cherubs and angels encrusting its immense ceiling, a statue of Saint Raphael with a scepter crowning a large monument at one end. It was remarkable, tremendous, but seemed somehow…misplaced. Normally, a building such as this would stand in solitary glory rather than encroached on all sides by the remnants of a rival faith. It was hard to ignore this blatant symbolic message about relations between the religions in past times.

Seeing the look on my face, Tatianne said, "Ah, my friend! You are shocked by the evidence of the aggression of the Catholic victors against the defeated Muslims. But this is how it was, eh? It was a different age! The Muslims, too, built on top of the holy buildings of the Catholics when they swept the Andalus in the 8th century. In fact, this very mosque is built over a 'W'isigothic Christian basilica!"

"All I can say," I said, "is that I hope we're past all that now!" I thought to myself, the God of all of us, Christian, Jew, and Muslim, could not have been much impressed by this behavior.

We said no more, but continued out of the Cathedral and back into the Mezquita, now approaching the *mihrab*, the niche facing Makkah. Around it on all sides were startlingly beautiful mosaics in sparkling gold glass fragments on a deep blue background, the inlay forming graceful loops of Arabic words. My eyes shot up to the dome above, decorated in similar fashion, so gorgeous that I instantly understood why people called Cordoba the "ornament of the world."

Mahmud stood beside me, pointing at the letters around the *mihrab*. "You see, Rachel? It is the *Asma Allah al-Husna*, the 99 most beautiful names of God." He quoted. "Allah! There is no god but He! To Him belong the most Beautiful Names!"

"From the Quran?" I asked.

Mahmud nodded. "Yes. Ta-Ha. Verse 8. And several others."

I was silent, and perceived something like a buzzing sound, though I seemed to hear it in my bones, rather than my ears. For just an instant, the golden letters of the names pulsed with light. Then, both sound and light passed. Mahmud looked at me and smiled.

After we left the mosque, we walked to the Café Sefarad, a favorite local restaurant that Tatianne had chosen for lunch.

Thinking of *the poem*, I asked Tatianne, "Are there any places where they might sell old books here? Old documents?"

A frown furrowed the skin on Tatianne's high forehead. "What kind of old books?

"Well, I'm thinking of books in Hebrew and Arabic."

"Mmm…there are not many. I cannot really think of a store where you could buy them. Remember, the great library of Cordoba was destroyed by fundamentalist invaders a thousand years ago. Is it for the poem, the one that Rawiyya mentioned?"

All ears and eyes were now on Tatianne.

"What did Rawiyya tell you about the poem?" said Yakub.

"Not much. But, of course, you knew that was why she was coming to visit me, when she…*Dios me ayude*…was murdered on the train? Achh…I feel like it was my fault!" Tatianne had her hands over her mouth and I could hear her hyperventilating through her fingers. I was afraid she might faint, but fortunately, we had reached the restaurant, and she was able to collapse at a table. I gestured to the waiter that she needed a glass of water.

The rest of us sat down around the table and, gradually, Tatianne revived.

"Achh…Yakub, I am so sorry. If it were not for me, your wife would not have been on the trains."

"Tatianne, my dear, you know that it is not your fault. Please, put your mind at ease!"

"But," she said, "I was the one who told her my intuitions about the poem, that she might find something here, in *el corazon* of Andalusia!"

"But you had no idea that terrorists would bomb those trains!" exclaimed Mahmud. "You merely wished to help!"

"Yes, that is true, but even so…" Tatianne took a deep sigh, and she looked miserable, an incongruous appearance for a face that was so obviously accustomed to smiling.

The waiter arrived, and Tatianne composed herself. Yakub reminded her that we would prefer no shellfish or pork of any kind. Tatianne nodded, "Ah yes!" she said. "Of course." She went on and ordered a medley of Cordoban specialties within these constraints, paella with meat rather than shellfish, gazpacho, *rabo de toro*, the oxtail stew for which the town was famous. "Ah, well, life must go on, eh?" she said, making an attempt at a smile.

After the gazpacho, a chunky mélange of tangy green and

red tomatoes spiced with cilantro, Yakub carefully approached Tatianne about the poem.

"So, Tatianne, *habibti*. What is it you told Rawiyya about the Andalusian poetry, exactly?"

Finishing off the last spoonful of gazpacho, Tatianne swallowed and wiped her mouth with her napkin, holding up one finger. When she'd finished her mouthful, she began, ""Well, I tell you, I have always had a suspicion, or more an intuition, you know, about a local poetess, from the 10th century."

"Poetess?" said Yakub, casting a glance over at me.

"Yes. It is the wife of Dunash ben Labrat. A Jewish woman. And they were not, how do you say, 'big' in the household, in the way of scholarship, at that time. That is why it was so interesting that this wife of Dunash, back in the 10th century, was able to write a poem of such beauty."

Yakub and I exchanged another glance.

"You know this poet already?" said Tatianne.

"Yes, we've heard of her," I said.

"*Si?*" Tatianne was surprised. "She is not well known, outside of Cordoba. How did you come to hear about her?"

"Some research we've recently done in the Cambridge library," said Yakub. "But there was not much information. I would like to see more of her poems!"

"Ah, *lo lamento*, that is the problem. There are no more records of her poems. But there are rumors, eh?"

"Rumors?" I said.

"Some rumors," said Tatianne, lowering her voice to a whisper and inclining her head towards me, "that her poems were collected by her son and hidden, buried perhaps, in an unknown location. Some have speculated Medinat al-Zahra, others the synagogue destroyed by the Almohades."

"Where was that?" Ruthie asked.

"Its location, *no es conocido*. Some believe that members of her *familia* continued to hide the documents through many generations. People speculate that *los poemas* are hidden somewhere in the Sinagoga down the block, a building completed in the early thirteen-hundreds. Like so many others, it was possessed by the Catholics in the great religious campaigns later that century. There were many riots, many Jews killed, *Dios proteja sus almas*. All the other *sinagogas* were destroyed at that time, but this one, she survived."

"So you've heard the poems may be hidden there!" I said.

Tatianne nodded. "And there is another rumor," she said.

"Yes?"

"These hidden poems?" Tatianne put her hand on my upper arm and squeezed it for emphasis. "They are said to have been of tremendous beauty."

"Oh!"

"A terrible loss." Tatianne sighed, removing her hand from my arm. "Ah well," she said, exhibiting what I was coming to recognize as her characteristic resilience.

Ruthie said, "So just let's clarify this. You're saying, these beautiful poems might be buried there, in the synagogue we're about to go see?"

"*Sí*, that is what some people say."

"Hasn't anyone ever searched for them?" She asked.

"Few people know about this, and it is difficult to dig around in an ancient historic building, no? But in *renovaciónes* over the past century, nothing has been found, eh? I think we cannot find them because they are buried in a way according to *la tradición de los judíos*. No one knows these traditions here anymore. You see?"

"Yes, I see very well," Ruthie said, and I was thinking, *Well, the locals may not know them, but I do!*

The oxtail stew arrived, lacing the air with its rich, meaty aroma, the chunks of tender meat flaky in a dark brown broth. We served ourselves white rice, which the others drenched with ladles of the rich sauce and meat while I loaded on a generous helping of roasted vegetables.

Conversation slowed as we directed our attention to the delicious food. When we had finished, Yakub was impatient to leave for the Sinagoga, signaling to the waiter that we would like to pay. I could have used some coffee, but was restless myself to move on to the next clue in our treasure hunt.

We went outside. It was mid-afternoon, and the day was beginning to cool down a bit. By now, the storekeepers had returned from their *siestas* and reopened their storefronts. The streets were full of bright postcard displays and throngs of tourists, here for the winter holidays.

We continued up the cobblestoned streets, passing through the Plaza de Judah Halevi on our way to the Cordoba Synagogue.

Yakub asked Tatianne, "Have you heard anything about a

pupil of the poetess, Mrs. Dunash? An Arab man, with the same last name as mine?"

Tatianne shook her head. "Al-Shadi? *No específicamente,*" she said, "but I have heard that she was a great teacher, with *estudiantes destacados,* many devoted students. Have you heard something about this?"

Yakub described the letter we'd discovered, written by Dunash's son, and the *diwan* of Said al-Shadi's poetry, left in his care.

When he was done with his explanation, Tatianne stopped in her tracks and grabbed Yakub's arm, exploding, "*Que es fantastico!* What have you stumbled upon, *mi amigo?*"

We all paused for a moment waiting once again for Tatianne to recover. I looked around and saw we were standing in a small open square. There, a Spanish guitarist thrummed the strains of a malaguena to the frozen countenance of Moses Maimonides, whose life-sized statue sat in solitary court at the center of a tiny plaza.

Shaking herself from her rhapsody, Tatianne said, "Ah, the great *maestro judío,* Maimonides! The people of Cordoba honored him with this statue in 1935, at the 800th anniversary of his birth in this city."

The man in the statue held a book gently, his gaze and bearing soft and, as I read it, rather sad. No wonder, since, as Tatianne told us, he had been exiled from his hometown as a boy and forced to flee from place to place at the hands of fundamentalist Muslims, the Almohades, who seemed to find justification to abandon the Holy Quran's instructions never to coerce in matters of faith.

"If you touch his foot," said Tatianne, "there is a legend that you will receive some of his *prudencia,* his wisdom."

I went over and put my hand on the flat spot behind the pointy toe of his medieval-style shoe. Yakub followed, then Mahmud and Ruthie. The bronze was smooth where all the many hands had touched over the years. So many people, seeking wisdom.

Cordoba Synagogue, Spain

4:00 pm. Wednesday, December 20th 2006

Dr. Rachel Roseman, Prof. Yakub al-Shadi, et al

Leaving Maimonides, we walked another half block before arriving at the synagogue, an unassuming building with a white plaster exterior. The front door took us to a courtyard and from there into the prayer hall, a small space, perhaps twenty by thirty feet. Its walls were decorated with the intricate latticework design of Mudejar craftsmanship, the beautiful ornate detailing created by the Muslim artisans of Christian Spain. The plaster was faded and bleached white. Ringing the synagogue at the top of the walls were Hebrew letters.

Tatianne told us that, "It was so sad." After the edict of expulsion, the Synagogue had been used as a hospital for "hydrophobic patients," that is, unfortunates suffering from rabies, and later as a meeting place for the guild of St. Crispin, a group of shoemakers.

As she spoke, my eye was drawn to a single, small niche on the western wall, exquisitely carved and decorated with rosettes offsetting strings of Hebrew letters. Between the words, there were large gaps where letters had dropped off. In the side walls of the niche, Tatianne pointed out some subtle Arabic calligraphy: "*al-mulk lillah*, God is King." The center of the niche bore the faint outlines of a rose-colored cross, leftover from the days when it had been used as a Catholic shrine in one of its former lives. In its floor was a bronze plaque, apparently a memorial of some kind.

Tatianne said, "So interesting, the Hebrew letters that fell off the wall, they were painted the color of our skin, peach. And up there," she pointed to the south wall "was the women's gallery. We cannot go up there now, the stairway, it is not safe."

We walked the circumference of the synagogue as Tatianne continued to point out items of historic interest. Yakub and I scrutinized each object, to see if it might bear some clue of a hidden treasure. Nothing jumped out at us in the first twenty minutes. After this time, I noticed Ruthie and Mahmud wandering around aimlessly, looking decidedly fatigued.

I said, "Do you guys want to go back to the hotel and wait for us there while we snoop around here a little longer?"

Relieved, Ruthie said, "Great idea! I've been dying to take a swim in that pool on the roof of the hotel. But you guys, promise you won't get yourselves in any trouble, okay?" I promised, but that had never stopped me before.

Ruthie and Mahmud left, along with Tatianne, who arranged to meet us the following day to take us to Madinat al-Zahra, the former palace of the *Umayyad* caliphs, where she'd suggested we look for further traces of the poetry of Mrs. Dunash.

After they left, Yakub and I had the synagogue to ourselves. I looked up at the two rows of Hebrew letters lining the upper walls. "I wonder what those say? Could they be a clue of some kind?"

"They are likely verses from the Psalms," said Yakub.

"Yes, but which ones? I wonder if they have some info." I went back to the courtyard to check. On the way, I passed the stairs to the women's gallery, roped off now with a velvet cord.

The attendant in the courtyard did not speak English, but when I said "information?" he pointed out several books and pamphlets available for purchase. I gave him ten Euros in return for a small book describing the synagogue and its inscriptions, in English.

Back inside the empty synagogue, I traversed each of the walls trying to identify which passages of Psalms they contained. In the end, I circled back to the niche. It really was a beautiful thing. I stood inside, wondering what its original purpose had been. Avoiding the bronze plaque on the floor, which I took to be a burial site, I looked back up at the Hebrew letters encircling the upper walls of the synagogue. It was hard to read them from where I stood.

It occurred to me that we could see them better from the women's gallery. Also, there might be some other clue up there about the lost poems. But it was closed and we could not go up there. *Or could we?*

I motioned to Yakub. When he got up next to me, I whispered, "Want to be a little bad?"

He looked surprised. "My dear! Here?"

"Not that, you...silly person!" Momentarily distracted from our task, I blushed and looked down. *Was he also preoccupied with this?* Flustered, I rushed on, saying, "I'd like to see the inscriptions! I bet we can get a better look at them up in the women's gallery. Want to go up there?"

Yakub gave me a wicked smile, but letting the moment pass said, "I've been good for so long, perhaps I can afford to be a little bad now?"

We went back to the entryway. The attendant was dozing off on his stool out in the courtyard. I plastered myself up against the wall like some kind of James Bond wannabe, and Yakub did the same. We crouched under the velvet rope and crawled, as quietly as we could, up the steep stairs, which turned at a 90 degree angle after five steps. The stairway did shake around a bit as we went, but fortunately, did not collapse. When I reached the top, I raised my hand for a 'high five.' Not sure what that meant, Yakub took it and kissed it.

After this, I went across to the edge of the balcony, which was right up next to the Hebrew letters. They spread away from us along the top of the West wall, above the niche. Though some were missing, I recognized the beginning of the Psalm we'd read just that morning, on the train from Madrid. "*Shiru l'Adonai Shir Chadash, Shiru l'Adonai kol ha aretz…*" Sing to the Lord a new song, sing to the Lord, all the earth…I pointed this out, in a whisper, to Yakub.

Having settled that, I looked around the small balcony, once the women's gallery in this doomed synagogue. There were bunches of broken Hebrew words and letters on the floor.

I hardly got to look at them before I heard a sound. Someone was entering the Synagogue. They called out, "Allo? Allo?" Yakub and I froze, neither breathing nor speaking. The voice below said something else and then we heard steps retreating and the sound of the door closing. After that, we heard something we did not want to hear at all: the sound of a lock clunking shut.

I looked at Yakub. "*Uh oh!*" I said, in a whisper.

We descended the stairs. Yakub went and tried the door. It was, indeed, locked from the outside. We looked around. The windows were way too high up to access. We were definitely stuck.

Problems with our current situation began to dawn on us sequentially. Neither of us had a cell phone with us. Mahmud and Ruthie would be worried sick about us when we didn't return. We had nothing to eat or drink. We might get cold. It could get creepy in this place at night. How would we explain our predicament to the person opening up the synagogue in the morning?

On the other hand, we should look on the bright side! We had the place completely to ourselves, it would be light for perhaps another half hour, and we were with each other. We were safe, after all, our problem really one of embarrassment and discomfort rather than danger.

"Actually," said Yakub, "I always carry a candy bar and some water in my bag. And," he said, with a flourish, removing his keys from his pocket, "I also travel with a flashlight!"

He was looking downright pleased now, and he rubbed his hands together. "Let's really explore now, before it gets dark! If any poems are hidden in here, whether those of Mrs. Dunash or my ancestor, Said al-Shadi, now is our chance to find out!"

Given the season, the shadows were already encroaching from the four corners of the small synagogue.

"I, for one," said Yakub, "am most interested in the west wall, and particularly the niche. Does your pamphlet say anything about that?"

I opened the small booklet I'd purchased and scanned through a few pages. "Well, on the west wall above the niche, the inscriptions include the one line from Psalm 96, which we saw from upstairs. There are also portions of Psalms 22 and 27 in the lines below." I removed my little Psalter from my pocket, reading from Psalm 22, verses 28 and 29: *"Let all the ends of the earth pay heed and turn to the LORD, and the peoples of all nations prostrate themselves before You; for the kingdom is the LORD's and He rules the nations."*

Yakub went over to the inside of the niche and looked up at the little arches inside, and the words *al-mulk lillah, power belongs to God.* "It is intriguing," he said, "that this inscription mirrors that sentiment."

"It's also strange," I said, "that a verse like this occurs at the intersection of the numbers of letters in the Hebrew alphabet, 22, and the number in the Arabic alphabet, 28."

"Ah! Your Jewish mysticism!" He laughed, entering the small niche and examining it carefully from top to bottom.

"Yakub," I said, feeling a little superstitious, "I think you're standing on a grave." I recalled similar plaques I'd seen in the Mezquita earlier today, near some of the alcoves now used as Catholic sacristies.

He stepped off of the bronze plaque onto the terra-cotta tiles beside it. Curious, I crouched down to look at the writing, faded from centuries of wear and tear. I read aloud what appeared to be the name of the unfortunate individual buried below. "Shirah

Usfarim Ganuzim." I then read the second line, which said "Shenat Sheiveim v'Hamaysh."

"The year seventy-five," said Yakub.

"What? The year seventy-five? What do you think that means?"

"Why don't you see what your guide book says?" suggested Yakub.

I nodded and, in the waning light, opened the book, turning to the index. I perused it until I found the entry for "Niche – West Wall," and below it, "memorial plaque," and the page number, 60. Squinting and reading aloud, I quoted: "'In the floor of the hauntingly beautiful niche, there is a burial memorial for an unknown Jew, Shirah Usfarim Ganuzim, whose ashes are contained in a metal box sunk into the floor. The inscription date of '75' corresponds to the Hebrew year, 5075, or 1315, the year of completion of the *Sinagoga*.'"

Yakub nodded, saying, "Let's take a look at the Eastern wall." We walked across the length of the small synagogue to the other side. There, we saw two rough niches hewn into the stone of the walls, one in the center and one to the left.

"Tatianne said that the center niche used to house the Torah scrolls," I said. The niche was now empty, its base covered in rubble.

Yakub examined the alcoves carefully, especially the smaller one on the left. It was getting so dusky that you could hardly see anything. He directed his small flashlight to the space, illuminating it in eerie blue light.

"What are you looking for?" I said, my voice echoing in the growing darkness.

"I'm wondering," said Yakub, "If this might have been the genizah of this synagogue." In the blue light of the flashlight, I saw him pushing on the sides of the niche, and then heard him make a sound of disappointment. "There is nothing here, just solid stone," he said, switching off the flashlight.

He returned to me, where I stood near the niche for the Torah scrolls. I was shivering, whether from cold or nervousness in the shadowy space, I couldn't tell.

"You're freezing!" said Yakub with concern, putting his arm around my shoulder and pulling me in next to his chest. "Don't you have a sweater with you?"

"Yes," I said, "It's in my backpack, over by the door."

Yakub switched on his flashlight again, and we returned to our backpacks, retrieving our sweaters. Yakub took out a water bottle and handed it to me. I took a few sips then handed it back. He drank sparingly. We sat a few minutes, chatting about our findings, our eyes growing accustomed to the darkness.

All at once, something hit me.

"Yakub," I said.

"Yes, my dear?"

"That memorial plaque in the floor of the niche. It doesn't make any sense."

"Why not?"

"It just doesn't jibe with Jewish tradition," I said.

"Why not?"

"Well, first, Jews don't believe in cremation. So why would they bury ashes here? Also, it seems really unlikely that they would bury someone in the synagogue at all. The whole idea is for people to decompose back into the earth, 'dust to dust.' And also, that name, Shirah Usforim Ganuzim…it's strange."

I thought through each of the names in the sequence. Shirah. That sounded like a feminine Hebrew name. But it also had a meaning: poetry. Then it all became clear.

These were words!

"Yakub! The name! It isn't a name!"

"What?"

"Think about the Hebrew!"

Yakub repeated the words aloud. "*Shirah*: poetry, *u'sefarim*, 'and books,' *ganuzim*, 'hidden'… Rachel! You're a genius! *A genizah for poetry and books!*"

"Exactly!"

"But then why did people think it was a grave?"

"That's what people here expect to see! It's what's in all the cathedrals and churches! But, as Tatianne mentioned, people don't know much about these Jewish customs here anymore, since the Jews were all expelled. I bet you hardly any Jews at all have moved back to Cordoba."

Yakub jumped up and began rummaging in his backpack. He removed something and then turned back to me. "Come on!"

Using the blue beam from the flashlight, we returned to the niche.

"Can you hold this for me?" said Yakub, handing me the flashlight. I took it and directed it down to the bronze plaque on the floor. Yakub knelt, and I saw that he held a large Swiss Army knife, bristling with gadgets.

"How'd you get that through security?" I asked, to take my mind off the upcoming task, which seemed remarkably much like grave robbing.

"I had it in my check-in luggage." Yakub extracted the flat-tip screwdriver blade and took a first tentative run along the edge of the plaque. "I thought we might need it today."

He worked the blade into the seam between the terra-cotta tiles and the metal, then ran it all along the edge, making sawing motions when he encountered resistance. He continued along all four sides of the plaque, which was about two feet wide and a foot high. After he was done, he wedged the screwdriver tip under one corner and leveraged upwards.

There was a scraping sound, as the bronze plate tilted. Yakub grasped its edge with his hand and, with a grunt, pulled it hard. It stuck for a moment, then suddenly let go, tipping over onto the tile floor with a loud clanging sound.

In its place was a gaping hole. Fearfully, I turned the beam of the flashlight down into it. There, I saw the surface of another metal plate, this one rusted and dusty. It looked like a large metal box. On one side, there were two big hinges, rusty and forbidding.

Yakub reached down and tried to pry up the lid with his fingers. It moved just the tiniest bit, before stopping on the fused hinges.

"Uh oh," I said, for the second time that night.

Yakub moved to squat next to the hinges, and began working away at them with the tip of the screwdriver blade, attempting to scrape off some of the rust. After a few minutes, he tried the top again. No luck.

"I think we need some oil," I said.

Yakub sat for a few moments, index finger to his lips. "Do you by any chance carry lip balm with you?" he asked.

"Usually." I tried to remember if I'd done so this time. I went back to my backpack and searched through the front pocket. Yes! There it was! My Vaseline lip balm!

I returned to Yakub and handed it to him. He squeezed generous dollops into the hinges, waited a few minutes for the

Vaseline to seep down into the insides of the hinge devices, then tried the lid once more. With a shriek, the hinges let loose their hold, and the top of the box lifted. Once again, I moved the trembling beam of the flashlight down into the blackness.

There, I saw a pile of what looked like grey ashes, with larger chunks of...something mixed in, elongated solid forms.

"Yuck!" I said. "It *is* someone's remains."

To my amazement, I saw Yakub reach his hand down into the ashes and grasp one of the elongated objects.

"What are you doing?" I squeaked, every superstitious nerve in my body screaming.

Ignoring me, Yakub pulled the object out and began examining it with his flashlight. Dusting off the grey ash, he looked closely at what I took to be a long bone.

After a moment, he said, "As I suspected. It is made of wood."

I released my breath in a big gush. "What?"

"It's the spindle of a scroll."

He reached down again into the box, and carefully probed amid the ashes, pulling out another object, which he carefully placed on the ground.

"A book!"

Yakub nodded. "A Jewish prayer book."

He extended his arm down into the box once again and probed around some more. This time, his hand connected with something and he grunted. "Hmm!" Getting a better handle on whatever it was, he pulled it up out of the floor and placed it in front of him.

I saw a metal box, about 8 by 11 inches, and 2 inches deep. Yakub blew the dust off its surface to reveal a filigreed illustration in hammered metallic gold and silver wire: sun, moon, and stars surrounding three letters, in Hebrew, at the center.

"*Dalet – Nun – Shin,*" I read aloud.

"Dunash!" exclaimed Yakub.

He carefully blew the dust off the top once again, and then placed the fingers of each hand along the edges, jiggling gently until it came loose. I shone the flashlight beam down into the box. It held a single sheet of paper, dark characters visible on its surface.

"That's it!" I cried, my eyes squinting to make out the words on the shadowy page.

Yakub gestured for the flashlight and shone it onto the page, his voice trembling. "We should not touch this paper, in case it is fragile and crumbles." He shone the flashlight onto the page, scanning it from top to bottom, then said, tendrils of disappointment lacing his words, "It doesn't look like a poem." He sniffed, then continued: "It's Judeo-Arabic, semi-cursive script. The writing is rather scrawled. It appears to have been written in haste."

"You can read that, right?"

He nodded, and began to read out loud. *'For one who comes after me, in God's name, on this terrible night of Tisha B'Av, year of One Hundred Fifty One, I, Rivkah bat Avraham, of the house of the Meshorerah, greet you. My parents, my young brother, and all those I love have been murdered. I flee now, and take the contents of this box to the family of the Nagid in Fustat. Pray that I make it to them alive."*

"That's all it says?"

"Yes," replied Yakub.

"It's not the poem."

"No."

Slowly, Yakub read the note again. Then, he commented, "The person who wrote this, Rivkah bat Avraham, says she's of the 'house of the meshorerah.' The poetess. Given the initials on the top of the box, I assume this means the family of the poetess, Dunash's wife. This must be the box that once held the treasured *diwan* of Said al-Shadi, and possibly other poetry by Mrs. Dunash herself."

I said, "And that year, 151. I assume this means 5151, according to the Jewish calendar? Since we just learned that the year 5075 corresponds to the year 1315 on our calendar, that means…" I calculated, "it was 1391."

"The year of the pogroms in Cordoba."

I nodded. "I wonder who was the *nagid* in Fustat at that time?"

"In 1391? It would have been David II Maimonides."

I nodded, as this small puzzle piece fit into its place. "Given that Said al-Shadi's *diwan* ended up in David's genizah, I guess she must have made it there."

"Yes."

"But why did she choose to bring the documents to the Maimonides family, specifically?"

"Well, for one thing, the family had its origins in Cordoba, and likely there was still a connection with the Jewish people here. Fustat may have seemed the only safe haven to this young woman, who had just lost her entire family to the mobs. Perhaps she was also hoping that the great *nagid* could shed some light on the poetry itself."

"That makes sense. And that's all that's in the box now? Just the note?"

I saw Yakub's head nodding in the darkness. We both sat a moment, letting this sink in.

"Maybe there's something else inside the genizah," said Yakub. He got up and returned to the hole in the floor, then lay down and rummaged through the ashes, which we now knew, thankfully, to be the remains of books, not humans. It was not a terribly large box, and Yakub succeeded in pulling out only a couple more prayer books, a torn scroll of Esther, and half of a Bible codex.

After forty five more minutes of sifting through the paper fragments, he gave up. "All of the Dunash family documents must have been in the ornamented box."

"Then we have nothing. Only the note."

"Well, it is still a very promising lead!" said Yakub. "Look on the bright side! We know that the contents of the box did arrive in Fustat, and that they made it into David II's Genizah."

"But that's the problem! How are we going to find that genizah? No one knows where it is!"

"We have several possible avenues. We can look for evidence in other libraries, as our librarian, Margaret Tibbs, suggested. Or perhaps, once the two pages of the document we found at the Cambridge Library are separated, the hidden page will reveal some information about the genizah's location."

I nodded my head. I'd been so excited to read the poetry, and now I would have to wait again. I sighed, gesturing to the metal box. "What should we do with that? We can't take it with us, it belongs to the synagogue."

"Yes, you're right."

Yakub went to retrieve his notebook and a pen, then set about transcribing the note's contents. After he was done, he replaced the note in the box and returned it, along with the books and scroll, to their former location, covering them once again with the hinged lid of the genizah and the metal plaque.

"Someday," he said, "we'll publish our findings, along with, *Insha Allah,* the poem to redeem the world, for all mankind to see. But for now, we must keep this discovery a secret. We cannot forget the warning of our unseen 'friend' at the Cambridge library, and his less-than-friendly message in *The Protocols of the Learned Elders of Zion.*"

"But that was probably just a prank," I said, feeling spooked. This sensation was amplified by the dark space around us and the remembrance of all the people who must have died violently in this place at the time the author of our letter fled to Fustat.

Despite my sweatshirt, my teeth began to chatter again. Noticing this, Yakub said, "Come on, let's sit close and keep each other warm."

I did not argue, but followed Yakub to where he settled down in the southwest corner of the building, somewhere between Psalms 96 and 22. We sat close to each other, our shoulders touching. Yakub's body felt warm against my side.

"You know, Rachel," he said, after some minutes, "we're facing towards Jerusalem."

I said, "But shouldn't you be facing Makkah?"

Yakub spoke in Arabic, words I could not understand.

"What did you say?" I asked.

"The Quran says, 'To God belongs the East and the West. Whichever way you turn, there is the face of God.'[10] So you see the idea. God is everywhere. For the sake of our religious path, we face one direction, but we might just as well close our eyes and face inwards, because God is inside us as well as everywhere else."

"How do you know all these verses from the Quran?" I asked, curious.

"My dear, I know the entire Quran. What poet would not? It is the greatest, the most sublime writing. None can imitate it. But to only reflect some of its light! That would be heaven."

"And yet you feel this way," I ventured carefully, "despite what happened to your wife?"

Yakub paused so long I thought he might not answer. At last, he said, "Rachel, the Quran is not the cause of the misfortunes of Rawiyya and my family. They are caused by people who do not

---

[10] Qur'an 2:115

really care about its true message."

Though I could not see Yakub in the dark synagogue, I felt his body tense.

"If what you say about the Quran is true," I said, "then these people have done the world a terrible injustice."

"Yes, that is so," said Yakub, his voice tight.

Changing the subject, I asked, "Is there a name for someone who has memorized the whole Quran?"

"The term is *Hafiz*," said Yakub. He took a breath, and I sensed him willing his body to relax. "You know, Rachel," he said, "I haven't told you very much about...Rawiyya. And me."

I said, uncomfortably, "You probably miss her terribly."

Yakub did not respond to this statement directly, but instead said, "I wish I had treated her better when she was alive. I was...I suppose you'd say, I was a bit of a boor. Like most men, I was sure that my work was more important than anything she might do. Ironically, in the end, she is the one who was closest to the hidden trail of this poem. I didn't give her any credit. I won't do things that way again."

He stopped talking. We sat in silence for awhile. The twelve windows ringing the upper walls of the synagogue admitted just the faintest trace of the evening lights of Cordoba.

"Now it's your turn," Yakub said. "You haven't told me anything about your husband. Remind me again of his name?"

"David."

"And he died about seven years ago? In a house fire?"

"Yes." I wasn't sure I wanted to talk about this. For a long time, I could hardly think about David at all without wanting to scream. Though the keen edge of the grief had gradually dulled, it still had the ability to pierce me at unexpected times. I did not want that to happen now. I tried a few words. "I was very sad for a long time. And," I surprised myself by admitting, "also a little angry."

"Angry?"

"Yes."

"Why were you angry at David?"

I paused a moment, fearful of the emotions this might call up. But I also sensed the possibility of some long-overdue healing. Tears sprang to my eyes as I went on. "You know, I've never mentioned this to you, but years ago I was told that I can't have children."

"Ahh," said Yakub. "I'm sorry."

"Thanks. Anyway, not long before David died, we did all this medical testing. We found out that the infertility was my fault. And that made me feel really guilty, I guess, and also jealous. How come David could have children, but not me? And anyway, where did my infertility come from? Maybe it was some infection David passed on to me? I was angry at him, and asking questions, and then he died, right in the middle of all of that."

My voice had risen, and the shrill words rang in the air of the small synagogue. I took a breath and began again. "David went and died before we ever settled this issue."

I felt Yakub's breathing calm me a little. He said, "Why did you want a child, Rachel?"

I was stumped. "I don't know. It's only natural, isn't it?"

"You had your work, your medicine. And you had been a great athlete."

"I just couldn't stand being a failure," I said, "at anything."

"A baby is not a trophy, Rachel." Yakub's voice was gentle. We sat quietly while I thought about this.

"The thing is," I said after a few minutes of silence, "I did love David so much. Since I never got a chance to resolve the questions I had, my anger about that got all tangled up in my grief."

"I understand," said Yakub. "Grief is not a simple thing."

After a few minutes more of silence, he said, "Would you like some chocolate now?"

I laughed. Chocolate sounded like the perfect antidote to grief. "Sure!"

Yakub fumbled in his bag while I shone the light. He reproduced the water bottle and a Milky Way bar, which he ceremoniously unwrapped and sliced into eight pieces with his pocket knife. We ate and drank, passing the water back and forth. I had never had such a delicious Milky Way bar in my entire life.

Once we'd consumed both water and candy bar, Yakub and I went in search of a bathroom. Afterwards, chilled once again, I was glad to return to our place in the corner of the synagogue and sit side by side with Yakub, the warmth from his body a welcome haven in the eerie darkness.

"Rachel," said Yakub, as if he had decided on something in the brief interim of our separation. "I have something for you."

"What?" I said. "It sounds important!"

"It is," he said, and I heard the rustling of paper. "Here." I felt the edge of a piece of paper in my hand. I grasped it.

"What is it?" I said.

"Why don't you look and see?" suggested Yakub.

I pulled out the flashlight and pinched it, so that its unearthly blue glow illuminated the page. On it, I saw the familiar figures of the Roman alphabet. English. At the top, there was Hebrew.

I looked over towards Yakub, just a darker shadow in the blackness. "What does it say?"

"It's a poem." said Yakub. "The one I mentioned the other day. The first poem I've written since Rawiyya died. Go ahead and read the title."

I read, "'The Well,'" and then stumbled through the Hebrew, "'*At habe'er, venofeil letocheych.*'"

"Do you know what that means?"

"You are the well and I am falling into you?"

"Correct." He went on then, reciting the full poem from memory.

The Well

את הבאר ונופל לתוכך

From Shur to Haran
Your mothers stood
by silent wells
in rocky ground.
Eyes turned, they watched
to catch sight from afar
the beloved approach
to drink from their jars.
You stood
in ashes.
When I saw you, I fell
into you.
Falling still,
I sense the darkness
at your center.
Will you feed me there
Grow me in that dark place?
Will I become a lily,
twining upwards

To curl around the rosebud
Of your heart?
Will I fall like tears
honeydrops
on your eyelashes?
Or will I flow from your breasts
like milk?
Will your lips speak
with my voice?
And will God hear
and laugh?

I sat, speechless. "No one's ever written me a love poem before," I said, finally.

"Then I will write you more," said Yakub, and then he kissed me on the lips for the first time. I leaned towards him, and my hair fell in a curtain over him, releasing a fragrance of fresh flowers. He continued kissing me while pulling me down towards him. His chest felt bony, and his arms, wrapping around me, were strong. I smelled the familiar scent of cinnamon and lanolin, much stronger now up close.

After several minutes, respecting the place where we found ourselves, a sacred space for three faiths, we ended with just kisses.

My lips still burning, I asked Yakub, "What is *habibi?*"

"That is 'my dear,' or 'my beloved'".

"You are *habibi.*"

I felt his face against mine and his arms around me, and I felt his cheeks were wet. I heard him murmur in my ear. "I think we should get married."

"What?"

Yakub sat back. "You didn't hear me, *habibti?* I said I want to marry you."

I tried to speak, but I couldn't seem to make my speech apparatus work. Finally, I was able to say, "Yes."

"Yes what?" said Yakub, "Yes you did hear me, or yes you want to marry me?"

"Yes," I said, "I want to marry you!"

We laughed and hugged each other. .

Yakub said, "Where will we marry? I want to marry soon! Madrid? London?"

"I don't know!" The prospect seemed so fantastical, I

didn't even care about the details. "We'll think of something!" But then, that little nagging voice in my mind started up, and I said, "What about your family? Will they mind that you're marrying a Jew?"

This was a situation we had avoided discussing until now.

"This is a bit of a problem," I continued, "isn't it? Are you sure you want to do this?"

"Even our blessed prophet, Muhammad, married a Jewess," said Yakub.

"Really?"

"Yes. Her name was Safiyya."

"But I imagine she had to convert."

"Well, legend had it that she had already converted by the time she married Muhammad. But it is not required for a Jewish woman to convert when she marries a Muslim, as long as she is devout and the children are raised Muslim. Since, as you have told me, you cannot have children, this is not a problem in our case."

After this, we talked a long time, going over all the thousands of delicious details involved in arranging our wedding. Eventually, Yakub brought his bag over as a pillow, and we lay down on the floor, our arms wrapped around each other, and fell asleep.

After the ecstatic profession of new love, the nightmare that came to me was as discordant as it was horrible.

I dreamed that I was in this synagogue. Men in prayer shawls filled the space around me, and upstairs I could see the faces of women and children in the gallery. All at once, from outside, came the clamor of marching footsteps, the din of drum and trumpet. The doors flung open and in walked a group of men, several of them dressed in long white garments and black cloaks. One of the men held a large book in his hand. Beside him, I saw another man. He was all shriveled and disfigured, bent sideways like a comma. When this man turned around, I saw he had a lock of silver hair at the front of his forehead. Two guards wearing helmets and royal insignia on blue tunics stood by the door, full-length crosses flanking them.

The mis-shapen man whispered to the man with the book, who then spoke, his words wafting into the air like black mist. Then, they were both gone. Abruptly, two priests went and stood in front of an elderly man with a white beard and prayer shawl. They held a book out and gestured for him to place his hand upon it. Others in the synagogue pulled back and pressed towards the doorway, where the guards pushed them back, kicking and jabbing those who drew close. The man in the prayer shawl remained frozen, like a statue. A wild man wrapped in chains went and found a young boy in the crowd, not more than a toddler. He lifted him up to chest height, grasped him by his ankles, and in a quick motion, whipped him in an arc that smashed his head against the wall.

I awoke, a scream ringing in my ears. From the feeling in my throat, I judged it had been my own voice that had woken me up. Around me, the air of the synagogue was cold and silent. I lay gasping, struggling, suspended between dreaming and waking. At last, my mind fully surfaced from sleep, and I saw that Yakub was on his knees, his hand on my shoulder, his face close to mine.

"What is it, Rachel?" he said, alarm in his voice, "Are you ill?"

I swallowed to clear my throat. "A dream," I said, rubbing my eyes. "A terrible dream."

Yakub lay down again beside me, facing me, stroking my hair to comfort me.

"It's over now," he murmured as he continued to stroke my hair.

I nodded, my head against his chest, as I fell back asleep.

When I woke again, I was disoriented for a moment, not remembering where I was, nor why I felt such an odd mixture of dread and joy. The early-morning light was just entering the twelve windows of the synagogue. I looked at Yakub. His green eyes were open.

"Good morning, Rachel!" he said. "I have been up watching you sleep for the past forty five minutes, waiting for you to wake up so I could ask, 'Did I dream it, or did you really say you would marry me last night?'"

"I was just wondering the same thing!" I laughed, pushing remnants of the nightmare back down into my subconsciousness.

"You are alright this morning?" Yakub asked, "You have recovered from your bad dream?"

"Yes."

"What was it?"

I rolled onto my back and stared at the ceiling. The details of the dream were already receding. "I can't really remember."

Yakub kissed me then, and I felt that melting sensation in my center, more powerful even than I remembered. Reluctantly, after a moment, Yakub stopped kissing me, moving his lips to my cheek, and then leaning on an elbow and looking at me, brushing my hair back from my face with one tender hand. "*Insha Allah*, you will have only pleasant dreams from this point forward," he said, then sat up. "We should likely move back to the women's gallery soon, in case the caretaker comes early."

He stood and went over to the niche, looking down at the bronze plaque. He swept some dust over the top in an attempt to make it look undisturbed.

"We have to find that genizah," I said.

"David II's genizah?"

"Yes."

"Well, perhaps we'll find out something very soon about its location from the document we left with the research department at the library in Cambridge."

"But what if it doesn't say where it's located?"

"Faith, Rachel," said Yakub. "That is all we have."

With this somewhat dubious reassurance, we began to collect our bags and other evidence of our overnight sojourn. We then went upstairs and sat down amidst the broken letters.

Not long after, we heard the lock rattle, and both of us sat very still. We listened as someone came in downstairs. They clattered around a little bit, but didn't seem to notice anything amiss. The footsteps soon retreated back outside to the courtyard, the location of the ticket kiosk. Street noises came in through the open door. Sometime later, we heard the first visitors enter. Yakub and I crept down the stairs, mingling with and escaping several minutes later amidst a group of brightly-clad American tourists. Feeling free as birds, we flew down the street to the hotel.

When we arrived at the entrance to the hotel, we saw trouble. A police car was parked in the circular drive, light spinning. Mahmud stood beside a policeman along with Ruthie and the hotel desk clerk, who was translating. Poor Mahmud looked distraught. I realized how awful he must feel, believing he had lost his only remaining parent.

He was the first to catch sight of us. I wish I could have captured and bottled the joy that spilled from him when he saw us.

"Baba!" he called out, forgetting the police and running over to hug him. His outpouring of relief soon gave way to questions.

"Where were you, Baba!" he said, "We worried about you all night! And something terrible has happened!"

"What is it?" asked Yakub.

"While we were out swimming yesterday afternoon, we think someone came and broke into our hotel rooms!"

"Really? How do you know?" asked Yakub.

"The lock on Ruthie's room was broken, and some of your papers were disarranged, Baba. And also, you did not come home. We thought you'd been kidnapped." Mahmud turned to me. "Where were you?" he said.

"Uhhhh…" I said, not sure how to answer this. I didn't want the police to know we'd spent the night in the synagogue, no matter how noble our cause might seem to us.

"We'll talk about that later," said Yakub, answering on my behalf. "First, let's relieve this police officer of his concerns."

He went to talk to the policeman, speaking through the Spanish translator. The man peppered him with questions then suddenly gave a great guffaw and looked over at me. He closed up his notepad and got into his car, patting Yakub on the back and shaking his hand. He drove away, giving me a nod and a little salute on the way.

"What did you say to him?" I asked.

"I told him I asked you to marry me," said Yakub, loud enough for everyone to hear, "and that we spent the night in…suitable fashion, celebrating."

"Yakub!" I said.

Mahmud was now frowning. "Is this true, Baba?" he said.

"Not entirely but mostly," Yakub said, *sotto voce*. "You and I will talk later."

Ruthie was giving me the hand signal for 'A-OK!'

I rolled my eyes. "Oh brother."

"Show me what happened to our hotel rooms," urged Yakub.

Mahmud led us back to our rooms, walking ahead of us silently, his bearing stiff and disapproving.

Ruthie, on the other hand was full of questions. "Is it true?" she asked. "Are you really getting married?"

Yakub laughed happily and said, "Yes, that part is true." He leaned closer to her, in a pantomime of whispering, but in reality speaking loud enough for Mahmud to overhear. "The other part, about spending the night together in sin, is factitious."

"Really?" said Mahmud, stopping and turning around.

"Yes!" laughed Yakub. "The reality is, we got ourselves locked in the Cordoba Synagogue overnight. This is not something I chose to admit to our friendly local police officer."

A wide smile split Mahmud's face. "That's good!" Mahmud turned to me now, bowing slightly and saying with some formality, "I am so pleased you will be joining our family! *Masha'Allah* – blessed is Allah! And Baba, *insha Allah*, you will find peace now after the death of our mother. I wish you much happiness." Mahmud leaned over and kissed his father on the cheek.

"So!" said Yakub, clapping his hands together and beginning to walk once again, "We will marry! It remains only to determine when and where!"

"Baba, you are completely *majnun!* Crazy!"

"Crazy with love!" said Yakub.

"In Yiddish," Ruthie said, "they call it *mashoogena!* So how about if we call Rachel *Mashoogena* and smiley-face over here *Majnun*. Sound good to you?"

"Sure!" I said.

"Tell me about this burglary," said Yakub, coming back to reality as we approached our rooms.

"The policeman you spoke with took a report," answered Mahmud. "But given that nothing valuable was stolen, and the two of you were not, after all, abducted, *al-hamdu lillah*, I doubt he will spend much time investigating this."

"Who do you think it was?" asked Ruthie. "They didn't take any money or any of my jewelry. Only the locks were busted."

Arriving at our hotel room, Yakub said. "Well, let's have a look."

I searched around and, as Ruthie had indicated, found nothing missing.

When we reached Yakub and Mahmud's room, we found a locksmith working on the door. Yakub looked through his papers. Everything seemed in order.

The locksmith finished his job and packed up his tools. Before leaving, he demonstrated the working lock, and then he left, calling a cheery *adios*.

I sat down on the bed, torn between elation and worry.

"Okay, you two," said Ruthie, looking back and forth between me and Yakub, her hands on her hips. I could tell a scolding was coming. "From now on, no more flying solo. After this break-in, not to mention the prank played in Cambridge by that anti-Semitic creep, we're in this together! Okay? So any sleuthing you do, I'm coming along. Got me?"

I nodded. "I never could win an argument with you."

"You got that right! Anyway, did you guys find anything in the synagogue? Or was it just lovey-dovey all night long?"

Yakub laughed. "We did make a discovery." Yakub described the box and the note, and gave a brief synopsis of our other discoveries in the Cambridge Library, including the existence of David II Maimonides's genizah.

"So you're at a dead end now?" said Ruthie.

"Not exactly," I said. "We just have to find that genizah."

"Oh. Only that," laughed Ruthie. "A task at which the experts have failed, thus far. What are your chances?"

"Fair to good, I would say," said Yakub. "Rachel, can you check if anything has come to your e-mail from our librarian?"

"Sure!" I stood up. "I'll go get my computer."

I went back across the hall to my room, returning in a moment with my MacBook. We waited impatiently as it booted up. Finally, the desktop appeared. I signed into the hotel wireless for an hour of connectivity, then double-clicked on my e-mail program.

I watched as it downloaded my messages, all hundred and forty-seven of them. Mid-way down the list was a message from my fax provider, a small clip beside it signaling an attachment.

"Here it is!" I said excitedly, opening the message and double-clicking on the paperclip. The document reader program opened, and I saw a cover letter from Margaret Tibbs. I read aloud:

"My dear genizah detectives: it appears you have hit treasure once again, as you will see upon viewing the attached document. You were, of course, correct about the existence of a second page, attached to the one listing the contents of the private genizah of David II Maimonides. And you will be pleased to hear exactly what this third page contains: *a map!* With that, I give you my best wishes for the success of your endeavor. Margaret Tibbs, Chief Librarian, Taylor-Schechter Genizah Collection, Cambridge University Library.

PS - My apologies, but I have not been able to further research the source of the prank involving the distasteful pamphlet, whose title I will not mention here. My assistant, Eugene, has been inexplicably absent from work these past two days. I will keep you apprised of any additional information that may come to light on this matter."

"What's with the assistant?" I wondered, clicking on the small arrow leading to the next page of the attachment. "That seems very odd. Do you think he might be the one who put the *Protocols* in the box?"

"It does strike me as suspicious," said Yakub.

"Maybe I should suggest this to Margaret Tibbs. I think I'll e-mail her."

But the thought was completely driven from my mind as a ghostly diagram sprang into view on my screen. Containing a number of squares and lines, buildings and roads, as I deduced, I saw that it was, indeed, a map. And there, in the very center, the treasure hunter's apex experience: a large black X.

X marks the spot!

"Yakub!"

He was three steps ahead of me already, leaning down next to me and peering at my computer screen. "May I?" he said.

"Absolutely!" I vacated my seat so he could look more closely.

"It is Judeo-Arabic, once again," he said. He grabbed the pen and phone pad on the desk, and began transcribing the words. It took him only a few minutes, since there was not much writing on the page, just a couple of lines at the top. When he was done, he sat looking at what he'd written.

"What does it say?" asked Mahmud.

"*For safe-keeping, I assign these books to the following location, until such time as it may be God's will that I return. David ben Joshua Maimuni, Aviv, Year of 158.*"

I did the calculations. "That's the year 5158 in the Jewish calendar, so it would be five years after Rivkah's note."

Yakub was still peering at the computer screen, examining the map in closer detail. In one of the large boxes, I saw the Hebrew letters *beit-kaf-beit-aleph*. In a smaller box nearby, the words *bayt ha-nagid*, which I knew meant "house of the nagid" in English.

"This must be a location in Fustat, since that is where the Nagid lived," said Yakub. He began sounding out the Hebrew letters, trying out words to fit. "Bayt, bayt..k...bayt Knesset...Bayt Knesset Ben Ezra! *Al-Hamdu Lillah!*"

"What?" I said.

"It's the synagogue where the Genizah was located, in old Cairo!"

"But that 'X' is outside the synagogue." I said. "Wasn't the Genizah inside?"

"Yes. But this is good news! We know the Genizah itself has been emptied. But our 'little genizah,' as we might call David II Maimonides' genizah, for simplicity," he pointed to the screen, "may still exist! And..." he stood up abruptly, "we must go there!"

"Wha..." I stammered.

"Yes!" Yakub clapped his hands together. He went to the phone and started dialing.

"What are you doing?" asked Ruthie.

"Calling Tatianne," he said. "We have to cancel our plans for the afternoon, and instead travel to Cairo. Tatianne will make the arrangements for us."

As he waited for her to answer her phone, Yakub turned to me, his face alight. "We will marry in Cairo!" He laughed a happy laugh. "I suggest you go and pack!"

A half hour later, we hauled our roller duffels out to the lobby, where Tatianne was waiting with Mahmud and Yakub. They had told her about our night in the Cordoba Synagogue and the room burglary, and also the news of our engagement and impending marriage. Tatianne gave me a huge hug, congratulating me.

"You have made me very happy today!" she said, kissing me on both cheeks.

Tatianne had arranged for us to travel the following day to Cairo. Today, we'd return to Madrid from Cordoba on the high-speed train. She rode over with us in the taxi to the train station so she could help us navigate the ticket change.

In the cab, Yakub described what we had found in the synagogue. "I don't know how, my dear, but you must somehow pass on to the synagogue owners that the plaque in the niche conceals something other than bones."

"And tell them that my American friends were just doing a little minor grave-digging, eh?" She laughed. "I will think of something. But perhaps I will not tell them yet, eh, Yakub? Not until the two of you are *acabado*, finished with your quest. This burglary, these people who follow you, they do not sound, how do you say in your English idiom, above the board."

Yakub laughed and nodded. "I'm afraid you're right."

"You will let me know when you find these poems?" she said. "Promise me!"

"Yes," Yakub promised. "Of course we will."

At the Cordoba train station, Tatianne arranged our ticket changes, then kissed and hugged us all goodbye one by one.

When she got to me, after letting go of her embrace, she grasped my arm and whispered in my ear. "You must be careful. This one has been hurt badly." She pointed to Yakub. "His wife, Rawiyya, she was a beeootiful woman. A soul with great *bendición*, blessing. You have blessing too. But love him strongly, eh? You will do that?" Tatianne had tears in her eyes.

Without smiling, I said, "Yes, I will. Very strongly."

"*Bueno.* That is very good."

We got on the train and headed back to Madrid.

London, England
9:00 pm. Thursday, December 21ˢᵗ 2006
Mr. Smith, to Eugene Smith (journal entry)

Once again, I am not well! My stomach cramps and I vomit up my food. Soon, I will waste away to nothing!

But my physical ailments are of no concern, my son! What wonderful news you have given me tonight! And now, you are on your way to Cairo and, dare I hope, the final leg of our four-thousand-year-old journey!

Oh, I delight to hear your stories of how you outwitted our friends, the poetic quartet! Following them to Spain, breaking into their hotel room, managing to hide yourself away in the radiator cabinet while they discussed their ill-fated plans. What a stroke of genius that was, and they never even suspected you were there!

I can hardly believe that our "friends" had the dull-wittedness to get themselves locked in the Cordoba Synagogue overnight. But even so, there seems to be no end to their vicarious good fortune, as they've discovered a box that once contained the *diwan* that we have been seeking, a goal which had eluded us these many years. We have long suspected that the *diwan* of Said al-Shadi contains, if not *the poem* itself, then the final clues to those intent on creating it. Once we destroy it, the al-Shadi's will have to start from scratch again, and I'm convinced that conditions will never again be favorable, as they were at the time of intersection of the great faiths in the court of Abd al-Rahman III in the Golden Age. No, our own plans to bring the Armageddon will certainly succeed long before any such collaborative understanding might occur.

How interesting and illustrative that the current *al-Shadi's* ill-fated wife died in the terrorist attacks in Madrid. A perfect example of our methods, demonstrating that our labors, though distant from the hand that lights the bomb fuse, still result in the death of our adversaries! Yes, our efforts among the fundamentalist Muslims have been remarkably fertile, and sure to bear more fruit in the future.

And apt, as well, that you returned to the place, Castille, where your ancestors once enjoyed such unmitigated success, where your forefathers trod the paths of righteousness, influencing those in the Catholic Church at the very highest levels! Yes, the truth is that their counsel to the church fathers incited the entire Iberian campaign, resulting in the conversion of over a hundred thousand infidels, Ishmaelites, and Jews, and the claiming of countless mosques and synagogues in the name of the church, particularly in the year of 1391. I would even credit the later expulsion of the Jews in 1492 to the after-effects of these efforts! I trust you enjoyed meeting his descendents there, in Cordoba? You will have to give me full details upon your return from Cairo. As I'm sure you will, in triumph, once you have found and destroyed the *diwan* we have so long sought, and with it, any hope of salvation for the masses.

Ah, Cairo! How apt the destination! How ironic and appropriate that the destruction of hope for the Jews should occur in the land of their oppression, the place from which they feel, in error, they have been redeemed! But God, in His goodness, works in poetic ways in all that He does.

As for the radiator burns you received during your concealment in the room of al-Shadi, I have suggested you use sheep's balm to sooth the sting and facilitate their healing, as I have done many times myself, with the burns inflicted by my father during my education. These and other pearls of wisdom I will continue to impart to you, until such time as God sees fit to take me from this world.

Cairo, Egypt
Morning of Friday, December 22nd 2006
Dr. Rachel Roseman, Prof. Yakub al-Shadi, et al

We left Madrid on Friday, boarding an early Alitalia flight heading East to Cairo, where we planned to spend the next four days. Tomorrow, we would explore the destination on our treasure map, near the Ben Ezra Synagogue, seeking the *diwan* of Said al-Shadi, and perhaps the poems of Mrs. Dunash as well. Sunday, we would marry. After that, who knew what fate would bring? Tentatively, Yakub and Mahmud were to leave for Makkah on Tuesday to perform the *Hajj*, and Ruthie and I would also head out on our own pilgrimage to Israel. But perhaps our plans would be interrupted. Yakub would find his clue, the key to unlock his creative powers of redemption, and thus create the poem to redeem the world. Or that was how I saw it, anyway.

Yakub had spent some time on the phone the night before, arranging for our wedding. Apparently, there were quite a few legal papers to be drafted and appointments to be made, but a lawyer friend of Yakub's cousin, Kareem, assured Yakub that he could take care of it all by Sunday. The reception would be at Yakub's Aunt Rima's house in Islamic Cairo.

On the plane to Egypt, I sat next to Yakub, Ruthie and Mahmud occupying the seats across the aisle. Despite the early hour, they were already engrossed in their scientific papers. Yakub and I talked about the plans for our wedding, held hands, and dozed, still recovering from our long night in the Cordoba Synagogue.

We changed planes in Milan, where I spent the two-hour layover exploring the duty-free shops. In the large, otherworldly shopping space at the center of the terminal, I found a bookstore selling many books in English, including, tucked away in a hidden corner of non-fiction, a paperback titled "The New Jewish

Wedding," by American author Anita Diamant. I purchased this book with my American Express card, tucking it away in my carry-on bag. Whatever happened in Cairo, I knew it would not be a "Jewish" wedding. Nonetheless, I wanted to see if there wasn't some tradition I could incorporate, something to tie me in to the traditions of my mother. My wedding to David, though we were both theoretically "Jewish," had been a completely secular affair, performed by a judge at my parent's house in New York. This time would be different.

I rejoined Yakub, Ruthie, and Mahmud at the gate, and together we boarded our plane, then flew across the Mediterranean to Cairo. As the plane descended, I thought I caught a glimpse of the pyramids, on the far side of an enormous river. It was a little after 3:00 pm, and the rays of the sun were becoming oblique, lending a golden glow to the city skyline.

Yakub and Mahmud still had active Egyptian passports, but Ruthie and I required tourist visas to enter the country. This turned out to be a surprisingly simple process, involving waiting in line at the visa office, and then showing our American passports and paying a fee. After we'd taken care of this, we collected our bags and went through customs, which took us another twenty minutes. By the time we came outside, it was late afternoon.

Yakub's cousin, Kareem, was there waiting for us at the curbside in an ancient blue Volvo station wagon. The air was warm and humid, but not excessively hot. The two men embraced, and Yakub introduced us. Kareem was dressed in western clothing of khakis and button-down shirt, and looked to be about the same age as Yakub. As we got in the car, I noticed him surreptitiously examining me. This made me uneasy. How would Yakub's family feel about me, a Jew?

Kareem did not speak any English, and my Arabic was far too rudimentary for real conversation. Furthermore, what little I did know was Modern Standard Arabic, not the Egyptian dialect spoken by Kareem. I knew just a few greeting words, however, so I decided I'd try them out.

"*Izayyak!*" I ventured, after Ruthie, Mahmud, and I had settled ourselves into the back seat. How are you?

Looking amused, Kareem turned his head slightly, saying, "*Kwayis! W'inti? Izayyik?*" I am well. And you?

"*Kwayisa, al-hamdu lillah!*" I am well, thanks to God!

Kareem laughed, turning back to Yakub and speaking to him in rapid Arabic.

Yakub said, "Kareem is pleased that I'm training you so well! Little does he know that I have nothing to do with it!"

"Yeah, right!" I said.

We had now navigated the busy airport access road and were heading out on a larger boulevard towards Cairo. It seemed to me that half the cars in Egypt must be on this highway. We inched along, side-by-side with an assortment of ancient, dented automobiles and buses stacked to their ceilings with people and luggage. Beside the road, there were only a few scraggly shrubs and trees with scattered yellowed and brittle leaves.

"Kareem tells me that it has been very dry," remarked Yakub. "The city is on water rations."

It took us forty-five minutes to travel the twenty-five kilometers to the city. As we drove, Yakub pointed out the landmarks: "Over there is Sadat's tomb! And there, in that area of town is the place I first moved with my father and mother when we came to Cairo! And here…it is the section of town we call Islamic Cairo." I saw a distinctive skyline of rounded domes and pointy minarets, their tips rimmed in green light in the early twilight.

I was transfixed by the Arabic writing all around, on road signs and storefronts, the sides of vans, billboards. I found myself sounding out the words as we passed by, though I had little idea of what they meant. I noticed Kareem still watching me in the rear-view mirror. Soon after we passed the ancient citadel, which Yakub informed us was constructed by the great emperor, Salah al-Din, in the twelfth century, we turned off at a large boulevard heading towards the Nile River, Salah Salem Street. When we reached the river, we turned right onto a street called Corniche al-Nil. In the darkening blue of the early evening sky, the lights on the far side of the river sparkled, appearing very far away.

We continued several kilometers north along the Nile, passing hotels as we went, eventually turning into the circular drive in front of a curved glass tower.

"What hotel is this?" I asked.

"I have booked reservations for you and Ruthie at the Four Seasons," Yakub explained. "I thought you would be comfortable here. And, I have a friend in the hotel's management who has given us a special rate. He will make sure you are well taken care of.

Mahmud and I will be staying at my Aunt Rima's house."

A uniformed valet attendant opened my door and a bellhop removed our luggage from the back, placing it on a rolling cart. Yakub accompanied Ruthie and me into a large lobby, tiled completely in marble. He attended us as we checked in, then turned to me, saying,

"So, perhaps you and Ruthie will dine in one of the hotel restaurants tonight, then have an early bedtime? Mahmud and I will be back in the morning for our excursion. What do you think? Around 8:00 am?"

"Excursion?" said Ruthie.

"Can you remind Ruthie where we're going?" I suggested.

"But of course! To the place where 'X' marks the spot! The Ben Ezra Synagogue, in Fustat, old Cairo!"

"Won't they be having services tomorrow?" wondered Ruthie. "It's Saturday. Shabbat!"

Yakub shook his head ruefully. "Alas, they no longer hold services at the Ben Ezra Synagogue. There are very few Jews left in Cairo today. The site has become a destination for visitors interested in the famous Genizah and in the history of our ancient city, which began in Fustat."

The bellhop was beginning to look impatient, glancing at his watch and gazing out the door.

"Well," said Yakub. "So. I will meet you, down here in the lobby, at eight am sharp. We will take the Metro to Fustat in the morning. Oh, and here." Yakub handed me a number of Egyptian Pounds and pointed out an ATM machine across the lobby. "You may want to stop there sometime."

Yakub bid us goodbye, remaining formal, with only a wave of the hand now, since we were in a public place in a predominantly Muslim country and were, as yet, unmarried.

Ruthie and I followed the bellhop to the elevator and ascended to the twenty-third floor. Our room was a one bedroom suite. On the table was a plate of fruit and cheese, including, perched on its edge, a small envelope and a card from Yakub's friend assuring us that he would do everything possible to make our stay comfortable.

I gave the bellhop a tip, hardly noticing as he said his goodbyes, my eyes so blinded by the view. Below, the Nile sparkled darkly, dotted with boats and barges with gay lights and, in the distance, a dark bulk against the late twilight sky, three triangular shapes. The Great Pyramids of Giza.

Ruthie and I plunked down in the easy chairs, our gaze fixed on the breathtaking view. After a few minutes, I went to get my small carry-on bag. I removed my travel candlesticks, two candles, and a book of matches. I lit the candles and, together, Ruthie and I said the blessings of Shabbat.

Cairo, Egypt
Morning of Shabbat, December 23rd 2006
Dr. Rachel Roseman

Saturday morning, very early, I woke and realized I had a minor problem. The map that Margaret Tibbs had faxed to me was still in electronic form on the hard drive of my computer. It would be very inconvenient to carry the laptop around with us, and it could also be difficult to see the map on the computer screen in the glare of daylight. On the other hand, I didn't want to send the map to the fax machine at the front desk, allowing the clerk on duty to see its mysteriously alluring contents.

I got up quietly to avoid waking Ruthie and snooped around the hotel room in the semi-dark, my bare feet noiseless on the thick Berber carpet. After a brief interval of searching, I found what I was looking for: an in-room fax. I checked the fax number, then turned on the computer, connected to the wireless network, and sent myself a fax of the map. Four copies.

Afterwards, I sat on the couch in the living room, gazing out the window at the lightening sky and holding the maps in my hand, thinking to myself, *would the world be redeemed by a fax?*

Several minutes later, I went to wake up Ruthie, taking her at her word that she wanted to participate in our treasure-hunt, accompanying us on our expedition to yet another synagogue. I prayed we could stay out of trouble this time.

After we ate some continental breakfast and got dressed, we headed down the elevators, stopping at the ATM machine before looking around for Yakub.

He and Mahmud were sitting in a small alcove near the entryway, a silver coffee pot on the table in front of them. They were both dressed in short-sleeve button-down shirts and khakis, which appeared to be the standard dress for male al-Shadi family members here in Cairo. Both of them looked fresh and ready for a day of adventure. Seeing Yakub after the overnight separation sent a thrill into me that stopped and lodged somewhere low in my abdomen. When he saw me, a large smile blossomed on his face.

"Rachel!" he said.

We headed out the front door, walking the broad tree-lined streets towards an open square, the Midan Tahrir, a park with surrounding hotels and impressive government buildings. Several men wearing caftans and *kufis* approached us in the street, asking if we would like tea or coffee, but Yakub brushed them off with a few polite words in Arabic.

"They are trying to get you into their shops," explained Yakub. "We don't have time for that right now."

Adjacent to the central plaza of the Midan Tahrir, we descended into the Sadat station, already busy on this early Saturday morning. We purchased our tickets, waiting several minutes for the subway to arrive. The station was remarkably clean and well-tended, as was the subway train itself, a sleek modern affair with an orange stripe along its side. The car was crowded, since Saturday was a regular workday here in Egypt, but we were able to find space together, standing holding onto the vertical metal rails as we sped out of the station and into the tunnel. After several stations, we arrived at Mar Girgis.

There, we descended from the subway, finding ourselves on an open station platform drenched with sunlight. We ascended a flight to the street, entering a large boulevard facing the wall of an ancient city. "This," said Yakub, gesturing at the church domes and spires across the street, "is Coptic Cairo!"

We began walking towards the northern entrance. Once through the gate, we navigated past a convent then down to a large garden outside the Greek Orthodox Church of St. George, a circular building which, Yakub told us, was built on the ruins of an ancient Roman tower.

As we walked, Yakub described to us the history of Coptic Cairo, also known as Fustat. "This is the earliest site of settlement in Cairo, some dating it back to 600 BCE. It became a Roman outpost before the time of Christ, called 'Babylon in Egypt.' There, you see remnants of another Roman tower." He pointed south, where a round tower was visible. "There is another entrance there, but the museum is under construction, so we cannot enter that way just now.

"It is really rather incredible how much sacred history and tradition there is concentrated into this one small section of town! This is where the early Christians fled from persecution by the Romans and where the first Christian church in Egypt was built. Before that, it is said that Mary, Jesus, and Joseph travelled here during the times of Herod the Great, when they were forced to flee to Egypt for safety. Believe it or not, but the religious history predates even that, for here along the banks of the Nile is reputedly where Pharaoh's daughter rescued Moses from the bulrushes."

As Yakub spoke, we walked through a large open garden, afterwards navigating narrow streets towards the synagogue. "Across the way, outside the walls," Yakub continued, "is where you will find the site of the Amr ibn al-As Mosque, which was established at the first conquest of Egypt by Islam in 640 CE, not long after the death of the prophet, Muhammad, peace and blessings upon him."

Ruthie said, "It is amazing that all of these things took place in this one small area of town!"

"Yes," agreed Yakub, "and equally amazing is the Ben Ezra Synagogue, where the Genizah was discovered in the late eighteen hundreds."

"What is that?" asked Ruthie, "A genizah?"

I explained, "It's a place where Jewish people store all their old books and written correspondence. Since written Hebrew is felt to be sacred, in particular the letters composing the name of God, we don't just throw the writing out in the garbage. And this genizah here apparently remained undisturbed for something like a thousand years, right Yakub?"

"Yes, that's right!"

Mahmud said, "But why? Knowing the value of many of the ancient sacred documents, I would think the Genizah would have been plundered by thieves!"

"Ah!" said Yakub, "But you see, there was a legend that the room of the Genizah was protected by an ancient curse, and that this curse took shape in the form of a giant snake who would attack any who entered!"

I shuddered. "A giant snake?"

"I hate snakes," said Ruthie, echoing my thought.

"It appears you both have at least one thing in common with Indiana Jones!" laughed Yakub.

We had now reached the entrance to the synagogue. It was a small, square building, its main entrance on the west side, a second entrance on the south side, accessible through a stairway and bridge. The entire building was surrounded by a high wall. As we entered, Yakub removed the faxed rendition of the map. The three of us also took ours out.

I peered at the map, trying to get my bearings. "It looks like the 'X' is around the back," I said. We walked along the side of the building, passing under the bridge to the upstairs entrance.

"Hmph" said Yakub.

"What?" I said.

"I believe the 'X' is *outside* of this wall." He pointed to the wall in front of us. Of recent construction, it appeared far too high to scale. "It would help if we had a modern map."

"Maybe they have one inside the synagogue?" I suggested.

We retraced our steps to the front of the synagogue and entered the building. Inside, it was cool and quiet, with just a few other visitors at this early hour. A caretaker greeted us. Yakub spoke with him briefly and the man went in the back. As we waited, I peeked into the synagogue. It was quite beautiful, the *bima* in the center and the Holy Ark with the Torah scrolls at the end of the room. Around the upper walls was a balcony, the women's gallery I presumed, enclosed by marble pillars and spacious arches. At the end, on the left side, was a ladder leading up to a door in the wall. I recognized this from photos at the library in Cambridge.

"Look!" I called to the others, "The Genizah!"

"Yes," said Yakub. "Completely empty now."

"Is the snake still there?" said Ruthie, joking but a little spooked all the same.

The caretaker returned with several brochures, saying in English, "No! No snake! Do not worry!"

He handed us the brochures. Yakub thanked him and we all went back outside.

"From the looks of the map in this brochure, we need to skirt the walls of the synagogue and find the Greek Catholic Graveyard," said Yakub. I followed him as he walked back out the gate. He was analyzing his brochure, and called out, "Look at this!

It's a map of the synagogue dating from the medieval period! The 'X' seems to correspond with the perimeter of a house outside the Roman wall, listed as the *Dar al-Nagid*. Do you know what that is, Rachel?"

"No!"

"That means 'house of the Nagid! From the end of the twelfth century up until the early fifteenth century, this is where the Maimonides family would have lived! Its location corresponds with the house drawn on our own map."

"That is really cool!" I said, thinking of the famous doctor whose statue we'd seen only two days before, the first successful synthesizer of Jewish faith, philosophy, and science, not to mention physician to the family of the great Muslim leader, Salah al-Din, and great-great-great grandfather to the author of the map we held. He had lived right here!

We were now skirting back along the wall of the synagogue. Ahead of us, we saw a cemetery with many ornate crypts and crosses. We entered and, once inside, headed back the way we had come, encouraged to see the roof of the synagogue over the wall ahead of us. I kept my eyes glued to the ground in order to avoid treading on the top of anyone's grave. There was no sign of any remaining Maimonides house at the corner where the two walls met.

Yakub looked around for a moment to get his bearings, then said: "So our 'X' must be"…he walked back to the corner of the cemetery walls, then strode in measured steps, counting, ten east, twenty-five south. He stopped. Where he stood, there was a small rectangular stone sarcophagus, unmarked. It looked like the coffin of a small child.

"Yakub!" I said, alarmed.

"Don't worry, it's not a grave," he assured me.

"How do you know?"

"There are no markings anywhere. No one would bury someone without a monument of some kind. And also, David II Maimonides," he pointed to the map, "has told us that this is a genizah."

"Maybe we're wrong about the location? Or maybe the gravestone fell off?" I said. No one answered me.

Yakub looked around, scouting out our surroundings to assess our next steps. Far across the cemetery, there was a canopy erected over what must be an open gravesite. Though the funeral had not yet begun, we saw several people, likely attendants, moving around the site in preparation. There was also a lone mourner, wearing caftan and head covering, kneeling at a grave about a hundred yards away.

"What we seek is interred in this sarcophagus," said Yakub, with certainty.

"So what should we do?" I asked. "We surely can't be grave-robbing in broad daylight."

Yakub put his hands on the stone lid of the sarcophagus. It was about four inches thick and covered in lichen. He gave a tentative shove, testing its resistance. It budged not the slightest.

Sighing, he removed his hands, brushing them off against the pants over his thighs. "We will have to come back in the dark at another time, bring a couple of strong men to help with the lid. Likely, we will need to bribe the cemetery guard as well."

"Aunt Rima knows a lot of people in Cairo," said Mahmud. "Maybe she can find someone to help us."

Yakub nodded. "An excellent idea. Let's talk to her and see if we can work this out."

"How much money will you need, to bribe the guard?" I asked.

"Hmmm. I don't know. I suppose it could be considerable," frowned Yakub.

"We can help," I said. "We'll get some more money out of the ATM at the hotel. Pool our funds."

"Yes, sure!" said Ruthie. "I'm good for that!"

"Excellent!" said Yakub.

"So what do we do now?" I said.

Yakub looked at me and Ruthie. "There is not much we can do at this point, likely not until after the wedding."

I nodded, and suddenly this idea erased all other thoughts from my mind, and I couldn't prevent a big smile from blooming on my face.

"Perhaps we should return to the hotel, have an early lunch along the way. Afterwards, perhaps the two of you would like to go shopping for the wedding? Do you need to buy anything?"

I thought of the wrinkled clothes, the assortment of sweat pants, running shorts, t-shirts, and jeans, along with the single purple velvet dress I had brought along. "I definitely need to go shopping."

Yakub clapped his hands together, rubbing them, saying, "Good! Let us return to the metro station. We'll have some lunch, then you two can go to the mall. Meanwhile, Mahmud and I will talk with Rima to see if she can help arrange to get us into the graveyard after hours. Once we've spoken with her, we'll have some idea of the cost, and Mahmud and I can stop at the bank to get some cash ourselves."

"Perfect!" I said.

The four of us walked back across the graveyard and out the gated entrance. The single mourner continued to kneel by the gravesite in solemn contemplation as we left the cemetery.

Engrossed in our own personal thoughts, the four of us retraced our steps back to the Mar Girgis Station. My mind returned to the sarcophagus in the Greek graveyard. I tried to picture what might be inside. Books, I hoped, plenty of books, and not a decomposed corpse. Soon, however, my thoughts jumped back to the wedding. *What would I wear? I needed a ring for Yakub…*

As we waited for the metro to arrive, I noticed the visitor we'd seen in the graveyard enter the station and stand down the platform. I looked at him and nodded a greeting. He nodded back then looked away. I wondered who he'd been grieving for back at the cemetery.

After returning to the Sadat station, we made our way back towards the hotel, stopping to eat lunch together in the pleasant shaded garden of a restaurant Yakub knew from his youth in Cairo. At the hotel, Ruthie and I each withdrew $500 from the ATM and handed it over to Yakub for the bribe money. He and Mahmud then left us to attend to their afternoon chore of organizing what seemed disturbingly much like a grave robbery. Before leaving, Yakub asked if we could meet him at the lobby tomorrow, 11:00 am. We'd go from there to begin the series of visits to official offices which would culminate in our marriage.

Ruthie and I went back to our room to drop off our backpacks, then headed out on our afternoon shopping expedition. The hotel concierge pointed us toward an excellent shopping mall within walking distance, and we spent the afternoon there, purchasing my wedding clothes, a new dress for Ruthie, and a ring for Yakub. I also replaced my decades-old frayed cotton underwear with more alluring silk and lace, perplexed to find that the recent decrease in running and increase in intake of rich food had caused my bra to go up two sizes. We found a beauty salon, where they trimmed my hair. It was dark and straight, and the way it swung in an arc across my back after they'd cut it made me feel like an Egyptian princess.

On the way back to the hotel, a light rain began to fall. I pulled my travel umbrella out of my purse, and Ruthie and I shared it, bowing our heads together and hurrying through the remaining two blocks to the Four Seasons. As we walked, Ruthie said to me, "Rachel, I'm so glad you've found someone. I thought you might never get over David. I was worried about you being alone."

"Well," I said, "I'd always have you!"

"Yes," said Ruthie, "that's true. But even though it's corny to say, a woman needs someone to love."

I laughed, marveling to myself how often corny things turned out to be true.

Back at our room at the Four Seasons, Ruthie and I checked the room service menu and ordered dinner. While we waited for it to arrive, we laid out all our newly-bought treasures on the coffee table, draping the clothes along the back of the couch where we could look at them. After dinner, to the sound of the steadily-falling rain, I opened Anita Diamant's book on the "New Jewish Wedding" and read it long into the night.

Later, while Ruthie slept, I also did a little research on the internet. Afterwards, I went into the bathroom, where I cut my nails very short and took a long bath, washing my hair and scrubbing myself with soapy water until every last inch of me was sparkling clean.

LOVE

Cairo, Egypt
Morning of Sunday, December 24ᵗʰ 2006 (Wedding Day)
Dr. Rachel and Ruthie Roseman

Early the next morning, long before dawn, the bedside alarm woke us, and together Ruthie and I dressed in t-shirt, sweatpants, and flip-flops, making our way quietly through the deserted hallways and up several flights of stairs to the rooftop swimming pool. There, we found that the rain from the night before had tapered off, leaving puddles of water on the pavement by the pool. The stars sparkled on their surfaces, and a ghostly crescent of moon hung in the space above the nearby buildings.

The internet research I'd done the prior evening had revealed that there was no working "mikveh," that is, Jewish immersion pool, anywhere in Cairo right now. However, while a mikveh was required by Jewish law to have a source of natural water, I had also discovered that it was acceptable to use a swimming pool for ritual immersion if no other option was available.

I had briefly considered doing my bridal mikveh in the waters of the mighty Nile River, which flowed by, in massive silence, just yards from the hotel where we stayed. I'd decided against it, however, recalling from my medical school days that the river was the source of a dangerous form of parasitic infection called Schistosomiasis, hardly an auspicious start for a wedding. Furthermore, I was exceedingly doubtful that we could attain the privacy required of a naked immersion in the public waters of a city of seventeen million people, regardless of the hour. The rooftop pool, almost certainly deserted at this time of day, and, by luck of fate, recently replenished by a supply of fresh rainwater, seemed a perfect, though admittedly less dramatic, option.

Next to the pool, there were a series of private cabanas, complete with shower, and we entered one of these. There, I removed my clothes and showered once again, scrubbing carefully in order to remove any last remaining dirt or grime that might separate my skin from the purifying waters of the mikveh. When I exited the shower, Ruthie handed me a towel, and I dried off. She then turned me away from her and began to brush my hair, carefully teasing the brush through until all the strands were straight and untangled. After this, she asked me to remove the towel, and I let it drop to the floor. She examined my back, and I felt her remove several stray hairs. I then took off my earrings and rings, placing them on a counter. I draped the towel around me once again, and we left the cabana.

Outside, we stood together beneath the stars and moon. Ruthie took the towel from around my shoulders, and I felt the air on all the naked surfaces of my body. I entered the water and, taking a deep breath, I submerged completely, allowing the water to touch every inch of skin, every strand of hair.

Surfacing, I released the air in my lungs and recited the Hebrew blessing, "Praised are you, Adonai, God of all creation, who sanctifies us with your commandments and commanded us concerning immersion."

I submerged one more time. This time, I floated below the surface, noting the sensation of the water on my skin. Opening my eyes, I felt the cold against the margins of my eyelids, saw the lapis lazuli blue of the water. "Here I am, God," I thought to myself. "Here I am." In answer, I heard the living silence of the water pulsing against my eardrums.

When the oxygen in my lungs ran out, I surfaced again, drew in more air, and repeated the blessing one more time. I then placed my hands on the concrete pavement by the pool and lifted myself out of the water.

Ruthie held the towel up, and I pulled it close around me. Between chattering teeth, I said my final prayer, called the *Shehecheyanu,* a special prayer recited at times of firsts and special events, such as weddings: "Blessed are You, Lord our God, Ruler of the Universe, who kept us alive and preserved us and enabled us to reach this time."

Ruthie gave me a giant hug, and we went back in to the cabana, where I showered one last time and put my clothes back on.

Afterwards, we sat in silence on pool chairs by the water, listening as the city of Cairo woke up: first, the Muslim call to prayer, then the increasing boat traffic on the river, and finally, the honking of horns and traffic along the Corniche. When we stood to leave, the sun was just coming up, huge and white, rising above the buildings to the east to join the moon as it descended to the horizon beyond the river to the West.

Back at our room, I ordered breakfast, and as we ate, Ruthie asked me to demonstrate some of my Arabic words.

"*Hal tureedeen al-qahwa?*" I posed.

"Same to you!" she said.

"No, would you like some coffee?"

"Oh, well, since you say so!"

Afterwards, I brushed my hair, applied makeup, and put on my new, silken-blue wedding dress. I realized I was nervous about meeting Yakub's family. How did they feel about his marrying a Jewess? I remembered Yakub's cousin, Kareem, watching me in the rear-view mirror of his car as we drove to the hotel the first day. Had Yakub told him all about me? What did he think?

As I dressed in our bedroom, I heard Ruthie making a phone call out in the living room. It was brief, but I heard quite a bit of giggling and murmuring.

After she hung up, she entered the bedroom and began dressing.

"Lenny Goldstein?" I asked.

"Yup," she said, pulling on her stockings and then her beautiful embroidered black dress. "Can you help me with this zipper?"

I came and helped her, zipping the fabric together over the curve of her low back and shoulders. She sat down and pulled on her black pumps, then stood again. Her legs were slim, and the skirt of the dress skimmed gracefully over her tapered calves. Lenny better watch out, I thought.

At last, the time arrived, and Ruthie and I were ready. My bag was packed and sitting by the door. The hotel had instructions to move it to our bridal suite after the room became available.

When we entered the lobby, we spied Yakub and Mahmud across the large marble-tiled hall, sitting in the alcove by the front door. They watched the whole way as Ruthie and I click-clacked across the stone floor in our high heels. When we arrived, Yakub jumped up, taking my wrap, which I had draped over my arm, and placing it ceremoniously around my shoulders. His eyes lingered a moment on my dress, moving up and down, and I felt heat moving out in both directions from my lower abdomen.

"Ready?" he said to me. I nodded.

As we walked to the entrance, I examined Mahmud and Yakub. They were both dressed in dark suits, Mahmud with a striped tie, Yakub's dark green, just a shade deeper than his eyes. In his pocket, he had a green handkerchief. They both smelled of aftershave, and their hair was combed carefully beneath their spotless white *kufis*.

As we walked to the car, Yakub asked me how we had slept. Taking this opportunity, Ruthie jumped in to say, "Well, your bride here had us getting up at the crack of dawn."

"Really? Why is that?"

"Some kind of ancient Jewish bridal purification ritual. Up in the swimming pool. All I can say is, she's really, really clean."

Yakub looked at me. "Is this true?"

I nodded.

"You did this for me?"

"Yes. And for me. And…" I paused.

"Yes?" said Yakub.

"And for God," I said, uncertainly, not accustomed to this type of talk.

He smiled.

Kareem waited at the curb in the ancient Volvo. He jumped out when we arrived, openly admiring Ruthie and me in our wedding finery. He made a comment to Yakub, who nodded towards us, still smiling. Yakub gestured that I should sit in the front seat next to Kareem. I got in. Yakub carefully moved the hem of my dress away from the door before closing it. Then, he got into the back seat, crowding in next to Mahmud and Ruthie as the three of them fumbled with their seat belts in the narrow space.

Kareem drove us over to the U.S. Embassy, only a few blocks away. Through traffic, however, this took about twenty minutes. On the way, Yakub described to me how he had planned the wedding for that day, to make sure I agreed with all the various steps involved.

First, we would get the legal, civil wedding done. Later at his Aunt Rima's house, we would sign a wedding contract, called a "*nikah*" in Arabic, and then do the transfer of vows, accompanied by the ritual exchange of rings. Yakub had asked his imam for approval to draft the *nikah* in English, so I could read and understand it. We would sign it in the presence of witnesses.

Remembering all I'd read in Anita Diamant's book, I asked, "Is the *nikah* like a *ketubah* do you think?"

"Yes, I believe so," said Yakub.

I was certainly no expert, but it sounded to me like we were covering most of the essential elements of the Jewish betrothal and wedding: the transfer of rings and vows, the signing of the *ketubah*, the witnessing of the ceremony by others... All the rest, the broken glass, the seven blessings, even the famous *chuppah*, all of these, though doubtless profoundly significant, were customs rather than law. It sounded like Yakub would also be covering the core aspects of an Islamic wedding.

We arrived at the building, a non-descript high-rise with a utilitarian appearance. We went to the U.S. Consular section, where I obtained a signed affidavit indicating that I was free to marry an Egyptian citizen. The attorney Yakub had consulted had prepared all the other necessary papers, including a copy of my passport and a document attesting to the fact that my husband had died seven years before. These papers were reviewed by the American clerk in the embassy. "Congratulations, Ms. Davidson," he said when he emerged from a side office with my signed affidavit.

We were then required to go to the Egyptian Ministry of Foreign Affairs, which was across the river in Giza, not far from the pyramids. There, I was asked to swear that I was Jewish. In return, I received a notarized statement confirming this fact. Apparently, it was alright for a Jewish woman to marry a Muslim man in Egypt, but not the other way around. Presumably, the theory was that the Jewish woman would adopt her husband's religion when they married, or at least raise the children to be Muslim. This could get complex, however, since in Jewish law, children of a Jewish mother were Jewish. Since we would have no children, however, I did not expend much energy worrying about this.

Finally, we got back in Kareem's car and headed across the river to the Egyptian Ministry of Justice Annex, which was close to the U.S. Embassy, once again miring ourselves in endless traffic as the car grew increasingly warm. We lowered all the windows, letting in a cross-breeze that stirred my hair pleasantly and carried in odors of the city: auto fumes, cooking lamb, Egyptian coffee. As we drove, I asked Yakub and Mahmud about what it was like to grow up here, and they told me stories of the city, which, of course, had changed dramatically since Yakub had first moved here just after World War II.

At the Ministry of Justice, more paperwork was required, along with payment of a fee for the marriage certificate. Kareem and

Mahmud both showed their Egyptian passports and testified that they agreed to the wedding. All our papers accepted, all documentation complete, the clerk said some words in Arabic, Yakub put a gold band on my right ring finger, and I placed one on his. In this way, Yakub and I agreed to be bound in marriage. With this exchange of vows, rings, and papers, we were now, according to Egyptian civil law, legally married.

It wasn't until I walked out the door of the Ministry of Justice that it hit me. I was legally married! A crazy joy struck me, and I turned to Yakub, saying, "You may kiss the bride!"

Standing on the steps of the Ministry of Justice, he did just that.

After this, we went to Yakub's aunt Rima's house in Islamic Cairo. Kareem navigated the narrow streets carefully, driving at walking speed to avoid running into any of the pedestrians or shopkeepers thronging the densely populated streets.

He parked in a dilapidated corrugated tin shed next to an auto garage. We all got out, walking a half block to a small, tidy two-story town house, its unblemished plaster surface painted pale yellow. It was the third in a line of six or seven similarly well-kept townhomes. Kareem unlocked the door, entering and calling out, "*Mama?*" From the back room, a small woman emerged, dressed in long-sleeved shirt and brocade skirt, wearing stockings and silk flat shoes. She wore no head scarf, and her silver hair was pulled back into a French twist. She looked like she was in her mid-seventies, and shared with Yakub the wiry athleticism and penetrating green eyes.

Yakub embraced her, and then turned to me, introducing us in English.

"Aunt Rima, meet my wife, Rachel Davidson al-Shadi."

I held out my hand, but she ignored it, reaching up around my neck to embrace me. Her skin, covered with many wrinkles, was soft and smelled like lilac.

"Rima is my father's little sister, and a teacher of English and Arabic literature herself, until she retired ten years ago, soon after she became a widow," said Yakub. "Aunt Rima, as I told you, Rachel is not only my wife, but the doctor who saved my life back in America."

Speaking in a clear, low-pitched voice, with a trace of a British accent, Rima fixed me with her penetrating green eyes, saying, "You are a friend of the al-Shadi family."

I didn't bother to tell her that I really hadn't done that much for Yakub in the hospital.

After this, Yakub introduced Ruthie, and Rima remarked on how much she admired her beautiful dress. "I have seen so many fashions come and go, here in Cairo," she said, "and now this obsession with modesty." She shook her head. "In my day, we fought for freedom for women. Now, we are forced to fight again, and more bitterly."

Rima led us into a living room whose open French doors led to a small yard, paved in stone, with many potted plants and flowers. The house was two stories tall, the upstairs all bedrooms, the downstairs composed of a kitchen, dining room, living room, and small guest bathroom. Rima gestured that we should be seated. We sat and chatted about the afternoon we'd spent, driving from government building to building. Rima laughed at our descriptions.

"Ah! Bureaucracy! Some things, at least, don't change!" She had placed a variety of sweets and savories out in bowls on the tables: dates, dried apricots, nuts, pickles, bowls of the seasoned brown fava bean paste (*fuul*) and pita bread, and we ate these as we talked.

As the sun began to set, the doorbell rang and Kareem went to answer it. I heard happy Arabic greetings in the front hall, and then Kareem returned leading in a group of four people, two men and two women, all dressed in Bedouin garb, except one, a man in his mid-to-late thirties dressed in light-weight slacks and cotton shirt. The women wore *abayas* and head scarves, sandals on their feet below light fabric pants. The last of the party was a small, elderly man in a kaftan, wearing a head circlet over a long white cotton head scarf. Beneath this, his face was dramatically-patterned with deep wrinkles, resulting, I imagined, from long days in the desert sun.

When Yakub saw him, he shouted "Muhtadi!"

As Rima, Kareem, and Mahmud embraced our new guests, a beaming Yakub introduced Ruthie and me to his uncle. I wasn't sure of proper etiquette, but Muhtadi held out his hand, and both Ruthie and I shook it. It felt tiny, like bird bones. As we made our greetings, Muhtadi examined me with penetrating blue eyes.

"*Ahlan wasahlan!*" Hello! I said.

Muhtadi, looking surprised and then pleased, responded,

"W'inti! Ahlan biki! Bikhayr?" And you? How are you?

"Al-hamdu Lillah! Wa anta?" I am well, thanks to God. And you?

"Al -hamdu Lillah!" Thanks to God, I am well.

He turned towards Yakub, raising his eyebrows. Yakub shrugged and nodded.

Yakub then introduced us to the others in Muhtadi's party: Muhtadi's grandson, Khalid, his daughter-in-law, Najma, and Khalid's cousin, Insaf. The latter was a woman of about fifty, her head and neck covered tightly in a scarf. She, too, examined me closely, her eyes impassive. Muhtadi spoke to Yakub, and then Yakub explained to us that Muhtadi's wife, Samiha, was too elderly now to make the long journey from Jericho. She sent her best wishes, along with gifts. These he now produced from within the folds of his kaftan.

The first was a beautiful, rainbow-colored woven wool shawl. I removed my own wrap, and Yakub helped me to place the new one around my shoulders. The wool was a very thin gauge, and the shawl settled pleasantly on me, light as a feather, the hue of its vivid blue thread drawn out by the azure color of my wedding dress.

The second gift was contained in a small, flat wooden box. This I opened, at Muhtadi's urging, finding inside a thick circlet of silver and, in the center, a pair of delicate silver dangle earrings in the shape of flat bells, their centers composed of interlaced tree branches, five tiny silver balls suspended from the base of each earring. As I admired them, Muhtadi spoke with Yakub, who then explained to me that these were traditional family heirlooms, passed from woman to woman through generations, most recently to Muhtadi's wife, Samiha. She wanted me to have them.

Yakub took the bracelet out of the box and snapped it into onto my wrist, then carefully lifted the earrings out, removing my own earrings gently and threading the delicate wires through the piercings in my ears. The feel of his fingers on my earlobes was mesmerizing. I moved my head and the earrings made small tinkling sounds, tickling the sides of my neck.

Muhtadi nodded in appreciation, saying something in Arabic to Yakub.

"What did he say?" I asked.

"He said you look like a princess."

"Shukkran jazilan!" I said to Muhtadi. Thank you so much!

After this ceremonial gift exchange, Rima found places for everyone in the small, comfortable living room, and soon the relatives were talking in rapid Arabic. At intervals, Yakub would translate for us. "I have told them about how I met you," he said.

Insaf looked over at me, her blue eyes bright in her round face. She smiled, and I felt warmth flow between us. *"Shukkran!"* she said to me, and I replied, *"Afwan!"* You're welcome!

After a half hour or so, Yakub and Muhtadi went off into the kitchen, where they remained for some time. When they emerged, Muhtadi looked euphoric. A large smile lit his face from corner to corner.

At this point, Rima motioned to Yakub, and she, Kareem, Mahmud, and Yakub went off into the next room. After several minutes, they returned. Kareem was carrying a piece of paper, which he placed on a small table with two chairs. They gestured that Ruthie and I should sit down.

"This is the marriage contract," said Yakub. "We want to make sure that both you and your sister get a chance to see it."

Ruthie and I sat down next to each other and looked at the document. It was a piece of light yellow parchment, beautifully ornamented in Arabic calligraphy. In the center, there were ten lines of text, written in clear English calligraphy. The words said that Yakub and I would take care of each other. That we would take no other spouses. That, if it ever came to it, we would each have equal right to be released from our marriage vows.

When I was done reading the contract, Ruthie nodded her agreement at me. Yakub and I signed the contract in the spaces provided for our names. Everyone clapped and laughed, and Rima hugged me. She took the document and placed it on a small upright frame, inviting everyone to come by and look at it.

After another half hour, Rima signaled again, and Yakub came to me bearing a filmy white veil. He placed this over my head, and then led us into the dining room. Through the gauzy fabric, I saw a place set for Yakub and me beneath a kind of ceremonial tent, the table cloth strewn with rose petals. When we were all seated, Kareem filled our two glasses with a pink-colored non-alcoholic drink, and I lifted the veil above my mouth to join Yakub in a toast. Yakub then showed me that we should remove the ring from each other's right ring hand.

Before placing the ring on my left ring finger, Yakub said,

"With this ring, you are consecrated to me as my wife."

I looked at the ring more closely now, admiring it for a moment. It was a gold circlet, inlaid with ten stones of different colors, the bezels inset so that the jewels were flush to the surface of the ring. In the candlelight, the colors of the jewels glowed.

Looking up from it, I reached out to hold Yakub's left hand, running my thumb over the knuckles, gently tracing the scar where his fifth finger used to be, bringing it to my lips. I took the ring I held in my right hand and said, "With this ring, you are consecrated to me as my husband." I pushed the ring and it slid easily over his knuckle.

Yakub removed the veil and kissed me.

Soon, Yakub's Bedouin relatives went to retrieve their instruments. These looked terribly exotic, one of them appearing for all the world like a coffee grinder, pestle and all. While Muhtadi chanted and sang, Insaf accompanied him. They recited and sang poems, and as they did, a kind of magic seemed to ensue, the walls of the room melting away like the flaps of a Bedouin tent gathered up on the desert sands to reveal the silent sky and distant stars, the moon a bright crescent, flocks of goats nearby, safe in their nighttime shelter.

Yakub told me that these were traditional poems and songs, the oral culture of his family, some of them very ancient, *qasida's* and *qit'ahs*, *ghazals* and *muwashshahs*.

"These have never been captured in writing," he said, "but have passed from generation to generation since before recorded history. They speak of our love for the One God. They are the poems of *hanifiyya*, those who followed in the footsteps of Abraham."

"And Hagar," I said.

He laughed, "And Sarah."

"Ishmael and Isaac," I completed the family tree.

Later, Kareem brought out an *'ud*, a beautiful pear-shaped instrument inlaid with mother-of-pearl, and everyone goaded us on to the first dance of the evening. Yakub stood and held his hand out for me. I got up, embarrassed to dance in front of strangers but at the same time thrilled, at last, to be able to hold Yakub and feel his body against mine. In the makeshift dance floor of Rima's small living room, the two of us turned slowly round and round in a tightening spiral, and I felt again that magnetic pull, as though I

were falling into the space between us, the very same sensation I'd
had felt the first time I met Yakub.

At the end of our dance, Kareem set down the *'ud*,
disappearing into the kitchen and returning with a large white cake,
complete with plastic wedding couple in Western dress. I laughed at
the preposterous confluence of traditions. Yakub and I held the
cake knife together and cut the first slice, halving it and feeding it to
one another with the usual messy gaiety of this ritual. When his lips
closed on the first morsel, I kissed his mouth, the buttery vanilla
frosting slippery and sweet on my lips.

Not long afterwards, Yakub's relatives packed us off, like
any young newlywed couple, into a hired limousine that had
somehow made its way down the tortuous streets to Rima's house.
Ruthie would follow later in Kareem's car.

In the limousine, I closed my eyes and rested my head
against Yakub's chest, feeling the warmth of his shirt, damp from
our dancing, and breathing in his scent, a mixture of cologne, spice,
and musk.

Back at the Four Seasons, they showed us to a new suite,
"Their best!" they promised, bubbling effusively about newlyweds
and honeymoons. Though we reassured the desk clerk that we could
handle Yakub's suitcases on our own, he insisted on sending the
bellman up with us anyway. We rode the elevator in silence,
watching the numbers rise ever so slowly until, after an interminable
period, we reached our floor. There, we trailed along the hallway
after the luggage cart until the bellman arrived at our room and
unlocked the door. The three of us entered, and the bellman fussed
some more with details about where to place the suitcases and how
all the appliances in the room worked until, at last, Yakub tipped the
man and he left.

When the door finally shut behind him, Yakub slowly
walked to each of the lights, the overhead, then the bathroom light,
and finally the bedside lamp by the window, turning each one off
with a "snap." The only illumination in the room now came from
the city of Cairo, and, here on the upper floor of this tall building,
the moon and the stars.

He stood by the window looking over at me, his figure dark,
all except his eyes, which caught the moon's light. I saw now only
the mysterious form of a man, outlined by stars. I went towards

him, and found him there, by the window, attracted by his warmth and the odor of his cologne.

When I arrived, I hesitated a moment.

"What is it, *habibti?*" he said, running his hand down the side of my face, a gesture that made my legs weak.

"I don't know…" I said.

"You don't know what?" said Yakub, putting his face close to mine and kissing my cheek.

"I don't know how you're accustomed to making love," I said. "I don't want to do something wrong."

Yakub chuckled, saying softly, his lips against my ear, "Do what you like, you are not a virgin…"

"No, but…it's been seven years since David died…"

"And over all that time, you never…?"

"No, never. And you?" I saw him shake his head.

There was a moment of silence, and then I lifted my hand, towards the white *kufi* on his head and, slowly, I pushed it off and it fell onto the floor. I leaned my body into his, and he pulled me towards him. I heard him make a sound. A word? I pulled his shirt out of his pants then began to unclasp each button slowly, and when I was done, I ran my hand inside his shirt along the muscles on the surface of his chest, leaning my head down to kiss the tender skin over his heart.

I felt Yakub's hands moving on the back of my dress and guided them to the zipper, which he pulled down slowly, running his hand over my skin in the gap created. I stood back and removed the dress, drawing it up over my head, my eyes momentarily blinded by the fabric. I pulled the garment free and, taking my time, draped it over a chair, then removed my shoes one at a time, standing before him, the starlight washing my bare skin with light.

I started towards him, but Yakub stopped me, murmuring, "Wait…I want to look at you…"

I watched as his eyes took me in, moving from my face down my body, lingering for delicious moments as he continued over its surface from top to bottom,. I received with pleasure this quiet visual exploration, recalling that when I was young, I had never wanted anyone to look at me this way, fearful of inciting any kind of passion, which felt unwelcome to me as a very young woman. And, of course, with David, we'd both been so young the first time, that everything was over in literally two minutes.

This time, both of us were experienced, and could afford the luxury of time, knowing by instinct the gifts of careful touch, the rewards of restraint and anticipation, the slow and exquisite advance towards the location of desire.

Yakub finished his slow visual exploration. He came over and, lifting me, carried me to the bed, where he set me down and stood in front of me, stroking my hair. I undid his belt, pulling it slowly through the loops, then shearing the shirt from off of his shoulders. I felt his fingers on the latches and clasps of my final garments, then his precious weight, and I had the remembered sensation of endless slow spiraling towards a dark center, the place where parallel lines converge. For an instant, I recalled fragments of a poem, written by another lover in ages past... *if only I could drape myself upon you, like a many-colored garment...my arms a bow upon your neck, my legs a girdle around your waist... you could not tell my end from your beginning...*

And then there were no more words, only bodies and ecstatic light.

Cairo, Egypt
5:15 am. Monday, December 25th 2006 (Honeymoon)
Prof. Yakub and Dr. Rachel al-Shadi

That first morning, I awoke to see Yakub in silent prayer, dressed in a pair of cotton pajama pants, his chest bare. It was dark, but a beam of light from the entry hall illuminated him as he kneeled on his prayer mat, eyes closed, lips moving. He leaned forward and placed his forehead on the ground in front of him. After sitting up, he leaned forward once again. He repeated these motions several times.

As I lay in the warm sheets, fragrant with Yakub's smell, I said a silent morning prayer myself, one I had begun to repeat each day immediately upon awakening: *Modah ani lefanecha...I render thanks to You...*

Yakub and I had a day and a half to spend together before we separated on our divergent pilgrimages – Yakub's to Makkah and mine to Jerusalem. I tried not to think about that right now. Instead, I stood up and went over by the window, where I completed my prayers, reciting the *Shema* and the *v'Ahavta* quietly, so I would not disturb Yakub. Afterwards, I looked out the window, perceiving just the smallest illumination along the horizon, jagged with spires. It struck me that the day was Christmas, and I wondered what happened in this mostly-Muslim city on this day. There were many Christians here, a sect as old as the age of Jesus himself.

I went and lay back in bed and considered our discovery of the day before yesterday. The ancient sarcophagus in the Greek Catholic graveyard, covered in moss and lichen and holding...what? A secret poem to redeem the world? Or a bunch of dusty bones?

Yakub finished his prayers, got up, and came to lie down next to me. He put his arms around me, and we repeated our lovemaking of the night before, slow and exquisite in the growing light of morning. Afterwards, we lay there many minutes, saying nothing as I listened to his heart beat, my left hand beneath his head, my right hand free to explore the contours of his beautiful face. Finally, he rose again and went to the phone, where he began to order us breakfast in Arabic. I admired him as he stood there, unclothed, the brown surfaces of his body defined by the rosy light of sunrise. I said another blessing. This would be a day of blessings, hundreds, even thousands of them.

Yakub finished our breakfast order in English, for my benefit, "And lots of strong coffee!"

He climbed back in bed and we planned out our day.

"What will we do today?" I said. "Until we get into that coffin in the cemetery, we're kind of stuck..."

"Yes, I know. Rima is going to make some inquiries today. We will likely go back to the graveyard tonight to attempt to open the sarcophagus."

I laughed.

"What is it, my dear?" said Yakub.

"Well, I just can't believe I'm here in Egypt, talking about sneaking into a graveyard and secretly opening a sarcophagus. It just sounds so...grade 'B' movie or something."

"You are right!" he laughed. "Is there anything you have a burning desire to see, here in my hometown?"

"You could take me to the pyramids," I said, "or the Egyptian Museum!"

"Yes," said Yakub, looking devilish, "or we could stay here today!"

"You're like a teenager!"

"Are you complaining?"

Yakub did, in the end, take me to the pyramids that day. After our breakfast, we went downstairs and found a taxi to drive us to Giza. Though it was Christmas Day, the site was still crowded with tourists and merchants, people offering to be our tour guides, to give us a camel ride, to sell us any number of shiny baubles. Yakub, a native of Cairo, was able to good-naturedly dissuade all of their advances, and we proceeded to the ticket line, where we took our turn to purchase passes to enter the Great Pyramid. This was the pyramid of the famous King Khufu, whom I had met under his Greek name of "Cheops" in my history books as a young girl.

After getting our tickets, we walked the grounds, looking at the mysterious pyramidal buildings, said to have been constructed in 2560 BCE, many hundreds of years before Abraham even existed.

Yakub and I braved the stuffy interior of the Great Pyramid, entering through a slightly down-sloping cave-like hallway, then beginning a steep ascent through the hewn rock. The passageway, lit by electric bulbs, was extremely narrow in sections, forcing us to scramble on hands and knees up the wooden planks of the flooring until we came out in the more spacious, though equally steep, grand gallery leading to the king's burial chamber, the heart of the pyramid of Khufu. The chamber, the size of a small bedroom with a very high ceiling, was empty, save for a few slabs of rock and an empty sarcophagus. Of course, the king was no longer there, all the contents long ago removed by thieves. We looked around for a few minutes, feeling the weight of the hundreds of thousands of tons of stone above our heads. We then retraced our steps down the steep passageway, passing by the queen's burial chamber on our exit.

Outside once again and feeling as though we'd returned from a trip to outer space, we walked over to the great Sphinx, seeing its familiar figure, its nose sheared off at some undetermined time into the sands of the desert. My mind conjured Shelley's poem, which, since childhood, I'd always associated with this structure: *Round the decay of that colossal wreck, boundless and bare, the lone and level sands stretch far away...* Here in the second millennium of the new age, it was no longer the "lone and level sands" that stretched away, but the equally desolate wilderness of civilization, teeming with neon signs and Golden Arches, encroaching now to the very margin of the ancient pyramid complex.

It was quite warm that day, and Yakub and I were tired and

thirsty from our exertions in the Great Pyramid. Yakub knew about a pleasant spot to rest in the town nearby, a place called the Mena House Hotel. We walked the half mile or so to the hotel and, there, shared tall glasses of ice water followed by a cream tea at the Khan al-Khalili restaurant. Our table overlooked gardens and, beyond those, the ancient stone of the mighty pyramids, and we sipped the dark Indian tea and ate scones topped with clotted cream and strawberry jam.

I lifted Yakub's hand from the table, lightly tracing the scar along its outside surface.

"Do you remember," I said, "When I touched your hand, at the hospital in San Francisco?"

"Yes!" said Yakub. "How could I forget that?"

"You do remember?"

He nodded and, with his mischievous grin, said "You were quite saucy, I thought!" He lifted my own hand and brought it to his lips.

"You know," I mused, feeling the slight tingling in my outside palm, the site of the mysteriously-healed laceration, "something happened to my hand that day. I had a deep cut. But after I held your hand, it was gone. Completely disappeared."

"Really!" said Yakub, taking my hand and examining it further, "I see nothing at all!"

"I know," I said.

Yakub kissed my hand once again, trailing his fingertips down the soft skin along the side of my forearm. I shivered.

"Strange things happen," he said, "when love begins."

After this, we started our journey back to the hotel, riding a ferry up the Nile in the late afternoon sunlight, standing on the deck and watching the many sailboats that skimmed along the river, a cooling breeze propelling them across its silver surface.

From the ferry terminal, we walked the several blocks back to our hotel, entering its elegant lobby, the stones cool beneath our fevered feet.

Upstairs in our hotel room, the red light on our phone was flashing. Yakub immediately went to retrieve the message. When he'd finished listening, he hung up and dialed the phone. Someone answered, and he asked for Rima. After a moment, he began speaking in rapid Arabic. His look became concentrated. They spoke for ten minutes or so, while Yakub wrote down words in a scrawl I could not decipher. At length, he said *Ma'es Salaama*, goodbye, and hung up.

"What was that all about?" I said.

Yakub was sitting, his two hands pressed together, index fingertips against his lips.

"Yakub?"

He looked up. "What? Oh! My apologies. I was trying to figure out the best course of action. We *are* on honeymoon, after all." He grabbed my hands and pulled me into his lap.

"What will we be doing?" I asked.

"Not we," he said. "Only me and Mahmud. Kareem will drive."

"What?"

"My aunt Rima has been able to arrange a meeting with two of the men who work at the graveyard in Fustat. We are to meet them at the entrance gate there tonight at midnight."

"But I'm coming with you!" I protested.

"No, you are not," said Yakub.

"But..."

"She was quite explicit. Only me and Mahmud."

"But why?"

"The main contact at the graveyard is quite reluctant to comply, despite our generous payment, but is obligated by a debt that Rima's friend is calling in to persuade him."

"Oh," I said, disappointment in my voice.

"Don't be so sad," he said, kissing my pouting mouth, then my throat, murmuring into my shirt, "we have many hours until I have to go..." and I soon forgot about poems and sarcophagi and anything but Yakub.

We spent the precious hours that followed in each other's arms. We had entered another kind of place, a special private pavilion made possible by love, an edifice created only with God's grace and whose presence seemed, if only temporarily, very close. In the rare and infrequent moments of such times, fairy tales did exist, along with magic, happiness, and peace, and all the world seemed contracted to the expanse and temporary paradise of our hotel bed.

Cairo, Egypt
10:00 pm. Monday, December 25th 2006
Prof. Yakub and Dr. Rachel al-Shadi

At ten o'clock, Yakub arose from the bed and prepared to shower.

"Are you hungry?" I asked. "You'll need some food for energy, in case you end up running away from any mummies..."

"Yes, please order me some garlic cloves, while I go prepare the crucifix and the silver bullets."

"Ah!" I said, "You've been watching some grade 'B' movies yourself!"

"Seriously, I believe a little soup in preparation for our night-time adventure would be a very good idea. And some coffee, to wake me up."

While Yakub was showering, I went and checked the room service menu, then ordered something called "*moloukhaya* soup," coffee, and bread. I went and got dressed in t-shirt and sweat pants, watching as Yakub emerged from the bathroom and put on his clothes. I noticed he dressed in dark colors, and reasoned this was to serve as camouflage in the dark graveyard.

Afterwards, he came and sat next to me on the couch, leaning his body against me while I held him in my arms, his hair damp against the cotton of my t-shirt. Soon, the room service arrived, and Yakub seemed glad to eat the strange, thick green soup, into which he dipped the *xubz Arabiyy*, Arabic bread, while sipping water and strong black coffee.

At 11:15, Mahmud came and knocked at the door. When he entered the room, I noted that he, like Yakub, was dressed all in black.

"Hello, Rachel!" he said, his teeth very white against the black clothing. He looked at his father, and broke out in a grin. "We look like two burglars!"

"You are right!" laughed Yakub. "But the only burglar here is Rachel. I'm afraid she has stolen my heart."

Mahmud looked back at me. "As the poet said, '*my spirit is yours, yours to take...*'" (7)

"Ah!" said Yakub. "Quoting the master, Umar ibn al-Farid, near midnight on the threshhold of your first crime!"

"Well," I said, "You all might think this is all very poetic and romantic, but I am a little scared, now that I see you all ready to go." In fact, I felt a gnawing in my stomach that threatened to expand momentarily into an ulcer.

Yakub put a hand out and touched my hair. He pulled me towards him and gave me a hug, saying, "Don't worry, Rachel. We'll be back in no time! And then you will have a new problem!"

Holding Yakub around the waist, I said, "Oh yes? And what might that be?"

"Solving the riddle of the poem to redeem the world!"

"*God willing!*" I said, releasing him reluctantly.

He leaned to kiss me on the mouth before the two of them left.

After the door shut behind them, I went distractedly back to the couch and sat down. I knew I would not be able to sleep, and so picked up my Arabic workbook from the living room table, pouring myself a cup of lukewarm coffee. I already missed Yakub terribly. I didn't even want to think of what it would feel like to be separated from him for any length of time. I was also beset by a sense of foreboding. I couldn't escape the feeling that something terrible was going to happen to Yakub and Mahmud in the graveyard.

Though it was hard to concentrate on the Arabic words, I tried to force myself to pay attention, bending over the workbook and squinting at the script, which swirled meaninglessly in front of my eyes. Giving up, I found the remote and turned on the television. All I could find to watch in English was the 1950's rendition of "King Solomon's Mines." As I began to doze off, the images flashing on the television screen were less than reassuring: Deborah Kerr, in expedition clothes, and Stewart Granger, stumbling around among decomposing skeletons...

I must have dozed for awhile. The next thing I knew, I woke up to a sound behind me. I turned to see Yakub entering with Mahmud and Kareem. Letting out a yelp, I ran across the room, horrified to see my husband's handsome face swollen and discolored, a large bruise already closing his left eye. There was blood caked into his thick black hair.

I ran to turn on the overhead light so I could examine his scalp for lacerations. I found a big one, about an inch long, still oozing dark, half-clotted blood. "I knew it!" The sense of foreboding I'd been feeling had not been misplaced.

I ran to the bathroom and got a washcloth, returning and applying pressure to the wound. "You can lose a lot of blood this way!"

"But, it's just a small cut." exclaimed Yakub, plumping down on the bed.

"Who's the doctor here?" I gestured to Kareem, signaling that he should come and help by applying pressure to the wound with the washcloth, freeing my hands to examine Yakub. "Tell me what happened. Were you knocked unconscious?" I retrieved my pocket flashlight, checking his pupils for size and reactivity. I then examined his ears and nose for leakage of fluid. Everything looked alright, no sign of occult skull fracture.

Mahmud answered my question. "A man hit him on the head, in the graveyard."

Bypassing the adventure story for now, I stuck to questions on the medical facts. "Was your father knocked out?"

"I don't think so, but he was groggy and confused for a few minutes." Mahmud looked very upset and worried. I felt the same.

I went through the mental status exam, checking Yakub for orientation to time, place, and person. He checked out A & O X 3 (alert and oriented times three). "Do you feel sick to your stomach?" I asked.

Yakub thought a moment, checking himself for signs of nausea. "No. Mostly just sick with disgust at my own stupidity."

"Don't say that," I said, checking his reflexes and asking him to perform various muscle tests. Everything was fine.

I took the pressure dressing back from Kareem, lifting it briefly to check the laceration beneath. "This is going to need stitches," I said, putting pressure on the dressing again as the cut began to ooze. "What did he hit you with, anyway?" I said, "A saber?"

Yakub laughed. "No. It was some kind of heavy bag or something. In your old American movies, I believe they call it a 'sap'."

"Is there an emergency room nearby?"

"Yes, but I would prefer you to do it. You are an excellent doctor."

"Yakub, you beautiful *majnun*. I have no suture kit! How was I supposed to know you were going to go knocking your noggin all around Cairo?"

"There's a sewing kit in the drawer," he remarked. I couldn't tell if he was joking.

I explained, patiently, "I'm afraid that's only done in the movies. The threads in the kit are completely unsterile."

"Can't you clean the needle in a match flame?" he asked.

"It's not the needle I'm worried about, it's the thread."

"Is there nothing you can do?" said Yakub, plaintively. "I don't want to spend my last hours here with you in the hospital!"

I thought a moment then went to find my purse and rummaged through it. Thank goodness I never cleaned it out! There it was, at the bottom, in a crumpled plastic Glad bag: a small tube of Crazy Glue. Praying it wasn't all dried up by now, I pulled off the long plastic top and tipped the tiny tube upside down. A clear droplet came out.

"We can use this!" I said, showing Yakub the Crazy Glue. In the hospital, we used this to close many lacerations these days. It came in breakable purple tubes, was called "cyanoacrylate," and cost over $100 a treatment. Or, you could use the hardware-store version I had for $3.99.

I applied pressure for another five minutes until the edges of the wound quit bleeding, then rinsed it with water, seating Yakub under the makeup mirror light in the bathroom. After drying the wound one more time, I quickly squeezed several drops of the clear cyanoacrylate into the laceration, taking a small bundle of hair from each side and wrapping these around each other, pulling the two edges of the wound together. I repeated this procedure several times. In the end, I was happy to see the wound entirely closed, edges well-opposed.

"One time," I said, "I did that to a patient in clinic, but used my fingers to shut the wound. The glue worked great except that it stuck my thumb and forefinger to the patient's skin for an hour before I could get it off!"

Yakub stood up and kissed me. "You are marvelous. And I wouldn't mind if you were glued to *me* forever."

We went back into the living room, where Mahmud and Kareem waited. Kareem examined Yakub's head wound, then gave me an appreciative smile. *"Gameel,"* he said, and I recognized a compliment. *Beautiful!*

I suggested Yakub lie down on the bed. Retrieving the

throw from the divan, I covered him up. He settled back comfortably, glad to be at rest at last.

"So, what happened?" I asked, now that Yakub seemed stable.

Mahmud and Yakub described their experiences in the graveyard while Kareem sat listening, nodding his head every now and then, even though I knew he didn't understand much English.

Kareem had dropped Mahmud and Yakub off on Mar Girgis street, and the two had walked to the graveyard entrance. As far as they knew, no one had been following them.

They had met the cemetery attendants there as planned, entering through a side gate. The men had brought a crowbar, and when they'd arrived at the sarcophagus, they had succeeded in prying the lid from the top.

"So?" I prompted. "What did you see? Was it empty? Or bones?"

"Neither of the above," said Yakub. "It was very dark. But with the help of a flashlight, we saw a mound at the bottom of the sarcophagus. It turned out to be two books."

"Only two? What happened to all the others?"

"I don't know," admitted Yakub. "But all we saw was two."

He looked over at Kareem and said something in Arabic. Kareem leaned down and pulled forward a blue backpack. Unzipping the top, he carefully removed a book with a black leather cover, gold letters faintly embossed in its center. From its pages, the edges of a sheet of paper protruded.

"Okay," I said. "That's one book. Where's the other one?"

Yakub looked away. The sides of his mouth began to tremble.

Mahmud continued. "The other book was taken from my father in the graveyard. A man came and stole it from him."

Yakub turned back to me, his face stricken. "It was my fault!" he said.

Mahmud looked at his father, anger in his voice. "It was not your fault!" he said, "It was the thief's fault!"

"But I stopped to look at the poetry! We should have left right away. I just couldn't help myself. I've waited so long…"

"Hold on, hold on!" I broke in. "What happened, exactly? Slow down, please, if you can!"

Yakub took a deep breath in an attempt to compose

himself. His face was desolate as he said, "After we opened the sarcophagus and found the books, we took a quick look at them. The first one, the one you see here, was evidently a siddur, and a rather common one, from the era in question. The second book, however, was *the* book."

"*The* book?" I repeated.

"Yes. As soon as I opened it, I knew it was a poetry journal, a *diwan,* written in a beautiful Arabic script. I simply had to look at it right away, even though it was dark and there was danger. I began carefully turning the pages, scanning quickly with my flashlight...and I think I remember turning to the last page, which I reasoned would be the logical place for *the poem*, because if someone wrote such a poem, why would they write anything after it?"

Mahmud interrupted. "He was crouched down, reading it on the ground next to the sarcophagus when the little man came along, grabbed the book, and hit him. I ran after the man, but he was very fast..."

"And he got away?" I said.

Mahmud nodded.

"What did he look like?"

"He was...well, it's hard to say, because it was dark, and I only saw him for a moment."

"But do you have any impressions? Did you recognize him?"

"No, I didn't recognize him. I did see his face for just an instant, though. It was...a strange face." Mahmud spent a moment remembering, then said, "It appeared that something was wrong with him. His chin was very pointed, and his whole face was...like a triangle, shaped sort of like a top. His ears were low-set. That's all I remember. He ran very fast, and his legs were thin."

"Hmmm..." I said, trying to recall if I'd ever seen anyone like this. The description seemed vaguely familiar, like something from a dream or déjà vu.

I turned back to Yakub, trying my hardest not to betray the impatience and urgency I felt. "So...did you see it? *The poem?* Before he stole it?"

"Yes...I think so," said Yakub.

"Think so?" I said, trying not to sound disappointed.

"He hit me while I was reading it, the last page. I can't really recall much." He turned his stricken face to me again, his eyes betraying both misery and wonder, all at one time. "It was beautiful. More beautiful than any poem I have ever seen."

"But you don't remember the words?" I said.

Yakub screwed up his lovely, bruised face with the effort of trying to recall it. Then, he let out a burst of air and sighed deeply. "Not right now," he said. "Give me time. Perhaps I'll remember something."

He closed his eyes.

Mahmud said, "We should allow my father to rest, shouldn't we? He has had a bad blow."

"Yes, you're right."

Mahmud spoke to Kareem, and the two men went to the door. I followed them, whispering to Mahmud at the door, "Do you think we should go to the police?"

He shook his head. "What? And tell them our property was stolen while grave robbing?".

I grimaced. "You're right. And I doubt they'd be able to locate this thief anyway."

"Precisely," said Mahmud. He squeezed my shoulder. "Don't worry. My father may remember the poem after all. He has a very good memory."

"I know." But I also knew the affect of brain trauma on recent recall. No matter how great his memory, the blow to his head might well have knocked any recollection of the poem from his mind forever.

Mahmud shook his head ruefully and checked his watch. "Five-thirty am. So, I'll be back this evening around seven to pick my father up so we can leave for our plane flight to Jeddah. Perhaps he can rest until then."

I nodded. "Alright. See you later! I'll keep you posted if anything happens."

After Mahmud and Kareem left, I went back to the bed and carefully folded myself into the space next to Yakub's body. He wrapped his arms around me, his uninjured cheek against the top of my head. "There," he murmured, "my dove."

He stroked my hair for a few minutes, his breathing becoming more regular as he drifted into sleep. I remained awake, watching him for signs of injury. All I saw was his calm sleeping face, and all I heard was the sound of his breath, regular and soft.

I let Yakub sleep for a few hours, rising when the time was respectable for a call to Ruthie. I needed to let her know what had happened to Yakub.

Her voice grew increasingly concerned as I filled her in on all the details of the incident.

"Are you sure he's alright?" she said. "It sounds bad."

"I know. I'll be checking him regularly before he leaves tonight, to make sure he's okay."

"Good thing he's got a doctor nearby!" said Ruthie.

"Maybe. Not sure how much good I'm doing."

"Of course you're helping. Anyway, I'll come over this afternoon to check on you guys. What time does Yakub leave?"

"Seven pm," I said, a hollow sensation in my stomach.

Sensing my feelings, Ruthie said, "Don't worry, Rachel. We'll have a great time in Israel, and you'll be back with Yakub in no time."

I said an unconvincing "Yeah," before we hung up.

I returned to the bed, climbing carefully in beside Yakub and lying there for another long bout of watching him breathe. Finally, at about ten, I figured it was time to check on his mental status and vital signs. It had been over four hours since my last exam.

"Yakub," I called softly, "Yakub."

He opened his eyes and looked at me, a smile spreading across his lips. "What a beautiful sight to see upon waking!" he said.

"How do you feel?" I asked, sitting up on my knees so I could examine him better. In answer, he put his arms around me and pulled me towards him, holding me tightly against his chest.

"We shouldn't..." I said, "It's not good for your injury."

"Alright, doctor," said Yakub, gazing into my eyes, and I saw that his pupils were fine.

"Do you know where you are?" I asked, checking for orientation.

"In heaven."

"Silly. And the date?"

"Eternity."

"You aren't helping!" I protested.

"Would you like me to count sevens backward? One hundred...ninety-three...eighty-six..."

"Alright, alright!" I said.

He smiled and pulled me in close to him again. We lay there together for a long time.

"What will we do without the poem?" I said, my mouth against the shirt in the hollow of his chest.

Yakub rolled his head to gaze up at the ceiling. "I don't know. But one good thing is, at least our pursuers will leave us alone. Now that they have the *diwan* in their possession, we're safe."

"That's really scary, though," I said. "Surely there's a reason that Mrs. Dunash's family was taking such pains to hide it. Maybe those Smiths will do something terrible now that they have it?"

"We'll deal with that when we come to it."

Cautiously, I returned to a sensitive subject, unable to restrain my curiosity "Do you remember any more about what you read last night?"

Yakub furrowed his brow, bringing a hand absently to the laceration on his scalp. "I almost remember something. It's just on the verge of my mind." He lay a moment, concentrating, then rose suddenly and paced to the window. "Ouch," he said, wincing and putting his palm to the side of his cheek and temple.

"Yakub!" I said with alarm.

"I'm fine," he reassured me, lowering his hand. "I just got up too quickly." He went and sat on the couch.

"Coffee!" I said. "And breakfast."

He looked up. "Yes! That would be wonderful."

I asked him what he wanted, then dialed room service and ordered. When I was done, I went and sat on the couch next to Yakub.

He leaned back and put his arm around me, but sat up again when he spied something on the coffee table. "Ah! I had forgotten about this!" he said, leaning over to pick up the prayer·book he had retrieved from the sarcophagus last night. "I was so concerned about the *diwan.*"

"Oh yes!" I said, remembering it myself for the first time. "It must be important too, otherwise why would David II have hidden it? Which makes me wonder again..."

"Yes?"

"What happened to all the other books from the 'little genizah'?"

"I've been thinking about that," mused Yakub. "Perhaps David Maimonides returned to collect the other books, but left

these two here, in case the rightful owner should return and claim
them?"

I nodded. "That makes sense. But in that case, they never
did return."

"But I did."

"Did what?"

"Return. Assuming the *diwan* belonged to my ancestor, Said
al-Shadi."

"Hmm," I said. "That's kind of spooky."

"This book, however," said Yakub, examining the prayer
book, "must have belonged to someone Jewish."

I moved forward next to Yakub to look more closely at the
book. The front cover had just a few flakes of gold adhering, and I
saw the ghostly outlines of the word *siddur*, Hebrew for prayer book.
Carefully, Yakub opened to the first page, letting out a small sigh of
relief. "Good! The dry atmosphere of Cairo has preserved the
integrity of these pages, *al-hamdu lillah.*"

After the blank binding page, there was a title page,
describing the *siddur* in more detail. "This is the prayer book of the
Cordoban congregation," Yakub explained. "It was likely used by
Rivkah bat Avraham, and brought here by her during her flight
from Cordoba." He turned to the loose page that protruded from
the edge of the *siddur*. Placing the book on the table, he opened it
fully, removing the loose sheet of paper and placing it carefully on
the flat surface of the table. He then turned his attention
momentarily to the siddur itself. "This is hand-scribed, of course,"
he said, "since the printing press was not invented until a half
century later."

I scanned the Hebrew, saw the words: *Tehillim Tzade-Vav.*
"Look, Yakub! The page marks Psalm 96, which is part of the
Friday evening prayer service!"

"Hmm!" said Yakub, distractedly. He was engrossed in
examination of the single page of loose paper. He got up to retrieve
his glasses, then sat down and returned to his scrutiny of the
document. It was about five inches by seven inches, stained with
brown splotches. On it, I saw a strange diagram, a large Star of
David with many sharp rays radiating out from it, three round
circles along the edge, several words written above in Hebrew, and
more Hebrew letters within the star itself.

My eye passed over the diagram of three dots once again.

The Star of David symbol, with its surrounding rays, a total of about four inches in diameter, was next to the middle one.

"What is this?" I said, gesturing at the diagram.

"I'm not quite sure. In those days, people often attempted to create amulets for magical purposes. They would frequently include symbols such as the hexagram and various combinations of words and letters. But this one is different, unique from any I have seen before. It seems to me no simple amulet for love."

He peered at the diagram, and then I heard him whistle. He got up and retrieved his magnifying glass, returning to the figure, his nose inches from the surface of the paper. He looked for all the world like some kind of Arabian detective.

"What is it, Holmes?" I joked.

Yakub did not look away, but said, "What? Oh! Yes, my dear Doctor Watson. Take a look at this Star of David."

I peered down at the photograph but saw only the usual 6-pointed star.

"I don't see anything," I said.

"Here!" Yakub handed me the magnifying glass.

When I placed it over the upper triangle of the Star of David, I saw the line of its edge separate out into irregular dots. If I squinted my eyes and really concentrated, I thought they might even be letters.

"Yes, they are letters!" said Yakub, confirming my unspoken thought.

"What does it say?" I asked.

"Well, look here." Yakub moved closer to me on the couch, and we tried our best to look through the magnifying glass together. It was possible if we held it at a distance of several inches from the page and then stood back. "See how these letters are highlighted, the Hebrew letters signifying the verse number: Tzade-Vav. Ninety-six, in regular numbers." he said. "It's Psalm 96!"

"Again!" I said.

"And look!" said Yakub, gesturing at the rays extending out from the star symbol.

I examined the diagram once again. There were many short lines. On closer inspection, I saw they were also words, this time in Arabic script. I could make out the words *al-Samad, al-Jabbar, al-Hakim, al-Magid, al-Wadud*...I said them out loud.

"'The Eternal', 'The Powerful', 'The Enduring', 'The

Glorious', 'The Loving'" translated Yakub. "These are among the 99 Most Beautiful Names of Allah!"

"Are there 99 rays around this star?" I asked.

Yakub took a few moments to count the lines. "Yes, there are!"

"And how about these letters here?" I said, examining the letters contained within the star. "Hey-Vav above, and Hey-Yud below, with an Aleph in the center. It's the four-letter name of God, in Hebrew. But how is the Aleph connected?"

Yakub shook his head. "It is a very great puzzle. It will take some time to solve it, I think."

"And what does this say here, above the line of three dots?"

"It says '*amudim shel shalom*', or 'pillars of peace.'"

He took off his glasses and pronounced, "My dear Rachel, I believe what we have here is a mystical amulet for redemption."

"Redemption!" I said.

Yakub turned the page over. The reverse side was blank.

Something struck me, and I said, "Yakub, do you have the copy of that letter, the one written by the son of Dunash?"

"Yes, of course." Yakub stood up and went to the small closet safe. He entered a combination, retrieved the copies, and returned.

I read through the last few paragraphs, searching for the item I'd remembered.

"Here it is!" I said, reading aloud, "*Over and over, she draws a strange talisman, a six-pointed star, with many wavy rays, telling me that this is where al-Shadi was going. Madness!*"

"Where al-Shadi was going..." repeated Yakub. He turned the page over and examined the diagram again. "Three pillars, and a Star of David." He shook his head.

"Wait," I said. "There was something else." I re-read the letter from the beginning. "Aha!" I read aloud once again: "*Al-Shadi had made a discovery of some kind, a breakthrough in his poetry, and now must travel to the 'holy land' to complete the work.*"

"Three pillars and a Star of David," repeated Yakub. "In the holy land. But which one?"

"Which one? What do you mean?"

"Well, if we are speaking of the Judeo-Arabic tradition, there are two holy lands. There is Israel, and there is Saudi Arabia.

And even more precisely, there are the holy cities, Jerusalem and Makkah."

I nodded. "Wow," I said.

"What?"

"That's where you and I are going!"

Yakub's eyes lit up. Both of us felt it. The mysterious intrusion of fate.

"As they say in your Psalm 37, 'the steps of a man are directed by the Lord...'"

"Assuming we are looking for the same thing Said al-Shadi was seeking, what do we look for when we get to those holy sites? Pillars?"

"It's possible. In fact, there are pillars on the Hajj, very important pillars, the *Jamarat*, where we throw stones at the devil, fighting the greater *Jihad*, that is, the war with our own ego. This is the central purpose of the Hajj. We must destroy the things inside us, greed, jealousy, anger, all those things that prevent our full submission to God."

"So you can look at the pillars on the *Hajj* and I'll look up on the Temple Mount."

"Yes!" said Yakub.

I sniffed. "I've never looked for a sign from God before. That's a little dicey, don't you think?"

"I suppose it is," admitted Yakub.

There was a knock on the door, and I opened it to admit the man with the room service tray.

After breakfast, I re-examined Yakub, checking his pupils and his mental status. He was still fine, though he looked tired, and I suggested he sleep some more. I settled him back in the bed, applying a cool cloth to his head. He looked at me gratefully before dozing again. While he napped, I went and took a shower, dressing in my favorite sweat pants and San Francisco Marathon t-shirt. Afterwards, I lay down carefully next to Yakub and watched him sleep once again.

At 4:00, I heard a soft knock on the door. It was Ruthie. I leaned my head out into the hall, to avoid waking Yakub.

"He's sleeping now," I said.

"Is he alright?"

"I think so. His neuro exam is fine."

"Do you need anything?"

"No, not right now, thanks. I'll definitely need a hug after he goes, though."

"You got it. When's he leaving again?"

"Around seven."

"So I'll come over after that. We can have dinner together. Maybe I'll spend the night with you in your room."

I gave what smile I could. "Thanks, Ruthie. See you later."

I let Yakub sleep until five-thirty, then woke him gently, repeating a brief neurologic exam. Everything remained fine. Yakub got up, put on his sweater, and took the documents out of the safe to review them once more. He made a sketch in his notebook of the Star of David and the pillars while I ordered more coffee.

When the coffee arrived, we sipped together in silence, sitting side by side, and then Yakub went to take a shower. I followed him into the bathroom, just to be with him a few minutes more. I watched him, a pale figure through the wavy glass of the shower door.

When he got out, I noticed his face was pale. He asked me for an aspirin. Concerned, I said, "Do you have a headache?"

"Only very mild," he said. "I simply want to avoid one later as we travel." His drawn face belied his words.

"Yakub!" I said, worried. "Are you nauseated at all?"

"No, no, I feel fine." He looked at my stricken face. "*Habibti!*" he said, touching the side of my face, "I just don't want to leave you! That's why I look unwell."

I went and retrieved two Tylenol tablets and a glass of water. "You should not take aspirin or other anti-inflammatories, not with that head trauma."

"What is this?" asked Yakub, looking at the red and yellow capsules in his palm.

"It's acetaminophen. It doesn't cause bleeding."

He nodded, and I watched as he took the medicine. I checked his head wound and pupils one more time. They still looked fine.

In a moment, we heard a soft knock on the door. I opened it to find Mahmud standing there. "I'm sorry to bother you," he said, "but it's time for my father and me to go."

"Yes, I know," I said. My words echoed hollowly in my

ears, like I was standing in a tunnel.

Yakub appeared, and Mahmud exclaimed, "Baba! Are you ill?"

"No, just sad. As for my medical condition, I've been under the best care in the world." He turned to me, his eyes brimming with tears. "Goodbye, Rachel." He embraced me once more.

"Do you really think you should go?" I said. "I'm so worried about you!"

"Rachel," he said, "I'm fine. I must go on this pilgrimage, as you know."

I nodded. Then I said, abruptly, "Wait!" I ran to the bathroom to get the Tylenol. "You may need more of these." I placed the bottle in Yakub's hand.

Turning to Mahmud, I said, "You'll need to keep an eye on him. If he shows any confusion, nausea, vomiting, alteration of consciousness, or extreme headache, get medical help immediately!"

"I will," said Mahmud. Despite his reassuring words, he looked worried too.

Mahmud took Yakub's suitcases, and the two of them departed. When the door closed behind them, it felt as though a spear had pierced my heart. I stood for several minutes, unable to breathe. Then, hoping it might take my mind off the growing panic I was feeling, I put on my jogging clothes and went down to the exercise room to run on the treadmill. Forty-five minutes and a sweaty five miles later, my anxiety level was astronomic.

Back in my room, I showered off the sweat, unsure what to do with myself next. Thankfully, Ruthie came, as promised, several minutes later. She had brought her suitcase and checked out of her own room.

We ordered room service again, then sat and watched TV for awhile, hardly talking at all. I had nothing to say. With Yakub gone, nothing much seemed to matter.

At last, it was bedtime, and I went and lay down in bed, thankful for the opportunity to escape. I soon fell asleep.

Far from being a respite, my sleep brought me only more agitation. I was in my clinic in San Francisco. There had been a disaster of some kind, and all kinds of traumatized patients, far too many for me to handle, were expected in the clinic at any moment. I heard the sirens approaching, their wails growing louder and louder. I finally perceived that it was my alarm clock ringing. My eyes opened, and everything came back to me in that instant. I wondered how I would possibly survive the next eight days without Yakub.

London, England
7:00 am. Wednesday, December 27th 2006
Mr. Smith, to Eugene Smith (journal entry)

My dearest boy, you have succeeded beyond my wild dreams! Do you know what you have done? Perhaps you are too young to appreciate its true import! My boy, you have rid our family, at last, of the pestilence that has plagued us for four millennia! Only God alone knows the joy I feel today! I glory to think of the news you have given me, about your successful encounter with al-*Shadi*. How easily you foiled his poorly-laid plans, followed him, from place to place, with never a suspicion by your unwitting foe! How simply you stole the document from his pliant hands! I regret only that you made use of force. So much better, son, if you can do these things without the laying on of hands. But you will learn, my boy, you will.

Thank you, my dear Eugene, for reading those ridiculous poems to me over the telephone last evening. Though it made me retch to hear them, as we both know, they are a revelation and a jubilation. Why? Because now you know the key to what *the others* hold most dear! And, in fact, we find this poetry is, itself, *incomplete*, as its own author admits!

Surely, my son, you will now be free to create the crowning achievement of our family, the final masterpiece to lead the world away from their blind gropings towards God! If you accomplish this, the people of the world will read your words and will be plunged further into evil and sin. At that glorious time, only the spotless members of our own family will be worthy to rise and live alongside God!

When you return, after your trek to Makkah, we will burn this poem together, ridding the world forever of its misguided promise of redemption for the rabble.

And now, Eugene, my dear, you travel to Makkah, where you will receive a hero's welcome from our brothers, who have lived in that place since ancient times, long before Muhammad ever saw its rosy peaks, when our ancestor, *al-Qayana*, first came to that land from the North.

Undoubtedly, *al-Shadi* and his side-kicks believe we are off the scent, since we have the *diwan* they so foolishly pursued. Well, *the poem* is clearly no longer a threat to us. But what good is triumph, without standing in victory over those you've vanquished? The time for justice has arrived! These people must be punished, for all the harm they've caused us.

As for me, I would like to take care of the woman personally. The thought of her irritates me beyond toleration. And I feel strong, at last, in the wake of your triumph! Strong enough to travel, even to the Holy Land. And there, I will take certain steps to ensure that she will pay, in fact, that she will die. It will prove no difficulty, as there are so very many who hate her kind within the walls of that great city. I anticipate no trouble whatsoever.

And now, I make my travel arrangements. How I relish the idea of walking in the outside air, cool breezes on my skin, the warm stones of Jerusalem penetrating to my very bones!

POWER

Tel Aviv, Israel
Morning of Wednesday, December 27ᵗʰ 2006
Dr. Rachel al-Shadi and Ruthie Roseman

After I extricated myself from the clinging tendrils of my nightmare, I did my best to turn my mind off completely, heading down for another perfunctory jog on the treadmill, returning after a half hour to prepare for our trip. Ruthie woke while I was packing.

Looking at me from the bed, she commented, "You don't look so good!"

"Thanks a lot," I said, throwing the final items into my suitcase

"Are you okay?" she said, sitting up.

"I miss Yakub," I admitted, slumping miserably down onto the bed. Ruthie gave me a long hug, then got up and started getting ready herself.

Forty-five minutes later, we were in the cab on the way to the airport. I became aware of the large numbers of women on the streets wearing black veils. I don't know why I hadn't noticed this before, but maybe it was because, with Yakub, I felt welcome in this country. Without him, I felt like a stranger.

As we drove through town, we passed a demonstration. A man in a *kufi* was addressing a crowd of men. Though I could not understand the Arabic words he spoke, I heard the name "*Amrika*" several times and, judging from the angry response of the fifty-or-so young men in attendance, I determined that they were not speaking favorably about my homeland. Who could blame them? How had we Americans gotten involved in this mess in the Middle East anyway? How had we, the country of the free, started even more wars, now in Afghanistan and Iraq, creating yet another opportunity for human cruelty in the world, where our own and others' beautiful children would be killed, and where evil would multiply and stain yet another generation with hatred? We had so much power to do good, to wage the real war, the war against human suffering. But instead, we had squandered the goodwill of the world on the usual confusions of nation versus nation.

I closed my eyes. I couldn't stop a tear from rolling down my cheek. I felt Ruthie take my hand and hold it.

My spirits revived somewhat on our plane ride to Tel Aviv.

In fact, right from the center of the pain and disillusionment I felt leaving Egypt, arose a new and powerful sense of hope. I had no idea where it came from, but I attributed it to some hardiness in my soul for which I could claim no personal responsibility. Was it somehow connected, after all this time, with the similar journey my own ancestors had made millennia in the past, crossing the terrain I now travelled by air, to end, after revelation, trial, and tribulation, in the Holy Land?

Israel! There was no explaining the thrill this destination caused me. I felt like I was coming home after a long absence, even though I'd never been there before. When we touched down, a prayer came into my mind, a *Shehechiyanu,* the prayer for miracles, ordinary and extraordinary. "God, thank you for bringing me to this day!"

We went through customs, and when we emerged, I heard Ruthie say, "Omigod!" as if, departing from the seventh, she'd now encountered the world's eighth wonder.

There, in the vaulted arrivals hall of the Ben Gurion Airport was Lenny Goldstein. On his face, he bore a giant smile, and in his hand, a bouquet of flowers.

"I thought I'd surprise you!" he said. "Looks like it worked!"

"Omigod!" said Ruthie again, rooted to her place as the people streamed around her, anxious to get outside and on to their next destination.

Lenny came over and the two embraced. Then Lenny, his arm still around Ruthie's shoulder, turned to me and said. "Hi, Rachel!"

"It's great to see you, Lenny," I said, "but did you really have to come all the way to Israel just to give me a patient report?"

He laughed. "Well, I'd like to report they're all fine. And so am I!" He looked at Ruthie. For once in her life, she was speechless. "Come on!" he said, releasing Ruthie's shoulder, handing her the bouquet, and grabbing both of our roller-duffels. "Let's get going!"

We trailed along after Lenny as he navigated through the airport to the garage. "This is my uncle's car," he explained when we arrived at a spotless blue Saab. "He was nice enough to lend it to me so I could come to the airport and collect you."

Able to speak at last, Ruthie said, "How long have you been here?"

"I got here the day before yesterday," said Lenny.

Lenny loaded our bags into the trunk. I got in the back seat, Ruthie in the front. "Omigod," said Ruthie, one last time for good measure.

"So!" said Lenny, "where are you guys staying?"

"King David Hotel," I replied.

"Good! The tour will begin now!" said Lenny.

"But I'd already scheduled a tour guide for tomorrow," I protested.

"Well," said Lenny, "you can call and cancel when you get to the hotel. And my services are free!"

"What about my patients? Who's taking care of them now if you're here with us?"

"Don't worry, Rachel! They're all fine! I signed out to our partner, Dr. Ambergrass. She owes me for covering her romantic fling last year, and was more than happy to help out. And as for Zeke, I made sure to talk to Adele, the nurse on the surgical floor. She'll keep an eye out for him and call Dr. Ambergrass if he bounces back into surgery."

"How about my little guy? The baby I was worried about?"

"Saw him two days ago. He'd gained a pound. I think his mom's finally getting the hang of the breast-feeding."

"Great!" I breathed a sigh of relief. It was good to know, though slightly humbling, that things could go along just fine without me.

As we drove the well-maintained highways from Tel Aviv to Jerusalem, a journey of about forty-five minutes or so, Lenny switched gears from doctor into "tour guide" mode.

"So, have you read the Torah?" he asked us, then said, "Well, I know you have, Rachel, but how 'bout you, Ruthie?"

"Not really," she admitted, and then, in the day's best non-sequitur, said, "What are you doing here?"

"I couldn't let you beautiful daughters of Israel come up to the land for the first time without a suitable welcome, now could I?" he said. "Anyway, it was actually the week of my own vacation, and I didn't have anything specific to keep me in San Francisco, and since I was able to find coverage for our patients, I thought, why not come spend the secular New Year in my favorite place in the world, with my very favorite people?"

"Have you been here a lot before?" I asked.

"Spent a year here when I was a rabbinic student, and then four years at med school in Beer-Sheba after I made the change. Half my family lives here, so I've also spent a lot of summers running around Jerusalem."

"You were a rabbinic student? You never told me that," I said.

"I have all kinds of secrets you don't know!" beamed Lenny.

We were traversing a large, flat valley, the late afternoon sky pale above us. "So okay," said Lenny. "Enough with the small talk. Back to my Torah lesson. So Rachel, tell us who Joshua was."

"Joshua son of Nun was the person Moses appointed to lead the Israelites into the land of Canaan. Moses had to pass on the torch before entering 'the Land,' since God had told him, as a result of what he did at Meribo, that he wasn't allowed to come in. He died before they crossed the Jordan River."

"Correct. Joshua was also in charge of the Hebrew armies that fought the people already living here when they came to Canaan. Though, I must say, it's my observation that even though they started out well, razing the walls of Jericho and all that, they sort of petered out on the idea of conquest after that, eventually living alongside all the inhabitants of Canaan. Precisely as God had told them *not* to do. But that's another story. Anyway, what you see here," he gestured out the window, "is the Valley of Aijalon, where the sun stood still and where Joshua fought the battle with the Amorites."

I looked out the window, hardly breathing to think that this very place was mentioned in the Holy Torah.

The road now began to slope gently upwards. Strung along the side, I saw groups of abandoned and rusted military vehicles. "Look there," exclaimed Lenny. "Those are the tanks that the Hagganah used when they were trying to reach Jerusalem before declaring independence in 1948. They kept throwing themselves against this blockade, but were vulnerable in this narrow pass. There were lots of casualties. Eventually, they found an old abandoned road leading up the valley and managed to break through. I've heard people talk about what it was like to see them drive into Jerusalem. They say it was like a miracle."

"We have to stop before the sign at the town limits of Jerusalem so that we can walk in," I said.

"Really? What for?" asked Lenny.

"It has to do with one of the Psalms. Rabbi Lehrer says it's traditional to read it before entering the city," I explained. "And it's important that we walk in for the first time on foot."

"Psalm 126?" said Lenny.

"Yes. How'd you know that?"

"Like I said before, I know more than you think."

I nodded. "Mmm-hmm. Well, if you know a tenth as much Bible as you know medicine, your knowledge must be formidable."

Lenny didn't reply, but he didn't contradict me either.

When we arrived at the large sign at the city limit, Lenny let us out, then went and parked up past the sign a few hundred feet. As he returned to where we stood, I took out my little silver Psalter, and we began to read:

Though he goes along weeping,
carrying the seed bag,
he shall come back with songs of joy,
carrying his sheaves.

Lenny recited the Psalm with us as we walked across the city limit and entered Jerusalem officially. Afterwards, I saw his eyes were full of tears. Then he broke into a song, dancing a little jig on our way back to the car, where we all piled back in.

It was about four o'clock in the afternoon, and the sun's rays were getting long.

"Come on!" said Lenny. "Let's drive up to Mt. Scopus, to the Hebrew University, where I can give you the best view of the city ever! A secret spot known only to locals!"

His enthusiasm was contagious, and both Ruthie and I agreed, no longer feeling one bit tired from our long day of travelling.

Lenny drove on through the steeply rolling hills of Jerusalem, and I saw the yellow stone of all the buildings, splashed with rosy light here at the end of the day. I felt the light enter my heart and begin to warm it up.

As for Ruthie, she was mostly just looking at Lenny.

"Will we see the Temple Mount from where you're taking us?" I said, as we turned right and began switch-backing up a curvy road to one of the city's peaks.

"Of course we will. That's the point!" laughed Lenny.

Given the opportunity, I thought I'd get a little info from Lenny about the Temple Mount, since I planned to go up there, looking for…looking for what? Three pillars and a Star of David? And then what? A sign from God? Oh well, I'd think about that later.

"Can we go up on the Temple Mount itself?" I asked.

"Yes, but only during certain very proscribed hours. It's a Muslim holy site now. And actually, I don't really recommend going up there."

"Why not?" I said, curious.

"It's just not very…I don't know…not very comfortable for Jews. It's better to leave it to the Muslims for now and just look at it from a distance."

"But doesn't that bother you?" I said.

"Not really," said Lenny. "After all, we're here!" he laughed, and gestured at all the buildings around. "As we say at the Seder, '*Dayenu.*' It's enough!"

"Well, anyway, I do want to go up there sometime. So it sounds like you have been there."

"Yes. I went a lot when I was young, but not much recently. The last time was about two years ago, I think."

"So, were there any pillars? Any writing or symbols on the buildings?"

"Writing? Symbols? Pillars? Doctor Roseman, what are you up to?" said Lenny, eyeing me in the rear-view mirror.

"That's now Dr. al-Shadi," I said, then spent the rest of the ride up Mt. Scopus explaining about the wedding, to Lenny's delight and astonishment.

We arrived at a garage near the top of the hill, entered and parked. We then went into the faculty building through the garage entrance, ascending four flights to the roof.

Stepping out the door, I saw a panorama of the city of Jerusalem with the golden dome in the center of my field of vision. It was a long way away, and from here, looked like a shiny cup you could take in the palm of your hand. I saw my arm reaching out, and heard a sound rising up. Then I realized that this sound seemed to be coming from my throat.

I found I had fallen forward onto my knees and covered my face with both hands. I felt hands on my back and opened my eyes to see the worried faces of Lenny and Ruthie. Turning from them, I looked back at the Temple Mount, squinting so I would only let in as much of the view as my eyes could handle. I identified a name for the feeling in my heart. I think it's called awe.

I could see that Ruthie was saying things, but I couldn't hear her voice. Lenny, on the other hand, had sat back onto his heels and was just watching me. He seemed to understand what was going on.

Gradually, the sound returned, and I could hear Ruthie saying, "Rachel, Rachel…are you okay? What's the matter? What is it?"

Ignoring her questions, I stood up silently and walked to the edge of the roof, now able to open my eyes fully and take in the sight: the golden dome at the center of a large, walled space, another dome in a smaller grey building at one end, and, all around, the hills of Jerusalem, carpeted with the glowing lights of many homes. *How beautiful are your tents, Oh Jacob, your dwelling places, Oh Israel…*[11]

Both Ruthie and Lenny were now silent as well, taking in this glorious sight.

When we got back into the car, Lenny drove in silence. After several attempts at conversation, Ruthie gave up, shrugging her shoulders and looking out the window.

Jerusalem, Israel
Evening of Wednesday, December 27th 2006
Dr. Rachel al-Shadi, Ruthie Roseman, and Dr. Lenny Goldstein

Lenny drove us to the King David Hotel, located a few blocks from the Old City on the top of a nearby hill. It was a large, stately hotel, composed of the ubiquitous yellow Jerusalem stone, its entrance adorned by tall and graceful palm trees, its lobby painted in shades of light and dark blue, the beams intricately patterned with medallions and a variety of geometric designs. The front desk staff was efficient and welcoming, and as we followed the bellhop down the marble hallway to the elevator, I noticed the floor tiles were engraved with the signatures of famous people who had stayed at or visited the hotel: Winston Churchill, Anwar Sadat, William Clinton. I felt dwarfed by the grandeur and history of this magnificent hotel.

Lenny accompanied us to our room, a comfortable space with two queen-sized beds and a sitting area with sofa and chairs.

---

[11] Numbers 24:5

Outside, there was a balcony overlooking the tennis courts and swimming pool. On the table by the sofa was a plate with grapes, apples, nuts, and a block of cheddar cheese. Lenny sat and nibbled while Ruthie and I unpacked.

We had made reservations at the front desk for dinner in one of the hotel restaurants. Ruthie and I got ready, dressing in the bathroom one after the other.

When Ruthie emerged, I had to whistle myself. She was wearing a brand new dress, one I hadn't seen before. She must have purchased this during her days on her own in Cairo. It was dark red, with a crossed v-neck bodice, tight waist, and flowing skirt. She had applied makeup and finished it off with the high-heeled pumps she'd worn at my wedding.

I looked across at Lenny. He wasn't saying anything, but he didn't need to. His face said it all.

Oh man, I thought. I hope we can make it through dinner without a scene from *Last Tango in Paris*. *Last Tango in Jerusalem*. How about that? It had a ring to it.

"Earth to Rachel!" I heard Ruthie say, then ask Lenny, "Is she going to be like this the whole time we're here?"

"Who knows? I think it's some kind of religious fervor!"

I laughed at them both. "Don't worry. It isn't catching, as far as I can tell."

"That's not what I've heard," said Lenny.

We walked down three flights of stairs to the main level hallway, turned right, then, after entering the grand lobby, turned right again and headed down another flight of stairs to the restaurant. It was small and cozy, with a view out onto the terraced gardens, its tables adorned with white tablecloths and crystal water goblets.

The waiter came and poured ice water, took our drink order, and told us someone would be by soon with bread.

Lenny took a sip of water, saying, "Tell me a little about this religious fervor."

Ruthie said, "I'd like to know too. What happened to you at Mt. Scopus?"

"I don't know," I answered slowly. "It's hard to explain." I struggled, groping for words.

Lenny was looking at me intently. "What did you feel, though?"

I made another effort to describe it. "When I saw the Dome, it felt like something that had been out of place moved back into proper alignment. Kind of like a blocked channel opened up. I was flooded, overflowing, completely inundated with...the feeling..."

Ruthie said, "All I can say is that it's a good thing you weren't over by the edge of the roof when you fell down like that."

I agreed with her. "That would definitely have been one quick way to meet the Maker." This seemed to be on my mind tonight.

Lenny said. "You know, the Temple Mount is where the Akeda, the binding of Isaac was supposed to have happened. Abraham saw the place, *ha-Makom*, from afar. Back then, it was just a mountain, without buildings or man-made structures of any kind. When he saw it, Abraham knew that it was where he would prove his love for God."

"By killing his son," said Ruthie.

"Yes."

"A helluva way to show you love someone," she said. "Man, the Jews are really something."

"It's not just the Jews," I offered.

"What?" said Ruthie.

"Well, of course, the Christians believe in this story of the test of Abraham. It's part of their own Bible. But what you might not know is that the Muslims also have a version of this tradition. God asks Abraham to kill his son to prove his submission. In this case, the Islamic legend says that it was Ishmael, rather than Isaac, who was offered for sacrifice."

"But that's absurd," said Lenny. "It's clearly Isaac who is offered."

"Why is it so ridiculous," I said, defensively.

"Because," said Lenny, patiently, "the Torah clearly states that it is Isaac who accompanies Abraham up to Mt. Moriah. 'Take your son, your only one, Isaac, whom you love, and go to the land of Moriah, and offer him there as a burnt offering on one of the heights that I will point out to you.'"

"Wow!" said Ruthie, "You know that by heart?"

"I'll do anything to impress you!" he laughed, and a look passed between them.

Ignoring their courting antics, I said, "Isn't it just possible that both stories are true? After all, quantum physics has shown that a particle can actually travel two paths at the same time."

"Hmm?" said Lenny, still looking at Ruthie.

"Ruthie, you're a physicist, you know that's true—"

But she was looking back at Lenny and not listening to me either. I tried one last time. "It's kind of like what we've learned about the spin of the electron. If you measure it, it's one thing only, but if you could measure it again, it'd be something else. So one time, you check it, and it's Isaac. The next time, it's Ishmael."

"Mmm-hmm," said Ruthie.

This was hopeless.

I gave up in frustration and downed my water in a gulp.

Fortunately, our food arrived, and we busied ourselves with eating. After we finished and the waiter cleared our plates, I said, "What are we doing tomorrow?"

Lenny at last removed his gaze from Ruthie and looked at me. "Well, I hate to say it, but we probably should go see the Holocaust museum, Yad Vashem, in the morning, then head over to the Old City and the Western Wall in the afternoon."

I nodded. "Okay," I said, "But I do want to go up and see the Temple Mount tomorrow. I found out that it's open from 2:00 to 4:00."

Lenny screwed his face up into a caricature of distaste. "Ahhh…Rachel, I really don't want to go up there. Last time I went, I just felt so…unwelcome. I vowed I wouldn't go back, not until we can make peace with Palestine."

I shook my head. "You could be waiting a long time. But anyway, I'm happy to go by myself. It'll only be for a couple of hours. You two would probably like to do something on your own for a little while." Actually, I was glad that I might be able to do my snooping without a witness.

"Are you sure?" said Lenny, considering this. "I don't know."

"You guys will be right nearby," I said. "I'll be fine."

"I could take you through the tunnels by the Western Wall," Lenny said to Ruthie. "They're incredible."

"Really?" she said, taking his hand.

"Mmm-hmm," he said, and I saw they were beginning to head off into lover-land again.

I said, loudly, breaking into the mood, "Good! So it's

settled! I'll go up on the Temple Mount while you two go through the tunnels. We can meet afterwards for coffee."

"Yes, great!" said Lenny, looking at me for just a moment before turning back to Ruthie.

That settled, I left them to enjoy dessert together, returning to our hotel room on my own.

I hadn't admitted this to them, but seeing the two of them together made me miss Yakub even more acutely. Back in my room, I lay down on my bed and gave in to my feelings. Every cell in my body seemed to miss him. When I thought about it, I realized I not only missed him, but was also horribly worried about him. Was he alright? Had his headache cleared up? Was his lung infection really healed? I began to fret about him more and more. What kind of doctor was I, to let him go off on this pilgrimage after all these illnesses? At the end of all this thinking, I was thoroughly convinced that something terrible was going to happen to him.

At length, with nothing else to do, I got dressed in my pajamas, brushed my teeth, and lay down in bed. I didn't leave a light on for Ruthie, since I was pretty certain she wouldn't be spending the night here. I lay in the dark awake for many hours, worrying about Yakub.

Jerusalem, Israel
6:30 am. Thursday, December 28th 2006
Dr. Rachel al-Shadi

At some point, I must have fallen asleep, but I awoke early, disturbed by formless dreams. Feeling fatigued yet also agitated, I ordered coffee from room service. I settled down then to read the Torah portion for that week, which was about the reunion of Jacob and Joseph in Egypt. It made me wonder: when Jacob left Canaan for Egypt with his family, did he know what he was getting them into? Four hundred years of slavery. Then, redemption. But here we were, all of us humans, still waging war and killing people. Confused about where that redemption had really gotten us, I strapped on my running shoes and headed outside for a jog.

I turned into a narrow lane, and then ran the several blocks to the *Eir ha-Attika*, the Old City, turning right and running down the hill along its ancient wall. I followed it all the way around, circumambulating the Old City and the Temple Mount. On my way, from far below on the street, I got a close-up view of the battered grey-blue dome of the al-Aqsa mosque, hardly believing that I was actually here, seeing the sights I had only seen before in posters at my synagogue in San Francisco. Despite the early hour, I passed many people, a strikingly diverse mixture of tourists, school children, orthodox Jews, and Arab street vendors. Before I knew it, I was around the full circumference and on my way back to my hotel.

At 8:30, after I had showered and changed, I heard a knock on the door, and let Ruthie in, fresh from her overnight escapades. She was wearing sweatpants that were way too big, and a t-shirt that said "Yo-Semite." On her feet, she wore some oversized flip-flops.

"Good morning, beautiful!" I said. "Nice outfit."

Ruthie laughed. She looked happier than I could remember seeing her before. "Came back to get my clothes," she said.

"Good plan."

After Ruthie had dressed in her own clothes, we went down to meet Lenny at the restaurant. Apparently, breakfast at the King David Hotel was legendary. They set it up buffet style, the plates of delicacies covering several large tables: dried and fresh fruit of every kind, nuts, hot and cold cereal, bagels, bread, jellies of ten varieties, silver warming pans full of blintzes, pancakes, potatoes, scrambled eggs. The only thing missing was bacon, which was okay by me.

There was a man taking custom crepe orders, and I requested a raspberry jelly crepe, watching as the man spread the white liquid over the bottom of the pan, the bubbles along the edge indicating its state of readiness. At just the perfect instant, he flipped the crepe over in the pan, browning the other side for a moment before tossing it onto a plate, spreading it with jelly and, with a few deft movements, folding it and sprinkling it with confectioner's sugar.

The crepe was still steaming hot when I brought it to the table and took a bite, the red jelly oozing out as the fork sliced into it. It was about the most delicious thing I had ever eaten. Ruthie, Lenny, and I chatted for another half hour or so, then Lenny went to collect his uncle's car and drive around to meet us at the front door.

The day was cool and overcast, and we drove together to Yad Vashem and the Har ha-Zikaron, the mountain of remembrance. Lenny pointed out the various sites along the way, taking a route past the area of the Knesset and the government buildings, ending up skirting a large green expanse, the Jerusalem Forest.

The Holocaust Museum, Yad Vashem, was a complex of buildings located on the crest of one of the hills of Jerusalem, with clusters of buildings located in tree lined pathways, each trail a memorial of one kind of another. Lenny parked the car along the access drive, several hundred yards from the main museum building.

As he put the car into "Park" and engaged the emergency brake, Ruthie said, "Remind me again why we are here?"

I looked over at her. Her face was ashen.

Though Lenny had his hand on the door latch, he removed it now and settled back into his seat, looking at Ruthie.

"Are you okay?" he said.

Ruthie nodded. "These kinds of places usually make me feel sick all day."

Lenny observed her for a moment. "I thought you should see this, so you could get a sense of why *ha-Aretz*, the land of Israel, is so important to us Jews. You almost have to see this first so you can understand."

Ruthie nodded. "But you know," she said, "our own family, including me, has been doing its very best to forget this, and *not* remember it, for a lot of years."

"And that," said Lenny, "Is exactly why you need to see it now. Every single person, even if they're not Jewish, needs to come acknowledge what we human beings are capable of. Humanity, as a whole, needs to process this trauma."

Ruthie took a very deep breath, letting it out with a sigh. Then she reached for the car handle and we all got out.

The first thing we saw, hanging out at the end of a severed track, was a railroad cattle car. The sign said that this was the kind of car used to transport Jews and others to the concentration camps during the Holocaust. The Nazis crammed more than one hundred people into each car, jammed together without food or water. Many died before the train reached its destination, the placard explained. I looked at the cattle car. It perched at the end of the track, as though hovering above an abyss.

Turning from this sight, we walked upwards along a winding path, ending at a large tent-like building whose sign said it was the "Hall of Remembrance." Inside, we found a single cavernous room, dark and shadowed, with a flame burning, ashes of holocaust dead before it, the names of various concentration camps carved into the stone floor. I closed my eyes and said a prayer.

From there, the three of us went to the entrance of the main exhibit, setup as a long passage cut into the mountaintop, a jagged skylight extending from one end to the other. At the entrance, I saw a plastic collections container, and suddenly remembered Rabbi Lehrer's twenty-dollar bill. Taking my book of Psalms out of my pocket, I removed the rabbi's money and dropped it into the plastic container alongside the other bills.

Feeling somewhat like a sacrificial lamb, I entered the museum. As I walked along, zigging and zagging from one room to the next beneath the central spine of the museum, the images and sounds in each of the rooms collected like iron nails in the empty space inside me. Photos like this were too horrible to process: piles of twisted bodies, nameless, pale and white under steel-grey skies; the faces of children through barbed wire, black and white images rendering the yellow six-pointed star grey, the word *Jude* in stark black at the center. At the end of the gallery, I felt so full of iron nails that I could hardly walk.

As I continued on through that seemingly endless hallway, I also had a strange sensation, as though someone were watching me. Uncomfortable, I looked back over my shoulder, probed the faces of the other visitors to try to detect the source of this sensation. Did I see a man more than once, far behind us, limping quickly away each time he was detected? No, I decided, I was just spooked by the place. I must be seeing Nazis everywhere.

The last gallery was a large, circular room, with photos extending upwards, covering the entire surface of the dome-like ceiling. This room was called the Hall of Names. The goal of the exhibit was to collect a name and biography for each and every Jew killed in the Holocaust. They were over halfway there, three million plus names. On a screen across the room, I saw images and words projected. One after the other, faces came on the screen. An old man, with grey beard and fringes. A woman, dressed for travel. A young girl with braids and ribbons, reminding me very much of my sister as a child. A dapper man, with a cravat and mustache, his information card filled out in Hebrew. In English letters, his name was Hayyim. Life.

As we left the hall, I took Ruthie's hand. She squeezed mine and leaned against my shoulder for a moment.

Outside, we entered a plaza overlooking Jerusalem. I thought to myself, "There is too much to remember. Too many names. Names and names and names." All of these names made me want to go into a room by myself and scream. To never stop screaming, ever, ever, ever.

I covered my face and let the tears overtake me. I had not had any family members who had gone to Auschwitz or Birkenau. Nevertheless, my family was affected. My Jewish family. In San Francisco, I suppose, it was possible to forget this and to hide. But there was no hiding, really, from this. It would find you wherever you were, Jew or otherwise.

When we got to where the car was parked, Lenny signaled that we should walk a little farther, past the cattle car, down another small path. Ruthie and I followed him along the narrow walkway, ending in a small garden, ringed by walls of lists. Each name on the list belonged to a person, a non-Jew, who had heroically risked his or her life during the Holocaust to save Jews. This was called "The Garden of the Righteous among the Nations." There were over twenty-two thousand names including, from my own country, Waitstill and Martha Sharp and a man called Varian Fry; from Albania, Mefail and Njazi Bicaku, a Muslim couple who, along with their fellow Muslim citizens, protected all the Jews in their country from discovery by the Nazis; over six thousand names from Poland alone; and, of course, the famous German, Oskar Schindler.

Beside the heavy nails that had collected within me, I felt a new sensation. It trembled there, fragile as an embryo. Hope.

We climbed up to the car, and drove silently back towards Jerusalem. As we did, I thought about the pamphlet from the library in Cambridge, *The Protocols of the Learned Elders of Zion*. The author of this book predicted that the Jews would perpetrate all kinds of horrors on the rest of the world. The irony now seemed staggering. The only ones who had actually caused the kind of things they predicted were the ones who theoretically exposed them! Was the Holocaust world the kind of world the authors of *The Protocols* desired? Was this the humanity they wanted to be, once the "Jewish problem" was eliminated?

Jerusalem, Israel
Afternoon of Thursday, December 28th 2006
Dr. Rachel al-Shadi, Ruthie Roseman, and Dr. Lenny Goldstein

Lenny drove us back to the King David Hotel and parked his car. From there, we walked the several blocks to the Old City, entering through the Jaffa Gate.

Inside, there was a large, cobblestoned courtyard and, on the far end, a narrow street, glittering with color and sparkling gold baubles, the Arab market place. We entered, descending down the street as vendors invited us to join them in their shops for a cup of tea, undoubtedly hoping to entice us with their wares as we sipped. Recalling Fatima's advice to wear a head-covering on the Temple Mount, I asked Lenny and Ruthie if we could stop at a store displaying gaily-colored scarves, which fluttered in the breeze created by the many passersby. They agreed, and we entered the shady interior of the shop, where I selected a beautiful, deep azure-colored scarf with small flowers embroidered along the edges.

After completing the purchase, we continued further into the Arab quarter, and Lenny selected a small open-air restaurant where we sat down for lunch. The somber mood that had settled on us at Yad Vashem had receded, and the hope I had felt earlier had continued to grow. Sitting in the open air, feeling the pleasant breeze on my skin and seeing the yellow stone of the ancient buildings all around, domes, spires, and turrets peeking out above the walls across the way, I had that uncanny sensation again, though in a less intense form this time, the same feeling as I'd had when I saw the Temple Mount for the first time. That feeling of wholeness.

Lenny ordered us Falafel sandwiches and coffee, along with bottles of fizzy water. The food came. Despite my large breakfast earlier today, I felt hungry again. The crispy falafel, perfectly fried, paired with the fresh soft pita bread and tangy *tehina* was among the best I'd ever had.

As we finished up our coffee, my attention was drawn to some strange noises coming from behind me, the sound of slurping, then a kind of strangled swallowing, as if someone were choking with every bite.

Turning to make sure that whoever was making these sounds was not actually in need of a rescue maneuver, my gaze

settled on a man several tables behind us. Thanks to my medical
training, I knew immediately that this man suffered from some kind
of dysmorphic syndrome. His body was thin, almost emaciated. He
was of average height, about five foot nine, but oddly, one side of
his body, the left side, looked bigger than the other. Or perhaps it
was his right side that was shriveled. His head had the appearance of
a large top, broad at the dome and narrowing to a point at the
bottom, the jaw small, almost absent. His hair was dark, but in the
center of his forehead was a lock of stark white. Low down, almost
on his neck, his ears protruded with the appearance of small, dried
apricots. Most startling, however, were his eyes, which were an icy
pale blue color that shone eerily against his translucent skin.

The man's features were so misshapen it was impossible to
even determine his race or nationality.

With a look like this, I figured this man might not have all
his marbles. But when he opened his mouth to order coffee, his
speech was surprisingly refined, a punctilious English, devoid of
accent. After ordering, he looked at me and smiled. I found the look
oddly unsettling, but smiled back at him, turning around again to
rejoin the conversation with Ruthie and Lenny.

Lenny was telling Ruthie about the next stop on our
itinerary, the Western Wall, known to some as the Wailing Wall and,
here in Jerusalem, as the *Kotel ha-Ma'aravi* or just "The Kotel."

"It's quite a scene," said Lenny. "Especially if you've never
been there before. It's really just the exposed portion of the western
retaining wall of Herod's Temple. But because it's the Temple, the
most holy building in all of Judaism, it's still sacred to us."

"Why's it such a scene?" I asked.

"You'll just see all kinds of people there, from tourists to
sages. It's always kind of a festival at the wall. People praying,
crying, laughing, dancing. They put notes in all the nooks and
crannies between the stones in the wall. Even if they don't believe in
God, they want to give it a try, just on the off-chance God might be
checking…" Lenny laughed.

"How about these tunnels?" Ruthie asked.

"Now those are really fascinating. It turns out that a lot of
Herod's ancient Temple wall is actually still buried. The tunnels
follow the wall below ground level."

"Gosh!" said Ruthie. "Can you actually go under the
Temple Mount there?"

"No, no, no. That's not allowed. That is very sacred space, not only to Judaism but to Islam and Christianity as well. But it's really amazing just to see the wall. Some of the stones are as big as school buses. So big, the Romans couldn't even knock them down when they destroyed the Temple in 70 CE."

We paid our bill and left the restaurant. The odd man was still sitting at his table watching, and he waved at me as we left. I raised a tentative hand in farewell.

From the Arab section, we walked now to the Jewish quarter, descending through the city a number of blocks until we reached a road skirting the southern boundary of the Old City. From there, we turned left, entering a line of people waiting at the security screening. Soon, we emerged into the large plaza next to the Western Wall.

I noticed that there was a barrier extending westward from the wall. On one side, the color of the people's clothing was predominantly black. On the other, it was bright and varied, like a rainbow. Men on the left, women on the right.

Ruthie and I went to the right, making our way through the crowd of women until we reached the stones of the wall. They were light yellow, flush one to the other, each about the size of a refrigerator, some chipped and broken on the edges, with tufts of grass poking through the cracks.

I closed my eyes and said a prayer. What kind of prayer? The only kind that seemed possible, here in this sacred place. A prayer for peace. But I didn't write it on a piece of paper and stuff it between the cracks in the wall. The goal of my prayer did not seem up to God, but to us people.

After twenty minutes or so, I checked my watch. It was 1:55 pm. The Temple Mount opened at 2:00, and Ruthie and Lenny's tour of the catacombs began at the same time. We said goodbye and separated, arranging to meet back here at the Western Wall again a little after 4:00 pm. Just before they left, I remembered they didn't allow visitors to wear religious symbols up on the Temple Mount. I removed my Star of David and handed it to Ruthie.

The entry to the Temple Mount was right next to the Western Wall and, at precisely 2:00 pm, I entered through the security gate, then walked up the stairs and across a wooden bridge, entering the site through the Maimonides Gate. Once there, I tied my blue scarf inexpertly around my head.

I stopped a moment longer in the space just outside the entrance, reminding myself of what I was looking for up here. Something to do with three pillars and a six-sided star of David. That was all pretty vague, I realized, but that seemed to be the *modus operandi* of these signs from God, as far as I could tell.

I started off, then, walking across the open space in front of the al-Aqsa Mosque, recognizing that my job seeking a sign for world redemption up here on the Temple Mount would be somewhat hampered by the fact that I, as a non-Muslim, was not permitted to enter any of the buildings. I consoled myself by reasoning that most revelations happened outside in the open air, and not inside. That's where Abraham had his hand stopped by the angel, where Jacob saw the angels ascending and descending the ladder, where Moses noticed the burning bush, where the people of Israel saw God speak in thunder…

I admonished myself to pay attention. No more dreaming off. Look for pillars!

I surveyed the space around me. The area was only sparsely populated at this time of day. Ahead of me, there was a set of stairs leading up to the Dome of the Rock, arched colonnades at its top supported by graceful pillars. Three of them. Suddenly alert, I scanned the plaster surface above them for letters or symbols. There was nothing. I decided I would circumnavigate the octagonal Dome of the Rock, going counterclockwise. Briefly, I wondered if Yakub was similarly ambulating far away in Makkah.

At the eastern entrance to the building, I came upon an odd structure, a sort of miniature replica of the Dome, but with open walls, the roof supported by elegant pillars. I decided I would walk around the full circumference of the larger building before exploring this smaller structure. I continued walking, admiring the beautiful and intricate tile-work. I knew that the script ringing the top, just below the dazzling golden dome, composed Quranic verses.

My steps brought me back to the odd dome next to the larger building. The first strange thing about this building was that it had eleven sides, each roof angle supported by its own pillar. Also odd was the small dome on top of it which was another shape entirely. I counted its sides. Six of them. This was a hexagon! Like a star of David! Pillars and a Star of David!

Was this the sign? But I didn't feel anything. Ugghh! All this looking for signs was infuriating!

Nevertheless, I kept on going. I entered the structure, examining it carefully and spying a small niche, decorated on each side with a pillar inlaid into the surrounding stone. Above it, I saw more of the graceful script, a long verse in Arabic. *What could this be?* I took out my notebook and wrote down the Arabic letters. It took me about a half hour to finish transcribing all of them. When I was done, I still had no idea what it said. Perusing what I'd written, I decided I hadn't yet had a sign.

Looking up, I was startled to find a man standing next to me. I had not heard him approach. The Temple Mount had emptied of people and was now completely deserted, which made his presence near me all the more unnerving. With a shock, I recognized the man I had seen in the café.

"Hello," he said, in his oddly bland English, limping closer to me. I noticed now that it was definitely his right side that was atrophied, causing his limp. I wondered, was it some form of cerebral palsy?

"Hi," I said, not wanting to encourage conversation.

"Are you American?" he said.

"Yes." I looked back down to my writing, attempting to discourage him from further talk.

"I don't really have a nationality," he continued, though I hadn't asked. "But at the moment I live in London."

"Hmmm," I said, momentarily considering the option of running away, but then abandoning it. Given the man's limp, I figured if anything happened, I could get away from him easily.

"I noticed you in the coffee shop earlier," the man continued. "Are you a doctor?"

"Yes," I said, now curious, in spite of myself. "How did you know?"

"The way you looked at me. Like you were worried, and saw something to worry about. I'm afraid I do have a digestive condition."

"I'm sorry," I said. "Are you alright?"

"For the moment, yes," said the man. "But I don't know how long that will last."

"Well, I wish you a good recovery," I said, putting my notebook and pen away and beginning to walk towards the Dome of the Rock.

The man followed me. "Were you writing down the poem? Above the niche in the Dome of the Chain?" He pointed back at the small dome we'd just left.

"Yes. Actually, I don't think it's a poem. It's probably verses from the Quran."

"Hmm. Yes. Do you like poetry?" he asked.

"Yes, I do. But anyway, I really have to go." I sped up a little, surprised that he had no problem keeping up, despite his limp.

"I know where there are more poems," he called out. "Would you like to see them?"

This stopped me for a moment. I thought about it. Could this man be somehow connected to the *sign* I was looking for?

"It's alright," the man said. I saw his face fall. "Most people don't want to talk to me. Especially women." A tear splashed onto his cheek.

Despite myself, I felt a pang of pity. "Do you really know where there are more poems?"

He looked up eagerly, saying, "Yes! Do you want to see them?"

"Alright," I said, feeling misgivings, but still going along with him. I was becoming increasingly convinced that something about this meeting was related to the sign I was seeking. I reassured myself by reasoning that I had plenty of patients like this, and even had a special gift with them, I thought. This had never failed me before.

The man turned back for a moment, pointing to the small dome where I had transcribed my poem. "This is called the Dome of the Chain. Also known as the dome of *Dawud and Suleyman*, or the Dome of Judgment."

"Does that mean David and Solomon?" I asked.

He nodded, saying. "To the Muslims, the dome is considered the umbilicus."

"What, of the world?" I said.

He nodded again, and made an expansive swinging motion with his arms. "The whole world."

"I thought that was Makkah?" I said.

But my guide did not seem to hear me. He was already walking rapidly forward. "Come and see this!" He said.

He went and stood up against the side of the Dome of the

Rock, next to one of the windows. It was covered with mesh wiring. "Look here!"

Reluctantly, I looked through the window, though all I could see was darkness.

"Can you see?" he was standing close to me, his finger pointing through the metal mesh. "It's where Muhammad ascended to the seventh heaven!"

Vague structures began to emerge from the building's dark interior. When I realized what we were doing, I sprang away. If I was not welcome in this building, I certainly did not want to "steal" a look through the window.

"No," I said.

My guide looked dismayed. "What? You don't want to see it?"

"No. Not like this."

"Alright, then I'll show you the poems now," he said. "Come and have a look, and some coffee. I'll bring them to you." He took my elbow with his left hand, and I felt my flesh recoil from his touch. Sensitive to his vulnerability, however, I did not pull away.

"It's not far," he said. He let go of my arm and began walking again.

Feeling sorry for him and still convinced this man might be the sign from God that I was seeking, I followed him, out through a gate in what, with my rudimentary sense of direction, I deemed to be the northwest corner of the Temple Mount. We came out into a busy street of shops in the Arab Quarter. My guide was chattering on and I hardly listened, but he obviously had a destination in mind, and I felt safe among the bustle and crowd of people.

After about five minutes of walking, I asked my guide how much farther we were going. He said, "Soon! It isn't far!" The streets were now empty, only the occasional store or café.

He pointed up ahead. I saw a small cluster of tables outside a storefront with a green awning. Several people sat there. When he saw them, he waved and they waved back. He took my arm again in his left hand and guided me towards the table.

"Now we'll have coffee," he said, and I did, indeed, see coffee on the tables as we approached. But in one of those moments of clarity, as the world tips instantly and oh-so-easily from good to evil, I also saw one of the men stand up quickly from the table. His motion was *too* quick. At the same time, my guide's grip on my arm grew tighter, like a vice. Someone came from behind me and pulled my head against his chest, clamping his hand tightly over my mouth. The man from the table grabbed both my wrists. He quickly wrapped a black nylon rope tightly around them. Immediately, my palms pulsed painfully.

In a nightmare scene, I caught sight of a white sedan, just as another man popped open the trunk. They pushed me in, and the man behind me released my mouth for a moment. I screamed once, but the sound was deadened in the confined space of the trunk. The man slammed his hand back over my mouth while, with the other hand, he took a dirty cloth out of his pocket and then used both hands to stuff it into my mouth. It was dry, and I could not push it out. I retched. He wrapped a checkered cloth around my face to hold the gag in place.

Meanwhile, the man who had tied my hands was now tying my feet. Thus, with relatively little fuss, I was completely bound and helpless, lying in the trunk of a car. I saw the four faces of the men looking down at me. My would-be poetry guide was speaking. *"Her father is rich,"* I heard him say.

Just before the trunk slammed down, the man leaned towards me, and I heard him whisper something in my ear. "You should know," he said, his whispered tone silky, "that poetry you found in Cairo, the *diwan* my son took from your husband, is utter nonsense. There is no poem to redeem the world." A cruel smile curved his thin lips, though an instant later, something else showed in his eyes: an odd look of confusion, it seemed to me. Then the trunk slammed down and it was dark.

And just that way, in a single moment, I went from a free woman with a future to a prisoner with no hope. I was going to die. I heard the engine start, the car begin to bump over the cobblestoned ground.

That man's son had obviously been following me and Yakub for some time. He was the one who'd stolen the *diwan* of Mrs. Dunash. What a stupid, stupid person I was! And it was all for nothing, as his father had just told me. *There is no poem to redeem the world.* And he must know. He'd heard Said al-Shadi's poetry.

The significance of his other words, which had not really registered at the time, suddenly hit me. *Her father is rich!* What...? My father may have been well off, but he certainly was not rich, and now he was dead, his money tied up in trusts, legally protected by contracts more impenetrable than Makkah to the Jews. The man was lying to them! But why?

Whoever said that kidnappers had to be honest?

I registered this with horror. Did these kidnappers think they would be able to get a lot of money from my father? What would they do when they found out that they couldn't?

My brain worked furiously to discover some method of escape. I searched around with my heels and the fronts of my feet to see if there was any hole in the bottom of the trunk. Maybe I could drop out some personal item that would show people I had been here? No, no, that was stupid. Who would see it? Who would even know I was gone?

Lenny and Ruthie would be waiting for me at 4:00. That was probably still an hour from now. We could get a long way away from Jerusalem in that time.

But if these were Palestinian terrorists, as I'd feared, and we were heading to the Palestinian territories, surely, in that case, we'd be going through a checkpoint? When the car stopped, I would slam my feet into the top of the trunk and alert the border guards! And didn't they open trunks anyway at those checkpoints? Surely so? How could they propose to smuggle me across? With a sinking heart, I realized they must have some plan for this.

I found out soon enough. After only a short time, the car stopped. I did begin slamming my feet against the trunk lid, but it soon opened, and I saw one of my captors standing there, an ironic smile on his face as my kicking legs connected only with air. The other two men came to help him. I did not see my "guide" among them, and realized he must just have been the "delivery boy." Two of the men lifted me out of the trunk, while the third leaned over and fussed around with something inside it. I saw that we were parked in a rocky, deserted stand of trees by a dirt road.

The man at the car removed a 3-foot-wide carpet-covered square of wood. Then the two men brought me back over to the car. There was a box, just large enough for a body the size of my own, a rectangular coffin, of sorts. They forced me into it and placed the carpet-square over my head. The wood pressed painfully into my left side and shoulder. They must have screwed it on, because when I pushed up, it would not budge even the tiniest bit. I realized now that even if we passed a checkpoint, the trunk would appear empty. And I couldn't move enough to make any sound inside its mercilessly cramped confines.

I knew I would die of suffocation or carbon-monoxide poisoning in this terrible place. All because I was stupid, stupid, stupid, and stupidly went in my stupid gullible American way believing the world to be a safe place. Safe to search for poems and marry Muslims and act as if redemption were possible. How could I have ever believed that human beings, savage genocidal beasts that we are, could ever actually be capable of loving one another?

With these despairing thoughts, in the darkness and the foul-smelling air of my new prison, I suddenly saw, clearly as day, the face of my beloved Yakub. *I will see you again, whether in this life or the next.* With that, my consciousness began to slip away. I felt a pain in my left pelvic bone. *What is that?* I realized it was the metallic cover of the book of Psalms given to me by my rabbi. Despite the discomfort in my hip, this thought made me feel ever-so-slightly better.

Jerusalem, Israel
Thursday, December 28th 2006
Mr. Smith, to Eugene Smith (journal entry)

My son! It is done! As I had anticipated, here in this place, it was not difficult to find people who sufficiently despise the Jews and the Americans to jump at the chance to destroy them, particularly if they think money is involved. Once I made the first contact, people were more than eager to grab the bait. It just took a word here, a word there, and it was done. I was fortunate to locate a group known for its brutality and rigid adherence to fundamentalist Islamic beliefs. I'm certain that the woman will die under their *hospitality*.

And yet…I am hesitant to even put this into words, because I do not know what it is I am feeling. I thought I would feel triumphant, victorious, here in the city of God, standing tall, the sword of justice held high in my outstretched hand! Instead, I feel…what is it I feel? Well, I admit, I had not expected this Jewish woman to be beautiful.

But it is her eyes I keep remembering, peering from the trunk of the car. Her eyes! My son, despite my unspeakable act, they gazed back at me, with a look so startled and yet so soft, like drops of summer rain on parched ground. My God, is this the look they call compassion?

UNDERSTANDING

al-Khalil, Palestine
5:07 pm. Thursday, December 28th 2006
Dr. Rachel al-Shadi

When my kidnappers unscrewed the lid of my compartment and released me from the trunk of their car, I found myself in an alley behind a dingy, stucco house. They hustled me through the door quickly.

"O God!" I said, in my mind, "Help me!"

The fact that I had said these words, even if silently, terrified me even more. How many holocaust victims, fathers, mothers, children, the most helpless and innocent of people, had said these same words, and with what effect? *Hey, stupid! Remember? God doesn't bother with these kinds of details!*

Stumbling through a hallway, my mind consumed by images of beheadings I'd seen on CNN, I reached a living room, and my captors threw me into a chair. One of the men untied the gag from around the back of my neck. He removed the rag from my mouth, and, wincing at the slimy saliva that covered it, held it between his thumb and forefinger, as if it contained anthrax. He said a few words to the other man and then left.

The second man sat down in a chair across from me. Next to it was a huge black gun. He picked it up, resting it over his knee. He looked quite comfortable with this gun. I wondered if he had ever used it to kill anyone.

The gunman sat and looked at me. He smiled. I did not smile back. He was a young man, good-looking, with dark hair. He wore one of the ubiquitous white *kufis*. I estimated he was around twenty-five.

"What do you want?" I said. Oh no! I didn't mean to sound angry. "I mean, what can I do for you?" This was just the first of many pitiful things I said in my desperate attempt to please my kidnappers.

He shook his head, shrugging his shoulders.

"No Eenglish" he said.

The ropes were beginning to seriously hurt my wrists, and my shoulders also burned. I thought about screaming, but obviously, I was in a place where they felt it safe to remove the gag, and so realized I would only look ridiculous or pathetic by doing so.

I wanted these kidnappers to see that I was tough and resilient and, overall, a very nice person. Way too nice for anyone to shoot or behead. Did they behead women? I couldn't remember, no matter how desperately I rehashed my mental catalogue of CNN clips. I tried speaking again, hoping my guard might know just a little English, despite what he'd said.

"Where are we?" I asked.

He shrugged. I remembered a word I'd learned in my second or third Arabic class.

"*Ayna?*"

The guard looked surprised.

"*Nahnu bil- Khalil,*" he said, searching my face to see if I understood. *We are in al-Khalil.*

Al-Khalil. I had no idea where that was. But I said "*Shukkran!*" anyway. *Thanks!* For nothing.

"*Afwan!*" said my guard. You're welcome!

We were having a real little chat here!

My guard went on, "*Btihkii Arabi?*" I didn't quite recognize this dialect, but reasoned that he must be asking if I spoke Arabic.

"*Qallilan,*" I said, using the Modern Standard Arabic I'd been learning, "a little." I made a reflex attempt to raise my hands in the measurement gesture of thumb and forefinger before remembering they were tied behind me.

My guard said something else in Arabic. I could not understand one word. I shrugged. He tried again, same outcome. I realized I didn't even know how to say "I'm sorry" in Arabic.

He looked away, disgust on his face. Soon, he began jiggling his foot in boredom.

In just a minute, a young, very pregnant woman entered the room bearing a tray with a pitcher of water and some candied pineapple. She placed it on the table then gestured at it to ask if I would like some. I nodded my head, but raised my hands up behind my back to show my bonds. She looked at the man in the chair and he made a motion of assent with his chin.

The woman came over and began to work on loosening the knot. Soon, I felt my wrists released. I felt a wave of gratitude for this young woman, though when I looked at her in thanks, she reciprocated nothing. That was when she told me her name was Iman. "*Ismiyy Iman.*"

I placed my hands, now free, in my lap. The muscles of my

shoulders would not work well, so I could not reach for the water. Though I hadn't drunk anything in some time, the coffee I'd had in Jerusalem had caught up with me, and I desperately needed to use the bathroom. I called out, "Excuse me!"

She turned to look at me, her face blank.

"Do you have a bathroom?" I said.

"No Eenglish," she said.

I tried to pantomime what I needed, but neither of my captors understood, or perhaps making me sit there in discomfort was part of the plan. Several minutes later, I heard a knock at the door, and then voices as a new visitor entered. In a moment, a heavy-set man in western clothes came into the room accompanied by a man wearing army fatigues.

Another woman, slightly older than Iman, entered. I noticed the two women called the man in fatigues "*Baba,*" "father." I thought the older daughter shot me a look, maybe sympathy, but it was so brief that afterwards, I wondered if it had even happened. Her father said something, and the woman left, returning several minutes later with a tray containing a pot of coffee and a number of small glass mugs.

The visitor was watching me, saying nothing, and I felt a horrible creepy-crawly feeling. I didn't want his eyes on me. I didn't want the vision of me anywhere in his body. I wanted to scratch my image off his retinas so there wouldn't be anything of me inside him. After several minutes, he spoke to me, in English.

"So," he said, "I think you know why you are here."

No, I wanted to say, *I have absolutely no fucking idea.* But I said nothing.

"And I am afraid," he continued, "though you may love your life, you must pay for what you have done."

"But sir," I said, "can I know what crime I'm guilty of?"

"You know very well."

"But will you tell me please?"

The man looked angry but seemed to compose himself, with effort. "You are a rich, spoiled, American, Zionist, imperialist, feminist, Jewish, woman." He spat the words out one after the other, if anything infusing the last word with even more vitriol than the others.

He continued, "You have sinned against the world and desecrated God. But here, you will have a chance for redemption."

I sat silently. I had no idea how to answer these accusations, particularly since so many of the 'charges' were things I couldn't possibly change, even if I'd wanted to.

I swallowed. "Are you going to kill me?"

A smile crossed the man's face, as if this were a very pleasant thought that he would like to daydream on for a bit. Then he said, "We do not need to discuss our plans at the moment. For now, you have a task to do. You must speak to your President, your countrymen, your father, and your fellow Jews about what they have to do to enable your release. You must ask them to set our sons and daughters free from prison. You must ask them to provide a ransom for your life. You must say, with conviction, that all Zionists must leave our country.

"We will return to tape your statements on a daily basis. In between our visits, you must study and learn the ways of the Prophet so that you may live, or die, and be redeemed. Perhaps you will come to understand that this is the only way. Or perhaps you will remain an infidel. That is up to you."

Having said this, the heavyset man turned away. The elder daughter approached him with a cup of coffee. He accepted, and a curious look passed between them. I had the odd feeling that she wanted to throw the hot coffee in his face. But then she continued around the room, offering coffee to everyone else, including me.

Abruptly, the heavyset man set his coffee cup down and turned to the young man who had been guarding me. The man grasped his gun and, without a change in expression, walked quickly over towards me. He grabbed my arm and roughly raised me to my feet, upsetting my coffee cup. Absurdly, I fixated on the problem of the spilled coffee. *Someone will have to clean that up*, I thought. The man pushed me down, forcing my forehead onto the floor. I felt the hard end of the rifle tip behind my ear.

The heavyset man said "You had best stay still." He said this with an infuriating calmness, as if he terrorized and tortured women every day.

With my face smashed against the floor, I could see the things in only a very limited view. I swiveled my eyes in the direction of the voice, saw the legs walking over towards me, then the face of the heavyset man, close to mine. I felt his breath on my cheek. It smelled of half-digested meat. He had clean-shaven cheeks, and on the side facing me was a small brown mole covered over its surface with spiky hair.

He spoke in a very soft voice. "You will see now that your life is nothing but trash. That you and your people are trash. You have transgressed against God and desecrated the name of the Prophet, peace and blessings upon him. But now is the day of reckoning for you. You will be judged. But you should be grateful to us. In doing this, you will do your small part to right the wrongs of your nation and your people."

He stared at me, his muddy brown eyes smug. I cursed myself but could not prevent a tear from sliding out of the corner of my eye.

The man stood up. He waved at the gunman, who had been jabbing the rifle point into the bone behind my ear. I felt the metal move away. The man lifted me roughly and threw me back into the seat. So much for our friendly Arabic chat.

My upturned coffee cup lay on the floor, coffee spilling out around it in a dark puddle on the white carpet. No one offered me any more. The heavyset man paced back and forth.

"So. You will remain here, under the hospitality of this good family. You will be given every chance to prepare for the task you are to perform. Iman will be your companion. She is among the best of women. She will help you study the Quran. Abdul Malik," he gestured towards the man in fatigues, "will film several interviews with you. You will obey what he says. You will wear the *hijab,* that is, the head scarf, and the *abaya* and dress like a respectable woman. And that is all."

The man turned and left the room without another word. I never saw him again. I assumed he was the representative of whatever terrorist organization was masterminding this kidnapping. Abdul Malik, apparently my host, accompanied him to the door.

We sat silently. No one looked at me. I heard sounds, and realized that it was myself, whimpering. With an effort, I stopped. After several minutes, Abdul Malik returned. He had a book in his hand. He spoke to Iman, and she guided me to the bathroom, where she gestured that I should wash my hands. Without asking for permission, I used the toilet. Iman did not leave the bathroom, but looked down. I then washed my hands thoroughly, as requested.

She brought me into a small back room in the house, which was to become my living space and prison cell. It was dark already, its single window covered by rough boards. She retrieved a long black garment, gesturing that I should put it on over my clothes. She then draped a veil over my head. Only my face showed through. I was sure it was not a pretty sight. We returned to the living room.

Abdul Malik spoke for the first time, in English. "I have a great gift for you." He held up the book. I saw the word *Quran* on the cover. "You will read this book, and so become familiar with the beautiful recitation of the *Rasul*, Muhammad, peace and blessings upon him."

He handed it to me. It was the same English translation of the Quran that I had read just last year. Each page had both English and Arabic text, in parallel.

"I've read it," I said.

Abdul Malik looked surprised. "You have?"

"Yes."

"And yet you do not believe?"

"How do you know that?" I said, then regretted the words, which struck me, after I said them, as too challenging. "I mean, I'm Jewish. I believe in one God, the commandments, good deeds, prayer, and holy text."

"But what about Muhammad?" He said. I noticed his eyes were dark, almost black. They bore into me with an intensity of interest I had not expected. *Why did he care so much?* It struck me that if I could understand this, perhaps he would let me live.

"I believe Muhammad was a prophet. I believe, if I knew more about him, I could love Muhammad, just like I could love Jesus. But the religion of Islam isn't mine. I'm Jewish."

Abdul Malik was silent. His eyes continued to gaze at me, dark, impenetrable. It was as though I had dropped a stone into a deep well and had not yet heard the "splash." And that was the first of the strange theological debates I shared with Abdul Malik.

After this, my captors locked me in the bedroom with my Quran. They gave me a reading light.

Well, it could be worse, I thought. At least there was some hope. Maybe, if I could untangle this thing about Muhammad, they would let me live? Suddenly, as if someone were there in the room with me, I heard a voice. At first, I could not place it. Then it hit me. It was my rabbi, Solomon Lehrer!

"*Rachel,*" the voice said.

I jerked my head from one side to the other. Yes, I was alone. But the voice continued.

"You got yourself into a mess, didn't you?"

Fearing for my sanity, I replied. "Yes."

"I'm so sorry," sighed the rabbi's disembodied voice. "You really thought you could trust that guy at the Temple Mount. Did you forget what I told you about evil?"

"I guess I did, for a little while."

"Well, it is very *you* to try to make him feel better. Anyway, what's that you're reading there?"

"It's the Quran," I said. "These people seem to want me to read it."

"Hmmm," said the rabbi, then, "Rachel, do you remember what Maimonides said about forced conversion?"

"No."

"What? Weren't you paying attention?"

"Sorry, Rabbi! Remember? I didn't have time to take your class yet."

"Oh yes. Too bad. Well anyway, here it is, in a nutshell. If faced with forced conversion, the first thing to do is get the heck out of dodge. Vamanos. Well, you can't do that. So you're compelled to take the second best step, and that is to save your own skin. Life is the first priority. So say whatever you're forced to say with your mouth. In your heart, though, remain a Jew. Okay?"

"I think," I said, "that what I might do to save my life is just to try to understand."

"Ah...understanding," said the rabbi. And then he was gone.

Trying not to dwell on the fact that I seemed to be losing my mind, I turned my attention back to the Quran, taking the book and going to sit down on the edge of my mattress. When I did so, I felt the edge of the small book of Psalms in my pocket, surprised my captors hadn't searched me and taken it away. This book suddenly seemed more precious to me than any other thing I had ever owned in my entire life. I took it out of my pocket, running my finger over its filigreed surface.

I began to feel terrified that if my captors found it, they would take it from me. I could not bear that thought. I stood up and searched around the room for a hiding place, finding a loose section of carpet next to the wall under the window. I kissed the little book, running my finger over it one last time, then slid it under the carpet.

The light between the cracks in the boards over the window

was getting dim, and I estimated that it was early evening. Lenny and Ruthie were, by now, likely in a complete panic.

I didn't know what time the family ate, or even whether I'd be invited to participate. In fact, I had no idea what the future held. For now, I knew that perhaps my only chance of life was contained in the book set before me, the Quran. With every ounce of concentration and whatever intelligence I could muster in the state of abject terror, I sat back down and opened its front cover. I thought about my life back home, the freedom I'd taken for granted. I cried, and the words of the Quran swam in front of my eyes. I wiped the tears away with the sleeve of my *abaya* and began to read.

After I'd read about two Suras (chapters), the long ones at the beginning, I heard a key in the lock and then the door opened. Iman stood on the threshold. For the first time, I thought she looked pleased. She seemed to like the sight of me, crouching over my Quran like some cornered animal. She gestured with her hand that I should follow her.

The odor of cooked food reached me in the hallway. We followed it down to the kitchen. Through a door, I saw the three men sitting at the table in the dining room. They were smoking and drinking coffee. I could smell the bitter smoke of their cigarettes from the hallway.

In the kitchen, Iman's sister was washing dishes. On the table were the remains of dinner, some chicken bones picked over, now with just some largish scraps of meat attached, several bowls partially full, their sides caked over with dried food. There were three places set at the table. I realized this was our dinner. Apparently, the women got to eat the men's leftovers.

I thought about the list I had once showed Yakub, my "Religion Inventory." *These guys here*, I thought, *are violating almost every one of those rules, but especially:* slavery: "I am justified in taking away the fundamental rights of another person," and rank: "I am better than another person." Apparently, in this house, both attitudes applied, in relation to the women.

Nauseated, I said my *motsi* prayer anyway, though I could not eat anything. The two women watched me and said nothing.

After dinner, I helped the women clean up the kitchen. Then, Iman brought me to the bathroom one more time, and I figured that it was the last time for the night. This time, she allowed me to go in the room by myself.

Alone, I thought about Yakub. How would he find out I was missing? The thought of that made me even more sick to my stomach. I leaned over the toilet and retched. After several minutes, the heaving finally stopped. I stood up, bathed in cold sweat. I splashed water on my face, then washed my hands. In the mirror, my face looked awful, pale and drawn.

Outside the bathroom, Iman gave no sign whether or not she'd heard me throwing up. She took my elbow firmly and guided me back to our room. The men in the dining room watched me as I passed. One of them said something, and they all laughed. I wondered what was so funny.

Back at the room, Iman gestured towards the Quran with a sharp upward motion of her chin. She then slammed the door after her. *What was the matter with her*, I wondered. Around here, you could make people hate you without even trying!

I resumed my reading of the Quran. I wanted to mark sections but didn't want to offend the book in any way. I found a box of Kleenex and ripped sections off, placing them between pages with important verses. About sixty pages into the book, I thought I heard a helicopter fly overhead. A small firework of hope burst through my chest. *Were they looking for me already?*

As happened countless times during my purgatory in that house, the hope died immediately, replaced by cold reason. *Well maybe they are looking for you, but even if they are, how could they possibly find you?* After that, I turned back with furious determination to the Quran.

Eventually, I lay down on the mattress, which was covered by a cheap cotton sheet and a pilled-up pink blanket. I pulled the blanket over me and closed my eyes. As I drifted off, I thought of the little book of Psalms, safe beneath the carpet. And I thought about Yakub, picturing his face, so precious to me that the vision of it fed my hope, even in this dark place.

It is hard to believe that I was able to sleep, but I think my mind just turned off, unable to handle the terror and dread. When I woke up that next morning, memories of my experiences came rushing back to me in full force, along with associated feelings of desperation. I saw that Iman had joined me in the bedroom sometime during the night, and she now lay, snoring softly, on a separate mattress next to me. My bladder was full again, but I knew I would have to wait until Iman woke up to use the bathroom. Just out of interest, I got up and went to try the handle of the door, walking carefully in my sock-covered feet over the scruffy carpet. The knob didn't turn.

I sat back down on the mattress and made one of my famous mental lists:

TASKS FOR TODAY

1. *Collect clues for possible escape plans.*
2. *Get to know my captors, convince them I am way too nice to kill.*
3. *Figure out how to convince Abdul Malik that I believe in God and Muhammad but am still Jewish.*

No problem! I'll just solve the problem of the world's religions right here and now! The hopelessness of my plan struck me. Nevertheless, it was the only plan I had. So I picked up the Quran and took it with me over to the window, where the first rays of daylight struggled through the cracks between the boards. I sat down and read for a half hour, my bladder growing increasingly uncomfortable. Finally, I heard Iman groan and make smacking wake-up sounds with her mouth. She opened her eyes and, in a moment, focused on me, sitting beneath the window reading the Quran in the dim light. She smiled.

Note to self, I thought, *Iman likes it when I read the Quran.* At first, this made me hopeful. But then, I began to wonder about her motives.

She sat up, stretching her arms up above her. Her body was slim, her round belly protruding in a tense ball. I estimated she was about seven months along. A couple months to go. She went and changed into a sweat suit, then placed her *abaya* over it, followed by the *hijab.* After this, we walked down the hall to the bathroom.

Now that it was daylight, I noticed a small window above the toilet. It was way too small to crawl through, but I climbed up onto the toilet seat anyway to look out. All I could see was a narrow alley, completely deserted at this hour. It was wonderful, however, to see the sky in the space above the buildings. *It's still there!* I thought, irrationally.

When I finished using the bathroom, Iman led me back to

the bedroom. She gestured at the Quran using the same impatient movement of her chin as she had the day before. She left, and I heard the lock click.

I opened the book. In my desperate quest for survival, I was looking for evidence that the holy text of the Torah was, to the Jews, a revelation on a par with the Quran for the Arabs. Already, I had found several verses to support this thesis, even in the first few chapters. There was sura number 3, verses 113-5: *There are among the People of the Book some upright men who all night long recite the revelations of God and worship Him; who believe in God and the Last Day; who enjoin justice and forbid evil and vie with each other in good works. These are the righteous men: whatever good they do, its reward shall not be denied them* and verse 4:131: *We exhort you, as We have exhorted those to whom the Book was given before you, to fear God.* And I thought I recalled, from later verses that I hadn't yet read this time, something about Moses receiving the book so that his people would be rightly guided.

But I had, as well, found some things that worried me greatly, at least with respect to my own sorry neck. For example, just within the first few chapters of my re-reading, there was verse 2:61: *"Shame and misery were stamped upon them (the Jews) and they incurred the wrath of God; because they disbelieved God's signs and slew the prophets unjustly, because they were rebels and transgressors,* and verses 4:160-1: *Because of their iniquity, We forbade the Jews wholesome things which were formerly allowed them; because time after time they have debarred others from the path of God; because they practice usury – although they were forbidden it – and cheat others of their possessions. Woeful punishment have We prepared for those that disbelieve."* And then, there was the famous "verse of the sword," 9:5, *"When the sacred months are over, slay the idolaters, wherever you find them."* I wasn't sure exactly where the Jews fit into the spectrum of "idolators," but regardless of the protected status of *dhimmi,* or "People of the Book," I was afraid many Muslims, including my captors, might still interpret their rejection of the religion of Islam in that light.

After forty five minutes or so, the door swung open with force and bashed against the wall on the other side of the hinges. Iman stood in the opening, her face set in a scowl like some kind of minion from Hell. She raised her hand and gestured for me to follow. My blood went cold. *Was this it? Was it time? Were they going to execute me on video now?*

Although this did not jibe with their efforts to get me to

read the Quran, I feared that their plans might be fluid and changeable, as the situation demanded. Iman grabbed my arm, clamping hard over a tender area on my biceps. I grimaced, but she did not notice. Instead, she pulled me quickly down the hallway to the living room.

The nervous young man with the rifle, apparently Iman's husband, was looking at me, and I also saw Abdul Malik, still dressed in army fatigues. He sat in an easy chair, and gestured to the chair diagonally across the coffee table from him.

"Please," he said, "*tfaddaliyy.*" Be my guest.

I sat down, with a little helping shove from Iman.

Abdul Malik examined me. "Good morning," he said, as if chatting with terrorists after a night in captivity must be the most normal thing in the world for me. "I trust you had a good night's sleep?"

I nodded.

"And you are well fed?"

I realized my stomach was empty, but I wasn't hungry, so I nodded. "I've been well cared-for," I said, attempting to impart the most sincere gratitude. How could you kill someone who was grateful? I tried not to look at the man with the rifle. I wondered what it felt like when a bullet entered your head. Maybe you wouldn't feel anything?

"It is time," said Abdul Malik, "for us to know more about you."

He reached into his pocket and removed my wallet, taking my California driver's license out. "I see that your name is Rachel Roseman, and that you live in San Francisco. You are a physician. You have several credit cards. You belong to a running club. You are a United Premier member. You like poetry. All correct?"

It's amazing how much a wallet can give away about your life.

"Not exactly," I said, afraid to contradict him but even more worried that he would be angered if I falsified any information. "My name isn't Roseman anymore. It's al-Shadi. Rachel Davidson al-Shadi."

"What?" he said, confused. "Why does your license not indicate this?"

"I only remarried a few days ago," I said.

Abdul Malik scowled and shook his head back and forth

rapidly, as if trying to make this compute. "You married an Arab man?"

"Yes," I said.

"A Muslim?"

"Yes," I repeated again. I wondered briefly if this would give me brownie points, but was soon disabused of that idea.

"He did this? Married a Jew?" Abdul Malik's eyes betrayed both keen curiosity and revulsion. I had never encountered this response before in a man. It was unnerving.

"My understanding is that Muhammad did so as well."

"Times were different then," said Abdul Malik. I did not point out his inconsistency: regardless of different times, most fundamentalist Muslims believed it essential to follow the example of the Prophet and his Companions. "What kind of a man is he?" he asked.

"Yakub is a wonderful man," I said, feeling tears spring to my eyes.

My host snorted. "What kind of a man leaves his wife to wander around alone in Jerusalem so soon after a wedding? You were not on, what do you call it in America..."

"Honeymoon?" I offered, ever helpful.

"Yes! On honeymoon?"

"We had to separate for several days. My husband is on *Hajj* with his son. It was planned for a very long time. And...necessary, for other reasons." I was thinking not only of the poem and the sign from God, but of Yakub's need to resolve his anger against the Muslims.

"Ah! And you did not accompany him?"

Confused, I said, "Well, of course, I can't...you know...I'm Jewish."

"And you remain Jewish, though married to a Muslim man?"

"Yes," I said.

Abdul Malik said nothing, but shook his head. This terrified me.

He continued. "What is your husband's full name, and what does he do?"

"His name is Yakub al-Shadi. He's a professor. He teaches Arabic poetry."

This engendered even more disapproval, and I considered

what I'd read about poets in the Quran: *Poets are followed by erring men...*[12]

"Alright. Is the fellow wealthy?"

For the ransom, I thought. "No, not particularly. He was a university professor. He taught out of love of language, not for money."

"And what is this?" he removed a piece of paper from the pocket in my wallet, unfolding it and holding it down on the table with the palm of his left hand. I saw Zeke's scrawled writing.

"It's a poem one of my patients gave me," I said.

"But it is nonsense," said Abdul Malik. "Why are you keeping it?"

"It's not nonsense to me," I said.

Abdul Malik flashed me an angry look. "And what are you doing here in Palestine?"

Not wanting to tell him anything about *the poem,* I said, "I came here to see the Holy Land. My husband is on *Hajj.* I am also on a kind of pilgrimage."

"To Jerusalem. I see." This did appear to make sense to him. "Have you found what you came here for?"

I thought again about *the poem* and the sign from God I'd been seeking. My odds of discovering anything more about these things now seemed about as likely as my chances of ever becoming pregnant: nil to impossible.

"Not yet," I admitted.

Abdul Malik smiled derisively. "You are not much of a success, are you?"

"I don't know," I said, "I guess not."

He shook his head. "But your father. He was successful."

"Yes."

"And he is wealthy?"

"Was. He's dead now."

Abdul Malik looked shocked and then angry. He spat out an Arabic word I couldn't understand, then said, "But your mother, surely she has inherited his wealth?"

"She died before he did," I said. "The only one left in my family is my sister, Ruthie, and all the money is in a trust fund with

---

[12] Qur'an 26:224

legal protections."

Abdul Malik stood up abruptly and left the room. In a minute, I heard him speaking in staccato Arabic on the phone, obviously expressing his disapproval and anger to someone on the other end of the line. I heard him slam down the receiver. He then reentered the room. I wondered if this financial news would make them decide that killing me on camera was the better use of my "talents." He face was unreadable. He motioned to Iman. Apparently, our interview was over.

Iman grasped my sore arm and hoisted me up. This harsh treatment appeared to please Abdul Malik, who said, "Iman is one you should try to emulate. Pray to be as righteous as her. She will soon be a martyr to Allah."

I turned back to Abdul Malik, aghast, and said, "What?"

"Yes! She will give herself to our cause," he said, "*Insha Allah!*" God willing.

"But she's pregnant!" I said.

"Of course," he said, as though I were an idiot, "she will wait until after the child comes. But then she will surrender, in glorious sacrifice, to Allah. She will be greatly rewarded."

I stumbled down the hall after Iman. *She was going to be a suicide bomber. What kind of woman would blow herself up after the birth of her first child?* I could not imagine that God would condone or demand this type of action. Something seemed tragically misinterpreted here. Some colossal mis-reading of holy text appeared to be going on.

Iman followed me to the room, watched me enter, and then slammed the door behind me without a word. The would-be martyr. Though I feared and disliked her, I still felt sorry. What kind of a world would this baby be born to, no mother, nursed on the bile of hatred? Was this what the Prophet, Muhammad, wanted? Surely not! Would this to be the new generation of Muslims? I kneeled down on the scruffy carpet and prayed. Then I opened the Quran and continued to read.

At lunchtime, I heard the Muslim call to prayer outside my boarded window. The sound was mixed with the chopping noise of helicopter blades, forming an odd medley. From the next room came the voice of men in prayer: *Allah hu Akbar...*

I felt cold fear in my heart and realized that this prayer would now, for me as for so many other people, be associated only with terror and memory of violent death. I prayed for a day when words of worship would be heard only with joy, that the ringing of church bells would never again arouse the fear of Inquisition and raise the specter of torture and anguish at the hands of those professing to speak in the name of the God of love.

Later that afternoon, Iman came to collect me once again, and brought me out into the living room. There was now a collection of men in army fatigues, most of them wearing headbands emblazoned with Arabic letters. One of the men was standing by a tripod with a small VCR camera.

"Oh great!" said a hysterical voice inside my head, "Home movies!"

Abdul Malik greeted me and politely asked me to sit down. He handed me a piece of paper. He asked me to read it and see if it met with my approval. Yeah, right. As if I'd argue with him with a bunch of men around holding rifles. If it was alright with me, I should memorize it and recite it aloud. I would be able to practice as much as I wanted, he said, but it was important I get it right.

I read the short passage through three times.

Hello. I am Rachel Davidson, an American imperialist Zionist spy. I came to Israel for the purpose of gaining information necessary to assist American forces in the destruction of the armies of Islam. In the presence of the righteous warriors of Allah, I see now the error of my ways, and take full responsibility for the selfish, evil, and promiscuous life that I have led. I hope only to right these wrongs, and demand now of the American President and the Israeli Government that all Palestinian prisoners of war be released immediately. Furthermore, my righteous captors must receive a ransom of twenty million dollars within forty-eight hours or I will be killed. You will be contacted later with further details. God willing, you will comply with these demands or I will die.

This was horrible. Meanwhile, Iman's nervous husband held a gun in his hand, the small black hole at its tip pointing directly towards my left eye.

"Have you finished memorizing it now?" asked Abdul Malik.

"Not quite," I said. "Give me a few more minutes." I tried to maintain some dignity in my voice, but it sounded a bit whiny despite my efforts.

"Take your time, take your time," said Abdul Malik, pacing

rapidly. He said nothing to the gunman, who continued to point his rifle at me.

"Say it a few times out loud," suggested Abdul Malik. I retched once or twice the first time, but by the end, was able to commit it to memory by adopting a kind of sing-song voice.

After the last time I recited it, Abdul Malik seemed satisfied, saying, "Good!" He then motioned to the gunman, who jumped up and ran over, whacking the back of my head with the metal rod of the rifle barrel just hard enough for me to see stars. After this, he poked the tip of the rifle into the space behind my ear that he so favored.

"Why did you do that?" I said, my voice a weak and whiny croak.

"You must be convincing," said Abdul Malik, "As if you've seen a sign from God."

I put my hand on my head, leaning it over to the side at is pounded painfully. This all could have been a sign from God, but it didn't feel like it.

"Are you ready?" asked Abdul Malik.

I picked up my script and read it through one more time. My eyes were blurry, but I remembered the text well enough. My gunman friend moved back, out of the camera line.

I nodded that I was ready, then winced as the pain lanced from my temple down into my neck.

Lights, camera, action, the man next to the tripod signaled me to GO!

In a monotone, my face streaked with tears, my voice a thin croak, I intoned the words they had assigned me. They meant nothing. They required just the one taping. I took some consolation from the knowledge that anyone who spoke English would realize that I was reciting a memorized statement that had no meaning to me at all.

The man with the DV recorder left. He was going to capture the video and e-mail a link to a friend who would forward it through channels to various TV stations. This was the tape that my sister and Lenny would see later that evening.

When Iman returned me to my room this time, I did not read the Quran. Instead, I lay on my mattress and nursed my sore head.

In a gathering mood of deep despair, I remembered the

final words that the man with the white forelock whispered just before the trunk slammed down and left me in darkness. *There is no poem to redeem the world.* He was right. The whole idea was absurd, now that I saw it all in perspective. Men were just animals, just beasts, with only one simple distinction over other creatures: the unfortunate ability to speak and create stories.

I must have dozed off, because I woke to the feeling of something hard poking into my shoulder, and opened my eyes to the unfriendly face of Iman, who was prodding me with her foot and saying, "*Isteekziyy!*" She jerked her head towards my Quran. Deducing by her motions that she was telling me to "get up!" I stumbled to my feet, noticing that the spaces between the boards on the window were now dark. Iman held a gun. When she sat down, she placed it on her knee, the muzzle pointing towards me.

She lifted the gun, using it to point towards my copy of the Quran. "*Iqraiyy*," she said.

Read. For once, I could understand.

I read the words out loud, in English, while Iman listened, holding her gun.

al-Khalil, Palestine

6:00 am. Shabbat, December 30th, 2006

Dr. Rachel al-Shadi

The next morning, I woke up and found Iman snoring beside me once again. I waited until she roused herself, then I used the "exploding bladder" hand signal I'd perfected to indicate that I needed to use the bathroom. Without a word, she put on her clothes and led me down the hall. I used the toilet, washed my hands, then rinsed my mouth out with water, finger-brushing my teeth with what I took to be toothpaste, though I could not read the Arabic text on the label. It tasted for all the world like minty Crest, so I imagined I had guessed right.

After we returned to our room, I read some more of my Quran, finishing it by mid-morning. I hoped I had enough information to guide me in whatever conversation or disputation Abdul Malik might be planning for me on the subject of religion. But I had my doubts. Understanding of this text required teachers and many years of study. I'd had the benefit of neither.

At lunchtime, Iman took me out of the room and down to

the kitchen. She motioned that I should help prepare lunch for the men. I placed hummus in small bowls and sliced up Arabic bread into quarters. Iman brought the plates of food into the dining room while her sister waited in the kitchen with me. She wore the *abaya* and *hijab*, but I noticed unruly strands of dark hair protruding out beside her face on each side, as if she'd put it on carelessly. We sat in silence until Iman returned with the leftovers for us to eat.

By now, I was very hungry and was able to eat with relatively little nausea. After we finished, Iman brought me to the living room. I heard the television, and when I entered, Abdul Malik greeted me. He was surrounded by five other men, including his son-in-law and several others whom I'd seen yesterday. They examined me with interest.

"Ah, Rachel! *Kul 'aam wa'anti bikhayr!* Greetings for the holiday, Eid al Adha, the day commemorating the submission of Abraham and Ishmael to the will of God! It begins this evening, in just a few hours from now."

"Thank you," I mumbled, ever polite.

"You are just in time! They are about to broadcast a message from your sister."

Shocked, I said, "What about?"

Abdul Malik smiled patronizingly. "About your release, of course. She hopes to speak to our softer side. To say some words that will unlock the rusted doors of our hearts and help us to see the light."

Before I could think about it at all, I saw the commentator on television, a slim, blond woman in a tight skirt, welcoming my sister into the studio. She said some introductory comments then asked Ruthie to tell us about herself.

The camera focused on a close-up of Ruthie's face and shoulders. There were dark bags below her eyes. Her voice sounded odd on the television. As she spoke, her words were transcribed in Arabic along the bottom of the screen.

Ruthie said some things about our family, indicating that she was glad that we were orphans and that our parents would not have to witness the terrible things that were happening to their daughter. Then, she looked at the camera and spoke to me directly:

"Rachel, I hope that you are hearing this right now. I pray that you are alive and that your kidnappers are treating you mercifully. You are a gentle soul, and have never done anything to hurt anyone. You've spent your life trying to help other people, many of them abandoned and forsaken by society themselves. Your kidnappers should understand that.

"And now I'm speaking to my sister's captors. You know that our government won't negotiate with terrorists, so it must be your intention to sacrifice my sister. I appeal both to your mercy and to your highest souls. I wish you to understand that in choosing such a sacrifice, you have truly selected an innocent for slaughter. I remind you that humanity has advanced beyond the time when human sacrifice was acceptable, and to simply point out that, as religious men, you should remember that Allah Himself substituted a ram in place of a man. Surely, there's a sign in this for you."

When she was done, they switched off the television. I looked around the room at the assembled men. They said nothing and I saw no indication that my sister's words had affected them in the slightest.

"Well," said Abdul Malik, "your sister is quite an intelligent woman. What does she do?"

"She's a professor of physics at Stanford," I said.

"My, my!" he said. "Perhaps she should stick to those areas with which she is familiar, since she evidently knows nothing about religion."

"What do you mean?" I asked, defensively.

"There are times, such as when your holy lands are occupied, that the word of Allah does justify, even demand, killing your enemies."

"Please tell me where this is written in the Quran," I said.

Abdul Malik recited: "*Permission to take up arms is hereby given to those who are attacked, because they have been wronged. God has power to grant them victory: those who have been unjustly driven from their homes, only because they said: 'Our LORD Is God.'"* [13]

"But this just says *take up arms* as a result of religious persecution, it doesn't say to *kidnap and kill innocent people*," I argued.

"Do not be foolish. We have been driven from our homes. Even now, my relatives' houses in East Jerusalem are destroyed every day. Their families, including the small children, are evicted to live, homeless, on the streets of Jerusalem. And so, why do you

---

[13] Qur'an 22:39-40

think you are innocent?"

"But I don't agree with that!" I protested.

"But what have you done about it? And did you not," he went on, "benefit from the money your father made as a result of the imperialistic commercial violence imposed on the nations of Islam and others? And did not those of your faith, the Jews, drive the Palestinians out of their homeland altogether?"

"But," I said, "About Palestine. Can't we share?"

I knew so little about this complex subject. Way too little to argue with someone like Abdul Malik. There were so many actions, reactions, and counter-reactions in this whole sad story that it all seemed hopelessly tangled.

"Ha!" laughed Abdul Malik, derisively. "That is such a foolish thing to say that I will not even bother to answer."

I thought of mentioning one of the Quranic verses about forgiveness, but I realized that it was no use. Who should forgive, and who should apologize? Palestinians? Jews? Wouldn't it be better for us *both* to forgive and apologize at the same time? And when the prophets of our faiths received the commandments regarding forgiveness, repentance, and loving your enemy, did God say it would be easy?

"And now," said Abdul Malik, "I would like to know, have you completed your reading of the Quran?"

I nodded.

"Good! Then let us talk." He looked towards the kitchen and called out some words in a loud voice.

In a moment, Iman's sister appeared with a glass of water.

When Abdul Malik saw her, he barked something in Arabic. Staring at the floor, she took her right hand and stuffed her hair back under her *hijab*. Afterwards, it still looked lumpy and lopsided, but at least no hair was showing. Abdul Malik dismissed her with a disgusted backward wave of his hand.

"Ach, that one. Rahima," he said with disdain. "She will never marry. It is a disgrace, to marry the younger before the elder, but Iman, the worthy daughter, should not wait forever on account of her older sister. Do you know what?" He looked at me.

I shook my head. I knew nothing.

"Rahima was chosen as spouse by the supreme leader of our *Jihad* movement, the man you met the other day. Rahima is not without her beauty, but her mind is flawed." Abdul Malik touched his forefinger to his head. "And she has disgraced us all by rebuffing his advances."

I compressed my lips and shook my head as if in sorrow, commiserating with the familial difficulties of my murdering host.

He roused himself from his angry funk, turning back to our discussion. My heart began to pound, as the stakes of this conversation struck me full force. I suspected my performance would determine whether I lived or died.

Draining my glass of water, I swished the last bit around in my mouth, which had grown very dry in anticipation. I took a deep breath to further calm my mind. Prepared in some small measure, I waited for Abdul Malik.

He said, "So, Rachel, how do you feel about our glorious Quran, now that you have completed it for the second time?"

"I think," I began carefully, "that it is the word of God. I think it contains beauty, wisdom, and truth. I think that Muhammad is the prophet who transmitted this recitation. I think that God exists as the light flowing through the words of the Quran, just as He lives in our Torah."

Abdul Malik was nodding. "So you are a Muslim now?"

"Like Abdullah ibn Sallam?" I asked, referring to the Jewish convert to Islam referred to in the notes of the Quran.

"Yes!" said Abdul Malik, pleased with my attention to his sacred book, "Like ibn Sallam!"

Thinking as hard as I could, I said, "If you mean do I believe in the One God and that Muhammad existed and was a prophet, I would say 'yes'. If you mean do I believe in the Last Day, that is, redemption, I would also say 'yes'. If you mean this as a profession of faith in the *religion* of Islam, I would say 'no'."

"Why?" he asked.

"Because I'm Jewish."

Abdul Malik let out an explosive word in Arabic, disturbing the five other men, who sat listening, though most, I could tell, did not speak English. When he explained to them what I had said, they stared at me, daggers flashing from their eyes. *They'd probably like to kill me right now,* I thought.

Composing himself, Abdul Malik said, a mocking tone in his voice, "And how, after reading what you say is a book filled with light, do you conclude that you should remain Jewish?"

I searched my mind, but though I had tried to memorize

some of the relevant passages, found the words had fled now under the duress of the interrogation.

I said, "May I please have my copy of the Quran? I used tissue to mark pages."

Abdul Malik called over Iman and asked her to retrieve my book. She returned in a moment and handed it to me, her eyes a challenge and a beseechment. I wondered, for the millionth time it seemed, why she cared so much.

Opening to the first quote, I read:

" *The righteous man is he who believes in God and the Last Day, in the angels and the Book and the prophets; who, though he loves it dearly, gives away his wealth to kinsfolk, to orphans, to the destitute, to the traveler in need and to beggars.'* [14] To me, this indicates that as long as you do the things described in this passage, you are considered righteous, whether or not your *religion* is Islam."

Abdul Malik nodded. "Go on," he said.

"Well," I said, "there are many passages along these lines:

" *'An apostle is sent to each community.'* [15] *'Each apostle We have sent has spoken only in the language of his own people, so that he might make his precepts clear to them.'* " [16]

Between each of these quotes, I frantically searched the pages, desperate to prove my point to this man. Surely I could convince him of the error in his thinking?

"And what do these passages mean to you?" asked Abdul Malik.

"Muhammad was sent to Arabia, Moses to the Jews, Jesus to the Christians. All paths are acceptable, as long as you do your very best to understand the messages brought by the prophets, as described in the holy texts."

"Ah, but too bad the Torah you profess to love so much is worthless, corrupted by the later editing and manipulation by ordinary men."

"What do you mean?" I said, defensively.

He quoted: " *'Ask the Israelites how many conspicuous signs We*

---

[14] Qur'an 2:177

[15] Qur'an 10:47

[16] Qur'an 14:4

gave them. He that tampers with the gift of God after it is bestowed on him shall find that God is stern in retribution.' [17] The Jews have tampered with the word of God. Your holy scriptures are no longer valid."

"But that's wrong!" I cried. I recalled a quote by the Italian Kabbalist, Menacham Recanati, something my rabbi had mentioned in one of his classes: 'The Letters of God's name and of the Torah are the mystical body of God, while God, in a manner of speaking, is the soul of the letters.' (4)

How could something that Jews believed to actually embody God, be corrupted? But this whole line of argument was hopeless, I realized. I could have been the world's greatest Bible expert and still not been able to argue the historical facts necessary to disprove Abdul Malik's thesis. Bottom line: you either accepted the texts as holy or you did not.

"Well, anyway," I said, "clearly, Muhammad professed that as long as you believe in the One God, enjoin good, avoid evil, and believe in the Last Day, you are alright. You find this in this passage from the Quran, Sura 2, verse 62 *'Believers, Jews, Christians, Sabaeans – whoever believes in God and the Last Day and does what is right – shall be rewarded by their LORD; they have nothing to fear or regret.'*"

When I looked up from my reading, I saw that Abdul Malik was looking at me with a self-satisfied smile, as if I'd conveniently fallen into some kind of carefully-laid trap.

"Ah!" he said, "if only it were so! But you see, this verse has been clearly abrogated by another."

"What?" I said. "Abrogated?"

"Do you not know of this phenomenon? The replacement of one verse or holy text by another?"

"How is this justified?" I asked.

"Only by the word of Allah," said Abdul Malik, sarcastically. *"'If We abrogate a verse or cause it to be forgotten, We will replace it by a better one or one similar.'* [18]"

"So," I asked, "that means that the verse about the Sabaeans and the Jews is cancelled out by another one?"

"Exactly," said Abdul Malik.

---

[17] Qur'an 2:211

[18] Qur'an 2:106

"Which one?" I asked.

Abdul Malik smiled malevolently, finally ready to produce his trump card, the verse that would lay to waste all my silly conclusions about the Quran. "*He that chooses a religion other than Islam, it will not be accepted from him and in the world to come he will surely be among the losers.'*"[19]

I had actually thought about this verse before quite a bit, and I had an answer. If I'd known the response this would provoke, I might have kept my mouth shut. But words are impossible to gather back in, once spoken.

"Well," I began, "I still don't see this as a problem."

"What?" said Abdul Malik, incredulous. "If you do not become a Muslim, you will suffer in Hell for all eternity!"

"I don't see it that way," I persisted, succumbing, dangerously, to my innately Jewish tendency to quarrel over the meaning of holy text.

"How, pray tell, do you see it, then?" said Abdul Malik. "Enlighten us, please." He gestured around at his companions, as if they understood what we were saying. He was smiling smugly, convinced there was no way I could possibly wriggle out from this argument.

"Well," I continued, "it says 'he that chooses a religion other than Islam'. If you translate this literally, you could say 'he that chooses a religion other than submission to God.' So if your religion, or how you practice it, calls for or brings about true submission to God, then you are okay. As I see it, this is referring here to a *belief,* rather than to a specific practice. As it says later, '*For every community We have ordained a ritual which they observe.*'[20] The Jews simply observe a different *method* for submission, *Islam,* than the Muslims. But even though we argue a lot, like Abraham, by the way, when he argued with God on behalf of the people of Sodom and Gomorrah, we also *submit,* as professed in the famous Psalm,[21] 'I set God before me at all times,' and the daily prayer, Adon Olam, *'in Your hands, I surrender my soul...'*"

---

[19] Qur'an 3:85

[20] Qur'an 22:67

[21] Psalm 16:8

I was chattering along, oblivious, and didn't notice that Abdul Malik was becoming increasingly infuriated until it was too late. He jumped up, and the next thing I knew, I was kneeling, hands behind my back, a rifle shoved into the back of my head. He was shouting something in Arabic, and I saw the man with the DV recorder run and grab his camera and tripod from the floor and set them up.

When he was ready, Abdul Malik said in a shout, "What do you say before you die?"

Staring death in the face, I saw my beloved Yakub. Abdul Malik continued to shout things at me, but my ears blocked out his words and I heard only a very loud ringing sound. I opened my mouth, and these words came out: *Hear, Israel, the Lord is our God, the Lord is One*...I continued to recite the prayer in Hebrew, starting over a second time when I finished.

Shocked, Abdul Malik lowered his gun, and looked at me, a wild confusion on his face. "Iman!" he yelled, "Get this dog out of here!"

Apparently, Abdul Malik found it impossible to kill a woman kneeling and declaring God's unity. At least, that was how he felt right now, though it could certainly change.

Iman rushed in, pulling me up from the floor. Her face was grim. She was unhappy with me too. She pushed me in front of her, kicking me several times. When we reached the room, she flung me forward by the arm so that I fell onto the floor. She spat out *"Halla, tamuutiyy!"* then left the room.

I had no idea what this meant, but it sounded like it had something to do with mortality. I was certainly making a terrible flop of getting everyone to like me so that I could live.

London, England

10:30 pm. Saturday, December 30th, 2006
Mr. Smith, to Eugene Smith (journal entry)

Eugene, my son, what have I done? May God forgive me!

On the BBC and CNN, I have watched the news on the "hostage situation" in Israel, the beautiful American doctor, kidnapped, held for ransom. Rachel, Rachel Davidson al-Shadi, so many names I once despised, but now...Now I do not know what to believe! I look inside but find no hatred, its searing coals quenched by the cooling rains of her compassion.

I thought I would exult to see her severed head, held high by the servants of the *intifada*, that I would delight to contemplate her terror as she waited, kneeling before them, and they stood, butcher knife in hand, a knot of hair clenched around bulging knuckles. Neck, so tender, smooth and white, bared and curved in tension to the executioner's sharp blade...

But no, please God, not that! In Palestine, I touched her arm. I touched her. And she looked at me. Rachel, whose children cry for her. I too cry out, destroyed by my own pride!

Oh, my son, Eugene! Do not continue in this course! I beg you, hear me! I may never have the opportunity to speak with you again, since I fear my end is near, and you have followed al-Shadi and his son to Makkah. I entreat you now, in writing: abandon all these words of hatred! If I had the chance, I would destroy my own, but it is too late. Oh my son, the compassion of a stranger has taught me this: seek love, not hatred, for it alone is our redemption.

Eugene, I die. My gut spews blood, it comes even from my mouth, I vomit blood, there is no end to this blood inside me. Yet I welcome death, the only respite from my folly now.

al-Khalil, Palestine

Evening of Saturday, December 30th 2006 (Eid al-Adha)
Dr. Rachel al-Shadi

I lay on the mattress a long time, pondering the impulse that had stayed Abdul Malik's hand. Had he really been moved by some small remnant of compassion, held captive in his stony heart? Or was this all part of the plan?

Hearing the sound of Arabic prayers through the thin wall once again, the beginning of the Islamic festival of Eid al-Adha, I dozed off and must have slept. Sometime later, I woke to the feel of a gentle hand on my shoulder. When I opened my eyes, I was blinking at the face of Rahima. She kneeled beside me, her index finger pressing against her lips.

"Quiet!" she whispered, in perfect English. "They may hear us!"

My mouth dropped open, and my look of astonishment

brought mirth to her eyes. "Yes, yes, I know. You thought I was a silly, brainwashed Arab girl." She moved her hand impatiently. "But we don't have time to talk about that. We must plan your escape."

Continuing in her beautiful English, she said "Iman says she's too disgusted to spend the night with you here again, so that is good. My father is planning, without doubt, to kill you tomorrow, for the benefit of a worldwide audience. He will overcome his temporary reluctance towards your execution, of that I am sure. I believe that has been his plan ever since he learned he had been deceived about the money by the man with the white forelock, though a witnessed conversion and profession of faith towards his twisted cause would not have been a bad thing either, from his perspective. But obviously, that won't happen."

She looked at me with admiration.

I asked, "Isn't it way too dangerous for you to help me?"

"Don't worry about me," she said. "Just be prepared to go when you see me slide this," she held up a piece of pink construction paper, "under the door. It will be about three or four hours from now, maybe two or three in the morning."

"I'll be ready," I said.

Rahima left as quietly as she had come, and I thought, *Hey Maimonides, you said to get the flock out of there! You bet your booties!*

Almost exploding with excitement, I paced back and forth, trying to be as quiet as possible in my stockinged feet. This reminded me of something bad. I had no shoes! How could I escape without shoes? I prayed that Rahima would think of this. I went and lay down on my mattress, obsessing about my lack of shoes and envisioning everything that could go wrong.

Alert to all the sounds in the house, some interminable time later, I heard a small creaking sound, then saw the pink paper slide quietly under the door. On it, I saw words written in black magic marker: *Go to the front door. You will find me outside. Rahima. N.B. I have your shoes.*

Bless you, Rahima! I thought, as I gathered up my Psalm book and put on my *hijab* and *abaya*. I took Rahima's note with me, afraid to leave anything behind that might incriminate her.

As quietly as possible, I turned the knob of the door. It opened soundlessly. Outside, the passageway was dark. I crept down the hall, past the closed doors where I prayed that my captors were sleeping soundly, on by the living room, the bathroom, the dining room, the kitchen, to the front door, my heart beating wildly. I carefully turned the knob. The door opened without resistance. I closed it quietly behind me.

Outside, I felt a chilly breeze, and I inhaled the air into my lungs gratefully. The first breath of freedom! I saw a car parked in the narrow street. Fearful, I spied the silhouette of a head in the driver's seat. I looked around me nervously. Was this a friend, I wondered? Or a guard?

A voice behind me whispered, "Do not worry, he won't bother anyone now!"

Rahima was standing there, in *abaya* and *hijab,* holding my track shoes out towards me. Through the opening of the veil, I saw the dim white oval of her face, but could see no more. There was a three-quarter moon, but it did not cast much light here in the street, which was crowded with dark buildings.

I asked, "Is he…?"

"No, he is not dead. Just a little drugged!" She could not suppress a giggle. "He thought he was going to get lucky with me, but I slipped him something before he could get anywhere. Come on, get your shoes on, we have to rock and roll!" She rolled her rrrr's as she said this. *Rrrrock and rrrroll!* "I will take you as far as the edge of town, and then return before they miss me."

I quickly jammed the running shoes on my feet, tightening the laces with shaking fingers.

We hurried away from the doorstep, slinking inside the shadows beside the buildings. "If anyone sees us, they will probably just think we are prostitutes, sneaking home after a job!" laughed Rahima. Our shoes were soundless on the cobbled pavement, and we moved quickly through the deserted streets.

As we hurried along, I saw that the area had an unkempt look, as though uninhabited. After we had walked about fifteen blocks or so, Rahima slowed down a little.

"Where are we going?" I asked.

"I am taking you to the road to Kiryat Arba, a Jewish settlement. At the end of the road, you can go forward, but I will stay back, since to them, I am the enemy. When we get closer, I will have you remove the *abaya* and *hijab*."

"Alright. Just let me know what I need to do." We continued to walk rapidly through the dark, deserted streets.

"Let me tell you a little about my father," Rahima said, "and perhaps you will not judge him too harshly. When he was a young man, his heart was stolen by a woman, tall, silent, beautiful, brilliant. They had a happy marriage, two children: me and Iman. But the woman, my mother, was killed on a bus approaching al-Khalil, and my father's heart was stricken with bitterness. A Palestinian terrorist group was responsible for this atrocity, but still, his hatred was against the Jews, for he reasoned that without them, the problem would not exist. This occurred twelve years ago, and he has multiplied his anger and hatred since that time."

"That's very strange," I said. "My own husband's former wife was also killed by terrorists. On the trains in Madrid." I was silent, thinking about the very different responses of the two men.

"Really? And now he has married you?"

"Yes," I said.

"He is one of the *mustaqimun,* the righteous," she said.

"Yes, he is," I agreed, then asked, "where exactly is al-Khalil?"

"You have likely heard of it by its Jewish name, Hebron. The longtime home of Abraham, and his final resting place. The name, *al-Khalil,* refers to Abraham since, in Islam, he is considered 'the friend,' *al-khalil,* of God."

"Oh yes!" I said, memory dawning. "Abraham is buried here! Along with Sarah and Isaac!"

"Yes," said Rahima, "they are all buried at the *Haram al-Khalil.*"

This was also where Sarah had received the news of her miraculous pregnancy from the angel of God. She had laughed here, and Abraham had argued with God for the people of Sodom and Gomorrah.

Rahima and I walked quickly, side by side.

I don't know why it struck me at that moment, but since Rahima seemed so knowledgeable, I asked, "Do you know the Dome of the Chain, on the Temple Mount in Jerusalem?"

"Of course." she said.

"There's writing, probably a Quranic verse, above the prayer niche. Do you know what that is?"

Rahima thought a minute, then said, "It is about David, from Sura 38, '*SaD.*' '*O David, We did make thee a vice-regent on Earth, and so judge now between men in truth.*'"

Intrigued, I said, "Are you a *Hafiz*? Someone who has

memorized the whole Quran?"

"Yes," she said. "Please, take off your *abaya* and veil now. We are almost there."

I took off the garments and handed them to Rahima. She folded them and put them under her arm. "Where you are going," she said, "you won't need these anymore."

She raised her other arm, pointing in the direction of sparkling lights ahead.

"There is Kiryat Arba. When you get near the check point, yell out 'Shalom! I am American!' With luck, they will not shoot you."

"How far is it?" I asked.

"About three quarters of a mile," she said. "Please go. I must return, or my so-called friend, the fellow in the car, will awake and raise the alert."

"Alright," I said. I stopped just a moment longer, to give Rahima a farewell hug.

"Goodbye," she said, "I will likely never see you again. And Rachel?"

"Yes?"

Rahima looked back over her shoulder at the dark streets behind her. "Just in case someone might be following, I recommend that you *run!*"

I turned around and did just as Rahima said.

My legs were stiff at first from all the recent inactivity, but they quickly warmed up. As I raced along the dark street, I began to notice what appeared at first to be a strange optical illusion. The lights ahead seemed to be veering to the left, and every time I tried to point my trajectory towards them, my feet pulled me in another direction. Added to this was the strange occurrence of my accelerating pace and the ability to go faster and faster. The cross-streets seemed to shoot by me as quickly as if I'd been in a car. Glancing over my shoulder, I noticed the lights of Kiryat Arba receding farther and farther behind me.

I soon passed the dark shape of a large square building. I thought this must be the place where the patriarchs were buried, the cave of Machpelah. Suddenly in giddy high spirits, no longer concerned about my cockeyed navigation, I waved at my Jewish family, Abraham, Sarah, and Isaac, as I streaked by. After this, I saw ahead of me only more dark streets, and then the edge of town, and finally a rocky open field, sloping down to what looked like a cliff. I was a mountain trail runner, so I kept running, down over the lip of the precipice.

Far below, I saw the mirror-sheen of a large body of water. Through steep ravines, I flew, racing past a mountain waterfall, a cave, and then the lush palm trees and vegetation of an oasis. On and on I went, and when I reached the plain beside the water, I turned right. I no longer looked behind me. Like Hagar, I ran.

WISDOM

Be a pilgrim to the Ka'ba inside a human being, and Makkah will rise into view on its own.

Jelal al-Din Rumi

Jeddah, Saudi Arabia

5:30 am. *Wednesday, December 27*[th] *2006*
6th *of Dhu al-Hijja, 1427 AH*
Mahmud and Prof. Yakub al-Shadi

After a two-hour layover in Alexandria, Mahmud and Yakub embarked on their final leg to Jeddah, Saudi Arabia. Mahmud allowed his father to sleep during most of the two-and-a-half hour plane ride, hoping that the rest would allow him some recovery from the head injury he'd suffered the night before. He knew that his father would need all the strength and stamina he could muster during the arduous six days ahead.

As his father slept, Mahmud thought about the Hajj, rehearsed its meaning and specifics. According to custom, Abraham himself had initiated the first call to Hajj, after he and his son, Ishmael, completed building the *Ka'ba*, the square-shaped structure at the center of the *Masjid al-Haram*, the sacred mosque in Makkah. He and his father would begin there tomorrow, performing the *Umrah*, the circumambulation of the *Ka'ba* and associated rituals, then undertaking the long journey to the various "stations" of the pilgrimage, first out to Mina, and then the plain of Arafat, returning via Muzdalifah to Mina, where they would perform the stoning of the pillars symbolic of the battle with the devil, and the sacrifice commemorating the *thabiyy,* the near-ritual-slaughter of Ishmael.

As Mahmud had once explained to Rachel, the Hajj was one of the five pillars of Islam, and must be performed by every able-bodied Muslim with sufficient means to complete the journey. Muhammad himself had performed the Hajj in the tenth year after his migration to Medina, the year of his death.

Overall, the Hajj was a purifying ritual of the soul, a recommitment to the service of God and responsibility to the Muslim people.

Despite the importance of this ritual, however, more than once, Mahmud questioned the wisdom of their following through on the *Hajj*, with his father in such an uncertain state of health. As the Quran itself said, the obligation for performance of *Hajj* is removed if one is in a state of illness.[22] Mahmud worried terribly that his father would have difficulty on the arduous pilgrimage, particularly the thirteen mile walk out to Arafat from Mecca and the fast-paced walking from Muzdalifah to Mina on the 10th of Dhu al-Hijja[23], the throngs of people a danger even to those in the peak of health.

As the plane touched down in Jeddah, Mahmud shook his father's shoulder. "Baba," he called, "we're here!" Yakub opened his eyes, seeing that their plane had landed. Mahmud noted that Yakub looked worse than ever. Even beyond his physical ailments, he appeared to be in the grip of some strong emotion, one that Mahmud could not identify. Though he did not like to question his father's integrity, he knew that such a state of mind would make it difficult for his father to enter the state of mental tranquility and peace, *ihram*, required for the pilgrimage.

The two men disembarked from the plane and entered a terminal designated specifically for *Hajjis,* pilgrims. This was constructed to process the over one million air travelers who arrived each year during the *Hajj*.

Before claiming their baggage, Mahmud and Yakub joined thousands of other pilgrims in long lines at the passport and *Hajj* visa check point. They waited close to two hours, watching the passport officers interrogate the pilgrims in front of them, carefully checking documentation. At last, their own turn came, and they submitted to the questioning and document review, clearing immigration without difficulty.

At the baggage claim, jostled by the pressing crowds, Mahmud got a further clue about the mental state of his father. Seeing his bag emerge from the chute of the conveyer belt, Yakub went forward to claim it. Simultaneously, another pilgrim raced for his own suitcase, crashing into Yakub, who moved more slowly. Yakub winced, the pain of his hidden bruises flared.

He turned on the man, yelling in Arabic, "What is wrong with you? Do you think every moment is *Jihad?*"

---

[22] Qur'an 2:196

[23] December 31st, 2006. Because the Islamic months are calculated on the lunar calendar, the date of the pilgrimage changes every year, just as Jewish holidays fall on different days of the Gregorian calendar from year to year.

Abashed, the man apologized quietly and slunk away with his suitcase.

Mahmud made no mention of this outburst to Yakub, but it greatly increased his worry. He rarely, if ever, saw his father angry. Why here, in the city of God?

They waited outside for a taxi in a long line of exultant pilgrims. Despite his father's dour mood, Mahmud felt a growing sense of elation as he joined this group. So many travelers, from so many distant places, all brought to Makkah for the same purpose: to glorify God, and to fulfill the obligation of pilgrimage.

The atmosphere at the airport was so jubilant that Mahmud could even forget the traumatic and disappointing experiences in the graveyard in Fustat, at least for a little while.

While waiting for a taxi, Mahmud spoke with the woman in front of him in line. She was a divorced mother from Dallas, Texas, previously a Catholic but now converted to Islam. With her was an Iraqi woman, a fellow member of her mosque in Houston. They talked about their journey and their growing sense of jubilation about the upcoming spiritual quest. When she reached the curb, next in line for a cab, she turned to Mahmud and Yakub, bidding them goodbye.

"*Assalaamu 'alaykum,*" she said, to which Mahmud replied, "*Wa 'alaykum assalaam!*"

When they got in their own cab, Mahmud told the driver that their destination was the Makkah Hilton. They entered a long line of slowly moving traffic travelling the distance from the King Abdul Aziz Airport in Jeddah to the city of Makkah. Here, in this caravan of mixed vehicles, including gaily-painted buses, taxis, stretch limousines, and private automobiles piled high with suitcases, Mahmud had the sensation that he was already at the beginning of the pilgrimage.

The car travelled west towards Makkah, a distance of approximately sixty miles. Their progress was slow and it was over three hours before the Holy City came into view, a little after noon. Following the sign that said "Muslims Only" directing them into the city, Mahmud felt his spirits soar.

His elation grew when the jutting peaks of Makkah and the famous skyline, familiar to him from countless photos of the city, came into view. He was here! The place he had dreamed of all his life! His *qibla,* his direction of prayer! It was almost unreal to him.

Alight with joy, he turned to his father. Yakub's face remained impassive.

Crestfallen, Mahmud asked, "What is it, Baba?" for the hundredth time, it seemed.

"I miss Rachel," his father said, simply, and Mahmud believed him. But he suspected there was something else as well, something his father hadn't yet told him.

They turned off the highway, entering the streets of Makkah. As they neared the city center, Mahmud saw a glow rising up from the ground, and he knew it was *al-Masjid al-Haram*, the Sacred Mosque, though he could not yet see it. All around them, the streets were thronged with people. Brightly-adorned storefronts on either side displayed wares of clothing, prayer beads, and exotic foods from many countries.

The travel agent had chosen the Makkah Hilton because it was adjacent to the Sacred Mosque. The hotel lobby was crowded, and everyone was speaking in excitement about the pilgrimage, passing on advice and information about the various ritual ceremonies and the particular details they knew. "It's forty seven stones you throw at the *Jamarat,* the pillars," said one, and another corrected him, "No! It's forty nine! Six times seven, plus seven!" "Well, I heard," said someone else, "that you're supposed to throw seventy on the final day, to make sure the devil is good and dead!"

It was early afternoon when they reached their hotel room. Mahmud could hardly contain his excitement. He was like a young boy again, bounding from thing to thing, exclaiming with each new sight, "Look at this! Baba! Look!"

Out the window, he could see the three domes in front of the *Masjid al-Haram* along with the many spires of its minarets, lit up in colors of white and green. If he peered hard, perhaps he could even make out a black spot. Could it be the *Ka'ba* itself? He looked at the hills above the city. In one of these hills, Muhammad, peace and blessings upon him, had received his first revelation, had seen the angel Gabriel on all horizons and then, in terror, crawled back to the arms of his wife, Khadija. *This all happened here! Right here!*

Mahmud knew he had to calm down. He went and sat in an easy chair, turning it around so he could sit and look out the window. He took a deep breath, and then another.

After a few minutes, he looked over at his father. He was lying on the bed, his eyes closed. Was he sleeping? Or...?

Mahmud jumped up and went over. He peered down at his father, then called out softly, "Baba?"

No response.

His heart began to pound. He shook Yakub's shoulder. "Baba?"

His father opened his eyes. "What is it, Mahmud?" he said.

With relief, Mahmud said, "I was worried about you! Rachel said I should keep an eye on you, because of the bump on your head."

"I'm fine. I just didn't get much rest last night. I'm tired. Perhaps I should sleep." He closed his eyes again.

Mahmud had wanted to go over immediately to perform the *tawaaf*, the circling of the Ka'ba, but he saw that his father needed to rest, and felt obliged to stay with him. So he went and sat down in a chair by the window, listening as his father's breathing became regular. Soon, Mahmud went to retrieve a book from his bag, a well-worn copy of *Tarjuman al-Ashwaq*[24], the love poetry of Ibn Arabi, written here in Makkah. He sat back down, quietly reading as his father slept and peace settled upon their hotel room.

Makkah, Saudia Arabia
Morning of Thursday, December 28th 2006
7th of Dhu al-Hijja, 1427 AH
Mahmud and Prof. Yakub al-Shadi

The following day, Mahmud and Yakub arose at 5:00 am for morning prayer. The sky was still completely dark. As the two of them dressed, Mahmud secretly examined his father's face. He looked better, but the small lines around his eyes and mouth still betrayed some perplexingly elusive emotion.

After morning prayer was complete, Mahmud and Yakub sat sipping coffee and eating breakfast, watching the sun rise, its rays defining the spires and domes of the *Haram* which filled the entire window. When the orb of the sun came up over the edge of the jagged horizon, it was huge. Already, Mahmud could tell it would be a very warm day.

---

[24] The Interpreter of Desires

In preparation for the *Tawaf*, the circling of the *Ka'ba*, they both showered, and then draped the white cloths of *ihram* around them, putting unstitched sandals on their feet. They were to perform the full *Hajj*, the *Hajj al-Tamutu'*, just as Muhammad himself, and as Islamic legend held it, even Abraham and Ishmael, had done in millennia past. This meant they would enter *ihram* twice: once today for the *Umrah*, the lesser pilgrimage, during which they would perform several rituals at the *Masjid al-Haram*, and once tomorrow, at the beginning of the *Hajj* proper, the greater pilgrimage, the three-day journey peaking at its apex, thirteen miles away, in Arafat, on the *yawm al-wuquf*, "Standing Day." Wearing the two white cloths signaled their entry into both a physical state of purity and a mental state of tranquility, though Mahmud had his doubts about this latter condition in relation to his father, who remained tense and withdrawn.

After declaring their intention to perform *Umrah*, they recited the *Talbiyah*, the prayer of service to and declaration of God's oneness: *Here I am at Thy service O Lord, here I am. Here I am at Thy service and Thou hast no partners. Thine alone is All Praise and All Bounty, and Thine alone is The Sovereignty. Thou hast no partners.*

At last, they were ready. The two men stepped into the hall, entering the first small tributary in the collecting stream of people that ended at the *Ka'ba*. The stream swelled further as it left the hotel, a rushing river now of white-clad men and women wearing black or, occasionally, rainbows of bright colors. Mahmud was struck by a powerful feeling, the flow of something larger than himself yet also connected to these people.

By this point, it was as though there were two parts to Mahmud: the one in the "here and now," worried about his father, and the one sweeping towards the sea of humanity ahead, which Mahmud pictured as a kind of luminous river, its center a core of radiant light.

The stream of people brought them to the *Haram*, which they entered through the *Bab-al-Salaam*, the Gate of Peace, stepping with their right foot. As they went through, Mahmud and Yakub repeated the *Talbiyah*, followed by several other prayers, until, in a breathtaking instant, the *Ka'ba* was upon them. Seeing it, Mahmud stumbled. Yakub reached out his arm and grasped him and, for a moment, the two of them stood, gazing at the building, its geometric shape, a simple cube, draped now with a white cloth, an ornate golden door at one end.

Before they began their *Tawaf*, circling of the *Ka'ba*, they intoned together the words: *Allahu Akbar, la illaha illa Allah.* God is great; there is no God but God. Then, they walked as far as *al-Hajar al-Aswad*, the black stone, a silver-encircled object adhering to the side of the *Ka'ba*. This was a mysterious article, said to be a meteor from outer space, first placed in the structure of God's House by Abraham and Ishmael and then replaced again under Muhammad's supervision, when the *Ka'ba* was repaired many centuries later. Here, they paused again, speaking to God once more, declaring once again their intention to perform the *Umrah*, the lesser pilgrimage.

Together, they circumambulated the *Ka'ba* for the first time, skirting the semi-circular wall known as the *Hateem*. Islamic legend held that this was the location of the gravesites of Ishmael and Hagar. When they reached the fourth corner of the *Ka'ba*, they touched it with their right hands, then started the cycle over again. Around and around they went, repeating the circumambulation seven times. When they were done, Mahmud looked at his father's face. From the midst of his bliss, he felt a cold shock as he recognized the emotion at last. Rage!

"Baba..." he began, but his father stopped him with one icy look.

"Let's get to the *Maqam Ibrahim* and complete this," he said, his words clipped.

The two circled to the location of the Maqam Ibrahim, the boulder where Abraham had stood as he completed building the upper portions of the *Ka'ba*. The imprints of his feet still remain to this day. Mahmud and Yakub went and stood in this spot, praying. When they were done, Mahmud looked at Yakub once again, afraid for what he might see now. He was yet again baffled by his father's strange and shifting emotions. Now, Yakub stood looking towards the *Ka'ba*, his face pointed upwards, mouth open, tears rolling in rivers down his cheeks.

"Baba?" Mahmud said.

"God is here!" said his father.

Mina, Saudi Arabia
Friday, December 29th 2006
8th of Dhu al-Hijja, 1427 AH
Mahmud and Prof. Yakub al-Shadi

They completed their devotions of the first day by running, like Hagar, between the two hills of Safa and Marwa, just as she had done eons ago when searching for water for her dying son, Ishmael. After this, they returned to their room at the Makkah Hilton and removed the cloths of *ihram*. They then went for lunch at the hotel restaurant.

After they returned to their room, they spent the rest of the day in prayer and preparation for the greater *Hajj*, which would begin tomorrow. This included trimming the ends of each other's hair.

Mahmud took his time with this ritual, enjoying the feel of his father's hair, the appearance of the few silver strands that shimmered among the darker ones. He took care not to disturb the healing laceration, which still appeared a little red and puffy, though healing well.

Yakub made no sound as his son performed these ministrations.

The following day, the 8th of *Dhu al-Hijja*, began again before dawn, with the morning prayer of *Fajr,* followed by the ritual entrance into *Ihram*, this time with the declaration of intention to perform the greater *Hajj*. Today, the pilgrimage began in earnest, with the first five-mile leg of the thirteen-mile journey to Arafat, which they would reach tomorrow. They would spend the night tonight in Mina, completing a full cycle of five daily prayers there and leaving tomorrow for Arafat after *Fajr,* morning prayer. After that, they would return to Mina, by way of Muzdalifah, for the *Jamarat,* the stoning of the pillars in Mina, the day after tomorrow.

Their travel agent had arranged for them to send their bags on ahead to their tent in Mina, so they were unencumbered by possessions. As the sun rose, the two of them walked eastward, facing directly into the rising solar sphere. Yakub was quiet for quite some time. They stopped at several locations for water. Mahmud was still very concerned about his father, whose face looked pale and drawn.

Eventually, unable to contain his worry any longer, Mahmud said, "Baba, what was wrong yesterday? During the *Tawaf?* You looked really...angry, I suppose I would say."

As if to reinforce Mahmud's conclusion, Yakub spat out, "I AM angry." He looked away, pressing his lips together as if to prevent more words from bursting between them.

"Why, Baba? It is the *Hajj!* All humankind is joyful at this time!"

"It's precisely all humankind that I cannot abide!" said Yakub.

"But why?"

"Have you forgotten your mother already?" asked Yakub, perhaps unfairly. "These are the people who killed her! They found some holy word to justify it! It's intolerable!" Yakub's face looked like he himself would like to kill someone.

"No, I haven't forgotten my mother," said Mahmud, forcing calmness into his words. "Those people who killed her were wrong. But that doesn't mean that others aren't right or that humans aren't basically good. Not all the people here were involved in killing my mother. You have to forgive, to surrender to God, to dissolve in the *umma,* the people of Islam."

"I can't do what you say, Mahmud!" cried Yakub, his voice betraying his anguish. "I'm a pebble thrown into the water. It will not dissolve!"

"But what about God?" said Mahmud.

It seemed to Mahmud as if Yakub's face came apart, and he was horrified to see that his father was crying.

Finally, in a broken voice, he said, "How can I say this? I love God more than ever. Yesterday, when I stood in the footsteps of Abraham at the *Ka'ba,* I felt this great love, and, can I say it? I felt something *love me back!* But the disappointment and shame, that I can love God and not love his creation, humankind! It's a terrible, terrible thing! And I know this. I must resolve this, or I will die here on *Hajj.*"

Mahmud cried, "You will not die, Baba!"

Yakub simply shrugged his shoulders.

Several minutes later, Mahmud said, "But what about *the poem?* The one that will redeem humanity?"

His father laughed, a sound dripping with cynicism. "Who

cares about humanity?"

"Baba!" said Mahmud. "You don't mean that!"

"Yes, I do." he said. "Besides, the poetry is gone. Stolen. And now all we have is a memory I cannot remember, and a sign from God that will not come. I will never write this poem."

They walked in silence the rest of the way.

Before noonday prayers, they entered Mina, a virtual city of tens of thousands of white tents, temporary home to over two million people. At various entrances, there were large, multi-colored maps showing the locations of the diverse nationalities. Yakub and Mahmud located the Egyptian camp. After a bit of searching, they were able to find their own tent, which was air-conditioned and comfortable. They would spend the rest of the day and the ensuing night there, leaving the following morning for Arafat.

While Mahmud occupied himself by talking with other pilgrims, Yakub lay down on the cot in the tent and slept during all the intervals between their remaining prayers that day.

Mahmud was very worried about what his father had told him. He did not understand it in the least. From Mahmud's perspective, he found tremendous companionship and hope in the company of the other pilgrims. These Muslims were from all over the world, from every race, both genders, all ages. They were his "*umma*," his people. They were all equal, all seekers of God. He saw no terrorists here.

Yes, they would all soon enter *Jihad*, but this was the greater *Jihad* against the devils inside themselves. In less than 48 hours, he and his father would return to Mina and fight the battle with Satan. That was the meaning of *Jihad*, not the thing the political Islamists had twisted into a justification for the slaughter of innocents.

After dinner and before bedtime, Mahmud sat alone and watched the stars and moon in the clear sky above. The moon was in the stage between half and full, the time where its three-dimensionality is evident, where the contours of the "dark side" are imaginable though not visible. He marveled at the wonder of God's world, where so many things seemed to be created in pairs: good and evil; love and justice; reason and intuition; science and religion; free will and fate; man and woman, even Ishmael and Isaac. Is this what Allah meant when he said: *all things We have made in pairs, so that you may take thought?* [25]

He contemplated his father, his spirit as obscure as the moon's dark side. Would he remain there, unreachable? Would he find what he was looking for? Or would he, as Mahmud feared, succumb to the anger that had tormented him since their arrival in Makkah? Would he die, as he had said?

Arafat, Saudi Arabia
Morning of Saturday, December 30th 2006
9th of Dhu al-Hijja, 1427 AH
Prof. Yakub and Mahmud al-Shadi

The next morning, Mahmud and Yakub got up once again before sunrise, aroused by the voice of the *muezzin* in the morning call to prayer. Still wearing sandals and the two white cloths of *Ihram*, father and son set out on the eight mile walk to Arafat. They joined the throng of people, the men all dressed, like them, in white. On the highway beside them, throngs of buses inched slowly along in the rising heat.

After an hour or so of walking in silence, they stopped at a stand along their route and purchased some water and fruit. Yakub took several long drinks from the water bottle then placed it in his bag. He chewed on some dates. Mahmud was glad to see some appetite. Then, they continued on their way towards Arafat, walking in what seemed an endless stream of white-shrouded people, their clothes so bright in the sunlight it was hard to see them.

What occurred at the plain of Arafat was considered a kind of "rehearsal" for the *yawm ad din*, the day of judgment. The pilgrims, each and every one of them, were to make an accounting to themselves of their good deeds and of their sins, in preparation for the *Jamarat*, the battle with the devil, tomorrow.

Arafat was a broad, sandy plain which bore, in its center, a rocky prominence known as *Jabal al-Rahma*, the mountain of compassion. The entire plain and the mountain itself were now covered with men and women, all immersed in silent prayer.

Arafat is where Muhammad, peace and blessings upon him,

---

[25] Qur'an 51:50

gave his final sermon. After their arrival, standing amongst the millions of pilgrims, Mahmud and Yakub, too, heard a sermon that day, this one by the supreme authority on Islamic affairs in the Kingdom of Saudi Arabia, who spoke about a world at peace, and how only true adherence to Islam could make this dream a truth.

After this, Mahmud and Yakub turned their backs on the sun and started on their way to Muzdalifah, that place of darkness and mystery, an intermediate site between Arafat and Mina. They entered it under night's indigo veil. No longer subject to the comforting practicalities of logic and science, the world seemed to open up in all directions, the vastness of space yawning in the depths above them.

Here, they must collect the pebbles they would use in their battle tomorrow against the devil, and they must also take whatever small amount of rest they could before an early start back to Mina.

Yakub and Mahmud walked together, bending over to select stones then placing them in their pockets. Yakub said to Mahmud, "You know, I did sin greatly in my life."

"What?" said Mahmud, wincing. He did not think he wanted to hear what his father had to say.

"With your mother." Yakub took in Mahmud's expression and laughed. "No, don't worry. It wasn't infidelity. Neither of us succumbed to that devil. No, no."

"What then, Baba," said Mahmud, now curious.

"I didn't give your mother all the freedom she deserved," said Yakub. "I held her to a standard as mother and wife that forced her to set aside her own personal desires. When you become a husband, remember this. You must let go your grip on your beloved. Open your hand and set her free. Remember Muhammad, peace and blessings upon him, and how he loved his wife, Khadija."

Mahmud considered this in silence, then nodded, saying, "Thank you, Baba. I'm not ready to marry yet, but when I am, I will remember what you've said."

"This is the advice I will follow myself, now that, *al-hamdu lillah*, I have a second chance with Rachel."

Mina, Saudi Arabia

Morning of Sunday, December 31ˢᵗ 2006 (Eid al-Adha)
10ᵗʰ of Dhu al-Hijja, 1427 AH
Prof. Yakub and Mahmud al-Shadi

The next morning, the day of *Jamarat*, the battle with Satan, Mahmud and Yakub got up from their resting place in the deep darkness, well before dawn. Neither had slept. Today, they would pass down a narrow strait on their return to Mina.

They said their morning prayers then joined the horde streaming the three miles towards Mina. The tight packing of people emotionally charged to do battle with the devil caused Mahmud some considerable anxiety, worried as he was about his father's mental and physical state.

As for Yakub, he seemed irritable and on the verge of explosion once again. The gathering of people was obviously intensely distressing to his father. Mahmud also worried that Yakub was becoming fatigued. He walked as though dazed and stumbled frequently. This was disquieting, since on this occasion, rapid and focused walking seemed to be the order of the day.

Mahmud became particularly alarmed when his father had a hysterical altercation with another pilgrim. The man walked alongside them for a mile or so before speaking. His appearance was notable; he wore not only the robes of *ihram* but also a filmy white veil that covered all but his eyes. After a time, Mahmud noticed him lean over and whisper something, casually, to his father. Mahmud was startled when his father screamed shrilly, "It was you!" and then as the man continued to murmur to him, "Yes there is!" and finally, "Stop!" in a high-pitched wail. Horrified, Mahmud saw his father trying to grab hold of the man, and he rushed to apologize, but the man had disappeared already into the crowd of hurrying pilgrims. After this, Yakub sobbed for several minutes as he stumbled along, his breath rasping and irregular.

"That was him!" sobbed Yakub.

"Who, Baba?"

"The man from the graveyard! The one who stole the *diwan!*"

Mahmud whipped his head around but, in dismay, realized that there was no way to locate the man among the throng of people dressed in white. "Are you sure?"

"Yes!" he cried. "*Yà Allah! Protect us!*"

"But Baba, it is impossible…what would a man like that be doing on *Hajj?*"

"He's come to torment us! He's one of the *al-Qayana*! I'm sure of it! We have to find him!"

Yakub sped up, peering at each face as he passed, and Mahmud struggled to follow him in the pressing crowd. But neither of them located the man again.

Finally, to Mahmud's immense relief, they arrived in Mina. They sat in their tent waiting for their allotted time. They were among the earliest, their time to approach the pillars set at 8:00 am. Yakub continued to look around, scanning the crowd frantically for a sign of the veiled man, who did not rematerialize.

When their time came, they went to their meeting area. There the pilgrims seemed, if possible, even more emotionally charged than they had been on the walk to Mina. Mahmud saw the muscles around his father's mandible tensing, and his eyes were wild.

"Baba…," he began, but his father interrupted him.

"Let's kill these devils!" he spat, his lips turned down

They started off, walking at a rapid pace towards the *Jamarat*, each carrying his seven pebbles. They would gather their strength as they passed the first two pillars, then throw all seven at the third, doing battle with the devil, in hopes that they would deal a mortal blow.

Yakub and Mahmud passed the first pillar, walked another hundred and fifty yards or so then passed the second pillar. They did not throw yet. Mahmud was trying to focus on his sins, such as they were. They had reached the third pillar, the *Jamarat al-Akabah*. Mahmud took a pebble from his hand and threw it, hard. He heard the pebble hit with a satisfying "Click!" *Take that, Satan!*

He threw the rest of the pebbles, one after the other. Task complete, he became aware that his father was yelling again. "*I will kill you!*" he shrieked.

Alarmed, Mahmud looked over at his father. He was horrified at the sight that greeted him. His father stood, a hand upraised. Next to him, Mahmud saw seven pebbles scattered on the ground, his father's face frozen in a mask of terror. As though he knew something horrific were above him but was nevertheless compelled to look, Yakub slowly raised his gaze, his chin following, moving up, up...

"NO!" he screamed, his arms suddenly thrown above him. What happened next could not have been real, but Mahmud swore that it was. Something fell from above, piercing the ceiling, a dark streak, dreadful in its linearity, brutal in its velocity and momentum. Though many others stood immediately beside him, the dark arrow struck Yakub in the chest with terrible precision.

The impact knocked him down, and Mahmud saw the immense black spike protruding from Yakub's chest, extending up from floor to ceiling, skewering Yakub to the ground. Yakub lay supine, his eyes open. Mahmud ran over and knelt by his father. Before he lost consciousness, Mahmud heard him whisper, a look of wonder on his face, "*Alif!*" Then, his eyes rolled up and closed.

Aghast, Mahmud looked around frantically, calling out for help. When he turned back, he still saw Yakub's inert body, but the mysterious black spike was now gone.

"Who took that!" he screamed, but the pilgrims crowding around said nothing.

"It should not be removed!" yelled Mahmud, and now some people in official outfits, police perhaps, rushed over to determine the source of the disturbance.

At that moment, Yakub's eyes opened again, and he rolled his head from side to side. Mahmud looked at him, relief and confusion whirling inside him.

"What is happening here?" shouted one of the police.

Trembling, Mahmud cried, "I don't know! Something hit my father!"

"What?" said the policeman.

"A black...spike of some kind. It went right through his chest!"

"What? What are you talking about?" Now the policeman looked at Mahmud as if he were mad. "You are going to have to move out of here. It's not safe to stop in this area."

The two men grabbed Yakub and lifted him up. On his feet, he was wobbly, his eyes unfocussed. The policemen draped Yakub's arms around their shoulders and carried him forward, out of the way of the onrushing pilgrims. They walked several hundred yards then sat him down on a chair. One of the policemen gave him water. The other policeman took out a flashlight and looked in

Yakub's eyes. Apparently satisfied, he put it back in his pocket.

"Shouldn't we take him to the doctor?" Mahmud asked.

"There's a first aid station, in the tent city nearby. Take him there."

"Baba!" said Mahmud. Tentatively, he pushed aside the white cloth from his father's chest, terrified of what he would see. But all he saw was his father's unblemished skin. Puzzled, he looked back at his face.

Yakub was mumbling something.

"What, Baba?" said Mahmud.

"I'm just like them!" said Yakub.

"Like who?"

"The murderers. I wanted to kill him."

"What are you talking about, Baba? You are nothing like them!" This was crazy talk. "Baba, I'll take you to the first aid station!"

At the first aid station, the medic asked Yakub what had happened. "I don't remember," he answered. "I feel fine now."

The man turned to Mahmud and asked the same question. Mahmud felt strange telling him about the black spike. He did not mention that, but instead said simply, "My father fell down and lost consciousness."

"For how long?" the medic asked.

"Not long, maybe 20 seconds."

The man took Yakub's vital signs and, like the policeman, checked his pupils. He asked Yakub a few questions to see if he was oriented. He answered all the questions without difficulty.

"Dehydration," declared the medic.

That being the final diagnosis, the man watched Yakub drink a full bottle of water and then permitted him to leave. As they departed, Mahmud asked: "Do you have any pebbles here? My father hasn't yet completed this station yet."

"How many?" the man asked. There was a pile of them on one of the counters, left there, presumably, by pilgrims who had been taken ill before they could throw them.

"Seven," said Mahmud.

The man handed him seven pebbles. Mahmud gave them to his father.

The two of them returned to the third pillar. Yakub threw the stones, one at a time. Mahmud heard all seven hit the pillar. He never knew what devils his father defeated that day.

Afterwards, they said a prayer together.

The two men then returned to Mina, where they contributed funds for the sacrifice of a lamb, the festival of Eid al-Adha, the commemoration of the redemption of Ishmael. They would eat this lamb and what they did not consume would be given to the needy.

Afterwards, they went back to their tent. They trimmed each other's hair once again, this time very short. They removed the clothing of *Ihram* and put on their regular clothes. Mahmud was still deathly afraid for his father, who said little and moved unsteadily.

"Baba," said Mahmud, "I think we should take the bus to Makkah for the next *Tawaf.*"

Yakub shook his head. "No," he said. "We must walk, like Ishmael and Abraham."

"But Baba…" Mahmud protested. He did not get to finish.

"We will walk," repeated Yakub.

They set out on the five mile walk back to Makkah. Mahmud was alarmed by his father's frequent stumbling. His gait was wide and unsteady. At last, to his immense relief, the minarets of the *Haram* appeared in the distance. The sight heartened his father, who increased his pace. They entered once more through the Gate of Peace, saw the *Ka'ba* ahead, now draped with the black cloth of the *Kiswa,* ornate with golden verse, moving slightly in the breeze generated by the tens of thousands of worshippers who swept around it. The cloth held verses of the Quran, though before the time of Muhammad, peace and blessings upon him, it is told in legend that this cloth contained the *hanging verses,* the poetry of the Bedouin.

Mahmud was struck by the mass of people, so many you could not even see the individual faces.

He worried that his father's anger would be aroused again by the sight of so many pilgrims. But his face was now serene, and he entered the flow of people with tranquility. When they reached the *Maqam Ibrahim,* they stopped. Yakub stood in Abraham's footsteps once again. He looked towards the *Ka'ba,* and said, "They built it together."

"Who?" shouted Mahmud, to be heard above the sound of rushing people, "God and Abraham?"

"No," said Yakub. "Ishmael and Abraham. They built it

together. Ishmael forgave his father for sending him out into the wilderness." Mahmud saw tears on his father's face.

They walked towards the large building that housed Safa and Marwa, to complete the *Sa'y*, Hagar's running between hills, once again. On their way, as they arrived at the well of ZamZam, Mahmud saw his father begin to crumple, his knees buckling as though his legs no longer contained any bones.

In a sickening repeat of this morning's incident, but without the diversion of some kind of holy sign, Mahmud rushed up to find his father unconscious. He did not wake up this time. This time, paramedics came but could not revive him. They placed him on a stretcher and raced with him to a street outside the mosque, where an ambulance waited.

Since Mahmud was a family member, they allowed him to ride with his father to the hospital. As the ambulance crawled through the crowded streets, Mahmud watched his father's face. It bore an expression of peace. But despite the advanced medical equipment hooked up to him, Mahmud could not determine whether his father was alive or dead.

CROWN

There are as many paths to God as there are children of Adam.

Hadith

Somewhere in Southern Israel
Before Dawn on Sunday, December 31st 2006
Dr. Rachel al-Shadi

I ran. I had no idea of my destination and was not even particularly concerned about finding it. It felt so good to run!

The countryside was devoid of human habitation. Above, the moon hung in the sky, round and bright and, in the absence of buildings, it painted a silver light on the surfaces of the rocks, defining areas of shadow and light. Ahead of me, the path stretched on, a straight strip of silver leading to the horizon.

My feet followed this trail, and with each stride, I received new energy. I felt my heart beat, the air flow in and out of my lungs. I thought about the cave at Machpelah, about Abraham and his family. In the way one connects thoughts in this state of mind, jumping from idea to idea like stepping stones in a river, I recalled what my rabbi had said once when referring to stories in the Torah.

"They're like your dreams," he said, "and you are responsible for every character in your dream, whether good or bad. Not even that, you *are* every character in your dream! In the same way, we're also *all* the characters in the Torah. Both Moses *and* Pharaoh, both Israel *and* Amalek."

That may be so, I thought, but some seemed more prominent to me than others. Which ones? Abraham, who loved God more than anyone, so much that he would sacrifice his beloved son? Sarah, long-suffering beauty, mortally wounded by the actions of her husband and her son's submission? Isaac, the one who never laughs, dim of vision, the gullible "shadow-man"? Ishmael, silent, his hand forever against his brother, and yet patriarch of nations, just like Jacob? Hagar, proud "mistress," desperate mother, fleet-footed runner, confidante of God?

Of course, it was Isaac. I had always been Isaac. And as I ran through the strange wilderness, the meaning of his story became clear. What was important was not just Abraham and Isaac's submission to God, but Isaac's forgiveness. *Forgiveness.* Of God. Of his father.

This, I saw with sudden clarity, was the missing ingredient of redemption. If we could find forgiveness, then love would spread, like a wave, around the entire globe, a wave of mercy and compassion, of apology and restitution. In its aftermath, guns would be destroyed, knives melted and reformed into sculptures, cameras, pens. No more genocide, no more war. If there were a poem to redeem the world, either written, unwritten, understood or forgotten, I imagined this would be its effect.

But could *I*, Rachel Davidson al-Shadi, forgive and be forgiven?

And then, in that place in time and space, some indeterminate spot in the wilderness, I felt it rush through me, welcome as a stream of cool water. My father, Abdul Malik, Iman, her husband, the strange and terrible man from Jerusalem, my dead husband David -- all the pain was consumed, dissolved within this torrent of forgiveness.

Now, with the joyous and effortless movement of my legs, I thought that God could only be running through me. He could see the sights I saw, the beauty of His world, the sun now rising and illuminating the stones, the echo of my footfalls on the path, the taste and feel of the moisture in my mouth, the tensing and contracting of my muscles in perfect synchrony as I flew over the dusty ground. In my mind, I said a blessing. *Holy One of Being, Your Presence is Creation! I bless You for the You that is me and the me that is You.*

I ran, and my feet beat out a rhythm against the ground, a poem I had once known: *that LOVE is ALL there IS is ALL we KNOW of LOVE...* (5)

And then, as far as my eye could see, there were pillars. They were not tall, about twice my height, and their shadows made diagonal streaks across my path. One by one, I crossed these shadows. To my right, I saw a scintillating light, and I stopped. My body radiated warmth, and in it, I could feel the immense heat of the first moments of creation, the impact of an explosion of unimaginable dimension that was still exploding through me.

I stood by the shimmering light before the pillar. The light condensed and so became like a mirror. The features of the face of the person in the mirror gradually emerged, like a reflection in a pond after rippling its surface with a stone. When it clarified, I was surprised to see that it was not my own face. A pain ripped through me.

It was Yakub.

He looked at me from the other side of the mirror, and the ache I felt was reflected in his beautiful face. A tear dropped from each of my eyes, and I lifted my hand to wipe them away. As I did, Yakub's hand also came up. But of course, if I was lifting my left hand, he was lifting his right, as is the case with mirrors. Simultaneously, we looked upwards and I saw, etched into the pillar, a single word. Together, our lips moved, forming a sound:

סלאם

Salaam, the Arabic word for peace, in Hebrew letters. And our speech caused a thing like mist to float from our mouths. As we raised our heads to watch it disappear into the starry sky, I became aware of music, and realized that it was coming from myself. The whirling of the electrons, the oscillations of the particles in my body was creating a song, and then there was a harmony, perfect, sublime, arcing in a magnificent spiral of sound that gripped me in a powerful force, holding me as the land disappeared and Yakub and I revolved around each other, the sound now radiance between us. I saw only dark open space, and the spiral extending up and below, infinitely vast and glorious. I felt Yakub's being enter mine, and we were no longer two but one. I was aware of light pouring through us, as we rose and saw the kindly faces of our mother and father, and finally, there was only dazzling darkness.

CLOSING

Outside of Beer-Sheba, Israel
11:00 am. Sunday, December 31st 2006
Dr. Rachel al-Shadi

When I next became aware of myself, I found that I was lying on the rocky ground, a strip of asphalt visible a few feet away in front of me. Sitting up, I felt my head spin with vertigo. After it abated, I was able to turn gingerly and take in my surroundings. I noted bright sunlight illuminating a highway, empty in both directions. On each side of the road, a flat expanse of rocky yellow earth extended to the horizon.

I felt like I had run a marathon, a mixture of extreme fatigue and elation. Aside from this, I also noticed that I was ravenous and faint with thirst. Presently, I saw a vehicle far off in the distance, and as it got closer, I discerned that it was a pickup truck. I could see three heads in the front seat, and noticed that the one in the passenger seat bore a head scarf. Fear gripped my empty stomach, and details of my recent abduction came tumbling back into my mind. *Oh no! Was this Iman and her father, come to re-claim me?* I tried to stand up, but only staggered and fell back onto the ground, sparks flying in front of my eyes.

The truck pulled up next to me, and I saw three strangers looking out at me, their faces betraying only surprise and concern. The woman rolled down the window, and the man called across her, "*Shalom! Mah scholmaych?*"

I tried once more to get to my feet. Head spinning mightily, I staggered on cramped muscles over to the side of the truck and leaned against it heavily. Unable to maintain even this posture, I collapsed onto my seat on the ground once again.

The three people jumped out of the truck and ran around to me. As the man and woman continued to query me in Hebrew, holding my shoulders and peering into my face, the third passenger, a teenage boy, went back to the truck and retrieved something from behind the seat. Returning, I saw that he had a canteen in his hand. He held this up to my lips, and I felt cool water. Grabbing the canteen, I tipped it upwards, gulping water through my parched lips. I had never tasted anything so good in my entire life. It was like a miracle, elixir from heaven.

When I had drunk about half of the water, I lowered the

canteen, wiped my mouth with the back of my hand, and said, "Thank you!"

The boy squatted down and looked at me more closely. "You speak English?" he said.

"Yes."

"Are you hurt?"

I took stock of my body, finding only stiff, fatigued muscles and a massive gnawing in my empty stomach. "No, I'm fine. Do you mind if I drink some more of the water, though?" I shook the canteen.

"*T'fadali!* Help yourself!" he laughed, revealing a pleasant smile and even, white teeth. "Finish it off!"

As I gulped at the water, he said, "They call that water 'the hidden treasure.' It comes from the underground reservoirs of the Negev."

I nodded, handing back the empty canteen. "It tastes better than anything I've ever had."

The boy nodded, understanding.

I looked him over more closely now. He looked to be about sixteen or seventeen. I noted that he wore western clothing, and seemed to be dressed up for some kind of special occasion.

"Are you feeling better?" he asked me. "Do you feel like you'd be able to get into the truck?"

I nodded. The boy and the man supported me as I got to my feet.

"Where are we?" I said.

The boy gave me a strange look, and said, "You don't know where you are?"

I shook my head.

Content to let that question stand for a moment, the boy replied, "We're in Nitzana, near the Israeli-Egyptian border. Just over there," he pointed to a small hill, "is a landmark called Hagar's Heel."

I took this in, nodding.

"I was at the youth center down the road. My parents were picking me up for the Eid, the holiday, today."

I noticed that the man was staring at me. He spoke in surprised Arabic to the boy, who also began to examine me carefully, his eyes registering shock and recognition.

"Saydati," he said, excitedly, "are you the woman from the

television? The American hostage?"

I paused, thinking quickly. Should I admit this to them? They seemed very nice, but what if they were in cahoots somehow with the kidnappers?

Without waiting for an answer, the boy cried, "You are! I recognize you!"

The next thing I knew, I felt the woman's arms around me, and she was crying out "*al-Hamdu Lillah!*" When she stepped back, I saw tears streaming down her face.

The boy was beaming, but began to ply me with questions. "But how did you get here? It has to be fifty kilometers from Hebron!"

Confused, I looked down at my dusty running shoes and sweat pants. "I don't know," I said. "I think I ran."

"You ran?" he said, incredulous. "Fifty kilometers?"

I shrugged. "That's all I remember."

He shook his head. Giving up on the question for now, he said. "Well, come on. We better get you back to our house. We'll figure out what to do when we get there."

"Where's your house?" I asked.

"It's in a town called Drijat. Have you heard of it?"

I shook my head.

"It's a *fellaheen* village, about an hour north of here by car. Come on, jump in."

"*Fellaheen?*" I repeated. I'd heard the word, but wasn't sure what it meant.

"Palestinian landowners and farmers," said the boy, opening the door of the truck.

Looking to the cab, I said, "But what about you? There's only three seats!"

"I'll sit in the back," he laughed. "I do it all the time. I'm one of eight children, so I'm used to it!"

I climbed in, and the Arab woman got in next to me, the man entering the door on the other side. Before the boy slammed the truck door, he said, "You have a treat in store for you! It's *Eid al-Adha* today! There'll be a feast waiting for us when we get home!"

As we pulled away from the side of the road, I noticed now that the man and women were dressed in very fine clothing, the man in a long white caftan and spotless *kufi*, the woman in a pale, beaded *abaya* and white head scarf, shimmering with fine threads of gold.

They smiled when they noticed me admiring them.

"*Mah shmeych?*" the man queried me. Now that my head had cleared, I was able to understand this simple Hebrew. *What's your name?*

"*Shmie Rachel,*" I said, using the English pronunciation, then correcting myself, saying the Hebrew version, "*Rach-ayl.*"

He nodded, then pointed at himself, saying, "Rashid," and his wife, "Amina." Pointing his thumb over his shoulder to the boy riding in back, he said, "Yusuf."

"*Tasharrafna!*" I said in formal Arabic, and the man smiled broadly.

We talked a bit more, the three of us, until the extent of my Arabic and Hebrew ran out, and then we rode in silence, the man glancing at me every so often and smiling. I tried to assess his character, to estimate the chances that he might be in collusion with the kidnappers. I also looked surreptitiously over my shoulder periodically at Yusuf in the back. He had said they would figure out what to do with me when we got to their house. What did he mean by that?

Feeling fatigue overpower my worry, I turned my head back to look out the window to my right. The woman, Amina, was looking at me. She smiled, patting her shoulder, and I realized that this was an invitation for me to lean my head against her and sleep. She had an exceptionally-friendly face, a mother's face, with laugh lines radiating around her eyes and mouth.

Gratefully, I leaned against her and closed my eyes. As my mind drifted off into sleep, I thought, *surely people like this could not turn me over to terrorists?*

I awoke to feel the tires of the truck roll to a halt, and hear the sound of car doors opening. Opening my eyes, I looked around. Amina was examining me to see if I was awake, and when she saw that I was, she patted my hand and smiled.

Outside, I saw a two story pale-rose-colored house on a street of pastel-painted homes. We were at the center of a small town, several blocks of similar houses surrounding us, and a square mosque with a minaret and a small green dome on the next block. There were a few people on the street, and they stared at me curiously as I got out of the truck.

Amina called out a friendly greeting, but nevertheless scooted me into the house. I was grateful for her effort to delay what would surely be a sensationalist response to the arrival of a celebrated hostage in their small village.

Inside the house, there were crowds enough: a grandmotherly woman, her elderly husband, and a number of children, younger than the teenage boy I'd ridden with. As they gawked at me and gathered around in wonder, Yusuf introduced the elderly couple to me as his "Giddo and Tetta," explaining that they were his father's parents.

"My mother's parents lived in Gaza," he went on. "It's too difficult for them to travel here for the *Eid*." He introduced me to all of his brothers and sisters, including his older sister, Jamila, a graceful young woman of about twenty, dressed, like her mother, in shimmering pale *abaya* and *hijab*.

While Yusuf made his introductions, I noticed his father, Rashid, speaking earnestly to his parents and gesturing towards me. I saw the shock on their faces as they registered his words, and then the woman rushed over, hugging me and showering me with profuse "*al-Hamdu Lillahs!*" and before I knew it, she had installed me on the couch with a cup of strong, hot tea in my hand.

Yusuf sat down on the chair next to me, acting as translator for all the myriad of questions posed to me by his many young siblings, the smallest of whom simply sat at my feet gazing up at me, her small, pudgy hand resting on my knee. Meanwhile, I saw Rashid slip out of the room, heard him talking on the phone in the room next door.

Who was he calling?

For a moment, I felt my fear and uncertainty return, but it receded quickly as I took in the friendly faces around me.

Soon, Rashid came back in the room and spoke in Arabic to his son, Yusuf, who turned to me, saying, "My father has called the IDF. They're dispatching a unit from Beer-Sheba to come over and pick you up. Which means," he looked at his grandmother, "we'd better eat now!"

He repeated this in Arabic, and she sprang up, hustling us all into the dining room, where I saw a feast set out on the table: Arabic flat bread, and spreads of every consistency and color, heaping plates of olives and dates, glasses filled with brown, creamy liquid, which I recognized as the delicious *sharpat* I had drunk at my wedding just a few days before.

Someone had already added a place for me, seated between

Rashid and Yusuf, and as I sat down, Jamila entered with a large platter of steaming spiced meat, her mother following with a huge bowl of rice. They set these on the table, and everyone became silent as Rashid led us in a blessing, reminding us, as Yusuf translated on my behalf, that all these gifts came from God.

The family then fell on the food, passing it around the table amidst laughter and happy conversation. As the platter of redolent brown meat approached us, Yusuf explained to me, "You know, this is not just any meat. My father sacrificed this lamb himself this morning, after his morning prayers at the mosque. We do this to commemorate the submission of Abraham and Ishmael to God's will, and God's compassion in substituting a ram for the human sacrifice. It's important to know this."

The platter arrived, and Rashid placed heaping piles of rice and meat on my plate. Foregoing my preference for vegetarianism for this special occasion, I raised my fork and took a bite. In my famished state, I cannot remember ever tasting anything so delicious.

Soon, the family began to ply me with questions once again. Not about the kidnapping, but about myself: where I was from, what I did, what my family was like. When I mentioned that I was a doctor, I was happy to learn that Yusuf's sister, Jamila, was also studying to be a physician. Next year, she would be entering the medical college in Beer-Sheba.

Yusuf, on the other hand, was passionate about environmental studies. He had just completed a three-month session at the youth center at Nitzana, an exciting new program for teenagers from the Arab villages of the Negev where they taught these young men and women how to harness alternative energy sources, most particularly the power of the sun, along with special courses in astronomy, physics, biology, and ecology.

Curious, I asked him what had stimulated his interest in environmental studies.

"Initially, it was because of what's happening here in this village," he explained. "Did you know that this house is powered by solar energy? So are all the houses around us. Even the mosque! Soon, the whole town will be completely powered only by the sun! It is very exciting!" As if to prove his own words, he jumped up. "Come on! I'll show you!"

"But wait, we're not done eating yet," I protested, looking at

Yusuf's grandmother. She laughed and waved us on, smiling at her grandson's enthusiasm. *"T'fadali! T'fadali! Yalla!"*

I got up and followed Yusuf out of the room, feeling like the pied piper as all his younger brothers and sisters tumbled along behind us. We went out the front door, circling around to the back of the house. There, he showed me the rows and rows of black, shiny solar panels, busily processing the invisible energy of light. The children laughed, pointing at the panes, jumping and dancing around in the sunlight.

After a few minutes, we reentered the house. I saw that the table had been cleared, the main course replaced with plates stacked with cookies and pastries. Before we could sit down, however, we heard the sound of vehicles pulling up outside. Soon, there was a loud knock on the front door.

I followed Rashid out of the dining room as he went to open it. Four soldiers stood there, two men and two women, and beyond them, I could see a line of army trucks. The soldiers were dressed in full army gear, their hands on the butts of rifles slung over their shoulders. Rashid introduced me to them, and they greeted me joyfully. One of the women even hugged me, saying *"Baruch ha-Shem!"* – *"Thank God!"*

I felt relief, but not surprise, to see that it had, after all, been the IDF that Rashid had called. And I also felt a huge sense of embarrassment for having disrupted the peaceful *Eid* here in this Palestinian home. This feeling was only compounded further, as the soldiers set in to question the members of the household in regard to the possible role they might have played in my abduction.

This went on for about forty-five minutes, while I continued to reassure them that these people had been part of my rescue, and not my abduction. Eventually, the soldiers seemed convinced, and they asked me to accompany them back to the base in Beer-Sheba, where I would begin the formal intelligence process.

Before leaving, I said my grateful good-byes to my rescuers. I wished Yusuf luck with his studies, and best wishes for success in bringing solar power to Drijat and beyond. I also invited Jamila to visit me in San Francisco, if she ever had the opportunity to do a family medicine rotation abroad. Before leaving, Yusuf's grandmother pressed a parcel into my hand, an item wrapped in gaily-colored wax paper.

"Al-Salaamu alaykum," she said, and I saw tears in her eyes

as she leaned in to give me a final hug.

"*Wa alaykum al-Salaam*," I replied, taking my parcel and following the soldiers out to the waiting truck.

Once underway, I unwrapped the small parcel. It contained a supply of date- and walnut-filled shortbread, which I shared with the soldiers in the truck. I felt a curious sense of tranquility, as if this small gesture had somehow tipped the balance in some giant scale of good and evil.

After about a forty-five minute drive, we arrived at the army base. There, a group of young military people, men and women, greeted me with a cheer as I got out of the truck. They took me to the commander's office.

After that, I only remember a series of questions, different faces, people plying me with food, clothes, water. Soon, the first news team showed up, followed by several more.

My story, I have to admit, was rather unbelievable. I told them that I'd managed to escape by picking the lock on the door to my room in my captor's house. After that, I had been just plain lucky that no one saw me sneak out of the house. I didn't mention Rahima, worrying that if Abdul Malik found out about what she did, he would probably submit her for non-voluntary "suicide" bombing.

I went on to tell them that the guard outside had passed out in his car, maybe drunk. When I got by him, I just ran, and somehow got outside town and into the hills above the Dead Sea. I described the path I'd followed, and everyone looked skeptical.

"That sounds like Ein Gedi," said one of the officers.

Someone else said, "Impossible. She never could have come down those cliffs at night."

I shrugged. I agreed with him. Nevertheless, here I was.

I described what I could of Abdul Malik's home, and the meager environs visible through the small window in the bathroom. All of this information would be relayed to IDF intelligence, who had already assigned a task force to work with the Palestinian Authority in an attempt to locate my abductors.

Despite the seriousness of the situation, nevertheless a kind of a festival atmosphere prevailed at the base, as the Israeli soldiers celebrated my escape from the terrorists. In the matter of my journey down here, they chalked the unlikely story up to shock or post-traumatic stress. Surely I had not run all the way here, but had hitched a ride from someone on the way. In my own mind, when I did the calculations, it did seem impossible. How had I managed to run fifty miles, without even noticing?

Eventually, the questioning ended, and a soldier named Hulda was assigned to help me get re-situated with my life. She asked me if I had any family in Israel. I told her about my sister, and we went to Hulda's office to call her. She dialed the King David Hotel and asked for Ruth Davidson. I could hear the phone ring, then a voice on the other end. "Hello?"

Hulda handed me the phone.

"Ruthie?" I said, "Ruthie?" I couldn't talk anymore.

"Is this...is it...on the TV just now, I saw that you'd been recovered, you escaped...I didn't believe them..." She was crying too.

Ridiculously, we cried over the telephone for almost five minutes. Finally, Ruthie said, hoarsely, "I have to tell you something."

Oh no. This sounded serious.

"It's about Yakub. Mahmud called me just a little while ago from the hospital."

No.

"It's bad."

I started crying again.

"Yakub had some kind of...stroke, I think."

Sobbing, I managed to say, "He's alive?" I felt a thin thread of hope enter my heart.

"Yes he is," said Ruthie.

"Is he conscious?"

"No. He's been in a coma since mid-day. They're planning surgery any minute."

"What kind of surgery?" I asked.

"Something like, they're drilling a hole in his skull. I don't know."

A subdural hematoma! "Actually, that's really good news!" I said, feeling the hope begin to flutter and grow in the place just below my ribcage. A subdural hematoma happens in the layers of brain coating, often following head trauma, and is not a bleed into the brain substance itself. As long as the surgeons were able to drain all the blood and as long as there was no associated damage to the actual brain tissue, he would likely recover full function. I needed to see Yakub right away, to make sure they were doing everything possible.

"Where is he?" I asked Ruthie.

"He's at a private hospital in Makkah."

Oh no! How could I possibly get into Makkah?

"Man oh-man!" I said, suddenly realizing something. "He must have developed the subdural when that guy hit him on the head in Cairo!"

"Really? Yeah, I bet you're right!"

"Anyway, I'm coming back. I'll be there…" I said, looking at Hulda, who motioned with her fingers. "Around 8:00 pm."

"Great!" said Ruthie. "Are you hungry?"

Thinking of the feast I had recently enjoyed, I said, "Not really. I just ate. But we can talk about that later."

"Okay," said Ruthie. "And Rachel. I have some other news for you."

"Really? What is it?"

"I'll tell you later."

She hung up.

Before leaving the base, I informed the commander that I needed to go to Makkah, Saudi Arabia, immediately. Could he help me arrange this?

The base commander, a big, muscular man with a chest like a barrel, only laughed at me, shaking his head. "*G'veret, ee-efshar.* Impossible. You are Jewish?" I nodded. "You cannot go there. You know this."

"But surely they can make an exception in my case? My husband has had brain surgery. I'm a doctor. I need to be there!" My voice was rising an octave with each word.

The commander held out his hand and moved it up and down, signaling that I should lower my anxiety level down a few notches. He was still shaking his head. "There are no exceptions. You cannot go there." If I had been a private in the army, he would have said "dismissed." In any case, I knew he was done with the discussion. But I wasn't done yet. I'd just keep trying with the next person up the line in authority.

I returned to Jerusalem by armored vehicle. The hotel entry

was swarming with television crews but, fortunately, the hotel staff would not allow them into the lobby. A few of them managed to snag me on the way in the door, and I said a few words about how I was feeling before my IDF friends managed to stave them off.

"She will arrange interviews later, after she's recovered," they said, their semi-automatic rifles leaving little room for negotiation. I was glad I didn't have to talk more to the news people that day. I didn't want to give something away that would put Rahima at further risk.

When I got to my hotel room, it looked vaguely familiar from what felt like someone else's life. Ruthie, Lenny, and I hugged each other for some time.

They had ordered dinner for us, and room service arrived with our food. Under protection of armed guard, we shared a delicious meal, compliments of the management of the King David Hotel.

My appetite revived already, I devoured my dinner of tortellini with alfredo sauce, capers, and herbs, eating piles and piles of crusty French bread smeared with butter, Ruthie cautiously asked me about what had happened to me, all the way back to the moment I had been kidnapped.

"Some...strange man turned me over to the *jihadists*. He followed me from the café where we ate in the Old City up onto the Temple Mount. He said he had poems." I recalled the man with the white forelock, his strange and disfigured appearance. Despite myself, I felt pity for him. "He said he was ill." I was starting to hyperventilate.

Concern springing to her eyes, Ruthie said, "It's okay, Rachel. You don't have to talk about it anymore, if you don't want to."

I nodded. It was amazing how fast the images receded from my mind. I'd have to deal with this at some time, whether I liked it or not. But not right now.

I asked Ruthie and Lenny what they'd been doing.

"Hmm. Good question," said Ruthie. "Well, we were a little put out when our plans to visit the Dead Sea and Ein Gedi were bollixed on account of my big sister's abduction by Islamic fundamentalists. But other than that, we had a great time."

I laughed, then looked at Ruthie. "So. When are you going to tell me this mysterious 'news' you alluded to on the phone?"

"News? What news?" said Ruthie, batting her eyelids infuriatingly.

Lenny said, "Let me tell her. Is that okay?"

Ruthie nodded.

"Okay. Before the three days from Hell began, something amazing happened. We were waiting at the Western Wall to tell you when you failed to show up."

"You were?"

Lenny looked at Ruthie, and now could not suppress a large grin. "I changed my mind. You tell her."

"Okay," agreed Ruthie. "Here it is, in a nutshell. Your little sister finally managed to snag herself a doctor. A fact that would have made her mother proud!"

"Really?" I said, the truth dawning on me. "You're getting married?"

"Yup!" said Lenny, beaming.

"Ruthie!" I cried, "That's fantastic!" I got up and hugged them both.

"We were going to go get a wedding ring, here in Jerusalem, but then Armageddon started and we haven't had a chance."

"I'm so sorry," I said. "But still…you're getting married!" I raised my glass of ice water and said *Mazel Tov! L'chaim!* They followed me, then Lenny said, "Oh, Heck! Let's break out some bubbly from the mini-bar! I bet the King David will be good for it!"

Lenny retrieved a demi-bottle of Brut from the small refrigerator. When he popped the cork, it flew across the room and hit the wall, the champagne spilling over the top as he poured it into three wine glasses. We toasted again, for real. "To your safe return!" said Lenny. "May you live to doctor another day!"

"And to the good news" I replied, "of my sister's long-anticipated marriage! To a doctor, no less!"

"And to the New Year!" said Ruthie, for good measure.

The phone rang, and Ruthie went to answer it. I heard her say, "Hello? Yes? Mahmud! Yes, yes, she did." Pause. "Today, around 7:00 pm."

She said, "Yes!" And then I heard her pause again. "Mahmud, are you still there?…It's okay! Rachel and I cried about two hours when we first talked." She waited a little longer. Then she said, "What?" Her face lit up. "He did? Yes, she's right here."

She handed the phone to me. "It's Mahmud."

I picked it up. "Mahmud?"

"Rachel, you're safe! *Al-hamdu lillah!* Thank God! You heard about my father?"

"Yes," I said. "How is he? He had surgery today?"

"Yes. He returned from recovery about two hours ago."

"How is he doing?"

"The surgeons were very encouraging. He's still asleep right now, but they anticipate that he will revive sometime during the night. They're allowing me to stay with him, so I can be here when he wakes up."

"And you're in Makkah still?"

"Yes."

"They say I can't come there to visit."

"That's true."

"I'm going to figure something out anyway."

Mahmud sounded skeptical. "Okay," he said.

"No, really, I am."

Mahmud laughed. "I believe you! While you may be very nice, I've noticed that you also tend to get what you need most of the time."

We said our goodbyes. Realizing I was completely exhausted, I also said good night to Ruthie and Lenny, and without even taking off my clothes, went and lay down on one of the two double beds and was instantly asleep.

Many hours later, the sound of the telephone woke me up. My eyes fixed on the clock by the bed. It was 4:30 am.

Instantly alert, I grabbed the phone. "Hello?" I said.

"Hello, may I speak with Rachel please?" It was Mahmud.

"It's me. Has something happened?" my heart was racing at about 200 beats a minute. "Is Yakub alright?"

"Would you like to speak with him?"

"Wha...speak..." I stammered idiotically.

I heard a pause, some scrabbling sounds, then the sound of a familiar voice, a bit weak, but definitely Yakub.

"Rachel."

For the second time in twenty-four hours, I cried on the phone. Maybe even longer this time.

Jerusalem, Israel
Monday, January 1ˢᵗ 2007
Dr. Rachel al-Shadi

The only issue on my mind after I spoke with Yakub was how I was going to get to Makkah. I couldn't think about anything else. It felt to me like half my body had been torn off. Despite this fixation, however, I was required to do a number of press conferences, and to spend most of the day at IDF headquarters in Tel Aviv assisting with their investigation into my abduction. I must have seemed like a complete imbecile to them, since I couldn't focus on a single photo or question.

When I first arrived at headquarters, I asked the officer in charge whether he could arrange for me to go to my husband in Makkah. I received the same answer as I had the day before down at the base in Beer-Sheva. *Absolutely not.* I kept asking people repeatedly throughout the morning, always with the same response.

Early in the afternoon, as I was flipping disconsolately through photos, the officer in charge of my interview put a hand on top of mine. "Stop," he said.

I looked up at him. He was a young man, an American Israeli, and when I looked in his eyes, I was encouraged to see empathy.

"What's the matter? You seem completely disoriented."

I repeated to him my story about Yakub.

"And if I can somehow arrange for you to be with your husband, do you think you'd be able to concentrate?"

I nodded, feeling a small burst of hope.

"Alright," he said, standing up. "This might take me a little while. Please, continue to review the photos while I'm gone." I nodded, and he turned and left the room.

He returned an hour later with encouraging news.

"They can transfer your husband to a private hospital in Jeddah. It's only an hour's drive from where he is now, and so should be safe for him, medically."

"Is it a good hospital?" I asked.

"The best. In fact, they specialize in neurosurgery."

"Where exactly is Jeddah? Is it in Saudi Arabia?"

"Yes. Since it's the entry port to the country, they're more accustomed to foreign visitors. The Saudi authorities will allow you to fly there, but not to travel anywhere else in Saudi Arabia."

I nodded. The officer continued. "We've arranged for a special visa for you. You realize however, doctor, that it is not safe for you in Saudi Arabia. The organization responsible for your abduction most likely has connections there. Are you really sure you want to risk it?"

"I have to be there," I said.

"Alright. As a security measure, we'll announce publicly that you'll be remaining in Israel for another week. No one will know you've flown to Jeddah. But I do recommend that you and your husband leave the country as soon as medically possible. In the meantime, the Saudi government will assign you police security coverage. It's not in their best interest to have an international terrorist incident involving a high-profile American visitor, so they're motivated to keep you safe."

"So when will they move Yakub?"

"Tomorrow. You can fly to Jeddah in the afternoon and meet him there. The hospital will provide housing for you. Only one more question."

"Yes?"

"Do you have an *abaya* and a thick veil? You'll need them."

I laughed. "I'm getting kind of used to that by now! No, I don't have my own."

"It's not a laughing matter," said the officer. "It's a matter of law in Saudi Arabia. I'll arrange to get you these items before you go."

I stopped smiling. "Thank you. You have no idea what this means to me."

"Good. And now…" he pulled out the photographs again.

With the knowledge that I would be re-united with Yakub tomorrow, I found I was able to concentrate almost one-hundred percent. I spent the rest of the day looking through photos.

I was able to recognize the man I'd seen on the first day, a notorious anti-Israeli activist and mastermind of a number of well-known kidnappings and bombings, but as for Abdul Malik, the other men in his group, and the strange man with the white forelock, I was not able to identify any of them.

Thinking it through, I reasoned that the last one, the strange disfigured man, was probably one of the elusive *Smiths*. I told the intelligence officer the al-Shadi legend, suspecting that it sounded patently absurd. The officer confirmed my suspicions by shooting a surreptitious glance at his assistant and raising one eyebrow as I spun the tale.

The following morning, I returned to the IDF intelligence headquarters for one last session before leaving for Jeddah. I had packed my bags that morning, and bid Lenny and Ruthie goodbye. They were staying another few days in Israel, returning to San Francisco the following Sunday.

When our session was done that morning, the officer who'd arranged my travel handed me a packet which he informed me contained the items of clothing I would need in Saudi Arabia. He and another officer then drove me to the Ben Gurion Airport near Tel Aviv. From there, the second officer accompanied me on the flight to Jordon, remaining with me on the second leg to Jeddah.

After we arrived at the King Abdul Aziz Airport, he handed me off to the local Saudi police officer who would be in charge of my security here in Saudi Arabia. The man looked at me askance when I first emerged from the jet way, since I hadn't yet put on the veil and *abaya*. After preliminary introductions, he asked if I had brought any more modest clothing. I showed him the packet the officer had given me in Israel. Relieved, the policeman suggested a female police officer accompany me into the bathroom to ensure that I put them on properly.

I discovered that the veil the Israeli officer had given me was even more severe than the one I'd worn in al-Khalil, covering not only my head, neck and hair, but my entire face, leaving only a slit for my eyes. I felt rather strange, navigating the world in a black bag, but I was too excited about seeing Yakub to give it any thought.

From the airport, we drove through the city of Jeddah to the King Faisal Specialist Hospital, where Yakub had been transferred earlier today. It was late afternoon, and the lights were just coming on in the modern buildings of the city. I noted, with interest, that there were virtually no women walking the streets. What few women I did see were dressed as I was, and always accompanied by one or more men. The two Saudi policemen were silent as we drove.

The staff at hospital reception greeted me warmly, asking if I'd prefer to stop off at my room in the visitors building or to go immediately to see my husband. I, of course, chose to see Yakub. They made a call. Several minutes later, a man dressed in western clothing appeared.

Speaking in flawless English, he said to me, "Dr. al-Shadi? Welcome to the King Faisal Specialist Hospital! I am Dr. Abdul Rahman al-Hassan, your husband's physician. It is a pleasure to meet you!"

He reached out his hand, and I shook it, saying, "How is my husband doing?" My voice sounded muffled through the thick veil, and I wondered how the Saudi women doctors managed to navigate their work in this get-up.

"I just completed his admission examination. He is doing wonderfully!" said Dr. al-Hassan. "Come and see for yourself!"

He chatted on pleasantly as we ascended the elevator and walked the hallway to Yakub's room. I asked him where he'd done his training, and he informed me that he had attended Yale Medical School, and then gone on to internship and fellowship in neurosurgery at Harvard, completing his training here in Jeddah five years ago.

He filled me in further on Yakub's condition. "Your husband is in excellent shape!" he assured me. "Absolutely no problem, neither with the surgery nor the transport. He is strong as an ox!"

"I know," I smiled. "When do you expect he can travel?"

"Oh, I imagine he should stay in the hospital another couple of days, and then he can move in with you and his son in the apartments. If all goes well, I estimate he can leave the country in four or five days."

We had reached Yakub's room, number 365. I felt my heart racing as Dr. al-Hassan pushed open the door.

I spied Yakub, sitting up in bed, a white bandage fixed around his head. Mahmud, his hair cut very short, sat in the chair beside him, reading aloud from a book of poetry. The two men looked over at me, quizzical expressions on their faces. I realized they could not tell who I was, in my concealing veil. I didn't speak immediately, wishing to hold that tableaux in suspension as long as possible, the first sight of my beloved.

He looked at me, and I took in all the familiar features, cherishing each: his mouth, his nose, his green eyes. When he met my gaze, he said, tentatively, "Rachel?"

At this, I came over and lay my cheek down on his chest, carefully avoiding his bandages, just so I could hear the sound of his beating heart.

Jeddah, Saudi Arabia
9:00 am. Shabbat, January 6th 2007
Dr. Rachel al-Shadi

As Dr. al-Hassan had predicted, Yakub remained in the hospital another two days. Mahmud and I shared a two-bedroom apartment in the visitors housing next door, guarded 24-7 by our Saudi police escort. The apartment was very pleasant and modern, with a fully-equipped kitchen and a swimming pool. Inside, I was permitted to remove the *abaya* and veil, but anytime I went outside, I was required not only to wear them, but to be accompanied at all times by a male attendant. "Otherwise," Mahmoud warned me, "the *mutawwa* might get you!" The *mutawwa* turned out to be the morality police, hired by the government to ensure the ongoing virtue and purity of the Saudi population. "If you wear your *abaya* wrong, they may attack you with their nightsticks!" This sounded like a joke to me, but it was, in fact, absolutely true. I was extra-specially careful about my clothing after hearing this.

On Friday, Dr. al-Hassan released Yakub from the hospital and he moved into the apartment with us. Earlier that day, Mahmoud and I had extended the perimeter of our travels beyond our usual route from the apartment to the hospital, visiting the well-stocked local supermarket. Our police guards did not want us to risk walking, and so provided us with a ride to our destination. Under their protective surveillance, we were able to purchase all supplies necessary for a festive welcome-home celebration dinner for Yakub.

That evening, Yakub, Mahmud, and I shared our first family dinner together in the small apartment. Mahmud and I had prepared a simple meal, and after we ate, Yakub rested on the couch for awhile, then I settled him in the bed, getting in next to him and switching off the light. In the warm darkness of our bed, *abaya* and veil removed, I nestled close to Yakub, careful to avoid any sudden movements. The doctor had warned that intimacy was not advisable for another two weeks, so we waited, and for now, experienced the quiet joy of lying in each other's arms.

Saturday, the doctor permitted Yakub a brief walk, and our Saudi police sentry, warming to our small family, offered to drive us out to the Corniche, the boardwalk that followed the shoreline of the Red Sea. In the early evening, just as the day was cooling off, we ventured out on our expedition, driving the three miles to the coastline in the squad car. There, Yakub and I walked along the beach, holding hands, while the policeman and Mahmud followed a few yards behind. There were many other couples strolling the Corniche, the women dressed, like me, in *abaya* and veil, other couples riding in romantic horse-drawn carriages, the cool breeze from the water bringing the scent of sea mist and living things.

As we watched the sun go down beyond the horizon, Yakub said, "Rachel, do you know anything about the city of Jeddah?"

"No," I said, "tell me something about it!"

"Well," he said, "first, like many places in Saudi Arabia, Jeddah is considered a holy city."

"Why?"

"Pre-Islamic legend says that when Adam and Eve were expelled from the Garden of Eden, they were thrown separately out into the world. Adam landed in what we now call Sri Lanka, while Eve landed here in Jeddah. Tormented and lonely, they wandered alone for centuries, until God finally took mercy, allowing them to reunite in Makkah."

"I figured they must have met again sometime, since they didn't have any children until after they left the Garden of Eden, right?"

"That's right. It was after they were found each other again that they created all the children of the world."

"And all the trouble began," I laughed.

Yakub nodded, agreeing with a smile. "When she finally died, Eve was buried here. And so the city is called *Jeddah*, which means grandmother, or maternal ancestor."

"A very excellent story," I said.

"I have more!" said Yakub.

On the remainder of our walk that day, and on our return the following afternoon, we did not discuss our experiences while separated from each other. We didn't even discuss the poem. We just strolled, as I listened to Yakub's stories, taking in the rising moon, the sound of the waves, the smell of the sand. Serious things could all come later.

Monday, to the relief of the Saudi authorities, Yakub was cleared by Dr. al-Hassan to travel, and we made arrangements to return home.

San Francisco, California
Afternoon of Tuesday, January 9th 2007
Prof. Yakub, Dr. Rachel, and Mahmud al-Shadi

Yakub, Mahmud and I returned to San Francisco together on a foggy Tuesday afternoon. Yakub's family, including Farid, Hana, her mother Fatima, and their three children met us at the airport.

"Jaddi!" the two boys yelled when they caught sight of Yakub. They ran to him, jumping up and down, grabbing onto his legs and arms.

"Careful!" cautioned Mahmud, "Your grandfather has been sick!"

The boys stopped jumping, but still held onto Yakub's legs, one on each side.

"It's alright," said Yakub. "I'm fine now!" he looked down, and put a hand on each of the boys' heads. "How are my two boys?"

"Jaddi!" they said, looking up at him, leaning their small bodies against him.

Above their heads, Farid embraced his father carefully, saying, "Baba! How do you feel?"

"*Al-hamdu lillah,* I am well!" he looked at me and smiled.

Farid turned to me. "Doctor Rachel!" he said, "Congratulations! Or should I call you...Mom?"

"Rachel is fine," I laughed. "Though 'Doctor' is a little too formal now, I think..."

Hana and Fatima hugged me, and I got a chance to kiss little Zahra's fuzzy head while she beamed at me from ear-to-ear.

Yakub said, "Boys, you are going to have to let go, or I won't be able to walk anywhere!"

Reluctantly, the boys released their grip on Yakub's legs, and we made our way to the car. We rode back to Yakub's house together, crammed into Farid and Hanna's mini-van, using up all available seatbelts.

When we arrived, everybody piled out together. Once inside, Hana and Farid insisted I accompany Yakub up to the living room while they prepared sandwiches, unpacked Yakub's bag, and started a load of laundry.

We ate upstairs in the living room together, perched on various sitting chairs, while Yakub, Mahmud, and I told stories about our trip.

"Jaddi, did you see any mummies?" asked the older boy, Isma'il.

"No, no. Not even any bones," said Yakub.

Isma'il looked disappointed.

"We did see a graveyard, though," said Yakub, "and even opened up one of the graves!"

"You did?" said the younger boy, Hisham, his eyes wide.

Yakub nodded.

"But you didn't see any bones in it?" Said Isma'il.

"No. Just books."

"Books? Why were there books in there? Can I see them?"

Yakub went to his travel bag and located a parcel wrapped in soft cloth. He unwrapped it and showed the two boys the prayer book he'd discovered in the Greek Catholic graveyard at Fustat. Trembling, Hisham reached out his hand.

"Oop!" said Yakub. "Don't touch it! It's very valuable! Let me show you." He opened the cover carefully, and showed them the page where the "amulet for redemption," as he'd called it, had been located. He then went and retrieved the amulet itself, which he had placed in a plastic folio and protected further in a three-ring binder.

"You see how this is wavy?" he said, pointing to the edge of the Star of David. The boys nodded. "It's a Psalm. One of the poems from the Hebrew Bible. And these rays," he pointed to the lines extending outward from the star. "...are the *Asma Allah al-Husna*, the 99 most beautiful names of God."

"Oh!" said Hana. "That is fantastic!"

Yakub nodded at her.

"And what are these?" said Isma'il, pointing to the three dots.

"Those are *Jamarat*, pillars," said Yakub.

"Baba, is this diagram the poem you were looking for?"

asked Farid.

Yakub shook his head, regretfully. "No. We...we probably didn't find that yet."

"Probably?"

Yakub looked at me. "Rachel and I still have to talk about it."

I nodded.

Hana came and picked up the notebook with the diagram. She sat down on the couch, placing it on the table in front of her.

"This hexagram, it's interesting. A very ancient symbol. The two interlocking triangles often symbolize the union or harmony of opposites. Fire and water. God and man. Man and woman. In this case, the triangle pointing upwards is man, and the one pointing downwards is woman. And these Hebrew letters, what are they?"

I came to look over her shoulder. "Let's see." I concentrated on the diagram. "Hey-Vav in the upwards-facing triangle, Hey-Yud in the downward one. Hu-He," I said, experimenting. "Oh!" I covered my mouth.

"What?" said Hana, eyeing me with curiosity.

"Those sounds mean 'he and she' in Hebrew! It goes with what you said about the two triangles being symbols of male and female union! Though the actual spelling would include an Aleph, in both cases..."

Yakub came and looked down at the diagram. "Aren't those the letters of God's name?"

"I never noticed that before...the holiest name of God contains 'he and she'! (6) Is that how unification happens?"

"I don't understand," said Hana. "What do you mean?"

"In Judaism, we have a belief that when God's name is unified, the world will be redeemed. Here, it looks like the message is that unification of male and female elements brings about this unity."

"'*She shall be a garment to him, and he shall be a garment to her,*'" said, Hana, quoting the Quranic verse Yakub had first mentioned after reading the poem by Mrs. Dunash in Cambridge.

Yakub and I looked at one another, realizing that something

profound was falling into place, though unsure yet what it was.

Farid sat down on the couch next to Hana to get a better look at the diagram. "What are these *Jamarat,* these 'pillars of peace,' as I see they're called?"

"I don't know," said Yakub, "Rachel and I need to talk about it, to compare notes."

"Fascinating!" said Farid, shaking his head in wonder. "Tell me if you discover anything more!"

"I promise," said Yakub.

Yakub had brought home gifts from Cairo, and he gave these to the children now. For each of the boys, there was a treasure map on papyrus, an ancient coin, and a wooden box painted with hieroglyphics. They removed the wrapping paper, murmuring to each other in hushed tones as they viewed each item. After they finished opening their packages, they ran off to another room to begin their adventure.

For baby Zahra, he'd brought a soft, stuffed camel, which she took and squeezed against her face with a squeal of pleasure.

After we finished our coffee and dessert, Hana went down to transfer our clothes to the drier. When she came back up, the family said their goodbyes. Mahmud left along with them, to drive himself back over to Berkeley.

At last, everyone gone, Yakub and I were alone, here in what was to be my new home in San Francisco.

It was now late evening, and darkness had fallen. Yakub and I climbed the stairs to the roof, a scene I had envisioned infinite times during my confinement at the house in al-Khalil. I waited in giddy anticipation as Yakub worked the lock. At last, the door opened, and I could see the garden. Every rosebush, every tree seemed to be in bloom.

To Yakub's delight, we found that the single pomegranate had ripened in our absence. The tree bore the orb of scarlet fruit proudly. Yakub took it down and broke it with his hands, giving me one half. Together, we raised it to our mouths and sucked on the sweet juice. Afterwards, he handed me his handkerchief, and I wiped the redness from my lips. We went and found our place under the trellis, sitting across from one another at the small table, the fragrance of roses all around.

"Do you know how many times I envisioned sitting in this place with you, while I was…" I stopped, reluctant to mention the house in al-Khalil.

Yakub took my hand across the table. "We're together now, *habibti*."

"Yes." I put his hand to my lips.

We went inside and downstairs to the master bedroom. The requisite two weeks had passed, and so I warmed myself up in the arms of my beloved at last, recalling, perhaps for just an instant, what I had felt during the time after my dream of seeing him at "the pillars," before dawn in the dark nothingness of the Negev.

Later, in the smooth sheets of his bed, the fragrance of clean linen under my head, I lay and looked up at the ceiling. It was time to talk about *the poem,* and our experiences while separated.

I started to speak, but Yakub was already one step ahead of me. "This might sound peculiar," he said, "but I thought I saw you, when I was at the pillars, during the *Jamarat*. Of course, I had passed out just before, probably from the bleeding in my head, or..." he trailed off.

"Was it a hallucination?" I asked.

"I don't know. It was very vivid. More real, even, than anything *real* I've experienced."

"What happened?"

"I was standing, ready to throw the first stone. You know, it's meant to be a reenactment of Abraham's battle with the devil. But I wanted to kill someone, really *kill* someone, not just my own devils. I was looking for someone I could hit with that stone. That was when I realized how far my anger had gone. No matter what else I become, or how much I feel someone may deserve to die, I do not want to be a murderer."

"Yakub, you're the gentlest person I know."

Yakub took my hand. "You may think so. But all humans are capable of error. Even murder."

I said, "Was that all? Or was there more?"

"More." Yakub gazed at the ceiling, recalling the scene. "All at once, despite the crowds, I was alone, standing by the pillar. I saw a shimmering light before me, like a mirror, and when I looked at what should have been my reflection, it was not my own face I saw but yours. A single tear fell from each eye, and when I raised my hand, so did you. And when we looked up at the pillar, I saw it." Yakub gave an involuntary shiver. "It was a fearsome thing."

"What?"

"I swear, in Allah's name, that an *Alif* fell from above and pierced me right through the heart."

"What?"

"An *Alif*. After that, I saw a bright light, the brightest I've ever seen, and realized that it was not coming from outside, but from myself. I was shining like the sun! Light was emanating from you as well. Everything disappeared, and we were spiraling around each other as though we were one being..." He turned his head and looked at me. "It was ecstatic."

I lay silent a long time.

Yakub laughed, a low chuckle. "What is it? Are you afraid that I am crazy, that you must send me away for treatment?"

"No. It isn't that."

"What is it then?"

"Do you think that this was the sign we were looking for? The *Alif*?"

Yakub became thoughtful, his brow furrowed into lines, visible in the filtered light from the window. "I don't know. But if it is, what does it mean?"

Using my fingers to smooth his forehead, I said, "I need to tell you, I had a similar vision, after escaping from Hebron." I thought back on that morning, trying to remember what it was I saw. "First, I was running. I ran a long, long way. But it went very fast. Then, I saw pillars. It seemed like there were millions of them, extending out to the horizon in both directions. And I also saw a mirror, and I saw you in the mirror, just like in your vision. We both looked up. But I didn't see an *Alif*."

Yakub got up on his elbow so he could look at me. "What did you see?"

"It was a word."

"What word?" asked Yakub.

"I think it was..." I put my hand to my head, the images coming slowly. "I think it was the word *salaam*, the Arabic word. But it was written in Hebrew letters. And the Aleph was kind of...funny. Different, very large. I said the word, and the letters floated up into the sky." I looked at Yakub. "And then there was music, the most beautiful music you've ever heard. It was coming from inside us, connecting us to each other."

"Light and sound," said Yakub, his voice soft. "What day

was it that you escaped?"

"It was," I thought about it a moment, "...it was early in the morning, the day of your festival, *Eid al-Adha*. I remember one of the kidnappers mentioning that the holiday began at sunset. I left later that night, in the dark. The sun came up while I ran."

"*Ya Allah,*" said Yakub. "That was the same time I was traveling from Muzdalifah to Mina, and when I went to throw the stones at the pillars."

"Are you saying our experiences were simultaneous?"

"They must have been."

"I wonder," I said. "The locations where we saw the pillars: the *Jamarat* at Mina, and the place where I ended up, Hagar's Heel, according to the family that found me. Are they somehow connected?"

Yakub thought about the legend, the one his uncle, Muhtadi, had told him twelve years ago in Palestine. About Hagar's pounding feet, and how she ran into the wilderness near Beer-Sheva and ended up near Makkah, before seeing God's angel and finding water for Ishmael. "They do seem to be connected," he said, "perhaps in some other dimension."

Now, I turned to a more tender subject. "Do you still believe in *the poem?*"

Yakub hesitated. He said, "You know, I saw the man who stole the poem. He followed me on *Hajj*. He wanted to make sure I knew the poems he'd stolen were useless."

"His father said the same thing. At least, I think it was his father. The weird man in Jerusalem, the one that turned me over to the kidnappers." My heart started pounding, as it did now whenever I thought about him.

"These must have been the Smiths," said Yakub.

"But should we believe them?"

"I don't know." Agitated, Yakub sat up and swung his legs over the side of the bed. "I'm remembering," he said, after some time. "Something about the poems I read in the graveyard."

I waited for him to speak.

"The poems were...very beautiful. But as we discussed before I left for the *Hajj*, Said al-Shadi was looking for something more. Though his poems did not, themselves, include the *actual* poem to redeem the world, they made it clear, absolutely clear, that there *is* a poem to redeem the world! But it's not...an ordinary kind of poem."

"Yes, you've said that before. But what do you mean?"

"I'm not sure yet."

San Francisco, California
Monday, January 15th 2007
Dr. Rachel al-Shadi

I didn't have to return to work for several days, and I so spent that time tying up loose ends: closing up my apartment and terminating my lease, attending the final session of my "Introduction to Arabic" class.

When I returned to the Arabic school, I was a bit apprehensive about my pseudo-celebrity status as a famous hostage, acutely aware that my Jewishness was a long way out of the closet now. To my surprise, I discovered that the teacher, Ahmad, had not only been greatly relieved at my escape from the terrorists, but had actually, himself, been studying Hebrew for several years, which was why he'd shown such interest when I'd mentioned it at our first class. The truth was that Ahmad was a passionate devotee of language, and the Semitic languages in particular. Proving, yet again, that first impressions are often wrong.

I returned to work on Monday, glad to find that all of my patients were in good health: the baby had gained another two pounds, neither of my two third-term pregnancies had delivered yet, and Harry Blum's blood pressure was in good control.

My relief was short-lived, however, when Lenny called me late in the morning to let me know that Zeke had been admitted to the intensive care unit with a blood infection. He told me I should get up to the unit soon, since he didn't expect Zeke to survive the day.

Because he was in intensive care, Zeke was under the care of a specialist. Even so, I went up to check on him immediately. He was comatose, hooked up to the respirator, and I could tell from his splotchy septic rash that Zeke wasn't going to make it through the next twenty-four hours. He did not respond when I called his name.

After a few minutes, I had to go back to my other patients.

When my clinic ended, I went upstairs to check on him again. That was when a very strange thing happened.

The intensive care specialist in charge of Zeke's care had decided that further treatment was futile. He'd been unable to reach any of Zeke's family members, and so had been compelled to make this decision on his own, after consulting with me. At 8:30 pm, we extubated Zeke, turning off his life support machines and unhooking his monitors. I sat down by him in the chair by his bed, holding his hand and waiting for the end, praying it would come quickly.

As often happens at these times, Zeke revived momentarily. When he saw me, his face broke out in a radiant smile. "Doc Rachel!" he said. "You're here!"

"Yes, I am! Hi, Zeke!"

He examined my face, his eyes probing me like x-rays. Abruptly, his expression changed, and a look of joy overcame him.

"Doc!" he said, his chest rising and falling rapidly in excitement. "Doc! You did it!"

"What?" I said, my heart inexplicably beginning to palpitate. "What did I do?"

"You fixed 'em'!"

"Fixed 'em?"

"Yes! I see it!" he was nodding, his breathing labored, but his face radiant.

"Zeke, you're scaring me!"

Ignoring this, Zeke continued, "Did'ja...did'ja..." he bit his lip, closed his eyes, then opened them again. "Did'ja get married?"

"Yeesss...." I said, looking down at my ring finger. But Zeke wasn't looking at that. He was looking at my face. He gazed at me for just a moment longer, and then fell back, exhausted, onto his pillow.

"Good," he said. "Good." His eyes were closed, and he was breathing through his nose. "Then you'll have a baby."

"What?" I said. I laughed, an explosive blast from my throat.

"Yes," he said. His eyes opened again, and he gripped my hand, very hard. "It's the Aleph," he said, his body rigid, his face urgent. And then his head dropped back, his mouth gaped. He took three more shuddering breaths, each one louder than the last. Then he was still.

I don't know if it was grief or surprise, but the emotional shock was so overwhelming, I cried for the first time ever in County

Hospital.

A half hour later, in a state of great agitation, I made my way downstairs. Doubting my own sanity, I retraced my steps to the family medicine clinic.

"I must be crazy," I said, as I went to the lab and pulled out the pregnancy test kit. Thank goodness, the clinic was empty at this late hour. I went into the bathroom to collect the urine specimen.

Two minutes later, I was staring at a "plus" sign on the test's result window.

I waited two more days and tried the test again. Still positive. And again, on Friday. Positive. And now, I was even feeling the first tell-tale signs of nausea. Still, I could hardly convince myself this was true.

That Friday evening, after dinner, Yakub and I climbed up to our roof garden once again. Sitting amidst the fragrance of roses in our special niche, I said, "Yakub."

"Yes?"

I hesitated just a moment, afraid of anything that might threaten the fragile hope that trembled in me. Even words.

"I'm pregnant."

"What?" he said, looking at me strangely, as if he hadn't heard me.

"I'm pregnant!"

"You…"

"We're having a baby!"

"You've confirmed this?" he spluttered.

"Yes. Three times this week!"

Yakub jumped up, pulling me with him. We danced around the roof together, avoiding the rose bushes in our crazy *Jarcha*. We sat back down, our cheeks flushed.

"When did it happen?" said Yakub. "When is our baby expected?"

"September 22nd," I said, "Yom Kippur!"

"Do you think it happened during just that short time in Cairo, just after we were married?"

"It must be!"

"But you told me…"

"I know," I said. "You could say it was a miracle."

"Al-hamdu lillah," said Yakub, kissing my hands.

San Francisco, California
11:00 am. Friday, February 2nd 2007
Prof. Yakub and Dr. Rachel al-Shadi

Yakub and I had not had any discussion of our religions, that is, which one would "win out" in our marriage, if any. This was a question which had taken on more urgency, now that we were going to be parents. Still, at this stage, we were both re-examining the condition of our own faith. After our experiences at the pillars, our trust in God was as basic as breathing. But that did not mean that the *form* our religion would take was clear. In fact, I feared this problem of the religious orientation of the child of an interfaith marriage would not be easily solved.

Yakub had not been to his mosque in San Francisco since the death of his wife, suffering, as he had been then, with the unexpressed anger against other Muslims that so bedeviled him on *Hajj*. Now, I saw in him profound forgiveness, and an openness to reunite with the Islamic *Umma*, but only, as he said, "As a part of the larger *Umma* of humankind."

On Friday, midday, I took a half-day off from work so that we could attend the mosque together. When Yakub entered, he received warm greetings from many people, and when they heard he was a *Hajji*, they all congratulated him enthusiastically.

The mosque was exceptionally crowded. Yakub and I had to separate, since the men prayed at the front and there was a separate prayer space for women at the back. The *imam* gave a sermon about God's creation of the heavens and the earth, and humanity's responsibility in relation to these gifts. He pointed out that we were stewards, or vice-regents, of God's creation, and so far were doing a rather miserable job.

"The Holy Quran says, *'God has given you the earth for your heritage'* [26] and enjoined upon us, *'do not corrupt the earth.'* [27] And yet, every day we pour toxins into our waters and send noxious clouds

---

[26] Qur'an 6:165

[27] Qur'an 7:56

into the air that *Allah* has provided to all living creatures as sustenance. How can we combat this evil if we do not cooperate with other human beings? If our attention is diverted by war, our spirits twisted by hatred?"

A friendly woman in a blue headscarf helped me with the prayers. She was happy that I knew some Arabic words. I'd decided to continue to study Arabic, both because I found the language beautiful, and so that I could eventually speak with Yakub in his native language. Also, I was hoping someday to be able to actually read the Quran in Arabic.

After the prayer service, Yakub took me to lunch. Before we ate, we said a blessing for the food and for the viability of our growing child. Then, I asked Yakub something about the Quran that I'd been thinking about since my time at the house in al-Khalil.

"Yakub," I said, "why is it that in the Quran, God says that certain verses may be forgotten or replaced by better verses?"

"Ah," said Yakub, "the thorny problem of 'abrogation'. How did you run up against this?"

I described how the issue had come up in my conversation with Abdul Malik. As I spoke, Yakub's face darkened.

"I don't like to hear that someone treated you like that," he said.

"Abdul Malik is a sad man who hasn't learned that forgiveness feels better than bitterness," I said. "Maybe he will, someday."

Yakub took a deep breath and relaxed his hands. "You have much healing left to do. I hope that I can help you." Then he said, "Abrogation is not something accepted by most modern Islamic scholars. In fact, many reject the idea that a verse could be abrogated, believing instead that there is another interpretation of the verses on abrogation. Specifically, a later verse that contradicts an earlier verse does not replace it, but rather the newer verse illuminates some other aspect of the truth. The two revelations both spring from an ever living, never-changing 'higher' text, the 'mother of the book.' Each revelation has both a meaning specific to the time, and a higher meaning that transcends place and circumstance. There are other explanations for abrogation, but that is the one I prefer."

"I like that one too," I said. "But that interpretation is harder to grasp than the idea that one verse is replaced by another contradictory verse. I think most people are uncomfortable with the idea that truth contains actual contradictions. They want more certainty than that."

"But as Mahmud, my physicist son, continues to remind me, God has actually built creation on uncertainty. So knowing that we *don't* know is a very good place to start in religion," said Yakub.

I agreed, thanking him for his answer. At future times, we were to have many more conversations on this topic.

San Francisco, California
5:30 pm. Evening of Friday, February 9ᵗʰ 2007
Weekly portion of יתרו, "Jethro"
Dr. Rachel and Prof. Yakub al-Shadi

A week later, my rabbi called to invite us to join him and his wife for Shabbat dinner. Before the sun set, we walked the twenty blocks to his house. It had been over a month now since Yakub's skull surgery, and his thick silver-black hair had grown to the length of about an inch. On top, he placed a new white Kufi, one we'd bought together during an afternoon stroll along the Corniche in Jeddah. He wore a dark suit and emerald-green tie, and I was proud to be walking along the streets of San Francisco with him.

We arrived at the rabbi's house and rang the bell.

"Rachel!" he said when he opened the door, "My God! Here you are!"

He hugged me, giving me a large kiss on the cheek, his stubbly whiskers tickling my skin.

For the first time in the years since I'd known him, he seemed at a loss for words. His face looked set, and I saw tears flooding his eyes.

Finally, he said, his voice scratchy, "Rachel, you almost got yourself killed, didn't you? Just as I predicted. Sometimes, I hate to be right." He took out a cloth handkerchief, wiped his eyes and blew his nose. Then, he said, "How are you doing?" He peered at me through his thick glasses, his right eye looking off over my shoulder as usual.

"I'm doing better than ever!" I said.

The rabbi turned towards Yakub, and I introduced them. They shook hands, and the rabbi said, "Come in! Come in! Meet my wife!"

He led us through the hallway into a kitchen that smelled of fresh-baked Challah. There, we found a small woman with curly black hair laced with a few strands of grey surrounding what I perceived to be an exceptionally kind face.

She held out her hand and introduced herself. "Rachel!" she said, "I've so wanted to meet you! I'm Mahlah Lehrer!"

"Hello!" I said, taking her small hand and shaking it. She turned to Yakub.

"This is Yakub," I said, unable to suppress a big smile, "My husband!"

"Hello, Yakub! Call me Molly!"

"A pleasure and an honor to meet you, Molly!" Yakub said as they shook hands.

"Please," Molly gestured at the table, which was gaily set with a white tablecloth and bright blue napkins. Beside one place were two candlesticks, a *kiddush* cup and grape juice, and a cloth with the word "*Shabbat*" embroidered in gold Hebrew letters over a mound which I took to be the source of the mouth-watering smells.

Without delay, Rabbi Lehrer and Molly led us over, and Molly began the Shabbat blessings by lighting the candles. We continued with the *kiddish* and then the blessing for bread. Afterwards, we all sat down while Molly retrieved the casserole from the oven.

After we'd received our heaping plates of steaming food, I turned to the rabbi and said, "Rabbi Lehrer?"

"Yes?"

"I was wondering. Did you...speak with me when I was in al-Khalil?"

"Excuse me?" he said, looking as innocent as ever.

"I thought I heard you say something to me...about Maimonides..."

"You mean, telepathically or something?"

I nodded.

"Rachel," the rabbi said, raising a dismissive hand, "don't believe in all that '*abra cadabra*' stuff. It's hard enough getting along in *real* reality."

I started to protest, but realized I would only dig myself in deeper.

"So," said the rabbi, picking up his fork again and changing the subject. "Have you found it?"

"Found what?" I said.

"Well, let me see. The '*Afikoman.*' No! *The poem,* of course!"

Both Yakub and I shifted uncomfortably. "We're not sure," I admitted.

"Not sure? How can you be *not sure?*"

"It's a long story," admitted Yakub.

"Well, Molly and I are all ears!" said the rabbi, taking a piece of bread, salting it, and then looking at us.

Yakub and I began to tell our story, filling the rabbi in on all the adventures: the treasure hunt from the Cambridge Library to Cordoba and Cairo, the wedding, the graveyard, the theft of Said al-Shadi's *diwan,* and then the fantastic experience at the pillars.

The rabbi took all of this in with equanimity, and then, in characteristic fashion, in what seemed a complete non-sequitur, said, "So, Rachel. You know the Torah portion for today, right?"

"Sure," I said. "*Yitro.* The receiving of the Ten Commandments."

"Bingo!" said Rabbi Lehrer. "Up on Mount Sinai. Right. But lemme ask you a question. What do you think God *really* said to all those frightened people at the base of the mountain?"

"Ummm...*I am the Lord your God, you shall have no other Gods*, etc. etc, up to ten, and then all the rest?" I said.

"Good answer," said the rabbi. "But actually, you should know that there are dissenting opinions."

"What?"

"Yes. Some of the rabbis say God spoke all of the commandments, some say it was just the ten utterances. Still others argue that, no, it was just the first two while others say it was only the first word, *Anochi*, 'I'. But finally, one rabbi, Rabbi Mendl Torum of Rymanov, said it wasn't even just the first word, but only the first letter, *Aleph.* Can you say the sound of that letter for me, Rachel?"

"Very funny, Rabbi. You're the one that taught me that *Aleph* has no sound."

"Ah!" said the rabbi, his eyes large through his thick glasses. "But is this true?"

"That's what you told me!"

"But maybe there's more to it than that!"

"More to it?"

"Maybe the *Aleph* does have a sound! Like that little noise you make when you're just beginning to talk. For example, the glottal stop in your throat when you begin to say 'uh oh'?"

"As I do so often..." I laughed.

"Yes, I'm afraid so," the rabbi said, shaking his head in mock sorrow.

"So what are you saying, Rabbi?"

"Here's what I'm saying. When the people at Sinai received that sound, that *Aleph* from God, they had the terrible and awesome experience of God's *Self*. And from that single *Aleph,* all the other meanings, letters, words, commandments, flowed from God, into the Torah and all the holy books," said Rabbi Lehrer. "All meanings, all words emanated from that single sound. And there's something else really amazing."

"There is?"

"Yes. There are some people who noticed that the Hebrew letter *Aleph* looks like a human face: the two smaller arms are the eyes, and the long straight backbone is the nose. Furthermore, these components of the Aleph are themselves letters: two *yuds* and a *vav*. Curiously, the numerical value of these letters, which is ten plus ten plus six, or *twenty-six*, is exactly the same as the numerical value of the most sacred name of God, *Yud-Hey-Vav-Hey*. This calculation of numerical equivalencies is a form of Biblical interpretation we call *gematria*. So, by this method, you could say that the letter *Aleph* is equivalent to the most holy name of God, *Yud-Hey-Vav-Hey*, and thus contains, or unifies, that name...What's wrong, Rachel?"

I looked over at the rabbi, and realized I'd been rubbing my temples and squinting, something I do when I'm trying to work out a problem. "Oh, I'm sorry," I said. "I was just thinking about what you were saying. I've been trying to figure something out about the *Aleph* myself. So you're saying, the letters of God's name, *Yud-Hey-Vav-Hey*, equal the letter *Aleph,* numerically?"

He nodded.

"Did you ever notice that, if you reverse the letters, they spell '*hu-he*'?"

"As in '*he-she*'? Very nice! But where's the *Aleph*?"

"Exactly. That's what I've been trying to figure out! But if what you're saying is true, then when the male and female, the '*hu*' and '*he*' are unified, you both create and release an *Aleph*."

"Unity and separation all at once! Much like the act of creating a child! Yes, I see! Beautiful!"

"Thanks, Rabbi!"

"One thing, Rachel. I don't recommend you go around pronouncing that name, whether backwards or otherwise. You're gonna run into problems with another commandment if you do."

"Commandment number three, profaning God's name. I know. But you don't have to say it out loud to understand it."

"You're right. Very, very nice, Rachel! I love it!"

Yakub said, "Rabbi, may I…"

"Yes?" said Rabbi Lehrer.

"May I ask, what you said at the beginning, about the *Aleph* looking like a face. How does that relate to this?"

"Ah! An excellent question! This can help us understand what it means in the verse from today's Torah portion, when it says, 'all the people *saw* the thunder.' What they saw was God's name, *Yud-Hey-Vav-Hey*, united in the *Aleph*, the eyes and nose, on the faces of all of those around them." (10)

"So God is in the faces of all people?" I said.

Rabbi Lehrer nodded. "If only we remembered to look."

Yakub was listening intently, and now he jumped up. "That is really something!" he said, beginning to pace back and forth behind the table. "We have a similar tradition in Islamic Sufism. Our Arabic letter, *Alif,* is different than the Hebrew letter *Aleph*. It is just a single stroke, like a nose, or the number One. Even so, there are Sufi poems that speak of recognizing God in the face of human beings."

Rabbi Lehrer looked at him with interest. "Really?"

"Yes!" said Yakub. He began to quote. " '*In the faces of people, …a saint sees God's light. Yes – human beings are the face of God.*' This was written in the 1500's by a Sufi poet, Kahi Kabuli." (7)

"Are there more like this?" asked the rabbi.

"Rumi also composed something similar: '*I have no more words. Let the soul speak with the silent articulation of a face.*' " (8)

I was thinking hard, and it must have shown, because the rabbi said, "What is it now, Rachel?"

"Hmmm? Oh…I was just thinking about something a patient said."

"Yes?"

"It was a patient that died last week." I turned to Yakub, who sat back down at the table next to me. "Actually, he was the man who was rooming with you, the first time I met you." I smiled, recalling the day vividly.

"That poet gentleman?" said Yakub.

"Yes. Zeke Halvorson."

"Poor fellow! He died?"

"I'm afraid his habits finally caught up with him," I said.

"But what was it that reminded you of him?" Rabbi Lehrer prompted.

"Before he left, he gave me a poem. I don't have the copy anymore, because the...the man took it from me in al-Khalil. But I'd already memorized it anyway. It said, '*And now I say, that you must fix these, Yud, Vav, two-Hey ...*' "

Rabbi Lehrer whistled. "Was he Jewish?"

"Apparently his mother was."

"He was Jewish," said Rabbi Lehrer, with finality.

"But the thing that made me think," I continued, "is what Zeke said, just before he died." I took a sip of water, absently. "When he saw me, he said, '*you fixed 'em!*' and then he basically told me I was pregnant. Then he said something about an *Aleph*. And now, you're saying the *Aleph* unifies the letters, *Yud-Hey-Vav-Hey*, the holy name of God..."

But Rabbi Lehrer wasn't listening to my long-winded explanation. He was smiling at me, delight lighting his face. "Rachel!"

"Is this true?" asked Molly. "You're pregnant?"

I nodded.

"Rachel!" said the rabbi, his smile enormous. "But I thought...?"

"Even doctors can be wrong!" I laughed.

He nodded. "So, I'll repeat my question," he said, "*Have you found the poem?*"

"I believe," said Yakub, "that we are almost there."

After dinner, we walked the five blocks over to the Synagogue and entered the small congregation hall. Molly, Yakub and I sat in the front pew while the rabbi went in back to find the cantor so they could start the service. Molly asked Yakub if he had ever been to a Jewish prayer service before.

"Several times," he replied, "but never on a Friday evening. I understand they call it the *Kabbalat Shabbat* service. Is that because it has some kind of mystical significance?"

Molly inclined her head in a "yes and no" gesture. "*Kabbalat* just means 'receiving.' In this case, according to the traditional view, we're receiving the Sabbath. But the mystics do have a more esoteric meaning as well. They call it the *Kabbalat Shabbat* service because tonight, we greet the Sabbath bride, the *Shekhina,* the female presence of God. The mystics' great hope is that, as a result of our prayers and devotions, the male aspect of God, *Tiferet,* will descend, and the two will marry, uniting the worlds and repairing the universe."

"Ahh!" said Yakub.

The rabbi and the cantor entered, taking their place up on the *bima.* The cantor began to sing, accompanied on the guitar by a man wearing a *tallit.* We sang the Psalm, number 96, "Sing to the Lord a New Song, Sing to the Lord, all the earth." Several minutes later, we stood and turned to the entrance of the synagogue:

Come, beloved, to greet the bride, the Sabbath presence, let us welcome...

Inside me beat the secret heart of my child. I closed my eyes and pictured the tiny baby, blood coursing through its forming body. Just an ordinary miracle.

San Francisco, California

12:01 am. Friday, September 14th 2007
Dr. Rachel and Prof. Yakub al-Shadi

Our baby, a beautiful little boy, was born at the California Pacific Medical Center on September 14th, 2007, just over a week before the due date. Soon after the blowing of the Shofar at the end of mid-day services on Rosh Hashanah, my contractions began. The labor became difficult about six hours later, and I delivered our son at a minute after midnight the following morning.

Yakub and I decided we would name him after Yakub's father, Ibrahim. Yakub was also adamant we keep a part of my family name, and so his middle name became Davidson. Ibrahim Davidson al-Shadi.

He was a vigorous infant. After he had emerged completely, the doctor cut the cord, checked him briefly, then swaddled him and handed his precious tiny body over to Yakub. Together, we looked down at him, marveling at his ten tiny fingers with their miniscule swirls.

"Look!" I said, "His nose is straight and fine, just like an *Alif!*"

Yakub laughed, tears on his cheeks. "No! No! His eyes and nose look like an *Aleph!*"

And the truth dawned on both of us at the same time. God had, at last, given us a sign. Or perhaps we had only noticed it now, for the first time, in our own precious baby's face.

"What are you talking about?" said the doctor, puzzled, as she began massaging my belly to encourage delivery of the placenta.

"Nothing!" we both said.

San Francisco, California
1:26 pm. Shabbat, September 22nd 2007
Dr. Rachel and Prof. Yakub al-Shadi, et al

We circumcised our son on Yom Kippur at a ceremony held at our synagogue. In attendance were members of both of our families, including Ruthie and Lenny, Hana and her mother, Farid, Mahmud, and all three of Yakub's grandchildren. Rabbi Lehrer led the services, pointing out that it was not only Shabbat but Yom Kippur, the most holy day of the year, and he remarked that the *brit milah,* the ceremony of circumcision, was one of the few observances permitted on the Day of Atonement.

After Hana's mother handed the baby over for the circumcision, we all recited the words: "Blessed are you, Adonai our God, Ruler of the universe, who has sanctified us through your commandments and asked us to bring our sons into the covenant of Abraham our Father."

When we were all done, still holding our baby in his arms, the rabbi said, "So, Rachel, have you found *the poem* yet?"

I smiled at him. He always left me the easy questions. "Yes, Rabbi, we have. But as Yakub suspected, it wasn't just any ordinary kind of poem."

"Good!" Rabbi Lehrer smiled and kissed the fragrant top of Ibrahim's small head. He then handed him back to me saying, "Here he is."

And now, to my readers, please don't misunderstand me

and believe that I'm telling you that our little baby is more special than any other, or that I may even have delusions that he is the messiah. Don't worry! I don't.

My baby is certainly unique and, in my eyes, exceptionally gifted, but to believe that is only natural for a mother. Our baby is a miracle, a result of the joint creative processes of God and human being.

For those of a more technical nature, the complex explanation is this: The secret of the diagram of Said al-Shadi, the interlocking triangles and the letters, *Hey-Vav-Hey-Yud*, *He-She*, is that the *Aleph* is not missing at all. It's both contained within the letters, in their numeric value, as my rabbi explained, and separate, in the *Aleph* released by union of male and female. This is the paradox of creation, the secret of multiplicity within the One. And so the ongoing flow of evolution occurs, combining and separating, dividing and reforming, in an endless revelation of God's being.

For those who like things simpler, the answer is this: our baby is a poem, a metaphor for God, like all God's children, but not a messiah. Just a poem, a new song, like all of us, unique and infinitely beautiful, if we would only see. Like every human being, he bears on his face God's letter, the holy Name of God, conjunction of biology and word, the place where the speech of God and humankind unite.

London, England
3:00 pm. *Wednesday, October 10th 2007*
Eugene Smith *(journal entry)*

Dearest Lord, in this dark hour of my soul, I beg you for guidance. A most terrible thing has occurred. Today, I have learned a secret that must be contained at all costs, or it will destroy my family.

I admit, I knew my father was not well. His cruel disposition, coupled with his poor health and confinement, led to an extreme bitterness of spirit. His exuberance towards his punitive methods left me with little love for him. My mother, simple woman that she is, also could not abide the man. Nevertheless, I never doubted his single minded devotion to the redemptive aspirations of our family. Until today.

Why he got it in his head to travel to the Middle East on his own when a phone call would surely have sufficed was completely beyond my comprehension. Until now, I believed it was the arduousness of the journey that killed him. But in these long hours of the night I have just passed, I've discovered that it was something else, something vastly more corrupt, that brought him to his tortured end.

It was only after meeting with our solicitor yesterday that I became cognizant of the depths of his depravity and betrayal. It was all recorded in a journal, locked in sequesterment during the months of probate.

My father composed this revolting journal during his final months of life. Addressed to me, its purpose was to pass on his purported "life's wisdom" as he faced his imminent demise. Dear God, I wish that I had burned it before I read it!

Too late, I stumbled upon the evidence of my father's apostasy, lurking there in his journal like a cockroach. *Eugene,* he says, *Do not continue in this course! I beg you, hear me now! ... abandon all these words of hatred! ...Oh my son, the compassion of a stranger has taught me this: seek love, not hatred, for it alone is our redemption....*Rubbish! Nonsense!

Thinking back, I recall the surprise and disappointment I felt, upon returning in triumph with that *diwan,* waiting with such anticipation the joy of burning it in company with my father! Sad circumstance that, upon my homecoming, I found he had expired! Yet following his memorial service, I myself burned the abomination with joy, in honor of my father.

And now, I find he tells me I must stop writing, I must seek love, and other foolishness.

Father, I tell you now, if you could hear me, I will never stop writing! And love? It is just a fantasy, a diversion of weaklings lacking in intellect and courage. I am grateful that I was the only one to read your pitiful last scratchings. Once I destroy your journal, there will be no record of your turn of heart. I will have no further obstacles, and my path will be clear in all directions.

The poetry I wrested from the hands of that imbecile in Fustat, yes, I admit, it had some beauty. But its words spoke only that tired creed, the belief in man's creation in *God's image,* a verse proven, by my ancestors, to have been abrogated already in ancient times. God's image resides within the faces of my family alone, of that I have utter and complete certainty.

And so, the poet's talk of *signs from God* are meaningless, since we need no further signs from God. It is certain that we, the worthy, are destined for salvation. All the others will burn in Hell, but only after suffering great torment at each others' hands!

Yes, father, I continue my writing, and I am certain it will be a masterpiece, of higher order than anything yet created by the pens of our ancestors! Greater still than the *Protocols of the Learned Elders of Zion*, or even your own admittedly brilliant *Dangerous and Futile Nature of Poesy*. Of all the lessons that you taught me, the best is that the power of the pen is mightier than the sword, and I will never again harm another man in any manner of physical force. Now, I will go and burn your damning journal, and then return to my desk and my writing. Father, your words have not stopped me. They have only made me that much more determined to succeed.

In the Air

1:00 pm. Friday, October 12ᵗʰ 2007
Week of the portion of נח, "Noah"
Dr. Rachel, Prof. Yakub, and Ibrahim al-Shadi

I'm *en route* with Yakub and our baby, Ibrahim, on the final leg of our trip to Israel. Yesterday, we left San Francisco directly from the wedding of my sister, Ruthie, to Lenny Goldstein. My sister cried, and promised she would visit us soon in Israel.

Right now, we're flying from Frankfurt to Tel Aviv, and I'm watching from the window, eager, like so many before me, for my first glimpse of the land of Israel. I've left my job and all the things I know back in the United States to make *Aliyah*. Tonight, Yakub, Ibrahim, and I will spend our Kabbalat Shabbat at the Kotel, the Western Wall, and I'll pray again for peace.

Yakub tells me that tonight is also the beginning of an Islamic holy day, Eid al-Fitr, the end of the month of fasting called *Ramadan*. As the sun goes down, we'll enter a time of sacredness at that ancient holy place, as songs of both our faiths fill the air around us.

I'm thinking about *The Poem,* all we've lost and all we've gained. I know that the people who use words to obscure truth are still out there, still working and plotting to create hatred for their own exclusive view of redemption. They almost succeeded before, with *The Protocols* and the holocaust. What's next?

But what we've won is considerable. We have our son, our beautiful boy, product of true love, witness that only love has the capacity to transform reality. He's only a tiny baby still, and Yakub and I have yet to solve the dilemma of his religion. Will he be Jewish? Or Muslim? It's a hugely challenging paradox, one that we believed we'd never face when we first surrendered to love, that night in Cordoba. Ibraham's mother is Jewish, so he is Jewish. His father is Muslim, so he is Muslim. What should we do?

God willing, our son will be a believer in the God of Abraham. But which religion will he practice? The rites of Islam? Or Judaism? In the end, I believe, we will have to follow the advice of the Prophet himself, who told us that there is no coercion in religion. Ibrahim will choose for himself. Maybe he, like his namesake, will lead us to a new path, a way of glorifying God that is free of division. A mother can always hope!

Beyond this, as a result of all of our discoveries, Yakub and I are in possession of a truth of singular power and beauty. Our little boy bears it in his face, like all human beings.

The redemption we all yearn for, that is, the final unification between God and God's name, is completely in our hands. We accomplish it by recognizing God's name in the face of every human being, whether stranger or friend, whether *aleph* or *Alif.* The world will be redeemed when all people see that it is the *human being* that is the poem, the metaphor for God, each person unique, beloved, and treasured by God, connected with God at the root. . We are all capable of this unification, but we must turn ourselves to the task or it will fail. Redemption is as easy and as difficult as that.

I remember now that it's the week of Parashat Noach, which brings us back to the beginning, where the story of Abraham began, at Lech Lecha, when I first met Yakub a year ago. Parashat Noach contains not only the story of the flood, but also the shattering of language at Babel, and the paradox that even if all is divided and broken, it is really all one, unified in the light of God that exists within all creation.

When will humanity ever understand this? It isn't clear. But Yakub and I will do our part to announce this truth, to combat the lies of those who still bring hatred to life with their words. Because when God's poem, the human being is recognized, then at long last, the rainbow will shine over Jerusalem, and all humankind will sing the song that is him or herself. Everything will converge in the final unification of metaphors. God and God's name will be One. And the planet, all the rocks, the seas, the forests will sing.

CITATIONS
& SELECTED BIBLIOGRAPHY

1. **Muslim, Sahih.** The Book of Prayers (Kitab al-Salat), Book 004, Number 2008. [book auth.] Translator: Abd-al-Hamid Siddiqui. *Translation of Sahih Muslim.* s.l. : USC-MSA Compendium of Muslim Texts, http://www.usc.edu/dept/MSA/fundamentals/hadithsunnah/musl im/004.smt.html#004.2008.

2. **Franzen, Cola.** *Poems of Arab Andalusia.* San Francisco, CA : City Lights Books, 1989. ISBN 978-0-87286-242-5.

3. **Homerin, Emil.** *'Umar ibn al-Farid; Sufi Verse, Saintly Life.* New York, NY : Paulist Press, 2001. ISBN 0-8091-4008-X.

4. **Kushner, Lawrence.** *The Way Into the Jewish Mystical Tradition.* Woodstock, VT : Jewish Lights Publishing, 2001. ISBN 1-58023-029-6 (hbk).

5. **Dickinson, Emily.** That Love is All There Is. *The Complete Poems of Emily Dickinson.* Boston, MA : Little, Brown, and Company, 1924.

6. *Who is He? He is She. The Secret Four Letter Name of God.* **Sameth, Mark.** Spring, s.l. : CCAR Journal, 2008, Vol. LV.III, pp. 22-28.

7. **Fideler, David and Fideler, Sabrineh.** *Love's Alchemy; Poems from the Sufi Tradition.* Novato, CA : New World Library, 2006. ISBN-13: 978-1-57731-535-3.

8. **Barks, Coleman.** *A Year with Rumi: Daily Readings.* New York, NY : HarperCollins, 2006. ISBN-13: 978-0-06-084597-1.

9. **Adonis.** *An Introduction to Arab Poetics.* London, England : Saqi Books, 2003. ISBN 0 8635 331 7.

10. **Sells, Michael.** *Approaching the Quran; the Early Revelations.* Ashland, OR : White Cloud Press.

11. **Unknown.** *Sefer Yetzira.* [trans.] Aryeh Kaplan. Boston : Weiser Books, 1997.

12. **Carmi, T.** *The Penguin Book of Hebrew Verse.* London : Penguin Books, 1981.

13. **Matt, Daniel C.** *The Essential Kabbalah; The Heart of Jewish Mysticism.* New York, NY : HarperCollins, 1996. ISBN 0-06-251163-7.

14. —. *The Zohar - Pritzker Edition - Translation and*

Commentary by Daniel Matt. Stanford : Stanford University Press, 2004. ISBN 0-8047-4747-4.

15. **Hirtenstein, Stephen and Notcutt, Martin.** *Divine Sayings' the Mishkat al-Anwar of Ibn 'Arabi.* Oxford, England : Anqa Publishing, 2004. ISBN 0 9534513 5 6.

16. **Firestone, Reuven.** *Journeys in Holy Lands.* Albany, NY : State University of New York Press, 1990. ISBN-13: 978-0791403327.

17. **Bakhtiar, Laleh, [trans.].** *The Sublime Quran - English Translation.* 6th Edition. Chicago : Kazi Publications, 2009. 1-56744-750-3 pbk.

18. **Jewish Publication Society.** *JPS Hebrew-English Tanakh.* Philadelphia, PA : Jewish Publication Society, 2000. ISBN 0-8276-0697-4.

19. **Ali, A. Yusuf, [trans.].** *An English Interpretation of the Holy Quran.* Lahore : Ashraf Printing Press, 2001. ISBN No. 969-432-000-3.

SARAH ISAIAS has devoted her life to medicine, religious studies, writing, athletics, and family. Like the famous physician before her, and her most cherished role model, the great Rabbi Moses Maimonides, her writing elucidates the paradoxes of a belief system that sees no incompatibility between science and religion, reason and faith.

For many years, Dr. Isaias has dedicated herself to caring for America's medically-uninsured in an inner-city clinic. She has only recently turned her attention to another critical need - the call to peace.

Dr. Isaias is a family physician, an avid scholar of Arabic and Hebrew, a lover of Torah and Qur'anic study, a distance runner, and a poet. After raising five children, she lives alone now with their three dogs and her husband of 27 years.